DRIVEN

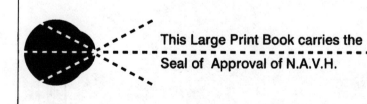

This Large Print Book carries the
Seal of Approval of N.A.V.H.

DRIVEN

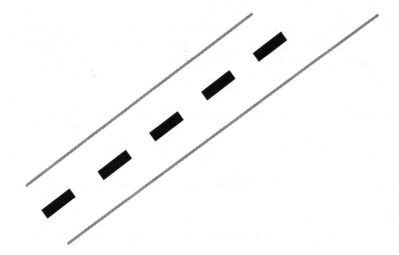

W. G. Griffiths

Thorndike Press • Waterville, Maine

Published in 2003 by arrangement with Warner Books, Inc.

Thorndike Press® Large Print Christian Fiction Series.

The tree indicium is a trademark of Thorndike Press.

The text of this Large Print edition is unabridged.
Other aspects of the book may vary from the original edition.

Set in 16 pt. Plantin by Elena Picard.

Printed in the United States on permanent paper.

Library of Congress Cataloging-in-Publication Data

Griffiths, Bill (William G.)
    Driven : a novel / W.G. Griffiths.
      p. cm.
    ISBN 0-7862-5552-8 (lg. print : hc : alk. paper)
    1. Long Island (N.Y.) — Fiction. 2. Serial murders —
Fiction. 3. Drunk driving — Fiction. 4. Large type books.
I. Title.
PS3607.R549D75 2003b
  813′.6—dc21   2003049976

For Bill and Dorothy Griffiths

As the Founder/CEO of NAVH, the only national health agency solely devoted to those who, although not totally blind, have an eye disease which could lead to serious visual impairment, I am pleased to recognize Thorndike Press★ as one of the leading publishers in the large print field.

Founded in 1954 in San Francisco to prepare large print textbooks for partially seeing children, NAVH became the pioneer and standard setting agency in the preparation of large type.

Today, those publishers who meet our standards carry the prestigious "Seal of Approval" indicating high quality large print. We are delighted that Thorndike Press is one of the publishers whose titles meet these standards. We are also pleased to recognize the significant contribution Thorndike Press is making in this important and growing field.

Lorraine H. Marchi, L.H.D.
Founder/CEO
NAVH

★ Thorndike Press encompasses the following imprints: Thorndike, Wheeler, Walker and Large Pr int Press.

— Acknowledgments —

First, I am very grateful to Markus Wilhelm, a father, a brother, my good friend.

I am also grateful to Rolf Zettersten, my publisher at Warner Books, for his generosity, confidence, and desire to publish this book, and to my editor, Leslie Peterson, for her suggestions and ability to do everything from gracefully rewrite rough lines to manage the production and schedule of the work.

I thank Roger Cooper for his extraordinarily high level of energy and enthusiasm through thick and thin and his personal oversight of the book club project, and Michelle Rapkin, who is like a sister to me with her constant encouragement, wisdom, and advice. Thanks also to Joan Sanger, who under extreme circumstances edited the first edition. I am also grateful to Barbara Greenman and her staff, who must work with microscopes, maps, and oil cans to keep the wheels turning.

I am indebted to my hard-working friends, Deputy Chief Gary Ruff, Captain Carl Sandel, and Detective Chris Grella (who begged me not to kill his character), and Pastor David Harwood, for their many unselfish hours and technical advice. Errors or inaccuracies are mine, not theirs.

I am very appreciative to Arlene Friedman for her valuable time and professional evaluations.

A very warm thanks to my first readers — Donny and Melissa Renaldo, Andrew Syrotick, Angelo Otto, Craig and Maryann Griffiths, Bill McCarty, Barry and Beth Mevorach, Shira and Jonathan Harwood, Kevin Cocchiola, Bill and Dorothy Griffiths, Phil Schlesinger, and Scott and Laurie Nicolich — for early feedback after suffering through some truly rough drafts.

Finally, my deepest gratitude goes to my beautiful wife, Cindy, who is always there to ask me for the next page, make fun of my spelling, and tell me, "You can't write *that*," and to my children, Stephen, Robyn, Luke, Willy, Peter, and Summer, for their love.

— W. G. Griffiths,
WGGriffiths.com

Be sober, be vigilant; because
your adversary, the devil,
as a roaring lion, walketh about,
seeking whom he may devour.

1 PETER 5:8

— 1 —

Krogan saw the police lights reflecting hazily in the rearview mirror and was about to crush the gas pedal of the oversized, over-powered 4x4 when he considered it might be more fun to pull over. The proud owner of the monster truck sat in the passenger seat, sucking hard on the last of a fatty joint held by a small lobster-claw roach clip. Powerful speakers pounded bass notes through their flesh. The air conditioning, on full max, did nothing against the thick cloud of pot smoke that filled the cab.

The truck slid to a stop on the grass off the parkway's shoulder. A half-drained pint of gold tequila spilled out of the console. Krogan snatched the bottle off the floor with a gorilla-sized hand and drank the few re-maining ounces. He then took another turn on the lobster claw as he revved the engine to the beat of the hard music. The metallic clack on his window went almost unheard.

"Oh, yeah. The cop," Krogan said, his voice deep and raspy. Never one for conversation, he lowered the window and heaved the empty bottle of tequila through the billowing smoke, glancing left just long enough to confirm the result: the puny cop was out cold on his back, blood oozing from a new and deep gash over his left eye.

Krogan hit the gas pedal and then the brake and shifted into reverse. He backed the rear tires to within inches of the cop's face and, laughing, shifted into first and punched the gas again, covering his fallen prey with a sticky gush of wet grass and mud.

"It's time," he said, flicking a nontwist beer-bottle cap off with his thumb.

The vehicle's owner nodded, staring blearily through slitted, bloodshot eyes.

"Ever . . ." Krogan guzzled and belched. ". . . kill a whale . . . on a Sunday?"

The passenger grinned. "It's been a while — maybe two hundred years. Don't know about Sunday."

"With a truck?"

"Never tried with a truck."

"Then it's the aquarium."

Laughter. "Yeah. Fishing at the aquarium."

With a roar, the truck was on its way.

— 2 —

Bubblegum. Detective Gavin Pierce didn't have to look down to know he'd just stepped on a chewed-and-spewed glob of fresh, sun-cooked bubblegum. Compliments of Coney Island.

On any other day of the week, such an irritant would normally result in a few choice words. But this was Sunday, a day steeped in tradition. Gavin set Sundays apart to be with the most important person he knew: his mother's father, Antonio Palermo. Grampa. Every Sunday morning, Gavin traveled back to his old neighborhood to pick up Grampa for church. Today was extra special. Today was Grampa's birthday. The old man was eighty-two. Gavin could hardly believe it.

Gavin stood watchfully behind Grampa as a young girl wearing a green-and-yellow concession hat handed the old immigrant two Coney Island hot dogs. Grampa nodded a thank you and received a warm smile in return. He had the knack for that — for eliciting smiles from complete strangers. Smiles just like hers had followed Grampa for as long as Gavin could remember. Upon occasion, Grampa could even crack Gavin's stone demeanor. Only Grampa.

Cradling the hot dogs with both hands, Grampa turned where he stood and paused before plotting out his way to the condiments counter just ten feet away. Gavin followed, allowing Grampa to fulfill the customary act of decorating the food. Gavin had switched from ketchup to mustard on his franks when he was a teen, but Grampa only remembered when Gavin had put ketchup on everything. Gavin was thirty-six, but today he would eat his hot dog with ketchup as he and Grampa took a walk down memory lane.

"You'd be having a dog for lunch even if I wasn't here, wouldn't you?" Gavin said as he received his. It looked and smelled enticing enough and for the sake of recapturing precious moments long past he would try to block out thoughts of the inevitable heartburn the deceptive little creature would surely bring. An antacid stand around here would be a gold mine, he thought as he watched someone pave a couple of hamburgers with mustard and onions. He briefly relocated himself protectively into the path of two laughing kids running toward them, then adjusted his position again when the threat to his fragile grandfather had passed.

Grampa had paused to answer Gavin's question, and Gavin reflexively leaned closer to hear over the popping balloons, game sirens, carnival music, and mechanical clatter of rides.

"I like," the old man replied decisively, his words punctuated with the lilting accent of his Italian homeland. He took a dangerously large bite of his hot dog, drenched in mustard and buried in sauerkraut and relish.

Gavin looked at his own ketchup-flooded food and sighed imperceptibly before biting. Grampa was waiting for the big *mmmmmmm* that always followed. Gavin obliged him. "They taste good, Grampa, but they're no good for you."

Grampa laughed. "What do you eat that is so good for you?"

Gavin thought. "Fish. Fish is good for you."

"What? I eat plenty of the fish," Grampa said, shrugging his shoulders.

15

"Baccala? That dried-up, salty leather? It's terrible for you."

Grampa shook his finger. "Only on holidays."

"Then what? Anchovies on your pizza?"

"Scungili," Grampa said with closed eyes and a smile, as if his hot dog had taken on a new flavor.

"Scungili's not fish. It's a snail. A big snail. A scavenger. It eats junk. It's a living garbage can."

"Like me," Grampa said, proudly tapping his chest, then winking at Gavin.

Gavin rolled his eyes and looked away, not wanting to encourage him. The old man did everything wrong. He never exercised, ate three eggs with sausage every morning and a liverwurst sandwich every night before bed, and drank coffee and wine like water. At least he'd given up those smelly, crooked cigars.

"Here, you take another ride?" Grampa said, motioning toward a huge disk that held its occupants upright with centrifugal force as it rose from horizontal to vertical.

Gavin shook his head. "If I go on another ride I'll throw up. Especially that one."

The rides at Coney Island hadn't changed much since Gavin's childhood.

16

The giant Ferris wheel was still there, as was the Cyclone, an all-wooden roller coaster that had once been the biggest and fastest of its kind. Now its questionable longevity made it scarier than when it had towered like the Swiss Alps in his little-boy eyes.

As they slowly walked past the Cyclone the ground vibrated and screams pierced the air, then were whipped away in a hairpin curve. Gavin's childhood ability to be tossed about in any direction and at any speed seemed to be long gone. Even the thought of another ride was making him queasy.

"I think it's time to go to the aquarium," he said.

"Huh?" Grampa said, cupping his ear.

"I said, let's go see the dolphins," Gavin yelled as the coaster rattled past again.

The New York Aquarium was in Coney Island, right next to the amusement park, and stopping by had always been tradition. The walruses and whales and other water creatures foreign to Gavin's everyday life had always intrigued him. Especially the dolphins, and there was a dolphin and sea lion show at four p.m., just an hour away. Gavin couldn't remember when he'd last seen a dolphin show with Grampa, but he did remember Grampa's astonished expression every time the dolphins had danced around on the water's surface with their tails. Gavin wanted to see that expression on Grampa's face again.

The walk to the aquarium was short in distance but long in time. Gavin didn't care. He had all day and was in no hurry for it to end, choosing instead to enjoy their stroll down the huge boardwalk that separated the business world from the beach world. It extended as far as he could see. The old decking had recently been replaced with new mahogany. After having had his own deck built with a much cheaper knotty cedar, Gavin wondered what it must have cost to redo the boardwalk.

Gavin was grateful for the overcast sky that kept the crowds away. There was, however, a small gathering around a middle-aged man handling a giant python. The man had a female assistant selling Polaroid pictures of anyone who would allow the man to arrange the snake on their shoulders.

"Grampa, are you afraid of snakes?" Gavin asked as they drew closer. The old man raised an eyebrow.

The circle of spectators opened to allow

Gavin and Grampa in. Grampa's eyes widened; he said nothing but was obviously taken aback at the sight of the huge reptile, at least eight inches in diameter, draped over its master's shoulders. It didn't seem to mind the small top hat strapped to its brick-sized head.

The python's owner eyed Gavin. "What do you say, young man? Would you like to have a picture of Sinbad giving you a hug?"

"I had something a little different in mind," Gavin said.

By the time Gavin and Grampa continued on their way to the aquarium, they were each staring at their own Polaroid. Gavin shook his head, wondering if there was anything Grampa wouldn't do if Gavin asked. The old man always argued a bit, but in the end he was a great sport. Gavin hoped there was a way to get Polaroids enlarged. If so, he would frame the picture of him and Grampa, arms over shoulders with the giant serpent draped comfortably across them.

Gavin carefully examined the photo. The evolution of Grampa-Gavin photos had reached the late stages. Gavin's eyes were no longer belt height and Grampa's hand no longer reached down to rest on his shoulders. In fact, Gavin's hand was now resting low on Grampa's shoulder. His somber expression was in stark contrast to his grandfather's wide smile. People had always told Gavin he reminded them of Russell Crowe. He would take the comparison as a compliment, but couldn't see the resemblance.

With fifteen minutes to spare before the dolphin show, Gavin and Grampa walked over to the aquatheater holding tanks. The holding tanks were a complex of three adjoining tanks that flowed into each other. One of the tanks was where the dolphin show would take place, but the two others were used to house whatever other sea creatures the show featured. Before and after the show people gathered in front of several large, thick viewing windows, amazed at the size and beauty of some of the world's most exotic mammals. The dolphins in turn would swim over and stare at the people as if mutually interested in the strange creatures that waved and squished their faces against the glass.

"The window at the end isn't so crowded," Gavin said, pointing to the glass closest to the parking lot. As they walked over Gavin glanced through the nearby chain-link fence to see a traffic cop directing cars in and out of the parking lot entrance about one hundred yards away. A cop himself, he was glad not to be directing traffic in Brooklyn.

As Grampa walked up to the glass a dolphin greeted him. "They always are smiling, Gavin. Just like you used to when you were a boy. My boy." He patted his grandson.

"That's because you always gave me something to smile about," Gavin said, putting his arm around the old man's shoulders.

"Nah," Grampa said, shaking his head slowly. "It wasn't me. It was you. You were always playing games and make believe that you were everything under the sun: cowboys and Indians, Superman and Batman. Always playing the good guys and bad guys."

"I'm still playing good guys and bad guys."

Grampa turned from his long-nosed admirer and looked at Gavin. "Except now you're not playing anymore. Your young dreams have come true."

Gavin hesitated before deciding not to correct the old man. He didn't want to soil their time with the realities of his world and how very little it resembled the dreams of his youth. If Grampa believed he was happy and fulfilled, Gavin would leave it that way. He would steer the conversation away from himself. "And your dreams, Grampa — have your dreams come true?"

"My dreams?" Grampa laughed, pointing at himself. "When you're young it's all dreams; when you're old it's all memories."

Before Gavin could respond to Grampa's comment, a loudspeaker announced the dolphin show would begin in five minutes.

"Let's go, Grampa. The show's about to start," Gavin said, just as he had when he was twelve.

"I'll see you later, Smiley," Grampa said to the dolphin.

By the time they rounded the holding tanks they found all of the seats in the first few rows had been taken, mostly by what appeared to be a group on a field trip. No problem. Although Grampa's eyes weren't what they used to be, they were still good enough to enjoy the show from one of the upper rows of seating that rose on steel girders above the holding tanks. And from that distance Grampa probably wouldn't get splashed by the dolphins, a prank the playful mammals seemed to enjoy as much as the kids.

Gavin slowly led the way to an upper row, allowed Grampa to enter a row off to the left, then followed.

He followed the old man to the end of the row, where they sat. There really were no bad seats and these gave a good overall view. The sun had finally broken through the clouds and the solid, blue security wall next to them afforded some shade; the rest of the spectators would be fishing for their sunglasses. The wall also gave them privacy from the parking lot and disguised the fact that they were about thirty feet above the ground from where they had viewed the dolphins before the show.

When most of the seats were filled, a petite blonde woman wearing the staff uniform of dark-blue shorts and a light-blue shirt introduced herself to the crowd as Bonnie. Wearing a wireless headset microphone, she spoke briefly of the New York Aquarium's history. As she spoke, Gavin could see the dark figures of the dolphins and sea lions entering into the main pool. One of the dolphins shot out of the water and did a flip, to the immediate applause of the crowd.

"Oh! That's Darla," Bonnie said matter-of-factly. "As you can tell, she's very shy."

Gavin glanced at Grampa. When Gavin

was a boy he had always been acutely aware of Grampa's watchful gaze — the clinical eye that determined whether or not Gavin was having fun. Now it was Gavin's turn. He was the one interested in Grampa's enjoyment. Fortunately, Grampa was obviously enjoying himself. He was watching the spirited dolphin with a boyishly wide smile and bright eyes, just as Gavin hoped he would. Just as Gavin had done some twenty-odd years earlier.

Suddenly Gavin's attention was caught by a voice yelling in the distance and the sound of a car skidding across pavement, followed by the loud roar of an engine with little or no muffler.

Bonnie's eyes shifted in the direction of the obnoxious roar, but she continued her well-rehearsed repertoire without hesitation. Her smile remained as she kicked a beach ball into the water for the dolphins.

But the engine noise was getting louder. Closer. Bonnie's voice over the loudspeakers could no longer be clearly heard. Outmatched by the competition, she stopped and stared disdainfully in the direction of the disturbance. People turned their heads toward the parking lot, but couldn't see beyond the aquatheater walls. They could only wait for someone else to take care of the problem.

Gavin expected to hear the engine stop and wheels lock up — perhaps some skidding — but no. There was no braking, just pure engine. Closer. Was something wrong with the car's throttle? Was it stuck? Was something wrong with the driver?

Suddenly there came a crash. The entire crowd startled in their seats. At first Gavin thought the vehicle had hit a parked car, but something sounded wrong — the engine was still roaring and there was an added clinking, scraping, grinding.

The fence? Apparently the vehicle had gone through the chain-link and was dragging it along. Gavin pictured sparks igniting off the pavement. He then heard and felt what he thought to be the fence's service gates ricocheting off the outer walls.

Still no braking. Full power ahead.

The impact felt like an explosion and jolted the entire seating area. Screams and gasps erupted from the spectators as the entire structure moved like one of the amusement park's rides. Before Gavin knew what was happening, the large safety wall next to them broke apart and fell away as if unhinged, revealing the parking lot below. In the next instant, the upper seating section they were in gave way, fell off on an angle, then caught itself briefly before slowly continuing its downward trajectory.

Gavin instinctively grabbed the seat to his left to keep from sliding. The collision must have somehow dislodged the main support posts for the arena seating. The entire upper section was moving in short, quick drops as it found temporary but inadequate support. The whole world was on a descending bumper jack.

Terrorism? The New York Aquarium?

"Gavin!" Grampa yelled as he began to fall away, his old fingers scrabbling and digging at his seat, but unable to anchor.

Gavin, one arm clasped around the back of the blue plastic seat next to him, grabbed a handful of Grampa's white shirt collar, his heart racing.

"I've got you," he cried. "I've got you."

The seats in the row in front of them bent inexorably downward. If only Grampa could find support.

"Bring your feet up, Grampa. Pull your feet up," he yelled.

Grampa's extra weight put a tremendous strain on Gavin's left arm and kept him from getting a better hold. The seat he was holding on to ripped out of the floor as Grampa tried unsuccessfully to step onto the seat in front of him. Gavin needed to pull him up a little further, maybe just inches. Cutting pain from the seat top digging into his forearm was making him dizzy, but no matter what, he wasn't going to let go of Grampa. If he did, the old man would certainly fall either into or just outside the holding tank three stories below.

Others in the upper section were screaming and holding tightly to their own seats or whatever else they could find. Gavin couldn't even look at them; his entire focus was on Grampa. His heart sank further as he heard metal grating and bending. With a loud snap, their section fell again and clanged to a jarring halt, jerking people free from their grasps and leaving the structure at an even steeper angle. Bodies emptied out of seats into the holding tank like cereal falling from a box into a bowl.

Gavin couldn't tighten his grip. Grampa's face was redder than he had ever seen it. The old man was gagging, choking on his own shirt collar, trying in vain to reach Gavin's arm. Gavin, who had been trained to deal with emergency situations with a cool head, felt panic seize his pounding heart as he realized that in trying to keep Grampa from falling, he was actually strangling him. The old man weighed about 170, but maybe, if Gavin pulled him closer, he could grab him under his armpit. At least then Grampa could breathe and maybe step onto the front seat.

Gavin pulled with all his strength. It seemed to be working. Grampa was getting closer. Or . . . was his shirt stretching? Gavin cursed, held his breath, and pulled, fingers digging. "That's it! We got it!" he yelled.

The collar Gavin was holding ripped. "Grampa!" Gavin screamed as crumpled linen came away in his hand. For an instant everything seemed to stand still as the old man reached frantically for something, anything to hold on to. Then he disappeared over the edge.

"Grampa! No!" A wave of numbing fear went through Gavin. He refused to think the unthinkable. He had to get down there. He had to find Grampa. He must have fallen into the holding tanks below. Frantic, Gavin began to pull himself up the chairs, one after another, trying to get to the aisle, where there appeared to be some stability. Hand over hand he fought with the smooth and slippery plastic seats. His breathing came fast and shallow and by the time he reached the walkway he was soaked with sweat. He raced down the sharply tilted aisle toward the pool, taking three steps at a time, grabbing seat backs for balance. The further down he went the straighter the stairs became, until they were level.

As Gavin leaped the final six steps down to the main level, he was amazed by the scene below him in the pool. The water was gone. Dolphins were lying helpless on the concrete, flailing and writhing desperately, screaming in high-pitched frenzy. What had happened to the water? The car must somehow have penetrated the holding tanks. But how could a car — even a big car — do that? The tank was reinforced with a thick concrete wall.

Gavin couldn't think about the dolphins. He couldn't think about terrorists. He couldn't think about the other people who ran screaming in every direction. He could think only of Grampa — of getting down into the tanks and finding him. He ran out through the aquatheater entrance and around to the holding area, cutting and darting through the obstacle course of confused people. A six-inch wave of water rolled over the pavement, engulfing the feet of and tripping baffled sightseers as they tried in vain to avoid it. Undaunted,

Gavin continued to sprint through the water until he turned the last corner and came to where he and Grampa had watched the smiling dolphin such a short time ago.

There Gavin stopped. He couldn't believe his eyes. The viewing glass was gone. In its place was a black-and-chrome pickup truck with waist-high mud tires. The front of the vehicle, all the way to the windshield, had crashed through the viewing glass and its surrounding concrete. The driver's door was halfway open and the airbag was still semi-inflated, but there was no driver. Beer cans were strewn about the interior and the ground outside the door. Gavin's fears of terrorists were slightly mollified — the scene looked more like a drunk driver accident than terrorism.

The driver of the mangled truck had apparently been saved by the airbag. The passenger had not been as lucky. One of the supporting posts for the bleachers had been ripped from its moorings atop the holding tank and was now lodged through the windshield and . . . through the passenger. The man, without the benefit of an airbag or, apparently, the sense to use the seat belt, had obviously hit the windshield just as the steel post smashed through the glass and into the middle of his upper back.

As a cop Gavin had witnessed some gruesome scenes, but this one froze him where he stood. But only for an instant, as he took everything in. Then he was running again, past a dozen or so people on the ground — some still, most of them moaning. He heard sirens in the distance and hoped they were for here; at the moment his trained impulse to rush over and begin emergency measures was completely supplanted by powerful devotion to the man he dearly loved.

"Grampa! Grampa!" he called, his eyes darting around in panic. Where was he? He jumped up and grabbed the top of the pickup's tailgate, stepped onto the rear trailer hitch with his right foot, and hurdled himself into the extra-high truck bed. Then, using the cab roof as a springboard, he dove for the cracked top rim of the holding tank like a basketball player going for the slam dunk. His fingers dug into jagged concrete as he pushed his feet against the tank's wall and pulled himself up.

He was stunned by what he saw. The fallen bleachers shadowed the tank, but the gloomy light was enough for him to see inside. Twenty feet below, a twelve-foot Beluga whale was laying in less than six inches of blood-reddened water, rocking back and forth in its death throes. Just to its right, close to the wall, were several people, some piled on top of others. One had struggled to his hands and knees in a daze, blood dripping down his forehead to feed the pink-tinged water. Others lay face down in the water, motionless.

Gavin peered past the arching whale. There! He could see black suspenders on a soiled white shirt. It had to be Grampa. His precious grandfather was face up and dangerously close to the confused whale's powerful tail.

Gavin straightened his arms, lifting himself slightly higher. "Grampa," he yelled, his voice echoing in the deep tank. He had to get down there. Pivoting on his waist to the inside of the wall, he pushed off. He hit the bottom hard, collapsing to the concrete on impact, sending a splash of cold, salty water into the side of the whale. He felt a sharp pain in his right knee as something gave, but ignored it, quickly rising. Cursing the pain that came with movement, he hobbled through the water and past the length of the whale. When he got to

Grampa he immediately positioned himself between the old man and the thick tail of the dying animal.

Grampa looked bad, his face bloodied from a head gash, his shirt ripped open to reveal lacerations that had probably occurred from hitting the top of the wall as he fell. Gavin cried freely at the sight. The old man was still — too still. His breathing was undetectable. Gavin quickly felt for a pulse. Nothing. Wait . . . There it was — slow and faltering, but still a pulse. Grampa was alive. But for how long?

The reflection of flashing lights appeared on the water's red surface as the sirens crescendoed and ceased.

"Help! In the tank! We need help in the tank!"

— 3 —

Karl Dengler had decided almost three years ago to take on a new name: Krogan. No official papers had ever been filled out or signed, but as far as he was concerned his name was Krogan. The name had come to him one night in an exceptionally vivid dream where he saw himself as a warrior dressed in ancient armor with a pewter helmet in the shape of a dragon's head. In the dream, his gray eyes were fierce and strangely hungry, more like the eyes of a wild animal than a man's. He rode a horse and carried a spiked mace. In the dream he took what he wanted whenever he wanted and from whomever he wanted. Wineskins and women were abundant. The languages spoken in the dream were foreign to Karl-now-Krogan, but he understood the actions and indeed had an insatiable appetite for them.

The day after the first dream, another

dream had filled his mind. Only then it wasn't so much a dream as a trance that caught him by surprise in broad daylight while working. Again he saw himself as a warrior, riding his horse through a fog in a foreign land of another time. Other warriors rode with him, but he was superior to them. They called him Krogan, and each time they attacked, they raised their weapons and wineskins and shouted, "*Shadahd!*"

In the following weeks these visions continued daily. Krogan looked forward to them. Each was different; in each he was dressed differently, speaking fluently in languages he had never heard and could not understand. But in all the languages his name had remained the same, as did the celebratory shout: "*Shadahd!*"

Soon he could barely remember anything from before the time of the first dream. His own past had become distant and obscure. Maybe it was the drugs and alcohol. Maybe it was because he spent little time thinking about anything other than the present moment. Whatever the reason, he didn't care. Memories were for the past. Live for today or die. Do what you want — period. Besides, the visions were satisfying. With them came the smell of blood, the fulfillment of violence. Maybe he was going insane. So what.

One night, after much drinking alone in his home, another vision came to Krogan. This time he was dressed in modern clothing — a T-shirt and jeans such as he currently wore. He saw himself leave his home and pick up a man whom he had never met, yet seemed to know. The man spoke the word — *shadahd* — that confirmed their relationship. They celebrated in the same raucous way as in previous visions. Krogan had no horse or spiked mace, though, so he took the keys to his new friend's car and drove it until he found a suitable victim to surprise — a night watchman in a guard booth.

At this point the vision must have ended, because Krogan didn't remember anything more. But the next morning he awakened in his bed bloody and sore. His clothes were dirty and torn. He immediately thought of the vision; had it been real? He soon found his answer in the morning paper — a watchman had been killed in a crash, along with the vehicle's passenger, who was the car's owner. The driver was missing.

Upon reading the news, an uncontrollable roar of laughter rose out of Krogan's belly and filled his house. He had actually done this thing. He felt invincible. Powerful. He felt like a god and looked forward to his next vision.

He had his new name tattooed between his shoulder blades as though his skin was a living football jersey. His telephone and electric bill might be addressed to Karl Dengler, the same name that appeared on his New York driver's license, boat registration, and house deed. But as far as he was concerned, his real name was Krogan.

— 4 —

Gavin sat, head in hands, in the waiting room of the intensive-care unit at the Coney Island Hospital, awaiting the news on Grampa. The circus atmosphere the Brooklyn medical center usually entertained was all the more intensified from the crash. Gavin's right knee was bandaged and propped up on a magazine table. The X rays had come back negative but the doctor had told him he'd probably strained a tendon and should have an MRI done to determine treatment.

"Detective Pierce."

Gavin quickly looked up from counting the multishaded green speckles in the white vinyl floor. Doctor Cohn, who had been working with the crash victims, was back. The doctor had been updating the packed room of family members all night. Over the last fourteen hours Gavin's gut had been wrenched in every direction as loved ones were delivered the good, the bad, and the still to be determined.

Gavin tried to see if the doctor was wearing his "I'm terribly sorry" face. "How is he?" he said, struggling up from his seat.

"Easy now," Doctor Cohn said warmly, putting a hand on Gavin's shoulder and taking a seat next to him. "Your grandfather's in critical but stable condition, although at his age that status could turn on a dime. X rays have shown a broken ankle and three broken ribs. He also has compression fractures of several of his lower vertebrae. Substantial inflammation, but as far as we can tell at this stage, there's no paralysis."

As hard as it was for Gavin to hear the list of Grampa's injuries, he was grateful not to be reading an autopsy report.

The doctor continued. "There was blood in his urine, probably the result of an injured kidney, judging by the deep bruise on his back. And he has a concussion, the severity of which we won't know without more test results. I don't think I have to tell you that he's lucky to be alive. After he hit the top wall he probably fell into a few feet of water before it all drained out. I don't think he could have survived that kind of fall otherwise. As you know, some didn't. Meanwhile he remains unconscious."

Gavin was momentarily distracted by a middle-aged man in a conservative tweed jacket. He was holding a notebook and apparently interviewing a woman on the other side of the room. He'd stopped while the doctor addressed Gavin. Gavin made him for a cop.

"If your grandfather was twenty-five I might be able to tell you we're almost out of the woods, but at his age . . ." The doctor finished his sentence with a shake of his head.

Gavin nodded slowly, then looked straight at the doctor. "Doc, I know he's an old man who probably doesn't have a whole lot of time left anyway. But he means a lot to me. Please call me when he comes to." He handed the doctor a white business card. "His wife's gone and most of his other close relatives have either died or moved away. I don't want him to be alone when he starts to hurt."

Dr. Cohn took the business card. "Sure . . . Detective," he said, reading the card. "I'll make sure you're notified immediately."

As the doctor shook Gavin's hand and

left, the man in the tweed jacket stood up and walked over.

"May I have a turn? I'd like to talk to you about what happened," he said, holding out a detective's shield. "I'm Detective Steve Rogers. I couldn't help hearing the doctor call you Detective. What job are —"

Gavin nodded before Rogers could finish his question. "Gavin Pierce, Nassau County."

"Which squad?"

"Homicide."

"Really . . . Look, I, uh, understand this isn't an easy time for you, but as you know, we have to ask dumb questions at bad times. If it's okay, I'd like to —"

"No problem," Gavin said impatiently. If he weren't so utterly consumed with Grampa's condition he would have been amused at the role reversal.

"I've got one question: did you see him?"

"Who?"

"The driver."

Gavin's eyes widened. "You don't have the driver yet?" How was that possible? He remembered the driver hadn't been in the truck, but he'd assumed the person was simply wandering aimlessly in a shocked stupor.

41

"No," Rogers said, then looked away, his disappointment overshadowed by anger.

Gavin's focus intensified. "Weren't you able to ID the driver through the truck?"

"It wasn't his," Rogers said, clearly frustrated.

"Stolen?"

Rogers shook his head. "Belonged to the passenger."

"The passenger?" Gavin said, surprised anyone would abuse a vehicle that badly with the owner sitting right next to him. "Did you check with the passenger's next of kin?"

Rogers looked at him blankly. "Of course."

"And?" Gavin said, not caring if he sounded like he was challenging the man's competency.

"I spoke to his widow this morning. It wasn't a pretty scene. But aside from that, she said her husband left in the morning to go fishing off the beach like he does every Sunday. Surf casting. All she could tell me was she was shocked he had been drinking. She claimed he was a recovering alcoholic and hadn't had a drink in two years."

"Nothing on the driver?"

Rogers shook his head. "The owner went alone and never mentioned anything about meeting up with anyone before he left. In fact, the wife said he preferred being alone. Said he would go to clear his head out. He was an auto mechanic — was putting in some long hours in his own garage and had one day off. He didn't care if he caught a fish or not. And we've got no priors on him whatsoever."

"Still, the driver's got to be somewhere," Gavin said, his voice rising. "He's got to be hurt. Did you check the local vendors, the park, under the boardwalk, other hospitals . . . the freakin' garbage cans?"

"We're doing the best we can. Believe me, we want this guy, too."

Gavin exhaled, limped to the waiting-room window, and stared intently into the lightening sky. "He'll turn up."

"He didn't last time or the time before that," Rogers said.

Gavin spun around. *"What?"*

"About a month ago we had a similar accident, although I'm using the term loosely. It wasn't quite as spectacular and didn't receive the press this one's gonna, but it was the same guy."

"What happened?"

"A movie theater. A multiplex down on Utica got rammed, killing two ticket girls. That one was a five-year-old Mercedes, and it had to have been flying. The passenger, a thirty-five-year-old professional woman from Manhattan, was DOA. No seat belt. Driver missing. Still missing. Passenger owned the car."

Gavin frowned and glanced around the room. "I'm surprised the Feds aren't here, too."

Rogers nodded. "They spoke to me earlier. There's too much wrong with the picture for them. Too much alcohol at the scene to consider religious fanatics. At best we might have some sort of copycat, but I don't think this guy has much of a cause. Personally, I think he just likes to wreck things."

"How do you know it was the same driver?"

"Prints, for one. Which is how we know for certain the driver's a male. They're big — really big. Prints on the door, on the wheel, on the beer cans and bottles thrown all over. And this," Rogers said, reaching into the side pocket of his jacket. He pulled out a plastic evidence bag and dangled it in front of Gavin.

"A crab claw?" Gavin said. It looked like something that had been taken from someone's Red Lobster dinner.

"Lobster claw, to be exact. It was used as

a roach clip. I found one just like it in the ashtray of the Mercedes. This one was in the truck. Have you ever seen a lobster claw used as a roach clip before?"

Gavin's mind was spinning, rage building at the thought that this disaster had been intentional. The pain on the faces around him and the memory of the dead and injured on the ground at the aquarium, some of them children, took on new meaning. The anguish was no longer a result of an irresponsible accident. And the one who had caused it was still on the loose. Free.

"No," he finally said in reply to Roger's question. "I haven't."

"Neither have I. Now I have three of them. The first one was from a Jeep that crashed into some people sleeping under the boardwalk. It didn't make the news, but with two dead homeless, one dead passenger, and a missing driver I got called in. The passenger, who owned the vehicle, was near pickled in vodka. The lobster claw was in the ashtray and wound up having the same fingerprints as the one found in the Mercedes. I don't have to tell you we just found the same prints on this one."

"A serial killer? You're telling me the

driver's a serial killer who uses cars and trucks instead of a gun?"

"Instead of a howitzer would be more like it."

"That's insane."

"Quite possibly."

"I mean, he can't care about his own life, either."

"Not if he's placing all his trust in airbags and seat belts."

"And you have no idea how to find him because he never drives his own car and the passenger's always dead."

"You're starting to get the picture."

"Why would anyone give him the keys? If they know him they've got to know he's nuts, and if they don't know him, they'd be giving their car to a stranger. It doesn't make sense."

"All the passengers were drunk. Very drunk. The Jeep passenger had .31 percent alcohol in the blood. The Mercedes woman was .29 and the truck guy .34."

"Point three-four? He must have been dead *before* the crash."

Rogers shook his head. "Unbelievably, no. Way too much blood at the scene to have come from someone already dead. At least he never felt that post go through him." He handed Gavin a business card that read "Detective Steven Rogers, Accident Investigation Squad."

Gavin took the card and looked in the direction of the ICU. "Yeah, wouldn't have wanted him to suffer any," he said bitterly.

Rogers paused, then looked with Gavin toward the ICU. "Hey, I'm real sorry about your grandfather, Pierce. We'll get this guy. He likes what he does. Sooner or later he'll turn up — probably dead as a passenger in his own car. If he has one."

"Right now, I'd rather have him alive," Gavin said, clenching his fist. "I'd rather have him alive."

— 5 —

Krogan drained the last few ounces from a stray fifth of Jack Daniel's he'd found discarded in an empty bait bucket. He put the cap back on the bottle and threw it overboard in the hope another boat would hit it. Two weeks had passed since he'd woken up inside a Coney Island Dumpster, reeking of fermenting garbage and in so much pain he could hardly move. Now the pain was gone and as usual he had only a spotty recollection of what had happened. He had heard the confirming news of the crash at the aquarium and was quite proud of the results.

He continued to cruise outside the mouth of Hempstead Harbor, paying zero attention to the new construction on what had once been called the Gold Coast, where famous turn-of-the-century money moguls' estates were now being turned into upscale waterfront developments. He had no interest in local or even global growth; he despised the old estates, the new homes, the builders, and whoever the new owners would be.

Instead he monitored his GPS, seeking to locate exactly where he had placed his hidden buoy and lobster trap. The technology of the unit meant nothing to him; it was nothing more than a tool. In fact, he would rather have used a surface marker, but then the traps could be pilfered as they had been when he used to work these waters with his father.

Krogan grimaced. He never thought about his father anymore. The man was long dead and gone. Krogan had never known his mother, who'd left him and his father when he was too young to remember. Krogan's father had spent his time either working the lobster traps or drinking. By the time he died of liver disease, Krogan knew enough to get by in his inherited business, which was all he cared to do.

Although his lobster boat was forty feet long with a huge beam and spacious work area that covered more than half the vessel, Krogan didn't look out of proportion in comparison. He was a big man — more than 280 pounds, six-five and muscular. His rock-hard right arm bore a tattoo of a speeding horse-drawn chariot with a cloud of fire in its draft. The chariot was driven by a man with a gargoyle's head and was pulled by a horse with bright yellow eyes — a souvenir of another night he couldn't remember. The demonic display reflected colorfully in the bright sunlight.

He pulled back on the throttle with a large, meaty hand, quieting the deep rumble of the rugged diesel that powered the boat, which he had renamed *Shadahd* — the password that, when spoken at the right time to the right person, unlocked doors he had not known to exist a few years ago. With a steady fifteen mile-per-hour wind from the stern, the boat drifted over the submerged buoy marker in the choppy summer waters of Long Island Sound. It was 11:50 a.m. and this was his first pickup of the day, which had started for him only an hour ago. Not that he had a schedule to keep — the lobsters didn't care what time it was, so why should he?

He leaned over and saw the buoy below the water's surface, right where he had planted it. He fished for the suspended line with a long gaff, snagged it, and pulled it up, his muscular forearms flexing as the old, barnacle-encrusted Styrofoam marker broke the cool surface. As he pulled the buoy over the side he noticed a sailboat heading in his direction. He recognized it instantly — the same cursed sailboat had cut too close to his bow three days ago when he was dropping the traps. He snarled at the boat. If it happened again, the puny moron trying to sail it would pay.

He picked up the line and wrapped it around the pulley winch. The clutch mechanism engaged and the winch began to pull the line. The first trap lifted into the air, water cascading back into the waves below. He pulled the trap onto the boat's ledge table and felt no special gratitude for the lone lobster he found inside. Stepping back from the trap he examined the creature — a three-pounder, flapping and snapping. He was about to band the creature's lively claws when a stirring sensation swirled through his head, as if a swarm of bees were using his brain for their hive. His gaze shifted from the lobster toward the sunlight sparkling on the nearby wave tops. The dancing light quickly fell into a hypnotic rhythm with the slow rocking action of the boat; he could no longer look away or even blink. The rolling of the waves appeared to slow. The sound of water lapping up against the side of the boat faded into a low hiss as the natural, conscious world in which he lived once again faded into a vision from the unknown.

In the vision Krogan saw a young woman — a waitress — scribbling orders on a pad as she stood at a table where four businessmen were seated, one of them pointing at the open menu in his hand. The waitress was shapely, dressed in khaki shorts, a white button-down shirt, and tan canvas boots with matching socks. She looked more like she was dressed for a safari than to wait tables. Her brown hair was pulled back in a French braid, revealing a gold, five-point star earring the size of a quarter. Krogan felt a desire to meet her — a hunger.

As he stared at the vision of the woman, Krogan heard a loud horn blast, then another. The vision began to break up. He blinked as the air cleared and the sunlit water reappeared. Overpowering the low rumble of his boat came another blast. He shook his head clear and turned in the direction of the intruder.

That same feeble sailboat had not sufficiently altered its course and was approaching rapidly. The man in the sailboat was having a terrible time handling his craft. Krogan was familiar with this particular forty-one-foot Morgan, having seen it many times in one of the slips behind the bulkhead in the harbor. An experienced sailor could have handled the boat by himself, but this guy was nothing but a rookie. Krogan despised him for that. His repulsion mounted as the man desperately ran back and forth trying to compensate for his inadequate skills. The fool had obviously miscalculated the wind and his angle of tack, and though he would probably miss hitting the stern of Krogan's boat, he would be dangerously close. Dangerous for the man, that was . . .

Krogan could care less about an accident. In fact, he enjoyed the thought and considered making it a reality. His boat was much stronger and heavier than the sailboat. He could motor out far enough for his powerful engine to get him to full speed and then ram the other craft dead center. He'd cut that wind-sucker in half like an ax through a watermelon, and hopefully the rookie with it.

The Morgan drew closer, entering Krogan's space. He could see now that the man was not alone. A young woman in a bathing suit designed for maximum sun absorption and minimum imagination stood up to see how close they were coming. She had the kind of looks most men would desire, but Krogan was unimpressed; if she was entertained by such an idiot as this inept sailor, then she deserved to share in whatever calamity befell him.

"Sorry," the man yelled in a clumsy attempt at camaraderie as the massive sails of his boat blocked Krogan's sun and they passed within fifty feet of *Shadahd*'s stern. The sexy passenger smiled and mouthed the same feeble apology.

Krogan wished he could reach out, pull the fool overboard by the throat, and drown him. But no — he would bide his time. For now, he would simply send his enemies a message. He stared them both in the eye, raised the three-pound lobster, and in a single movement ripped it in half with his bare hands as if it were a prophetic voodoo doll reflecting their own destiny. Without the least expression he crushed the tail in his hand, squeezing the raw meat into his mouth while the claws on the other half of the animal continued to twitch and snap in phantom reaction.

The inept sailor's eyes widened in surprise and his passenger looked away in apparent disgust. Krogan laughed loudly, with meat still hanging out of his mouth, until the mortified couple passed from earshot. He made note of the sailboat's name, written in script on the stern: *Playdate.*

"Enjoy it," he said. "It'll be your last."

— 6 —

Gavin stood under a large shade tree on a small hill less than a hundred feet away and watched. He was alone. He clenched his fists as the gravediggers tossed the first shovelful of dirt into the hole and he heard it land on Grampa's coffin. He wondered how many others associated with the crash had heard that same sound. *Thud . . . thud . . .*

Gavin was no stranger to cemeteries and coffins and mounds of dirt being shoveled into holes. His father had died of pneumonia when he was six, his mother of cancer when he was sixteen, and his fiancée of one day on a motorcycle ten years ago.

Earlier, while the casket had still straddled the hole, a lone priest had arrived to pay his respects. Gavin had briefly thanked him for coming but aside from that had nothing to say to him. Finally, the priest had mumbled a short prayer and left.

Gavin had not prayed. He had done his praying while Grampa was still alive. Grampa didn't need prayer anymore. Gavin had no doubt Grampa was with God and heaven was a better place with Grampa there.

The two gravediggers had waited patiently a short distance away while Gavin spoke with the priest and said his good-byes to Grampa. When Gavin finally stepped away from the gravesite, they had moved in and lowered the coffin into the cold, dark cavity. From the lack of mourners, they must have thought Grampa was just another nobody, unloved and forgotten. Gavin wanted to tell them they were wrong. He wanted to tell them Grampa was known and loved and would be remembered . . . and avenged.

The thought of Grampa's death still had not set in, and from past experience, he knew it would take a while. Three days ago, when he had first heard, awakened by the phone call at one in the morning, he had not believed it. There must be some mistake, he'd thought. He had just been with the old man twelve hours earlier and the doctors' and nurses' smiling faces had assured him Grampa was stable. He'd even been developing an appetite. The doctors, who had at first braced Gavin for the worst, had upgraded his grandfather's status, raising Gavin's hopes from doubtful to questionable to probable. The outrage of the crime had become almost tolerable when Grampa began winking at Gavin while being pampered by the young nurses.

But suddenly Grampa was dead. Assassinated by a blood clot. Dead without Gavin being there at his bedside.

All the rage tempered by Grampa's progress had returned. Stronger. Grampa had not just died; he had been killed — intentionally murdered. The blood clot could just as well have been the impact of the truck itself.

Gavin blinked. The workers were gone and the grave filled. An afternoon breeze cooled the sweat on his brow and leaves came to rest on the fresh dirt mound. Except for a couple of squirrels chasing each other around the trunk of a big maple tree and a few sparrows hopping on and off an old thin tombstone pecking at seeds, there wasn't a sign of life amidst the shallow rolling hills of this humble cemetery.

Suddenly, unable to contain his emotions, Gavin let out a sustained yell. How could God have allowed this to happen to

Grampa and those others? In his rage, Gavin almost kicked over the tombstone, but caught himself. No. He needed to leave this place and focus his anger in the right direction. He needed to get to head-quarters and check his messages. Maybe Rogers had called. If not, Gavin needed to get in touch with Detective Chris Grella, who had been on vacation for the last couple of weeks. Chris was Nassau County's answer for Brooklyn's Detective Rogers. Unless the accident was related to a previous case that belonged to another detective, it automatically became Chris's case and Chris was an old friend Gavin had had the good fortune to be paired up with in his patrol-car days.

Chris would have info, and Gavin couldn't wait to pick his brain.

— 7 —

"Oooooh, yeahhh! Punch it, baby! punch it!" the girl screamed, a beer in her right hand and a burning joint in her left.

Krogan held the Camaro Z28's leather steering wheel lightly, as if he wasn't really flying down Shore Road at 120 miles per hour. He glanced at the car's owner in the seat beside him. The girl with a gold star earring the size of a quarter rocked back and forth to the loud, heavy-metal beat pounding through the cloudy, air-conditioned interior. The music reverberated in Krogan's flesh.

As always, the one from his vision had already started drinking by the time they'd met in the flesh. He'd found the waitress already in her car, leaving the restaurant's parking lot. The nametag on the casual uniform shirt she'd been wearing when he first greeted her with the word *shadahd* had read "Lori," but as usual he had known her from another time and by another name.

As drunk as he was, he still recalled vividly the last time he'd partied with this one. She'd looked completely different then and even spoken a different language, but he knew for certain she was the same. He also recalled, just as vividly, knowing her in other times and other places — many times, each with a different face but only one name: Naphal. Krogan knew the next time they had a date she would be different again . . . but the same.

He nonchalantly crushed the brake pedal to the floor and eased the steering wheel fractionally to the right, sending the midnight-blue sports car into a screeching, tire-smoking skid. The speedometer plummeted to zero and the car slid sideways to a halt perfectly in line with the driveway entrance to the Hempstead Harbor Town Dock and Marina. When Krogan punched the gas pedal again, the car momentarily vibrated in place until the spinning wheels finally caught on the hot blacktop, propelling them into the parking lot and announcing their arrival with a loud squeal and reeking smoke.

Krogan reached behind his seat and found another cold can of cheap beer, which he immediately opened and guzzled.

He opened the window, tossed the empty can, belched loudly, and nailed the gas pedal again, driving to the rear of the parking lot and stopping in front of the pier. He turned the ignition off but left the key in the auxiliary position so the music could continue to blast.

"AC's not working," Naphal said, staring at the vents with narrowed, bloodshot eyes.

Krogan shut the fan off. Without the engine running the compressor, the air conditioner couldn't create cold air and the car was quickly getting hot and stuffy. He reopened his tinted window a couple of inches to let some of the smoke out, but not enough for anyone to see him. He didn't care about the lack of air in the car as much as he wanted to keep the front window from hazing up. He needed a good view for the night's grand finale.

"Better?" he asked.

"No," she answered.

He popped open another frosty beer and poured it over her head and onto her shirt. "How 'bout now?" he growled.

Naphal looked down at her drenched T-shirt. The cold beer was raising goose bumps on her wet arms. She smiled. "Much better," she slurred, then took a long hit on the burning joint.

"Oooh! Now it's cold," she said, stretching her arms to the ceiling.

Unwilling to be distracted from his primary objective, Krogan glanced back through the windshield to assess the view. Half the crimson sun had already sunk behind the trees that lined the hillside on the other side of the harbor. Along a fishing pier that jutted out from the parking lot, a few fishermen were making the most of the early evening sunlight. There was no sign of the boat.

He returned his attention to Naphal. She was rocking erratically to the high-powered music, out of step with the beat. Or maybe he was. Whatever. They had been drinking, smoking pot, and driving wildly for the last hour or so. Normally he would have treated himself to her, but tonight he wanted to keep a watchful eye on the bay. If the Morgan forty-one was on its usual schedule, the real fun would be starting any minute.

He took the shrinking joint from Naphal and fixed it into a small lobster claw, took a drag, then passed it back to her.

"Cool," she said, examining the claw with red eyes. She took another long hit, then passed it back.

Krogan sucked loudly on the last smoldering remains, then placed the claw into the ashtray, all the while looking through the rapidly clouding window before him. Naphal coughed spasmodically, her lungs unable to hold the smoke down any longer. Still coughing, she turned and reached behind the seat for another beer. As she rotated back around she paused to look at a tattoo on Krogan's left shoulder. It read, "LOVE HATE, HATE LOVE."

"I like," she said, then slowly leaned over and kissed the dark-green letters on his shoulder. "Mmmm, you're tasty. Where did you find this body?"

Krogan leaned back against the headrest and grabbed her hair, pulling her toward him, but then saw the silhouette of a large boat with its sails down, motoring home across the horizon. He pulled off his sunglasses, squinted, then wiped at the fogged windshield with his left hand. There it was. He reached for the ignition key, absently pushing the girl's head away, and started the engine.

"Hey!" Naphal said.

"Shadahd," Krogan said in a deep, lusty voice. The sound of the word leaving his lips generated its own energy within him, just as it always had and always would.

"Shadahd!" Naphal responded with a

sudden enchantment, then pulled the seat belt across herself and buckled it.

Krogan also buckled his seat belt, then looked out the front window with a cold, focused stare. His timing would have to be perfect. But of course it would be. Beside him, the girl lifted her beer and guzzled it down, then rocked aggressively to the driving riff of a lead guitar.

The sailboat began to slow as it approached the entrance to the marina just beyond the fishing pier. As Krogan watched them, a shadow moved briefly across his view. He looked up to see an ultralight plane flying overhead. He'd seen it before. Its graceful design, colorful fabric wings, and curious flying ability were wasted on him, though; as far as he was concerned, the man was a nuisance, tying up traffic on the boat ramp and attracting the attention of boaters that should be getting out of his way. Perhaps someday soon he would deal with that idiot, too.

He returned his attention to the boat. It was time. He shifted into drive and floored the gas pedal. The rear wheels screamed in search of traction, then grabbed. As they began to move Krogan slipped his hand over and unbuckled the girl's seat belt. The recoiling strap caught her under the arm.

"Hey!" she said. "What are you doing?" She tried to rebuckle, but the strap had locked and she would have to let it finish recoiling before she could try again.

The car blazed across the parking lot toward the pier. Those who had been fishing were now turning their heads. Krogan laughed as he saw their eyes widen. The Camaro's undercarriage sparked as the car hit the pier's entrance ramp. The fishermen dropped their poles and scrambled to get over the railing they had been leaning on. With one exception, they all jumped into the water a dozen feet below. A fat one, though, was having trouble climbing over the rail. Krogan veered slightly to give him a little help. The man had managed to get his left leg over the rail. With a loud, sickening whack, the car hit his right leg as the heavy fisherman lifted it, spinning him like a giant human Frisbee into the air, his leg unnaturally loose as he twirled.

The sailboat had just started passing by the dock about sixty-five feet out. The speeding car crashed through the railing like a sledgehammer hurled through a window, exploding the old wooden barrier into splinters and continuing on virtually unhindered.

"Shadahd!" Krogan yelled fiercely as the car flew silently through the air. With the sun glaring directly into the windshield, he couldn't see his intended victims very well with his natural eyes, but he saw them with perfect clarity in his mind. Experience had taught him to trust and enjoy the vision as it came. At first, he saw the moron sailor continuing to steer the doomed vessel as if he hadn't yet connected the inevitable. He had turned his head to see where the loud noise had come from and had not immediately recognized the approaching flying mass as being a car, or even as being out of place. In quick succession his blank expression gave way to surprise, shock, and finally terror. Krogan experienced a wave of delight as he saw the fear grab hold of the man, crippling his ability to respond logically — further proof his prey was worthless. Without good enough reflexes to escape, the man would now have only enough time to see his life flash rapidly before him.

Halfway to his target Krogan's focus shifted to the man's Asian-looking companion. She also had responded in frozen disbelief, gripping a nearby handrail tightly. Krogan could hear her thoughts, taste her confusion.

In the final moment before impact, Krogan lapsed into that familiar experience, a dimension that momentarily filled his being with euphoric satisfaction — a place where time slowed and consciousness soared. A dreamlike but acute awareness of previous crashes flooded his mind. Crashes that made him feel the immortal warrior he was.

He glanced at Naphal. She had given up on the seat belt. Both her palms were pressed against the dashboard to keep her upright in her seat as the front of the car tilted downward. Her face was relaxed and her stare trancelike. He knew she was experiencing the same acute ultradimensional reality he was.

The front of the car had just cleared the side of the boat. The moron's shocked, gasping face was suddenly clearly visible as the edge of the hood caught him under the chin. In his near-timeless state, Krogan savored a rush of violent hilarity as the man's head appeared to sit on the front of the hood like an ornament before disappearing downward into the grill.

Cracks formed in the center of the steering wheel and then opened, giving birth to the airbag, unfolding like a time-lapsed blooming flower before him. The silence fled with a rush of thunder. Naphal's arms buckled into the dashboard as she left her seat. The top of her head touched the sunlit windshield, creating bright striking lines of light in it before breaking through a hole that became larger as her shoulders passed through. With a final jarring, wrenching explosion of sound, the car slammed into the boat.

Silence returned as the car and boat rocked to and fro. The airbag deflated, having done its job. After a moment of stunned reaction, Krogan wearily unbuckled his seat belt. It was once again time to leave.

— 8 —

Gavin drew the attention of the crowd of on-lookers as he screeched to a stop in the Hempstead Harbor Marina parking lot and hurried from his car. When he'd heard the news of the crash he'd turned what should have been an hour-and-thirty-minute drive into fifty-five minutes.

Before the crash at the aquarium he had paid little attention to auto accident calls. But for the last two weeks he'd been listening carefully for them. Within moments of hearing this one he'd found himself shaking with anticipation. According to reports, the driver had mysteriously disappeared from a horrific, bizarre collision.

Gavin's pace was just short of a run as he swept under the yellow tape barrier that stayed the growing crowd. At his left were two ambulances with doors open and lights flashing. He wondered if there were any survivors — someone to make a connection back to the driver. He turned toward the water and stopped, his mind unable to take in what lay before him. The bizarre sight was eerily reminiscent of the monster truck spearing the viewing window of the holding tank. With a sweaty hand he tried to swipe what felt like icy-cold ants crawling up the back of his neck, then shuddered as the goose bumps continued down his spine.

As he watched a Marine Patrol boat struggle to bring in the sailboat with its unwelcome cargo, Gavin's hatred of the driver could not keep him from marveling. If the driver had actually been trying to hit the boat while it was in motion . . . what a shot. Was it just dumb luck, or was there actually skill involved? But how could there be skill involved? Even skill requires a certain amount of practice. How often could you practice driving your car off a dock into a moving sailboat? It had to be dumb luck.

The crime scene operation was in full swing. Gavin marched up to a uniform cop trying to keep unwanted traffic away.

"What you got?" he asked, his shield hanging in plain view from his sports jacket pocket.

The cop motioned toward the marina.

"We're searching the boat slips. If the driver's still alive and his body didn't get dragged out with the tide, it's the most likely place he'd be. The boats coming up the boat ramp are also being searched. Crime Scene's waiting at the dock for the Marine Unit to get the boat in. They've been having a rough time maneuvering that thing. Guess that's why you don't see too many sailboat car ferries. They tried pushin' it, then pullin' it, and now they're tryin' to tie up side by side and get it to the ramp dock."

Gavin looked at the floating ramp next to the boat ramp. On it were a team of forensic techs and print specialists watching the awkward rig being slowly brought to them.

"Their hopes of an undisturbed scene is shot to blazes on this one," the cop said.

"Anyone see the driver?" Gavin asked.

"Don't know yet. Maybe she did," the cop said, motioning to a stretcher being rushed up the boat ramp. "The patrol boat pulled her out first thing."

As the stretcher passed by, the uniform cop told Gavin the identity of the girl on the gurney was still unknown. She had apparently been thrown and was found unconscious. Her body was badly scratched and bruised and her head was strapped into place on the gurney. Her bruised and swollen face couldn't hide her Asian heritage. Gavin's eyes followed her to the ambulance. He hoped she made it. Maybe she could shed some light on who this maniac was. Any information from her would have to wait, though. As soon as the van's doors closed the ambulance sped out of the parking lot, lights flashing and siren wailing.

"Any other survivors?"

The cop closed his eyes and shook his head. "Not good news. The man at the helm lost his head."

"Literally?"

The cop nodded. "Yup, his neck was crushed by the bumper. The head's still missing. The girl in the car is dead, too. She might've survived if she'd been wearing her seat belt. They found it unbuckled and under her armpit. Looks as though she was trying to put it on."

Gavin frowned and looked in the direction of the wreck. "Or release it."

The cop's eyebrows raised. "Suicide?"

Gavin didn't answer. He wasn't thinking suicide. "Any ID?"

"I don't know. There was a handbag on the floor under a pile of beer cans, but we didn't disturb it. Oh, there's something else. On the beach there's a guy in some kind of homemade seaplane. He saw the crash from the air but, like everyone else, didn't see the driver leave. We've asked him to wait until the boats get out first; seems it takes him a while to break down his craft."

Gavin turned toward the beach and saw the seaplane the cop was speaking of. It looked more like a big kite than a plane. The pilot was kicked back in one of the craft's two seats, arms folded, watching the Marine Patrol recover the sailboat.

Gavin's attention detoured to an unmarked car that had stopped just behind the perimeter tape. He could see Detective Chris Grella through the windshield. Finally! Maybe now he could get some answers. Chris had been on vacation for two of the longest weeks in Gavin's life and Gavin was glad to see him back. The man was a good friend and a good cop. A hard worker, too, running his own business of emptying construction-site Dumpsters when he wasn't on duty. Gavin didn't know how his friend functioned on the little sleep he got, but Chris was always alert and chipper, a devoted friend who came to Gavin's aid without hesitation whenever the need arose.

"Hey, Gav! What are you doing here?" Chris said with a smile as he got out of the car.

"When did you get back?" Gavin said, figuring Chris would not have asked that question if he'd heard about the aquarium crash and Grampa's death. Chris knew how close Gavin was to Grampa.

"Just this morning," he said as his gaze wandered past Gavin to the shoreline. Gavin watched Chris's jaw drop. "Good grief! What happened?"

"*Who* happened might be more like it."

Chris turned back to Gavin. "An EDP?"

"No!" Gavin shot back. He didn't want the killer classified as an Emotionally Disturbed Person. An EDP would officially require more sensitivity and understanding than Gavin was willing to give. They were looked upon as extremely dangerous and unpredictable, while at the same time insane enough to escape responsibility for their actions. As far as Gavin was concerned, this psycho was going to pay with his life.

"What was he on? Missile fuel?"

"That and beer. There're cans all over the car."

"I hope one of 'em's cold," Chris replied.

Normally Gavin might have followed up that smart remark with one of his own. But the likelihood that this was the same lunatic who had killed his grandfather had sucked the life from what little sense of humor he had.

"Chris, I need a big favor," he said. "I need for you to request I partner up with you on this if it turns out to be who I think it is."

"Fine with me. Why?"

"I'll explain after we check out the scene. If the missing driver's who I think he is, I want him."

Chris's eyes narrowed. "You know I'll do whatever I can, but the lieutenant might not go for it. If he feels it's a revenge thing . . ."

"You can tell him you need me to help you catch up. I'm already involved with a Detective Rogers in Brooklyn on this one. I was there when this driver crashed into the aquarium's whale tank." Chris's eyes widened. "I'll tell you about it later. But you have to tell the lieutenant to take me off the charts. There's no way I can give this case the proper focus if I'm saddled with other cases."

Chris took a moment before answering. "If this turns out to be your guy, we are thinking of handcuffs as a first option, right?"

Gavin didn't smile. He didn't even blink.

"Okay, okay," Chris said, raising his hands slightly in surrender. "I'll tell him whatever you want, but the lieutenant's a pretty good detective himself."

"We'll talk. Right now I have to get down to that car," Gavin said, seeing the boat was almost at the dock.

As the two men made their way to the floating tragedy, Gavin heard the familiar sound of a helicopter. He looked back over his head as the chopper made a low pass, like a vulture sizing up its evening meal.

"The media," Chris sighed. "This is the kind of stuff they dream of. They're probably dispatching ground crews right now. Better watch the tape line. We're gonna have some pushy company soon," he said to a uniform cop passing them on their way down the ramp.

"Company's already here, Detective," the officer said, motioning toward the parking lot.

Gavin turned. "Perfect," he said, seeing Mel Gasman walking across the parking lot followed by a photographer. Gasman was an obnoxious pest who wrote for *The Daily Post*, a sensationalist rag that littered

New York City and the surrounding sub-urbs.

"Draw a line in the sand," Chris yelled to the officer as he hurried after Gavin to the boat. "If he crosses it, read him his rights." Gasman was already challenging the policeman.

"Wait up, Gav," Chris said, trying to keep pace. "Am I gonna need sneakers for our new partnership?"

Gavin didn't answer. He couldn't stop to explain what he was feeling right now. The closer he got to the boat the more he knew the crash had been caused by the same driver. *His* driver. He could feel it . . . taste it. Only this time it was in his jurisdiction and he could do something about it.

The floating dock, whose primary func-tion was to secure small boats for those who were either retrieving or parking their trailers, was dwarfed by the large sailboat being tied to it. The water wasn't deep enough for the boat's draft, and the blue wa-terline painted on the keel was revealed as the waves lapped against it. When the boat was secured, the forensic team boarded. The two FMIs had to climb over the aft cable rail; the natural entry was completely occupied by the Camaro's trunk, which cantilevered three feet off the side.

A couple of AMTs followed closely by a supervising assistant coroner were about to follow the forensic crew onboard. They turned as they heard Gavin and Chris approaching. Gavin, who was usually more cordial, quickly boarded the craft without so much as a nod of acknowledgment to anyone.

"Fellas," Chris said to the attendants as he followed Gavin onto the boat.

"Wow . . . That musta hurt," said one of the forensic team, breaking the silence of the others, who were staring in shock at the mess. Gavin stopped next to them, momentarily taken aback by the gruesome sight of the man with the crushed neck and no head. He had apparently been pulled out from under the car by the rescue team and left on the deck. Above him and still in the car was a dead girl, her head and shoulders thrust through the windshield, apparently restrained from going any further by the seat belt that went over her right shoulder and under her left armpit.

Chris stopped at Gavin's side, the assistant coroner and his attendants behind him, peering over Chris's shoulder.

"So, what do you think was the cause of death?" Chris deadpanned to the coroners. The forensic techs laughed as though they hadn't heard that line a thousand times before.

Gavin didn't laugh. He was busy looking from the body to the car. He needed to get to the driver's side door. He climbed around the front of the Camaro, surprised it hadn't cracked the side of the boat apart. The car door was wide open. When Gavin stepped around it he saw the deflated airbag drooping out of the steering wheel. Just as they'd said, there was no driver. His eyes quickly found the open ashtray below the radio. Nothing. Frustrated, he pulled a pen from his pocket and poked around in the cigarette butts and roaches. Maybe it had fallen out in the crash? He looked on the floor, pushing some empty beer cans around with the pen. Where was it? Maybe the killer hadn't used one this time. Maybe it was still on him, wherever he was. Maybe not. Maybe the thought of catching this maniac for Grampa was making him delusional? No. He was certain. This was him. He could feel it in his gut.

"Detective? Excuse me," said one of the techs. "Is there anything in particular you're looking for? Maybe it would be better if we —"

"A lobster claw," Gavin interrupted. "A little, freakin' lobster claw. I'm not trying to intrude in your workspace, but there's something I need to know now. Not tomorrow. Not in an hour. Now."

Gavin knew all too well that a crime scene had the potential of becoming its own war zone — detectives, forensic officers, and coroner's assistants all vying for priority. He could never be accused of innocent-bystander status in the tension between units, but today he was having an especially tough time keeping the big picture in focus.

"I know how you feel. I didn't have my nap, either," the FMI said.

Gavin shot a look at him. "Look, pal, I don't think you understand. I —"

"I know. I know. All you can think about is finding something that probably looks very much like . . . this?" the man said, holding up a clear plastic bag with a small lobster claw, burnt at the tip.

"Where did . . ." Gavin said as he plucked the bag from the man's hand.

"It's what we do," the man said with a smirk.

The man's sarcasm was lost on Gavin, who was unable to hold back his response. "Yes! I knew it was you!" he shouted, the bag clenched in his right fist.

"Oh, Gavin, me boy," Chris said from

where he'd been watching the exchange. "I think it's time you filled in a few blanks for me."

— 9 —

Gavin explained in detail what had happened at the aquarium and how Grampa had died. Chris, knowing the relationship Gavin had had with his grandfather, offered heartfelt condolences to his friend and vowed to help in any way he could, just as Gavin had expected. They now stood at the end of the fishing pier examining what had been the wooden railing that had supported a generation of elbows and fishing rods. The sun had long since set. Below and to the right, bright lights had been set up, to the delight of the media, to assist the forensic team. Below and to the left, the marina, with over a hundred boat slips, was swarming with police checking and double-checking every possible hiding place. Remembering the frustration and anger of Detective Rogers in the hospital, Gavin wasn't surprised they hadn't found anything yet.

"This guy's a real kamikaze," Chris said,

shaking his head.

"Kamikazes die," Gavin said dryly.

"So why won't this guy die? Everyone around him does."

Gavin knew Chris hadn't meant to be insensitive, but his comment instantly ignited flashbacks of Grampa's helplessness in the holding tank, his coffin lowering into the cold, dark earth. He quickly shook his head and brought himself back to the moment at hand. "Lucky, I guess. Alcohol? Air bags? Seat belts? All of the above?"

"Yeah, and a tough hide. This guy doesn't just survive. He —"

"How does he do it?" Gavin snapped. "To survive these crashes is one thing, but to escape . . . and then do it again . . . like this. Maybe he has help. Maybe he gets rescued. I don't know. How else could he do it?" At that moment, as much as Gavin wanted the killer, he wondered if he would ever find him. Would he always be one step behind, like Rogers?

Chris was silent for a long moment, then turned to Gavin. "How else could he have gotten away but by swimming? He either swam into the marina or he swam across the harbor. Either way it's a long swim for anyone, much less someone who just climbed out of that wreck. If he swam to the other side he should have been spotted on the beach."

"But he wasn't," Gavin said.

"Right. Then he swam into the marina. If he's hiding in the boats, he's ours. There must be twenty cops down there."

Gavin shook his head. "There are a dozen ways out of that marina and with all the attention the crash attracted he could have gotten away without being seen." He paused. "I know this sounds sick." He motioned toward the boat. "But I'm glad he showed up in *our* backyard. Now we can hunt."

"Maybe he was just passing through," Chris said.

"His trail's easy enough to follow."

"Hey, fellas. If it isn't my two friends Detectives Pierce and Grella."

Gavin and Chris turned to see Mel Gasman approaching, followed by his photographer. Gasman was a curly-haired little gnat of a reporter who would climb right into your cell phone if you didn't swat him away from time to time. He always seemed to be where you didn't want him, asking questions you didn't want to answer. On the upside, he wasn't nasty or belligerent and even had a work ethic to be admired. He never made a cop look bad in print; in fact, he often went out of his way to compliment. Although Gavin would never admit it to the man, Gasman's remarks had actually been instrumental in Gavin's promotion to detective. Someday Gavin would thank him, but not until he'd retired and no longer had to deal with Gasman at a crime scene. The idea of allowing Gasman to even think that either Gavin or the department was indebted to him was almost frightening.

From Gavin's experience, the tougher he was with the reporter, the easier he was to handle, although even then Gasman would wedge himself into anything that looked like a crack in the defense.

"We're not your friends, Mel," Gavin said.

"Oh, but you are. You guys might not want to admit it, but I know that deep inside you love me to pieces."

"Break you *into* pieces is more like it," Chris said. He leaned toward Gavin. "I don't think I can stomach this weasel right now."

"Forget him, Chris. We've got business to take care of. A lot's happened while you were away, sitting by a trout stream with a fishing line tied to your toe."

"How'd you know how I fish?" Chris said, pokerfaced.

"The fishing line is coming out of your shoe," Gavin retorted and turned to leave. Chris looked down at his shoe, then followed.

"Say, Pierce," Gasman yelled. "This is the second crazy accident you've been around in as many weeks. Do you think it's the same guy?"

Gavin didn't answer. Notoriety might be just what the driver wanted. More publicity could mean more accidents — more deaths. On the other hand, the exposure might scare him away entirely . . .

He looked again at the car imbedded into the sailboat. Was he losing his mind or had the killer purposely driven the length of the fishing pier as fast as he could, recklessly aimed for the fishermen, then crashed through the rail and into his target — a boat over twenty yards out? On second thought, he decided, it was unlikely the killer was afraid of anything, much less the media.

On his way back to the car Gavin noticed the man with the homemade seaplane, who had finally gotten his turn on the ramp. He had never seen such a contraption. It reminded him of a documentary on man's first attempts to fly. He watched curiously as the man drove the thing up the boat ramp. The engine was mounted high, the propeller built to push air like an everglade boat instead of pull it in like the planes Gavin was used to seeing. The colorful orange, white, and blue wing was also high, level with the engine, while the pilot sat underneath, all the way in the front in a small bucket seat, holding what looked like a video game joystick.

The engine noise was deafening as the plane pushed up the ramp. Once on the level surface of the parking field, the pilot throttled down and slowly made his way to the rear of a trailer, powering up onto it like a gargantuan dragonfly settling on a lily pad. The moment the dragonfly's engine turned off the propeller abruptly stopped and a stunning quiet filled the air.

"Excuse me," Gavin said as the man hopped off the trailer. "I'm Detective Pierce. You mind if I ask you a few questions?"

"Not at all," the man replied. "Do you mind if I work while we talk? I'd rather not break this thing down in the dark."

"Go right ahead. You need help?" Gavin asked.

"Why, that's mighty generous of you, Detective. Actually, if you could hold the end of the wing while I unbolt the struts, you'd save me a lot of time."

"No problem. What's your name?"

"Bill. Bill Goronwy," the man said, pulling a ratchet wrench from a small toolbox attached to the trailer.

"I understand you witnessed the accident."

"Sure did, and it was no accident. A shame. I don't know the guy who got killed, but I know the guy who chartered the boat out to him. I hope he's got insurance for something like this. He spent a lot of time fixing that boat up and a lot of money advertising it. For him, it was a business — his only business. I guess now he's out of work."

"Where were you when the crash happened?"

"About five hundred feet overhead," Bill said, loosening nuts as he spoke.

"I understand you didn't see the driver leave."

"Well, not exactly. I saw the driver's door pop open, but then I passed over and needed to turn so I wouldn't come too close to the high-tension wires; if I hit one of those I'd burn up like a bug in a zapper. The next time I looked, which was only a few seconds later, the guy was gone."

Bill put the nuts in the toolbox and instructed Gavin in how to help him place the wing in the trailer. They walked around to the other wing.

"What is this thing?" Gavin asked, taking his position at the tip.

"An ultralight. You don't usually find them in congested areas like this, but down south they're all over the place."

"Did you get this as a kit?"

"Actually, this one is a combination of several others. It's got Weedhopper wings, so I can get them on and off easily — if you call this easy. It has an old Hummer frame, a Full Lotus monofloat for a pontoon, and a Rotax 582 giving me all the power I need to take off with gear and a passenger."

Gavin hadn't understood a word of what the guy had said, except the last part. "You take passengers up in this thing?"

"Well, legally I can only take them if it's part of an instruction. But, yeah. You want to go up sometime?"

"No, no. I like it fine right here with both feet on the ground. I'm afraid of heights, especially in something like this," Gavin said as they pulled off the wing and placed it in the trailer by its mate.

"Thanks, Detective. I'm sorry I don't have more to tell you."

"No problem. Take my card and call me if anything else comes to mind."

With a wave good-bye, Gavin walked back to his car. He noticed before driving away that Chris was still talking to Gasman under the light.

— 10 —

Krogan felt weak but satisfied as he lay on a skinny mattress set upon a couple of lobster traps in the bow of his lobster boat. He was soaking wet and could only vaguely remember the swim that had brought him here. He did, however, remember the crash and savored the memory, replaying it over and over in his mind. He refrained from laughing aloud; he didn't want to be disturbed by the idiot police running around the marina, their busy footsteps creaking back and forth on the old wooden planks.

Several cops stopped outside the cabin and a diffused beam of light filtered through the porthole. Krogan knew they couldn't see him with the glass as dirty as it was, but he gave them the finger anyway, feeling the familiar dull pain of drunken soreness as he raised his arm. He heard voices but couldn't understand what they said; his cabin might be dirty, but it was watertight when locked, somewhat muffling outside sounds.

There was a thud and the boat rocked. Krogan smiled and reached for a twelve-gauge semiautomatic shotgun lying on a rotten net beside him. The outside of the barrel had rusty patches and the name *Ithaca* was pitted from salt and barely readable, but none of that would keep the buckshot from taking some cop's ugly face off the second the door opened.

The padlock on the door jingled as it was checked. Apparently Krogan hadn't forgotten to lock it, though he didn't remember. He looked at the hatch above and figured he must have come in that way. He must have tried the door first and left some kind of water trail on the floor outside. Was that what had made the cops curious enough to come aboard or were they checking all the boats?

Krogan raised the barrel of the gun until it aligned with the top of the door. At this point he would be disappointed if they left without a proper introduction. Maybe he shouldn't wait for the door to open. The thought of the shock the cops would express at the sight of a fellow cop's head exploding excited Krogan. His finger tightened on the rusty trigger.

The boat rocked again as the cops turned to leave the boat. They were even dumber than Krogan had first thought; either they hadn't noticed the water or had figured it hadn't evaporated yet from the day's work. They had also probably concluded the padlock couldn't have been locked from the inside. Krogan was disappointed. Couldn't the morons see the hatch?

He leveled the shotgun at the porthole, waiting for their silhouettes to appear through the glass. A nasty smile curved his lips as he heard the footsteps passing by. If he fired twice, he decided, he might be able to decapitate them. He was salivating at the thought of glass shattering and bodies dropping limply.

The instant the window darkened he fired . . . but the glass didn't shatter. There was no explosion. The gun was empty. The shadows disappeared along with the footsteps. Krogan cursed and looked across the cabin to where the box of shells sat on a shelf. He moved to get up but the soreness from the crash helped him realize the moment had passed. Instead, he dropped the gun back onto the netting and his head back onto the mattress, once again reliving his sketchy memories of the crash as he drifted to sleep.

— 11 —

Gavin awoke to his Golden Retriever's cold nose and wet tongue painting his face with saliva. Groaning, he pulled out the small sofa pillow his head was on and used it as a shield. He had fallen asleep watching the news and was still fully dressed except for the shoes he had kicked off when he first put his feet up. The morning news was now on, but he had no way of knowing if the report on the crash had been televised yet. No matter; he knew he could find a report from Gasman in the morning paper. As much as he despised the type of journalism the *Post* displayed, he subscribed to it for times like this. He needed to know what kind of hype to be prepared for.

"Go away, Cedar," he said from behind the safety of the pillow, knowing full well that when his dog had determined it was time to go outside he had no chance of going back to sleep. And sleep was all he wanted at the moment. Taking statements from the witnesses had gone well into the night . . . and for the most part had been fruitless. Nobody had noticed the driver exit and leave the scene of the crash.

Gavin slowly pulled the pillow downward until his bleary eyes could peer over its edge. Cedar's grinning face was barely far enough away for him to focus on.

"You got me again, didn't you?" he said.

Cedar barked, beating his tail against the couch for emphasis. Sometimes Gavin wondered just how much the dog understood. Sometimes he wondered if the dog wondered just how much Gavin understood.

"What time is it, Cee?" he asked, watching sunlight cut through a crack in the curtains and across the burnt orange carpet that had been chosen to match the dog hairs.

Cedar tilted his head and looked in the direction of the front door.

"I know. It's time to go out."

Cedar celebrated his master's keen perception with a couple of happy squeals and a puppylike circular dance that eventually spiraled him to the door.

"Who's got who trained, that's what I'd like to know," Gavin said, climbing out of the old cushions, which would retain his impression for a while before returning to their original shape. He hated sleeping in his clothes. Even though he'd slept for his usual six or seven hours, he still felt a little tired and a lot achier. He stood up and stretched, then popped the joints in his neck and back. A hot shower would help.

Gavin let Cedar out into the fenced-in front yard and picked up the paper from the stoop. Before he could open it he heard the phone ring. He picked up the cordless on the coffee table and plopped back onto the couch, watching the weatherman point at a map. "Pierce."

"Hey, Gav. Did you see the paper?" Chris Grella said.

"One second," Gavin said, tucking the phone into his chin to free his hands. He unfolded the newspaper on his knee. On the front page was a photo of Chris standing next to the boat. The title was typical *Daily Post*: "GHOST DRIVER KILLS AGAIN."

"Great," Gavin said sarcastically. "You *had* to pose."

"What's the matter? I thought you'd be glad. Someone might know this jerk and turn him in. They could read this and become suspicious of some guy who unexplainably turns up hurt. We could have his ass by lunchtime."

"Who told you that? Gasman?"

"I told me that. Besides, they were going to print the story with or without my help."

"It's the front page that bothers me. We don't know what drives this guy yet. This kind of publicity could inspire him," Gavin said as he turned to the story on page three.

NO ACCIDENT

Two people were killed and two others seriously injured yesterday when a sports car drove off the Hempstead Harbor Marina fishing pier at approximately 8:30 p.m. and crashed into a sailboat. The crash, which is under investigation, is alleged to have been intentional.

Mitchell Clayborne, a resident of Port Washington, was driving the boat at the time of the crash and was killed. His wife, Amber Clayborne, is in critical condition at Glen Cove Hospital. The Claybornes were on their honeymoon and apparently returning from a day of sailing when the accident occurred.

Witnesses who were fishing on the pier say the car, which had been in the parking lot for about a half hour, suddenly came racing toward them. One of the fishermen, James Carey of New Jersey, was unable to get out of the way in time and was hit by the car. He is listed in serious condition, also at Glen Cove. Carey claims the car purposely swerved to hit him.

The car allegedly continued on, shattered the railing, and smashed into the 40-foot sailboat as it passed by about 65 feet off shore.

Also killed was the passenger and owner of the car, Lori Hayslip, of Oyster Bay, who was a waitress at a local restaurant.

The search continues for the driver, who has mysteriously disappeared.

Coincidentally, in the bizarre July 24 crash at the New York Aquarium where four were killed and eight seriously injured, the passenger of the vehicle that caused the accident was also the owner. The driver in that accident was never found.

"All avenues are being investigated

and all findings are at this point confidential," said Detective Chris Grella. When asked if there was anything he would want to say to the driver, Detective Grella said, "Turn yourself in. You need help."

Police claim the likelihood of a terrorist connection is unlikely given the quantity of alcohol present and the absence of any group claiming responsibility. Anyone knowing anything about the accident or the driver is asked to contact Detective Grella at 212-555-1455.

Gavin stopped reading. " 'You need help'? Who are you? Dr. Chris?"

"I didn't know what to say. It just came out. I asked him not to print it."

"You asked Gasman not to print something. That's like asking him not to breathe," Gavin said.

"Well, there's no damage done. What's the plan of attack?" Chris asked, apparently wanting to change the subject.

"Some of the forensic reports should be in later today. In the meantime, why don't you follow up on Lori Hayslip, her job, her friends, her parents . . . the whole drill."

"Right. And you?"

"I'm gonna pay a visit to Amber Clayborne."

"I don't envy you if you turn out to be the guy who has to bring her up to speed with her new life as a widow."

Gavin didn't need or want to be reminded. Notifying the families of victims was the part he hated most about his job. He had never seen the same reaction twice and he remembered them all — vividly. It didn't matter how he delivered the news. As the messenger, he was instantly hated. Even if they didn't show it, he knew he was hated. He had been punched, spit upon, accused of lying, and cursed at, sometimes from people who wouldn't swear if they closed their fingers in a car door.

Trying to think about anything else, he remembered another practical matter that had to be dealt with: his car, a 1968 Sunbeam Tiger that was out of commission . . . again. This time it was the shift linkage. He'd bought the car five years ago. When the original owner had told him a Tiger was the same car Maxwell Smart drove in the old TV comedy series *Get Smart*, Gavin had been instantly amused and interested. When told the innocent-looking car had a worked-up Ford V-8 that could exceed 150 miles per hour and leave any production car in the dust, he was sold.

What Gavin hadn't been told was that the powerful engine was more than the rest of the car could handle, especially the small pretechnology drum brakes, which were barely adequate at normal speeds. He also hadn't been told about the maintenance. Gavin had never really gotten into personal automotive repair and trusted himself with little more than a tune-up and an oil change. The Tiger required a good mechanic and required one often. Fortunately, his local friend John Garrity was a real pro and knew the Tiger inside and out. And being the good friend he was, Garrity made house calls. He was scheduled to come by sometime today and have the car ready by tonight.

"Chris, I need a favor."

"Not your car again."

"Uh, yeah," Gavin said, embarrassed that buying the Tiger had turned out to be such an obviously bad decision.

Chris laughed as loud and as long as one could under the circumstances. "When are you gonna sell that stupid thing and get a car?"

— 12 —

The ride to the sixth precinct was as tor-
turous as Chris could make it. He spent the
time recommending backup mechanics and
stock bargains in fictitious tow-truck companies. Relief didn't come until they split up to
attack their respective to-do lists.

Gavin was glad to be back on the
hunt — and alone. He walked down the
hospital corridor, turning right toward
rooms 315 through 349. Amber Clayborne
was in 320, coming up on Gavin's right.
The good news was that she was still alive.
The bad news was that she was in a coma.
He paused before entering. There seemed
to be something wrong with simply
walking right into a woman's bedroom,
even if she *was* unconscious. But that
didn't concern him nearly as much as the
fear of her waking while he was there. He
didn't want to be the first one she saw. She
would have many questions, not the least

of which would be the condition of her husband.

He exhaled, then walked into the room's small hallway. From his viewpoint he could see only the furthest of the two beds and it was empty. He continued past the bathroom and stopped.

She appeared to be simply asleep. She wasn't wrapped in bandages or suspended in traction like so many other crash victims Gavin had seen. In fact, if you could ignore the intravenous tubes attached to her right arm and the monitor that signaled every heartbeat, you would think Amber Clayborne was simply resting. That she would open her eyes at the sound of her name.

Gavin stepped to the foot of her bed and studied her face. She was quite attractive. The length of her straight black hair lay hidden beneath her head. Her nose was straight and softly rounded. She looked somewhat Asian, but not completely. If the crash had stolen some of her beauty, it could not have taken much. She looked so peaceful; she must have been knocked unconscious before she knew what was happening, or at least before she could believe what was happening. The thought of the pain that awaited her grieved Gavin. He knew all too well what she would go through — the many stages one experiences after tragic news. He had seen and felt it more times than any man should have to.

"And who are *you?*" demanded a female voice from behind him.

Startled from his thoughts, Gavin snapped a look in the direction of the voice. What he saw left him momentarily speechless. He looked reflexively back at Amber Clayborne and then again at the woman before him.

"Detective Pierce," he answered slowly.

"Did you find the psycho yet?" the woman said.

"Uh . . . we're still —"

"Did you find *anything?*" she said impatiently, her hands on hips that were covered by a football jersey that fell loosely over well-fitting and well-used jeans. The Yankee's cap worn backward on her head and the challenging attitude could not disguise she was Amber Clayborne's mirror image. Gavin found her stunning. Not just pretty — beautiful.

"And you are?" Gavin said, hoping to establish at least some authority in her mind.

She rolled cat-green eyes, obviously annoyed by the question. "I should tell you anything? How do I know you're not the killer?"

Gavin frowned and pulled back the left side of his jacket, revealing his shield and holstered gun.

"Fine. I'm Amy Kirsch, Amber's sister. And if you couldn't figure that out, how are you ever going to find out who did this?" she said, pointing at her sister.

Gavin swallowed a defensive comeback before it left his mouth. It went down hard and left a bitter taste, but the last thing he'd come here to do was fight with a family member and cause more pain.

"Miss Kirsch, I want you to know that the department intends to —"

"Oooh, the department. I feel so much better now," she interrupted with her palm over her chest in mocking sarcasm. "Whenever the going gets tough and someone wants to pass the buck, there's always some kind of department, isn't there? Forget the department. What do *you* intend on doing? What are you going to do when you're done with your notes and interviews? Join the boys for a coffee at the doughnut shop? Or maybe catch them for a beer at the local watering hole? You'll have the best story to tell today, won't you?"

Gavin's neck and jaw muscles were clenched so tightly he had to speak through gritted teeth. "Lady, for the last month, every thought I've had has been polluted with this guy. I know what it's like to loose a loved one in a crash — someone who's been there for you your whole life. I know what it's like to lose someone you love to this beast. And what it feels like to want revenge more than anything else you've ever wanted."

Her eyes widened in surprise.

"You can rest assured that when I say 'the department' I'm talking *me*," he said, stabbing his chest with his index finger. "Whatever it takes, I'll find him."

"Wait a minute. You're not the detective that was in the aquarium crash last month? The one that was in the papers?"

His silence was answer enough. Amy's tiger eyes softened.

Gavin turned and walked toward the window. The last thing he wanted was pity. Pity paved the way for *self*-pity and opened the door for excuses. It had a way of dulling the edge and Gavin needed, now more than ever, to be sharp. No pity; no excuses.

"Are you serious when you say 'whatever it takes'?"

Gavin continued to stare out the window. He needed to cool off and suddenly felt he had said way too much already.

"Then let me help," she said.

Gavin exhaled quietly. "Well, you could be a big help by answering a few questions."

"Don't give me that garbage," she said, catching fire again. "I mean *help* help, not just telling you my sister had no enemies and her husband had never hurt a fly."

"What do you mean by help?" Gavin said, amused in spite of himself. He didn't want to be rude and say no just yet. He'd heard this sentiment before from victims' loved ones, and he would allow her to realize for herself the offer was appreciated but unrealistic.

"Give me the little bits and seeds of information you come across and I'll grow a tree with them."

Gavin arched a brow. "And how will you do that?"

"Mostly with my computer."

"I see. Thanks, but the department has its own computer system and trained —"

"Your department is living in the Dark Ages. One hand doesn't know what the other is doing and most of your trained personnel are lucky if they know how to type."

"Now just a minute. Wherever you got that information from —"

"I got it from me. I've been in your system."

Gavin looked at her sharply. "Been in the system?"

"You think operating a computer means typing in a name and then pressing Enter. The computer can lead you to all the information you need, but you've got to know how to find it."

"And you know?" he said cynically.

"I know."

"How do you know?"

"I was raised on a computer. My father's been importing computers from Japan as long as I can remember. A family business. My mother's Japanese. We import, custom-build, and program. I've spent most of my life going places you're not supposed to be able to go. I've explored the systems of half the companies on Wall Street, government systems, and yes, even Nassau Police."

"Now, wait a minute. You'd better not be saying what I think you're saying because that's pretty commonly known as illegal activity. Besides, you need a personal passcode to get into the department."

"Maybe *you* do. I get around it. If you gave me your passcode, it would save me about twenty minutes on a bad day."

In spite of his anger, Gavin knew what she was saying to be at least partially true. If he hadn't run across Detective Rogers in Brooklyn, he never would have known there were fingerprints to match up with or to look for the lobster claw. Sure, it was in the computer, but only in NYPD, not Nassau. But still . . .

"I don't think I want to hear any more of this, or I might be forced to take you down to the station and ask you some questions." He held up his hand to still her angry retort. "But in any case, it doesn't matter. To tell you the truth, we haven't got much of anything yet. That's why I'm standing here. Maybe your sister can help. Maybe she saw him or can tell us something that can help."

"Are you going to ask her before or after you tell her about her husband?"

"Look, I —"

"Just give me a chance. I want to see this creep nailed and I know I can help. I promise not to get in your way. And I won't do any hacking unless you personally give me permission to enter the system. Please."

She was giving him a look that was impossible to refuse. "I don't know. What you're suggesting is . . . illegal."

"You said whatever it takes."

"Give me your phone number, Miss Kirsch —"

"Amy," she corrected with a smile.

"Your number . . . Amy."

She rattled it off. "And give me yours . . . Detective Pierce."

"Gavin," he said, then immediately wondered if he'd lost his mind.

She smiled again. "I like that name. And your number?"

"I'll call you." He could feel a drip of sweat running down the back of his neck. "And I'll be looking forward to your sister's quick recovery."

Amy nodded, then looked at her sister for a long moment. She didn't get teary and sorrowful, as Gavin would have expected, especially from a twin. Instead, her steeled profile glowed with a different emotion even easier for him to identify with right now: hate.

— 13 —

Karianne Stordal was still shaken. Her legs felt rubbery as she walked the Long Beach boardwalk. Twenty-nine, she'd been a flight attendant for Globe Airlines for the past six years, and only once before had she ever encountered air turbulence as bad as today's.

After a bad flight, a walk on the boardwalk was usually enough to settle her down. The offshore breeze carrying the salty scent of the Atlantic Ocean reminded her of pleasant times with her parents at the beach. Thoughts of her uncomplicated childhood were always welcome and usually soothing, but today was different. Today she found herself considering additional help — the kind of help she so often ministered to nervous passengers: a drink. Not much. Just enough to take the edge off. Just enough to help her already pleasant surroundings ease her tension.

Her thought of leaning on such help was

not a simple one. She had not had a drink in over five years. As a recovering alcoholic, she'd done great. The fear of sliding backward into a repeat of past years of abuse had always overcome any serious temptation to drink . . . until today. For the first time in five years she felt like she had a good enough reason. Actually, she had earned it — deserved it. Any human being that had just spent the last hour in a glorified tin tube fifty thousand feet over the ocean, bouncing in and out of five-hundred-foot invisible air pockets and smiling while collecting half-full vomit bags deserved a drink.

The idea of a little liquid comfort had first come just minutes before setting foot on real ground and, as usual, had been immediately dismissed — or at least suppressed. But after going home to her Long Beach apartment she had still been trembling.

"It's over! You're fine," she had said to her image in the bedroom mirror as she slid her hairpins out and let her thick blonde hair fall to her shoulders. "You just need a hot shower."

But when a shower and change of clothing — into her ever-comfortable cut-off shorts and tank top — failed to help, the thought had returned. Very uncharacteristically, she now allowed the thought to linger at arm's length as she pondered it, trying to rationalize everything. Soon, the idea began to take on a logical, even friendly, feel — a sharp contrast to the addiction that had chased her for so many years. But that was then. Now she was stronger, more mature.

Her gait was as casual as a window shopper's as she passed by the stores and food stands that lined the boardwalk. She strolled by the Seahorse Tavern with barely a glance, reinforcing her ability to pass it if she wanted to. After all, she could easily have had a drink on the plane, or brought one of those little bottles home with her.

She leaned on the long pipe railing that protected passersby from falling to the sand six feet below and looked out to the ocean, shaking her head at the sight of approaching rain clouds. The weather forecast had mentioned the possibility of a late thunderstorm. The last thing she needed was more instability in her atmosphere. She held out her hand to see if she was still shaking. She knew she would be, but held it out anyway as if to show her strength to the eyes of another — her conscience. Then she looked over her right shoulder at the Seahorse Tavern, its grayish driftwood siding draped with old fishing nets. She could probably watch the clouds just as easily from the other side of that picture window . . .

She considered passing the tavern by again as she neared the door. Maybe another test was needed to show it was really she who was in control, and not her addiction. But, no. She'd already passed that test. And she could just as easily leave whenever she wanted, and would do just that — after one drink.

The wall of cool air brought immediate relief as she entered. To her left were a dozen tables, all but one empty. Two men in suits. They looked at her and smiled. She reflexively smiled back, but then, realizing her casual attire might appear a little too inviting, she turned away. She didn't want conversation; she wanted to unwind. Getting to know two guys whom she had never seen before didn't sound very relaxing.

To her right stood a long saltwater fish tank. Through its waving plant life and colorful fish she could see the bar. She could also see the seat she wanted — the last one next to the window. She passed the tank and caught the eye of the bartender, who was watching the TV mounted high on the wall.

"What'll it be?" he said with a friendly smile.

She looked to the ceiling as she took her seat, as if she wasn't sure. But she was. "Let's try a Bloody Mary. It's been a hard day at the office," she said, feeling the need to offer some explanation.

"One tomato and potato comin' up," he said, reaching for a bottle of top-shelf vodka.

She watched intently as the bartender made her drink. The clear liquor filling the gaps between the ice cubes and rising along the curved wall of glass sent a cold tremor through her chest. This was *her* drink he was making. She had a sudden urge to leave some money on the bartop and tell the man to forget it.

"Enjoy," he said with a wink, placing before her a tall red mix with a fresh leafy celery stalk planted in it. He went back to his stool behind the bar and continued to watch his golf game . . . like nothing had happened. But something had.

Karianne stared at the glass. Well, just drink some, girl. It's not as if it were Eve's apple. Lighten up. One drink in five years. Her salivary glands tingled with anticipation as her mouth remembered the taste of the liquor. She took hold of the wet glass and brought the cold rim to her lips, allowing the aromatic vapors to fill her sinuses. She looked at herself in the smoke-tinted, marble-grained mirror behind the bar. The reflected world was void of color, like a black-and-white TV. Her decision seemed anything but black and white. She closed her eyes and drank.

After her first swallow she looked left. She could see the bartender still watching the TV. In the mirror and through the fish tank she could see the businessmen chatting. Nobody cared. As she lifted the glass again she glanced to her right. She could see the clouds had suddenly arrived. They were so dark they appeared dirty, like the charred, billowing smoke of a huge oil fire. The coming storm had so dimmed the light she could see an eerily transparent reflection of herself in the window, her long Norwegian-blonde hair framing her face . . . and her blood-red drink at her lips. Bright, silver swords of lightning stabbed down at the ocean, further illuminating the unwanted reflection of her shame. Thunder shook the air and a fat droplet of rain smacked the windowpane. She continued to drink as other droplets followed, melting away her ghostly image and the reminding portrait of her sin.

Two hours and many drinks later Karianne was still sitting at the bar. Her shakes were gone. They'd left around the same time the tomato and potato became straight potato on the rocks. She leaned back and drained the glass again, allowing the ice to rest upon her lips until she was certain the cubes were dry. In her peripheral she saw a large black shadow walk by the window. She turned, but it had already passed. All she saw was wet darkness, the only light coming from a lamppost on the boardwalk fifty feet away.

"How 'bout just one more on the house, Sam?" she said, fishing clumsily through her black-leather fanny pack for money.

"Sorry, darlin'," the bartender said. "I've already bought you two. Besides, you've had enough."

Karianne didn't agree. She continued to look through her pack, but the only thing she could find of any worth was a football ticket. Giants vs. Bears, September seventh. It had been given to her by one of the players — a placekicker who had taken a liking to her on his way back from vacationing with his family in Norway. She wasn't much of a fan, but she'd been looking forward to congratulating — or consoling — the guy after the game.

She pulled the ticket out and stared at it, then brought it close to her face, hoping the words would come into focus. They didn't. She turned it over. He had signed the back: Norman Sorenson. She looked at her empty glass. Then, plastering on her never-failing smile and batting her blood-shot powder-blue eyes, she called again to the bartender. "Oh, Sam. Do you like football?"

"I do," said a deep voice behind her.

Karianne looked into the mirror and suddenly felt very small. The owner of the deep voice was standing behind her. He was huge. He wore an unbuttoned black leather shirt with cut-off sleeves and his blond hair was short and thick on top and shaved on the sides. Even in the gray-smoked reflection his gaze was intense, aimed boldly into her eyes. Something about his stare was instantly familiar. But the man himself was a total stranger. She found herself gaping and broke eye contact, regrouping as quickly as her intoxication allowed. Then she turned in her chair.

Again he locked onto her eyes, seized them with his own — wild, silver, hungry . . . and somehow familiar. But how? She would definitely have remembered if she'd seen him before; his tremendous muscle-laden body and ruggedly athletic face were not ones she was likely to forget. She noticed both his high cheekbones and chin were reddened, as though he had been in a fistfight. She also noticed he had a newspaper folded in his hand. A copy of the *Post*. On the front page a man's face had been circled in red.

Suddenly Karianne felt a chill flood her insides. It came from deep within, so deep the stirring shiver felt like it was touching her very soul. What was it?

"Give her another drink — a double. I'll take the same, whatever it is," the stranger demanded while continuing to hold her gaze.

The bartender hesitated, but quickly and clumsily submitted when the stranger shot him a look.

The newcomer was more menacing and dangerous in appearance than anyone Karianne had ever laid eyes upon, but to her surprise she didn't feel the least bit afraid or intimidated. On the contrary, she felt drawn to this monster of a man. And it wasn't simply his looks. Though he had spoken but a few words to her, she sensed a strange camaraderie. Maybe the alcohol was confusing her. His abusive attitude and demanding arrogance embodied what she naturally despised. She was nothing like that and she hoped she never would be and therefore shouldn't be feeling what she was.

The bartender placed the drinks and moved away, keeping an eye on the stranger as he did. He did not resume his relaxed position by the TV, but instead stayed close to a phone near the cash register.

"Drink," the stranger said in bold invitation as he took hold of the vodka placed before him. The tumbler appeared as small as a one-ounce shot glass in his giant hand. He poured his drink down in one motion, then slammed the glass down on the bartop. Even the ice was gone.

Karianne laughed, then drained her own glass, less the ice, and slammed it down in the same manner. The stranger said nothing. He just stared blankly at her.

"What? Do you think I'm going to do the same? Swallow my ice cubes? I think you've mistaken me for an old drinking buddy," Karianne slurred.

The stranger laughed. "You are an old drinking buddy." He reached into the front pocket of his faded jeans, pulled out a twenty-dollar bill, and slapped it on the bar. "Two more," he yelled, his attention remaining on Karianne, apparently confident his command would be followed without question. He took the seat to her left, his back to the bartender, and put his newspaper on top of the bar.

Karianne smiled, running her finger along the rim of her glass. "I don't suppose you've ever heard of the magic word?"

"Now," he yelled.

"That wasn't the magic word I had in mind," she said, shaking her head. "By the way, do you have a name?"

"Krogan," he said deeply but softly enough that only she could hear.

"Krogan? That's it? Just Krogan?" She gave in to a sudden, uncharacteristic urge to set her hand on his thigh.

"Krogan."

"Okay . . . Krogan. As long as you're buying, I'll drink with you. But I think you'll find more your type a little north of here . . . at the Bronx Zoo," she said, slurring her words terribly.

"Tonight we have a date," he said.

"A date? Getting right to the point, aren't we?"

He leaned toward her. "*Shadahd,*" he said.

Karianne frowned, but before she could ask him what he was talking about, another deep, cold rush filled her. She dug her fingers into his leg to steady herself. The bartender delivered the drinks and quickly left again. She stared at Krogan. "Shah-what?"

Krogan grinned and again poured the entire contents of his tumbler down his throat. "Drink," he said, the command more instructional than celebratory this time.

Karianne picked up her drink, wondering what kind of wild animal she was spending her time with — and enjoying. She brought the glass to her numb lips. She could no longer taste the vodka; she might as well have been drinking tap water. As she drank she peered over her raised glass and saw he was still grinning at her. Why? What did he see?

"Oooh!" she said, as another rush swept through, this one more intense than the others. She almost fell over. Krogan's smile grew. What was happening? He knew. Somehow he knew. What did he expect?

The room began to move. She thought she was going to pass out. She heard a crash. Blearily she looked down and saw her tumbler was no longer in her hand. Her head was spinning. The room was getting darker. She couldn't focus and wasn't sure she was sitting in her seat anymore. She shut her eyes tightly.

"*Shadahd,*" he said.

She moaned as another rush swept through her like electricity. His foreign word echoed through her mind. She opened her eyes and saw he was still there, his elbow leaning on the bar, seemingly enjoying her weakness. He hadn't repeated the word, but she could still hear it echoing in her mind, louder and louder, until she could no longer keep it inside —

"*Shadahd,*" she said. It just came out.

Suddenly the spinning stopped. Her vision was still blurred, but she was no longer dizzy because of it. The room seemed darker than ever, but she didn't mind; in fact, she liked it. Preferred it. She looked at Krogan. He hadn't moved, still intently watching her. She felt very different, and somehow Krogan knew that, too.

"Two more," she yelled, grinning widely. She couldn't remember the last time she'd felt this way, but somehow she knew she had — many times. Maybe she was dreaming. She didn't care. If it was a dream she was going to enjoy it. Really enjoy it.

The bartender brought over two more drinks, looking at her oddly, but didn't say anything.

"What's the matter, Sam? You don't get many interesting people in here?" she said sensually, locking her eyes on her old friend, Krogan.

The bartender didn't answer. He just retreated back to his usual distance.

Karianne and Krogan picked up their drinks together. She clinked her tumbler against his and poured the contents down . . . ice included. The cubes barely escaped getting caught in her throat and the pain that followed was so sharp the numbing alcohol in her bloodstream could do little to combat it. She grabbed at her throat and started to fall forward. Krogan caught her and pushed her back into the chair with a laugh.

"Maybe next time you'll take a body that can handle a little more abuse. This one's the best ever," he said, and pulled open his loose shirt, exposing his massive, muscle-ripped torso.

Karianne felt schizophrenic. Half of her knew what he was saying while the other half had no idea. Regardless, she didn't care. She was totally drunk and for some reason had plenty of energy. She reached up with her right hand and grabbed the thick hair behind his neck, then pulled his head toward hers and kissed him. Still holding his hair tightly, she pulled his head away and stared into his silver eyes. "Let's party."

"What kind of car do you have?"

"A new Jeep Grand Cherokee," she slurred.

"*Shadahd?*" he said, picking up his newspaper as he rose from his seat.

"Yes!" she said, suddenly knowing exactly what he meant.

— 14 —

Gavin pushed through the worn wooden door of the homicide department. Homicide 242 was a depressing hole in the wall. The carpet was so old, visiting retired detectives, some of whom were World War II veterans, could point to specific coffee stains and reminisce. The standard joke was that the local historical society had blocked the way for a new carpet.

The supervisor's office was partitioned off in such a way that no windows were available for ventilation or natural light. So as not to burden taxpayers or elected skimmers, an oscillating fan, powered through a creatively routed extension cord, was set upon a tall filing cabinet to assist a noisy, undersized air-conditioning system.

Chris was at his desk talking on the phone. He turned and held up an index finger. Gavin waited impatiently.

"Right . . . right . . . yeah," Chris was

saying while rolling his eyes and motioning that whoever was on the other end of the phone was on a needless verbal roll.

On Chris's desk lay a large white blotter decorated with data and doodles. Next to it sat a comic strip one-a-day calendar and one of those chrome toys that defied the physical laws of perpetual motion. Gavin usually made a point of stopping it whenever he walked by.

Gavin had no such entertainment on his own desk, just ten feet away — just a writing pad and photos of his parents, grandparents, and the girlfriend who hadn't lived long enough for him to marry. He was a jinx and the memorial on his desk was proof of it. Chris's desk also had photos, but they were all of living people — mostly people Gavin didn't know very well, which is why he figured they were still alive.

"Uh-huh . . . super. Thanks again," Chris said, then hung up.

"So?" Gavin said.

"That was your buddy, Detective Rogers from Brooklyn. He wants this guy almost as bad as you do."

Gavin knew that was impossible. "And?"

"You go first. How'd you make out at the hospital?"

"She's still in a coma. They'll notify me the moment she comes out of it."

"We should call them every day to make sure they don't forget," Chris said, pointing a pencil at Gavin.

"I don't think we'll have to. She has a twin sister who seems on the ball. Maybe a little too much."

"What do you mean?"

"Nothing. She's just the helpful type. What do you have from Rogers?"

"Good news, bad news. What do ya want?"

"Good."

"Prints are positive," Chris said as he handed Gavin the forensic report. "It's the same guy that introduced himself to you at the aquarium. And check out those prints. They're the biggest I've ever seen."

"So I've heard. What else?"

"We think he's blond. The girl had brown hair and there was short blond hair on the seat. Rogers is having the samples checked against hair found in the aquarium truck."

"They'll match," Gavin said without looking up from the report.

"Probably, but I don't understand how a guy that's this elusive isn't careful enough to wear gloves. He leaves his fat fingerprints everywhere. Maybe he wants to be known. Just not caught."

"What do you mean?" Gavin said, still reading.

"Well, maybe he wants the attention. I know the feds have all but ruled him out as a terrorist, but maybe he's a little jealous of all the attention they've gotten."

"I don't think so."

"Why not?"

"He's a Viking."

"A Viking?"

"Yeah. He lives for the moment. He could care less about tomorrow. The battle exists only for today. Yesterday was yesterday, tomorrow is tomorrow, now is now."

"Viking, maybe; stunt man, definitely. Instead of an ax and sword he uses cars and trucks. One of those Hollywood daredevil crazies that drive off ramps into a stack of piled-up cars."

Gavin looked up from the report to see if he was serious. At the moment nothing seemed farfetched.

"He'll probably turn out to be one of those wrestling dudes. Some of those guys will do anything for attention."

"They wouldn't do this," Gavin said.

"Well, probably not, but the media attention might spur on some copycats."

Gavin frowned thoughtfully.

"Whatever he is," Chris continued, "he certainly enjoys what he's doing. Nobody puts himself through that much physical pain if he doesn't have to."

"What did you find out about the girl?"

"That's the bad news. Nothing. She was a waitress at an archeological theme restaurant in East Norwich called The Dig. One of the other waitresses said she had complained about feeling shaky. She had a couple of drinks to try to settle herself down, then left before dinner was over."

"She left alone?"

"They think so. Nobody actually saw her leave and she didn't tell anyone she was going. And nobody recalls ever seeing her with any big guy with blond hair."

"Parents? Friends?"

"Not much. Everyone's in shock. A couple of close friends admitted she liked to drink at parties, but none would say she had a drinking problem."

"The blood test shows a .25. I'd say that constitutes a drinking problem."

"Point two-five?" Chris said. "I must have missed that. Another five hundredths of a percent and she wouldn't have needed the crash to kill her. I've never seen so much alcohol in someone who was still able to function. A seasoned alcoholic would've been out cold. She must have been unconscious."

"She had her seat belt halfway around her, like she'd tried to latch it. How could she do that if she was unconscious?"

"Well, then the .25 has got to be wrong."

"Tell them to do it over," Gavin said, dropping the report onto the desk.

"Why bother?"

"I don't know. We haven't got much and .25 stands out. It's odd. I can't see where it could bring us, but . . . it's odd."

"Done," Chris said, getting out of his chair. "I'll call them first thing in the morning."

"Headin' out?"

"Yeah. Pat's already fed the kids, but she's waiting for me with a juicy steak that needs grilling," Chris said, smacking his lips. "I suppose you need a ride home?"

"Yeah. My car's probably done and waiting."

"It's times like this I really miss being single," Chris said sarcastically. "You going home to that toolbox you call a car; I'm going home to my wife and that juicy steak."

Krogan smiled from behind the wheel of Karianne's Jeep when he saw the man that matched the face in the newspaper emerge through the glass doors. To take him out in the police department parking lot would be fun. The smart man in the paper deserved to be humiliated in front of the other cops.

Karianne, whom Krogan knew as Sabah, was more interested in the bottle nesting safely between her legs. It reminded Krogan of the first time he'd seen Sabah drinking, cradling a wineskin.

The cop from the newspaper entered a car with someone else. Two cops, Krogan thought. The more the better. He started his engine, but cursed when he realized the cops were parked next to the exit and he wouldn't be able to get to them in time. Whatever, he would have them soon.

Chris drove a white minivan — a family car for a family man. He and Gavin chatted and traded insults as he drove toward Gavin's place. At Gavin's, the garage door was open, the light was on, the car's hood was closed, and John Garrity was sitting back in a plastic patio chair with a bottled drink in his hand.

"Say, Gav," said Chris. "The transmission in this beast has been slipping a bit. Do you think your buddy would check it out for me?"

"You want my mechanic to look at your car? I'm surprised you think he's worthy."

"Hey. If he can get that thing of yours running, mine will be a piece of cake."

"Well, you can ask him yourself," Gavin said, seeing Garrity on his way down the driveway. He climbed out of the car, noticing as he did so a dark-colored Cherokee driving slowly by. Garrity smiled easily as he came up to the car.

"Hey, partner," he said to Gavin, then waved to Chris.

"How'd it go?" Gavin asked.

"Done. No big deal. I haven't been here long."

"Good. John, meet Chris. Chris, John," Gavin said. "Chris wondered if you could take a quick spin around the block and check out his tranny."

"Sure. Be happy to."

"Great," Chris said. "Gavin tells me you're the only one he trusts with his car."

Garrity laughed. "That's because he's scared how much the other guys would charge to work on that thing."

Chris and Garrity laughed as Chris slid over to the passenger seat and Garrity hopped behind the wheel.

"Hey, Gav. Wanna join me and the missus for dinner? There's a juicy steak with your name written on it," Chris said.

"Another time," Gavin said.

"Okay, but just remember when you're pulling out that last slice of salami from last week's cold cuts, I'm gonna be strategically placing sautéed mushrooms and onions on my hot, dripping steak. Then I'll follow it with hot mashed potatoes and —"

"Enough! Get out of here."

"— Greek salad with just the right amount of feta cheese. Hot, buttered asparagus —" Gavin shut the door on Chris's culinary barrage. Chris promptly rolled down his window and continued the abuse as they drove away. "Hot apple pie, à la mode . . ."

Gavin shook his head as he watched Garrity drive slowly up the block. He was about to turn away when he saw something that froze him in place. He could see the headlights of another car coming out of a side street. It was going much too fast to stop at the corner.

"No!" he cried, emptying his lungs as the car smashed head on into the driver-side door of Chris's van, slamming the car sideways until it bumped over the curb. As explosively loud as the impact had been, there was suddenly silence.

Dead silence.

— 15 —

Gavin's legs couldn't have gotten him to the crash any faster. All he could think about was Chris and Garrity. As he neared the collision he could see that the car that had hit the minivan was a Cherokee — the same one that had driven by them minutes before. He slid on the wet asphalt, stopping at the minivan's passenger door. His heart hammered as he grabbed the handle and yanked.

"Oh, God!" he cried, and meant it, as Chris's limp body fell toward him. Gavin caught him by the shoulders. He was out cold, but Gavin could feel his warm, shallow breath on his own neck. He pulled him out and lowered him gently to the hard concrete sidewalk, then went back to Garrity, who had been on the impact side. The interior light revealed Garrity facedown on the passenger seat. Steam from the Cherokee's radiator was billowing through the smashed-in door of the minivan, making it almost impossible to see. Gavin heard the creaking, popping sound of metal. It was the driver-side door of the Cherokee. A large shadow staggered across the fogged windshield.

Could it be the killer? At first the notion seemed absurd. But how absurd must the car flying through the air have appeared to Mitchell Clayborne before he was decapitated? But if it was the killer, what was he doing here? Had he followed them from headquarters? Were the hunters now the hunted? The sudden likelihood opened the door to questions Gavin had no time to consider. If he moved now he could catch the man, arrest him — or better, shoot him — and end it here. End this useless carnage of human life. He wanted that murdering scum so badly he was trembling.

He looked back at Garrity. Through the oily cloud of water and antifreeze vapor he saw blood spreading on the seat like spilled ink on a blotter pad. A coiled black cord led to a car phone lying on the floor. He grabbed it, pressed the power button, and punched in 911, praying for a connection. Instead he heard two low-toned beeps indicating the need to enter Chris's security code.

"I don't know the password," he screamed at the phone.

"Is anyone hurt?" called a voice from behind him.

Gavin turned to see an elderly woman standing in a nearby driveway.

"Call 911 and tell them to send an ambulance. Hurry!"

The woman stared.

"Go!"

The woman turned and hurried back up the driveway as Gavin turned back to Garrity and gently maneuvered him so his face wasn't buried into the seat cushion. The heavy limpness of his head brought tears to Gavin's eyes.

"Please, John. Hold on," he said, searching Garrity's neck for a pulse. Nothing. He grabbed the rearview mirror and ripped it off the windshield, quickly dried it off with his shirt, then placed it by Garrity's lips and nose. Nothing. No fogging. No breath. No life . . .

Gavin backed away from the car and looked at the sky. The dark clouds had broken up; moonlight illuminated their edges as they slowly scudded by.

"No! Not him, too. Not John," he sobbed, unable to control his emotions. "Why?" Why was this happening?

A groan. Gavin snapped his gaze toward Garrity. Another groan. It wasn't coming from Garrity. It was coming from the Cherokee.

He ran over to the passenger side of the other car. The door was hard to open, making the same metal-popping sound he'd heard when the driver's door was opened. Inside, in the dim light, he saw a girl moving slowly in her seat, groaning, her head hanging forward so that her very blonde hair touched her thighs. Her seat belt was unbuckled, but the airbag, which was now half deflated, had done its job.

As Gavin peered into the interior, his breath suddenly caught. A copy of *The Daily Post* was folded and wedged between the seat and the center console. Chris's face was clearly circled in red. Gavin reached past the girl and grabbed the paper. He opened to the print on page three and saw another red circle around Chris's quote: "Turn yourself in." Scribbled boldly across the page in the same red ink were the words "Here I am."

Gavin heard sirens approaching behind him and saw the reflection of flashing lights dancing on the macabre message in his hands. He folded up the paper and turned his attention back to the girl, grabbing her hair and pulling it back so he could see her face.

"Stay alive," he commanded through gritted teeth. "You're not dying on me, baby. I'm gonna latch onto you like a pit bull and you're gonna tell me who the driver is. And when I get hold of him, I'm gonna beat him to death with my bare hands."

Staring at the girl, he fought back the emotions that threatened to overwhelm him. It was then that he looked past her to the open ashtray and saw the lobster claw.

An hour later Gavin found himself once again in the emergency room at Glen Cove. Again he raised his head at the mechanical sound of the sliding glass doors opening. This time, to his dread, he was right. Susan Garrity. She wore gray sweats and slippers. She had probably been cozying up on the couch watching TV when she got the call. She took tiny, uncertain steps across the floor, clutching her chest with her right hand as if she were having a heart attack. Her black mascara ran down her face like burnt wax. She was sobbing, her eyes searching for answers in the faces around her.

"Susan." Gavin sprang out of his seat to

meet her. As he hurried over, he saw a nurse coming from across the room to intercept her as well.

Susan turned to his voice. "Where's John?" she cried in a pleading tone.

"I'm sorry," Gavin said. The words sounded ridiculously inane, but he couldn't think of anything else to say. He reached out to embrace her and she shook off his touch, bending over as if her stomach was cramping.

"I want to see my husband. I want to see John."

The nurse had tears in her own eyes as she looked at Gavin. He closed his eyes and slowly nodded.

"Your husband's in the other room, Mrs. Garrity," the nurse said. "I'll bring you to him."

Gavin stepped back and watched the nurse walk the grieving woman through the swinging doors, her arm at the small of Susan's back. They were the same doors Chris and the blonde woman had been rushed through earlier. The doctors had told him the preliminary prognosis looked good for the both of them. Chris appeared to have a mild concussion and a broken left arm. The girl had broken her left leg, but the air bag had saved her from any other serious injury. In fact, if not for the air bag, treating her broken leg would not have been necessary. She and Chris would both spend the night in the ICU and in all probability would be moved into private rooms in the morning.

"Pierce!" Gavin looked up and saw Mel Gasman hurrying toward him. Gavin smiled grimly.

"Gasman," he said. "You're just the guy I want to talk to."

Gasman looked as though he must have heard wrong. "You want to talk to me?" he said, pointing to his chest.

"Yeah! How would you like to help me catch the Ghost Driver?"

"I get the exclusive?"

"The story will be yours."

"Then I'm yours."

"Don't you even want to know what you'll have to do?"

Gasman shrugged. "What's the difference? As long as I get the story."

"Good. I've got breaking news. And I want tomorrow's front page."

— 16 —

After blindly fumbling with several buttons and switches, trying to quiet the buzzer on his new, overly optioned, alarm clock, Gavin gave up and reached for the plug. He wished he were a morning person. He had regularly tried to make the conversion, but it was hopeless. Morning people had regular bedtimes and seemed to enjoy snuggling under their covers at night and hopping out from under them in the morning. Gavin, on the other hand, found once he was asleep, he wanted to stay asleep and once he was awake, he wanted to stay awake. While awake, he didn't want to leave any problem unsolved and his mind would dig and search and build up and tear down until his cowardly eyelids gave in. Then he would sleep, so deeply that hurricanes and thunderstorms and sirens could rarely stir him to consciousness.

But not today.

Gavin immediately grabbed his phone, called the hospital, and was informed both Chris and Karianne Stordal were stable and asleep. Although she had no serious injuries, the flight attendant would be no good for questioning until later because of the high levels of alcohol in her system. Amber Clayborne, he was told was still in a coma.

Gavin then broke his usual morning sequence by heading directly for the paper. He couldn't wait to see what kind of impact his conversation with Mel Gasman had had. In exchange for all the seedy details and likelihood of more to come, Gasman had promised to emphasize a particular message Gavin wanted to send to the killer.

Gavin opened the front door. To his surprise, the paper wasn't on the stoop. He ventured out a bit further, wearing only a pair of *The Far Side* boxer shorts that he'd received as a joke gift from Chris for his last birthday. Standing with his hands on his hips and surveying his meager landscape of fenced-in lawn, he noticed a bicycle in the driveway. It was a mountain bike, full-suspension, expensive — a serious piece of equipment.

He took a few more steps toward the bike

and looked up the driveway toward the garage. Well, there was his newspaper, opened wide and being read by someone sitting in the same white patio chair John Garrity had relaxed in the night before. The paper shielded the trespasser's body, but he had an idea of who it was. Crossed below the paper were a pair of well-tanned, athletic, female legs wearing black biking sneakers.

"Can I help you?" Gavin said.

The paper lowered. It was Amy Kirsch.

"Detective Pierce. Anyone ever tell you that you look like . . . what's his name . . . Russell Crowe?"

Gavin grimaced. "What are you doing here, Amy?"

"Hey, I'm, um, really sorry to hear about your mechanic and partner," she said somberly. "I found out early this morning. The paper says you're all right. Are you?"

"I'm fine."

"Good," she said. "I was worried. I never know what to believe in the paper." She eyed him curiously. "It looks like you've got your own personal terrorist."

"Tell me about it."

"The paper also said the passenger survived." Her eyes suddenly filled with the intensity Gavin had first seen at her sister's bedside.

He nodded. "She's stable. I'll be seeing her soon."

"Can I be there?"

"Absolutely not."

"Hmm, but you'll let me know . . ."

"As soon as I know."

"You'd better!" she said strongly, then lightened. "An interesting slant in today's story. You made the cover."

"Really?"

" 'The brave live as long as the coward allows.' "

"That's the headline?"

"No. It's an old Japanese saying," she explained. She folded the paper in half twice, then stood up. She was stunning. " 'The brave live as long as the coward allows,' " she repeated, walking over and handing him the paper. She was tall enough to look him in the eye. "Nice shorts." She smiled and walked toward her bike.

Gavin reflexively looked down. His midsection appeared neglected compared to her rippled abdominals, which were obviously the product of hard and regular exercise. He, on the other hand, hadn't worked out regularly in six months and suddenly felt ashamed of his laziness.

He watched her walk to her bike, her thick, braided black hair sweeping her shoulders. Man, she was beautiful. He struggled to refocus on the paper. "GHOST DRIVER TAKES AIM AT INVESTIGATION . . . 1 DEAD."

"The paper quotes you as saying the Ghost Driver is a coward," Amy said.

"He *is* a coward."

"For sure, but if I didn't know better I would think you were trying to get him mad."

"Wouldn't want to do that," he said sarcastically.

"Okay, then your genius plan is to get him to come after you for insulting him?"

Gavin didn't respond.

"What if he catches you by surprise like he has everyone else?"

"I saw him check us out last night just before the crash. Next time I'll be ready."

"Don't you think he knows that?" she said, rolling her eyes.

"You idiot," he said.

"Excuse me?" Amy said, looking shocked.

"I was just helping you complete your sentence. Weren't you really thinking, 'Don't you think he knows that, you idiot?' "

"I didn't . . . Okay, I guess I did. Sorry."

Gavin didn't like being pushed by

anyone, beautiful or not. "Well, to answer your question, I don't think he really cares all that much. If he's half as drunk as his passengers are, revenge is probably taking a backseat to sheer recklessness. I don't know what the odds are. It's a shot. That's all. A shot."

He was angry. But he wasn't sure if it was her questions or simply because just talking about the killer made him mad.

"You better keep your eyes open, that's all. I don't want to lose my partner."

"Partner?"

"Yours is in the hospital, remember?"

Gavin let out a rare, albeit brief, laugh. "Thanks, but I don't need a partner. Chris will be back soon enough."

"I hope so. But like I told you before, you won't even know I'm around. I just need a little information."

"Like what?"

"The name of the passenger that survived. The paper said her name was being withheld."

"The paper was correct."

"I'm not going to harass her."

"Amy. Leave the police work to the police before you get hurt."

"What? You don't think I can do as good a job as you, Gavin Tremayne Pierce?"

"How did you . . ." Gavin hated his middle name. He never even included an initial when signing anything, even official stuff. She must have somehow found out what was on his birth certificate.

"It's Welsh — your great-grandfather's name on your father's side."

"Amy —"

"You have a ten-thousand-dollar credit line on your Visa, but rarely run up a tab more than a grand and almost always pay in full by the end of the first month."

So she'd found out his credit line somehow. You didn't need to be Sherlock Holmes to do that.

"And you don't have a steady girlfriend — at least not one you like very much."

"Now that's none of your business," Gavin said, not comfortable with her digging this far into his personal life.

"Sorry. But am I wrong?"

"You promised you wouldn't go snooping around without my permission."

"Already bored? I didn't even get to tell you about the scar underneath those cute shorts."

"Stop."

"So?" Amy asked, her eyes big and bright.

"So what?"

"So what's her name?"

"Why not ask your computer?" he said.

"Look, we both know I can find her name in the police or hospital files easily enough. But the sooner I get it, the better chance we all have of finding the killer. Besides, asking you is more fun," she said with a mischievous twinkle in her eye.

Gavin sighed and gave up. "Karianne Stordal. She's a Norwegian Airlines flight attendant. Anything else?"

"Your police passcode?"

"Forget it."

"Okay, okay," she said, mounting her bike. "What time is dinner?"

"What dinner?"

"All this work is going to make me very hungry. And we need to get to know each other better if we're working together."

"We're not working together."

"Six? Your place?"

"Here? I don't have any —"

"Look, I'll come by at six and we'll ride out to the supermarket and get some food. You have a bike?"

"Uh, yeah. It's —"

"Just make sure it has air. See you at six. Have an appetite."

Gavin watched her turn out of the driveway with a wave, wondering how he had just been talked into a date. Since the time of the aquarium crash until now, his interest in women — and pretty much everything else — had taken a backseat. Pain and death had a way of dulling the senses. With hatred and vengeance as a salve for his emotional wounds, life and its visual pleasantries had become little more than a big "So what."

Why, then, did he continue to watch Amy ride away until she turned out of view?

— 17 —

When Gavin looked up and saw the lieutenant storming toward him, he knew it had been a mistake to stop at headquarters instead of going straight to the hospital.

"What the devil do you call this?" Lieutenant Sandel said, dropping a copy of the morning newspaper onto Gavin's desk.

"You know Gasman, Lieutenant. He just got a little carried away."

"A little carried away? Chris got carried away . . . and you'll be next. What's wrong with that idiot? Doesn't he know that —"

Gavin didn't have to look up from the computer to know the lieutenant's face was metamorphosing with the revelation that his detective had set up the headline. He knew what was coming, too. Lieutenant Sandel was a reasonable man, but like everyone else he had superiors to answer to and wouldn't be found sticking his neck out far enough to get it chopped off.

"You worked out a deal with Gasman, didn't you? This was your idea," the lieutenant said angrily, hammering the newspaper with his index finger.

Gavin didn't deny it. He sat back from the computer and looked at his supervisor, then nodded.

Slightly mollified at the instant admission, the lieutenant sat down in the interview chair next to the desk and crossed his legs with a sigh. Gavin swallowed. Here it comes, he thought — the lecture.

"When Chris first asked that you be teamed with him in this case, I was reluctant because you were too close to it. I was afraid the death of your grandfather might cloud your judgment. Chris assured me your experience would be valuable and, if anything, you'd be more focused." The lieutenant's voice rose. "Now this guy has killed someone else you know and Chris is in the hospital where he can't keep an eye on you. And you're going over the edge!"

He angrily emphasized his point with a finger in Gavin's face. "And let me tell you something else. I've got others pulling your caseload, again at Chris's request. I can't say I wouldn't behave the same way if I were in your shoes, but if I did, someone would have to tell me what I've got to tell you now: I'm taking you off the case."

Gavin was shocked. This wasn't how the lecture was supposed to end. He'd been expecting a warning to calm down and be careful or else. But all he'd gotten was the *or else*.

"Lieutenant, I know I might have stretched procedures, but this can't be treated like a normal case. This isn't a hit-and-run where we find our man by matching pieces of broken light covers to find a vehicle or by following a blood trail to the local hospital. We have the cars. We have fingerprints. We have hair samples. So when we nab this guy the case will be iron-clad. But he's dangerous and he's still out there. If this paper can get him thinking about how to get me, it might keep him from thinking about crashing into someone else."

"Don't you think he'll know you're watching for him?"

"He won't care, Lieutenant. My gut tells me he cares more about wreaking havoc than he does about getting caught. We have his accomplice in the hospital and she's gonna make it. When she fingers him, we'll get him before he gets anyone else. If you pull me now, you're going to lose time bringing the next guy up to speed. In that time our psycho might decide to go on another joy ride." He sighed. "Believe me, I'm not trying to be a hero, but I am the best man for the job and you know it. You need this one caught, Lieutenant, and the sooner the better."

The lieutenant stared expressionlessly at Gavin. Then he closed his eyes and pinched the bridge of his nose. Gavin wasn't sure if the long pause was good or not. The lieutenant wasn't one to say no without an explanation; he could be forming the appropriate reasons for why he couldn't concede . . .

The nose massage stopped and the lieutenant opened his eyes. "No more scary surprises, Pierce. The feds are already nosing around this case. You do anything to embarrass me, you're not only off the case, you're outta here. Last chance. Got it?"

Gavin nodded, but the fire that burned white hot in his heart was less concerned with breaking rules and losing his job than with finding the maniac and making him pay.

By the time Gavin got to the hospital it was already two o'clock and he had little to show for his time. He walked straight into

Chris's room without a knock. A nurse was changing a clear fluid bag on an intravenous rack. Chris appeared to be asleep. He had a white bandage around his head, two black eyes, and a cast on his left arm that disappeared under his gown's sleeve but appeared to continue to his shoulder. As bad as he looked, Gavin was calmed by the fact he was breathing and that, according to the beeping monitor, his heart was strong and stable. Unlike Grampa, Chris had youth and health going for him.

The nurse turned and gestured for silence, putting her finger to her lips, then walked toward Gavin.

"He's just fallen asleep," she whispered. "His wife went home to rest a bit." She led him out of the room.

"I'm his partner. How's he doing?" he said softly.

"I think Doctor Fagan is the one you should ask. He's in the — Oh, there he is now." She motioned toward a clean-shaven, middle-aged man of medium build. As he approached he greeted the nurse with a pleasant smile.

"Doctor Fagan," Gavin said, extending his hand. "I'm Detective Pierce. If you could spare a few minutes, I need to ask you a couple of questions."

"Detective Pierce. I read about you in today's paper. I'm very sorry about Mr. Garrity," he said. "How can I help?"

"Well, first, Doc, how's Detective Grella?" he said, motioning toward Chris's room.

"He had a little bleeding in his left lung and a bruised left kidney. His concussion, though, seems to be less serious than we first thought."

Gavin grimaced, recalling the positive spin on Grampa's concussion prognosis. He shook it off, consciously reminding himself this was a different person, time, and place.

"Fortunately, your friend has a thick skull. He was in a lot of pain earlier, so we increased the Demerol a bit. Just enough for him to rest. As you probably know, the first three days after an accident are the worst painwise. Every cell in his body will ache. Also, that cast will be on for about six weeks. He'll be in here awhile, but we expect him to heal without any serious reminders of the accident."

Gavin nodded. "Maybe later you could put that bit about the thick skull in writing."

Fagan quirked his lips. "Of course."

"The other thing is that I need to question the woman, Karianne Stordal. It's urgent I speak to her as soon as possible. Other lives depend on it," Gavin said as seriously as he could.

"I suppose you could. She's not in much better shape than your friend, but she's in less pain. A fringe benefit of the cocktails. And speaking of the alcohol, she had an alarming amount in her. Point two-eight. I don't know how she was functioning. Anyway, she's in 318, just around the corner," the doctor said as he pointed down the long hall toward where Gavin knew Amber Clayborne had been placed. "You go on down there. I've got one more stop to make, then I'll join you."

Gavin thanked him and headed down the hall, thinking that the ICU was filling rapidly with people he knew. Turning the corner, he immediately saw a uniform cop outside Karianne's door. He nodded to the cop and then spontaneously continued on to Amber's room. As much as he wanted to question the flight attendant, he also wanted to see Amber. He wasn't exactly sure why and wondered if it had something to do with Amy. Of course, checking Amber's status had been on his to-do list. But he had to admit to himself there was more.

He stepped into Amber's room. There

she was, exactly as she had been the day before. Motionless, peaceful, and residing in an unreachable land. How long was she going to be that way?

With a sigh, he left the room. He was now well primed to see Miss Karianne Stordal. If it weren't for her, Chris wouldn't be in the hospital and John Garrity wouldn't be dead. It was her vehicle that had caused the damage. Maybe she'd even had something to do with Amber. Ready or not, Karianne was going to tell him everything he wanted to know.

He entered her room. She looked different than she had when he last saw her. Her face had swelled and her eyes had blackened. Her right leg was in a cast suspended in traction. All compliments of the airbag expanding into her at two hundred miles per hour.

Gavin was about to try to wake her when Dr. Fagan entered the room.

"She's still resting," Dr. Fagan said. "Maybe a little bit later would be better."

"Doc, every minute that goes by is another minute the killer has to do more damage."

"Surely the driver must be hurt also."

"Not so hurt he couldn't walk away from the crash . . . again. He had the protection

159

of a seat belt and the air bag. Besides, apparently this guy can really take a punch."

"Still and all, I find it difficult to believe that —"

"I know, but the fact is he's consistently been able to escape the scene before we can get there, and show up again — in this case by the next night. His ability to withstand this kind of physical punishment seems incredible, but so does the high levels of alcohol found in the passengers. If there's a chance we can learn his identity sooner rather than later, I can't sit back so one of his accomplices gets a little more rest. More rest for her means more rest for him. I must insist we at least try to wake her. If he's hurt, this would be the perfect time to get him." Gavin was trying to keep control of his anger.

"Very well," the doctor said and went to the bedside. "Karianne . . . Karianne," he said gently.

Gavin felt like yelling her name and didn't care if it stunned the entire floor. He imagined himself yanking the doctor out of the way by his collar, breaking an ampule of smelling salts under Karianne's nose, sticking his gun to her head, and screaming at her until she awoke.

"Isn't there some kind of intravenous

cup of coffee you could give her? Any-thing?"

"Detective Pierce, I understand your ur-gency and I will try to arouse her, but I must draw the line when . . . Wait . . . I think she's starting to come around."

The young woman had begun to frown and then stretch her neck backward slowly. She grimaced slightly and groaned.

"Karianne," the doctor repeated.

Her eyes slowly opened. At first they didn't move, then they gradually shifted to her suspended leg. She closed her eyes, as if they had seen enough for now.

"Karianne," the doctor said softly, like he was waking up his seven-year-old daughter for school.

Gavin was ready to explode. This woman didn't deserve to be daintily patted awake. What she needed was a bucket of ice water in the face and her rights read to her. That would wake her up — pronto.

Again, Karianne opened her eyes, then looked in the direction of the cooing doctor. Dr. Fagan smiled.

"You're going to be fine. You've been in an accident."

"That's not what I would call it," Gavin said.

The doctor shot a glare at Gavin, then

turned back. "This is Detective Pierce, Karianne. He needs to ask you some questions."

Karianne looked at Gavin. She closed her eyes and frowned, lips quivering, then opened them again. "What happened?" she asked hoarsely, tears welling up. "Is anyone else hurt?"

"You might say that," Gavin said. "One man is dead and another, my partner, is just down the hall. He's feeling good as long as they keep the Demerol pumping. And that's today's body count. We'll just add that to your friend's rolling tally." A competent detective would not normally have handled the initial approach with such an attitude, but the last thing on Gavin's mind was department etiquette.

Karianne tried to speak. Tears poured down her face as she quietly sobbed for what seemed like forever to Gavin. Not only was he in a hurry to get his questions answered, but he hated to see crying. He didn't want to let up, but he knew the tears would get to him. Unfortunately, the crying seemed to be causing her physical pain, which was probably prolonging the crying.

"What friend?" she finally asked.

"That's what we want to know. Who was

the guy driving?" Gavin demanded.

"Driving? Driving what?" she asked.

"The Jeep Cherokee."

Her eyes widened. "My car?" she said.

Gavin rolled his eyes. The last thing he wanted to do was tell her what she was supposed to be telling him. He was here to get information, not give it. But seeing she could not seem to remember a thing, maybe a few pertinent facts might jog her memory.

"Look. Maybe we should start at the beginning," he said as he pulled out a memo pad. He recounted what had happened so far, from when Garrity and Chris drove away from his house on back through the previous crashes. As he spoke, she stared at him without blinking. When he finished, she erupted.

"This is a nightmare. This can't be happening. It just can't. Not again . . ."

Gavin stopped. He and Dr. Fagan looked at each other, verifying without a word that they had heard the same thing.

" 'Again,' Karianne?" Dr. Fagan asked.

"Yes. The same thing happened to me five years ago in Norway. I woke up in a hospital and was immediately questioned about a crash. It was my car and the driver was never caught. I didn't remember any of it. I tried, but I never could. It's haunted me since, and now it's happened again. How? Why?" She began to cry again.

"No way. You're not going to tell me you don't know who the driver is," Gavin said, tossing his memo pad onto her bed in frustration. This was impossible. She had to know something.

She shook her head.

"Look, if you think you can protect this . . . this . . ."

"I'm sorry, but I don't remember! I don't know who you're after," she cried.

"Well, you'd better try," Gavin said angrily.

"Karianne," Dr. Fagan said. "What is the last thing you remember about yesterday?"

She exhaled and closed her eyes, apparently searching. She began massaging her temple and then the bridge of her nose. Finally she took her hand away and looked solemnly at the doctor. "I remember having a drink."

A drink? Gavin screamed silently. Now there's a monumental revelation. Your blood had enough alcohol in it for an entire Mardi Gras carnival. He opened his mouth to voice a retort, but the doctor held up his hand, apparently realizing

Gavin's struggle to maintain sanity.

"Who were you with?" the doctor asked.

"I was alone."

"Where?" Gavin said.

"Near where I live. In Long Beach. On the boardwalk. I think the place was called Seahorse."

Gavin picked up his memo pad and wrote it down. "Did you leave there with anyone?"

"I don't know."

"Big guy — blond?"

"I don't know. I don't even remember leaving."

"Great, we finally get someone who was with him and we know more about what he looks like than she does."

"What's wrong with me? Why don't I remember?"

"You apparently blacked out from too much alcohol. It's very common. All you've experienced has been sealed away from your conscious. Locked up," Dr. Fagan explained.

"Locked up," Gavin said. "Where's the freakin' key?"

"Yes. I was just thinking the same thing. If the events she can't remember are hidden within her subconscious, there are techniques that have been known to work.

But she has to be willing to remember."

"I want to remember. Believe me, I want to remember. I will do anything to stop this," Karianne said.

"What techniques?" Gavin said quickly.

"Hypnosis," Dr. Fagan said.

"Hypnosis?" An alarm sounded in Gavin's mind. He wasn't a particularly devout person, but he was a little iffy on the hypnosis thing. "And then a crystal ball and a palm reader?"

Fagan was not amused. "Hypnosis happens to be a medically accepted practice for reaching into a patient's subconscious and a viable therapeutic treatment for a multiplicity of suppressive disorders and addictions."

Gavin paused. His own reservations notwithstanding, the department frowned upon hypnosis. If this were the LAPD, there'd be no hesitation, but this wasn't California; New York was a different world. Then again, she'd said she was willing to do anything. And he'd long since given up trying to pretend he was playing this case by the books. He was out to find the killer — whatever it took.

"Okay," he finally said.

"Miss Stordal?" Fagan asked.

She nodded.

"How long is she going to be in here, Doc?"

"At least one, maybe two, more days."

"Then I'll arrange for a psychologist to meet us here tomorrow," Gavin said, determined he would if he had to kidnap one.

Before Gavin left the hospital to check out a bar called the Seahorse somewhere on the boardwalk in Long Beach, he stopped again to see Chris. This time Chris appeared to be awake, though it was hard to tell if his eyes were open or closed.

"Hey, pal. How you doing?"

Chris slowly raised his eyebrows to help open his eyelids. "Wonderful. I can't remember when I've felt better. So long as Nurse Barker keeps the good stuff flowing through the tube. Oh . . . sorry about John, Gav. How's his wife?"

"Don't ask. How's yours?"

"Ah. You know Pat. She's mad as can be — ready to go out and find the jerk herself."

"There's a lot of that going around."

"Did you see him?"

Gavin shook his head. "Nah. I was kind of busy."

Chris smiled weakly. "That's your problem. You're always busy. I heard that a girl survived. Did you talk to her yet?"

"Yeah. She didn't remember a thing, except where she was drinking beforehand. A place called the Seahorse in Long Beach."

"The Seahorse Tavern," Chris said. "A nice place on the boardwalk."

"I knew there was a reason for coming in here besides feeling obligated because you're my partner and all," Gavin deadpanned.

"Hey, I guess you were right," Chris said.

"About what?"

"About answering Gasman's stupid question about sending the killer a message. I guess he didn't like my advice."

"We all make mistakes," Gavin said as he looked at his watch. It was four o'clock. "And speaking of mistakes, I agreed to have dinner at six with Amber Clayborne's twin sister, Amy. I'll never make it."

"Where're you going?"

"My place."

"What's she like?"

Gavin thought for a moment before answering. "Besides being lights-out gorgeous, she's the type of person that would board a train to go somewhere and end up driving the thing by the time she got off."

"Sounds scary."

"Very."

"But how . . ."

"It's a bit complicated and I don't want to make you feel any worse. And, I've got to run," Gavin said. "I'll see you tomorrow. We're gonna hypnotize Karianne Stordal to see what she really knows. She's more than willing."

"Hypnotize?" Chris said loudly, then winced.

"You got it."

"Does the lieutenant know?"

"Nope. He can read it in your report when we're done."

"My report?"

"Of course," Gavin said, suppressing a smile. "We're partners, remember? Besides, the lieutenant will be easier on someone who's injured."

Chris furrowed his brow. "You know, Gav, you didn't used to be so . . ."

"Boring?" Gavin said, walking away.

"Safe," Chris said, looking down at himself in bed.

"Hey, if you want out . . ."

"Wonderful. *Now* you ask me. Look, I'm going to be there if I have to have them wheel me in. And Gav," Chris called. "I heard about what you told Gasman. Be careful, my friend. That guy's crazy."

"Who? Gasman or the killer?" Gavin yelled back.

"Both," Chris said.

Gavin didn't notice the fine craftsmanship that detailed the large, polished-brass clock mortised into the teak steering wheel — the centerpiece above the mirror at the Seahorse Tavern. What he did notice was that it was now ten till five. He had tried to call Amy on the drive down after conceding his schedule was sheer fantasy, but there'd been no answer at her home number and no machine to leave a message on. He had, however, managed to get a call through to Dr. Harold Katz, a criminal psychologist the department was familiar with. Under the circumstances, he had agreed to meet with Gavin at the hospital tomorrow at noon.

"What can I get you?" the bartender asked as Gavin walked up to the bar.

"A glass of water with a lemon wedge would be fine," Gavin said as he flashed his tin. "Would you happen to know who was working the bar yesterday afternoon?"

"That would be me. Why?"

Gavin pulled a photo from his jacket pocket and dropped it on the bar. The picture had been taken in the emergency room. "She look familiar?" Gavin asked.

The bartender put on a pair of glasses

and picked up the photo, holding it flat enough to catch the down-lighting over his head. Gavin watched the man's eyes widen as he drew the photo closer.

"Man, oh, man! What did he do to her?" the bartender said.

"Who?" Gavin shot back. "He was here? You saw him? You know him?"

"Don't know him," the bartender replied, slowly shaking his head. "Don't want to know him. But I can't say I'm surprised you want the guy. Figured he was wanted for something the moment I laid eyes on him." He continued to stare at the photo. "Is she going to be all right?"

Gavin felt like the bartender was speaking in slow motion. "Yeah, fine, although right now she can't remember a thing."

"Not surprised at that, either. By the time he came in, she'd already had better than half a bottle of vodka. I cut her off, but he came over and insisted she have more. A lot more. She was drunk, but he wanted her more drunk. I was amazed she was able to walk out of here."

"He insisted? Why didn't you refuse?"

The bartender looked down, obviously embarrassed. "I thought about it. Even thought of calling you guys. But . . . I can't say it any other way: the guy scared me. When he looked at me I, I just had to let him have his way. And it wasn't just that he was big. He looked wild, with fresh sores on his face, like he'd just been in a fight with a bull . . . and won. I was never so scared of saying no to anyone and never so glad to see someone leave."

The sincerity in the man's tone and the fear in his face were chilling enough to cool Gavin's intensity. "Okay. Tell me about him. Did you hear any of the conversation? Did you hear his name?"

The bartender shook his head. "Sorry. Like I said, I kept my distance."

"Well what did he look like?"

"Big. Mean."

"Blond?"

"Yeah. Short, kind of flat topped," he said, motioning with his hand over his own head.

"Eyes?"

"Scary, as if he could stare right through ya. I don't remember the color. As soon as he looked at me I wanted to turn away. Run away."

"It's him," Gavin declared, more to himself than the bartender.

"Who is he?" the bartender said.

"Could you help one of our artists with

a sketch tomorrow morning, say nine o'clock?"

"Sure. Just tell me where. I'll never forget that guy as long as I live. Enough to give me nightmares."

Gavin continued to question the man, noting details of everything the bartender could remember from the time Karianne walked in until she finally left with the man. Gavin wondered how much was exaggeration. The man the bartender was describing seemed more like a monster than anything human.

"Is there anything else you can remember?" Gavin finally asked.

"Well, there was something else that struck me as peculiar," the bartender said, massaging his chin. "When the big guy first came in, I could tell the lady didn't know who he was, but after a short while they were acting like they knew each other."

"What's so peculiar? After enough drink, everyone knows everyone," Gavin said.

"I know; I'm a bartender. But there was more to it. They even had a word they used when they clicked glasses — something I've never heard before. It was a funny word. In fact, I probably wouldn't even remember it if they hadn't said it a few times. And they said it loud when they left."

"What was it?" Gavin said impatiently.

"They were slurring, but it sounded like . . . *shay-dod*. Or *shah-dod*."

Gavin made a note of it as best he could. Finally. The case should wrap up fast now with as many clues as the big boy was leaving around. A little artist rendition and a little jogging of the flight attendant's memory and he would probably have a name and address. It was almost beginning to seem like business as usual. Almost.

— 18 —

Gavin was surprisingly glad and scared to see Amy's bike in the driveway as he drove in. Cedar stood at the gate dancing and wagging his tail. Beyond him on the lawn, laying on her side and leaning on her elbow, was Amy. Her lack of expression had him reciting to himself all the reasons that had made him late for their first date.

He got out of the car and walked to the gate, where Cedar was twirling in circles whining with joy.

"If you think I'm going to give you that kind of reception, forget it," Amy said.

"I'm sorry, but it couldn't be helped. We've got a decent description from a witness who saw them together before the crash and tomorrow when we hypnotize the girl we might be able to tag on a name and address."

"Hypnotize?"

"She didn't remember a thing."

"She's lying."

"I don't think so."

"Well, you're still late. And for punishment you have to tell me every little detail. And then I've got a few things to tell you. But first, I want to eat."

"No. Let's talk first, and then eat," Gavin said.

"You don't know me. I can't concentrate on anything when I'm hungry. Low blood sugar and high metabolism or something like that. All I'll think about while you're talking is food."

"Okay, okay. I can't even believe you're still here."

"You're not going to get rid of me that easily. Whatever it takes, remember. Besides, Cedar was good company and he told me a few things about you I can't believe."

"That so? How did you know his name? Did he tell you that, too?"

"Of course."

"Hmm." Gavin took Amy's outstretched hand and pulled her up.

"Just point me to the kitchen," she said, following Gavin into the house.

"Over there," Gavin said, motioning straight ahead. "Excuse the mess. The maid hasn't been around for a while." He started up the stairs to his bedroom to change.

Amy looked around, impressed at the cleanliness. "She hasn't?" Women were always impressed at the way he kept his kitchen. At least any women who got to see it, which lately was none.

Gavin continued to his room and five minutes later was stepping briskly down the stairs in khaki shorts and a T-shirt. His bare feet were breathing for the first time all day. Amy sat on a stool at the kitchen counter with her fingers steepled under her chin. The sight of a woman in his house was both alluring and troubling to Gavin. The fact that the woman was Amy Kirsch magnified his conflict.

"You get an A-plus in housekeeping. You also have all the fixings for a great meal. The only problem is you've got nothing to fix," she said.

"That's what I was trying to tell you this morning. What would you like?"

"Fish?"

"I'm picky with fish," Gavin said.

"So be picky. I'm not. We'll get whatever fish you love," she said, hopping off the stool and heading for the door. As she passed Gavin she grabbed him by the elbow. "Let's go, I'm starving."

"At least let me get something on my feet," he said.

On the road, Gavin was barely able to keep up with Amy and her mountain bike. She had a tendency to go up curbs and through debris that Gavin would have avoided. Gavin couldn't tell if she was showing off or just having fun. Either way, she exhibited a zest he could only envy. Maybe if he hadn't been so personally involved with the case, he would not feel so alien to her free spirit. He wondered, as she waved for him to keep up with her, what held the reins that kept him from being free with her? Was he really the head case some people said he was? Maybe if he hadn't become so tarnished by death he could share her enthusiasm for life.

So why, then, had he agreed to dinner with her? He could have been more resistant. But, on the flip side, how could he not be attracted to her? She was kind of pleasant — in a headstrong, slightly alarming, sort of way.

When they got to the supermarket, Gavin dismounted his bike, but Amy rode hers right to the door and waited for it to open.

"What do you think you're doing?" Gavin said, walking toward her.

"This baby goes wherever I go," she said.

"You're joking, right?"

"No, I always do this."

Gavin shook his head in disbelief. "If you're afraid it'll be stolen we can lock it to the lamppost."

"Nope," she said smugly.

"Well, what do you expect me to do, chase you through the store? Race you to the seafood section?"

Amy smiled. "Sounds like fun."

"Not to me."

"What do you do for fun?"

"Fun?" Gavin said, as if the word belonged in another universe. If God was interested in him ever having fun he would not have stuck him in a world with so much calamity. "I knit."

"Come on, Gavin. Let go a little. Where's your wild side?"

"I don't have one."

Amy's eyebrows raised. "That's not what I've read."

"Read? Where?"

"Your files."

"Department files?"

"From what I read, you can be quite aggressive when you want to."

"You should be arrested."

"Then cuff me," she said with dare in her eyes.

"Believe me, if I had cuffs with me I'd lock you and your bike to a parking meter."

"I'll tell you what, if you beat me in arm wrestling, I'll leave my bike out here."

"I give up. Bring the bike, but please walk it."

"Yes, sir, Officer, sir," Amy said, saluting. "But soon enough you'll see everything my way."

"Really. What makes you think so?"

"An old Japanese saying: 'Those who run with wolves learn to howl.' "

"That's Japanese?"

"Uh-huh," Amy said, nodding confidently.

"But there aren't any wolves in —" Gavin stopped when he saw Amy's eyebrow rise again. "Never mind. Let's get the food. I'm starving."

As it turned out, he had to admit to himself, and then begrudgingly to Amy, her bike was less of a disturbance than he anticipated. Maybe there was something to her Japanese sayings, or whatever they were. He wondered just how much she was used to getting away with. Even the cashier had met her with a smile. The bike might as well have been a cute baby.

Back at the house Gavin poured them something to drink while Amy made a sauce to go with the fish.

"That smells delicious," he said.

" 'The best sauce is a good appetite,' " she replied.

Gavin rolled his eyes. "Don't tell me. Another old Japanese saying?"

Amy smiled and nodded.

"What can I do to help?" he said, not used to watching someone else work in his kitchen.

"Nothing. Sit at the table and relax," she said, then turned to him as he stood there. "Relax!"

Gavin's dining room was small and simple, as was the old, refinished oak table on the stripped-oak floor. Amy found an old half-burnt candle on a kitchen shelf, lit it, and placed it on the table, where Gavin had found a seat. Cedar was lying down by the rear door, his eyes spending equal time between Gavin and Amy. Gavin wondered if the Golden Retriever-smile the dog was wearing displayed his approval of Amy or his relief that dinner was finally happening. Gavin guessed it was the dinner, since he could never resist giving Cedar a few morsels, even though it meant putting up with an occasional whine for more.

Although they had settled on catfish, Amy's method of sautéing the fish over onions in olive oil and garlic looked great, especially when her grandmother's secret sauce was added. The fish was set on a bed of rice with a side of lightly cooked shredded broccoli and carrots. As soon as the plates hit the table, they quickly sat and Gavin topped off their drinks. He raised his glass.

"To the hands that prepared this feast."

"To teamwork," Amy said, then clicked his glass with hers. " 'Where there's a will, there's a way.' "

"Japanese?"

"Of course."

They both ate heartily, not saying much until their plates were empty. Gavin had looked up from his dish several times to see Amy's bronze glow in the flickering candlelight. On the last glance, she caught him, acknowledging his gaze with a smile.

Apparently deciding it was time for business, she finally asked Gavin to detail his day. He retrieved his notes while Amy cleared the table of everything but their glasses.

Gavin knew the main tool of his trade was information. Information meant control and power and, in the end, validation. Under what he would consider more normal circumstances, he would have felt the need to establish a longer, more trusting, relationship before revealing what he knew. But he had no time for building trust. He had information and apparently so did she.

He swallowed what was left in his glass, pushed it aside, and asked her to resist asking questions until he was done. She agreed, eagerly bouncing back into her seat, readying herself for some note taking of her own. Gavin proudly presented the information his police computer had provided on Karianne Stordal, confident anything Amy had retrieved would only be redundant. Amy remained quiet throughout, though obviously straining not to interject when Gavin spoke about the hypnosis scheduled for noon. Finally, when told of the bartender's description of the killer, she ended her vow of silence.

"He didn't hear him tell her his name?"

"No," Gavin said, looking through his notes. "But there was a strange word he overheard. Oh, here it is. *Shay-dod* or *Shah-dod*, he said. And he said they repeated it several times."

"What does it mean?"

"I don't know. Maybe nothing. Maybe he heard it wrong. Could mean anything. A name, a place . . . who knows."

"I'll check it out first thing tomorrow morning," Amy said. "My turn now?"

Gavin nodded and sat back with folded arms.

"Well, the fact Stordal was in an almost identical crash five years ago in Norway is just the beginning."

Where had she found that? Gavin decided he didn't want to know.

"The vehicle that her car crashed into had five people in it. Three of them were killed. But one of the ones who survived not only saw the driver who escaped, but actually admitted to knowing his identity. The other survivor was the man's granddaughter."

"He knew him?"

"Yes! But," Amy said, raising her finger, "he refused to reveal the identity."

"Why?" Gavin said incredulously.

"The report surmised a possible fear of retribution."

"Really? He thought they would try again?"

"Sort of. He didn't want his survival or even the fact he had a granddaughter to become public knowledge. He was obsessed with keeping her within his sight at all times."

"The Mob?"

"I don't think so."

"A little temporary insanity?"

"More than a little and more than temporary. The entire rest of the time he was there, which was another week in the hospital, he refused to eat anything and even gave them a hard time when they tried to hook up the intravenous."

"Why the fuss?"

"I don't know."

"What about his granddaughter?"

"I don't know. All they say was he wouldn't let her out of his sight."

"Back up. What do you mean by 'the rest of the time he was there'? Was he visiting Norway?"

"Yeah. And that's the good news: we won't have to learn how to speak Norwegian to talk to him. He's from New Jersey. A preacher who was visiting Norway on some kind of ministry engagement."

"New Jersey? That's close enough. Maybe he was suffering from some kind of temporary paranoia and now that he sees his granddaughter has been safe for the last five years, he might open up to us."

"Maybe, but New Jersey was also five

years ago. He moved. He's no longer right around the corner. After the accident he sold everything he owned and moved up-state New York to a small town called Hamden, just west of the Catskills."

Gavin frowned in disbelief. "What did you do, tap into the Norwegian police department and the U.S. Postal Service?"

"Actually, the Norwegian police *was* one of my stops. But the IRS had more on him than the Post Office. Translating from Norwegian took a little time."

"You speak Norwegian?"

"Of course not. I get a little help from my friends," she said with a wink. "Anyway, the guy's name is Jesse J. Buchanan. Reverend Jesse J. Buchanan."

"Good job, Amy. I'll give him a call. Or are you going to tell me you've already done that and he's standing outside right now?" Gavin said.

Amy laughed. "I wish. Actually, I was hoping we might take a ride to the country and pay him a visit." She pushed back her chair, took her glass, and relocated herself on the living room couch. "It's not all that far away."

"A ride in the country sounds nice, but I wouldn't be much fun," Gavin said, picking up the cordless phone from the table. He punched in 411. "Yes, Hamden."

Amy handed him a folded piece of paper. He opened it and read, "Samantha's Farm." There was a number. He hung up and looked at Amy, his right eyebrow raised. She was ahead of him at every turn.

"Let me guess: Reverend Buchanan?" he said, motioning to the paper.

"Yup."

"You know, you've got to at least let me feel like I'm accomplishing something," he said. "What's Samantha's Farm?"

"He lives there, according to the local general store. There's no phone number under his name."

"Maybe it's unlisted," he said, refilling his glass and following her to the couch.

Amy shook her head. "Not even. Besides, his granddaughter's name is Samantha Buchanan. I wouldn't be surprised if she owns it outright. Either way, he's not an easy person to find. Maybe he wants to be left alone. Maybe he's hiding."

"Only one way to find out," Gavin said.

"You're calling him now?"

"Why not?" he said as he dialed.

The phone rang twice before an answering machine picked up with the voice of a child. "Hi! My name is Samantha and this is my dairy farm. Please leave the usual information at the beep. Thank you. Good-bye."

Gavin left a message and his number, then hung up and looked at Amy. He pressed the redial button and handed her the phone. "You've got to hear this."

"Gimme," she said. Her face went from serious to a smile to a giggle. "Very cute."

"Yeah, very cute. But what do you make of it?"

"A couple of things come to mind."

"Such as?"

"A sales gimmick? Honesty. Innocence. After hearing her voice, I know I'd do business with her."

"Maybe you would, but I'm sure there are just as many that think little girls and business don't mix."

"Men," she snorted with a roll of her eyes. "Well, maybe it has nothing to do with business. Maybe Samantha's Farm is just what they call the place."

"Hmm, sounds to me like you're still pushing for that ride in the country."

Amy smiled thoughtfully, made a few notes, then closed her pad and dropped it onto the coffee table. Gavin was impressed. Even if all her material turned out to be a dead end, he was still surprised she'd been able to get it — and so quickly.

He found he was actually starting to relax and enjoy Amy's company. He raised his glass for another sip, but stopped with the rim at his lips. He'd heard something — a roaring car engine. It wasn't far away and it was coming down the side street across from his house. He sat up and put his glass down.

"What is it?" Amy said.

Gavin suddenly remembered how relaxed he'd been when he was sitting at the aquarium with Grampa. And how he'd been caught off guard when John Garrity was killed. The engine got louder — closer. He could see the headlights illuminating the front window's curtains. In seconds the car would come crashing through . . .

"Gavin, what are you doing?"

He did not remember leaping toward her, but he had apparently seized Amy and was now shielding her with the weight of his body on the dining room floor. He opened his tightly shut eyes and looked behind him toward the living room. The lights were gone. The front wall was still there. The engine sounds were quietly fading up the block. He rolled off Amy and helped her sit up before looking again at the window, embarrassed, muscles still tense.

"Gavin. You're shaking."

"I . . . I thought . . ."

"It's okay," Amy said, tenderly sliding her hand along his forearm.

"I'm sorry," he said, not wanting to look her in the eye.

"There's nothing to be sorry about," she said, gently cupping his chin with her hand and turning his face toward hers. "You were afraid for me, weren't you? You tried to save my life."

"But you weren't in any danger."

"But you didn't know that," she whispered.

Gavin fought the urge to kiss her. His relationship with her was complicated enough. Besides, he didn't want to add Amy to a list of dead loved ones. For one reason or another, people he allowed himself to get close to did not have good life expectancies. He gently took her hand from his face. "It's my job to know," he said.

"It's your job to know?" she scoffed, pulling back. "You know, there's a time to work and there's a time to . . . not work."

"Japanese saying?" he said, trying to change the subject.

"Not this time," she said sternly.

"Look, I like a break as much as the next

guy, but as long as that psycho's breathing fresh air, I ain't punchin' the time clock."

Amy maintained eye contact with him for a long moment, then nodded slowly.

"We have a big day tomorrow," he said. "Maybe I better give you a ride home."

Amy clearly looked disappointed, but nodded. "I've got my bike."

"The bike will be safe with me. I promise not to ride away with it."

— 19 —

Karianne Stordal was sitting upright in her bed, alert on mild oral painkillers, the intravenous gone. The swelling in her face was barely noticeable and her black-rimmed eyes were almost fashionable. The most familiar people in the room she had known for less than twenty-four hours.

"Are you sure you're okay with this, Karianne?" Dr. Fagan said gently, his hand on her left forearm. Gavin wondered if he was like that with all his patients, or just the pretty blonde ones.

She nodded. "I suppose so. I want to know as much as anyone."

The criminal psychologist, Harold Katz, having completed final tests on video recording equipment in the corner of the room, aimed a microphone at Karianne. He was a tall man of about fifty years who wore a gray suit. His weak chin, large nose, and deep, droopy eyes made his face appear sad, even when he smiled — like a basset hound, Gavin thought.

Gavin sat at Karianne's bedside with his back toward the window. Although he'd already briefed Katz, he wanted to be close enough to communicate with the psychologist during Karianne's interview.

Chris was in a wheelchair at the foot of the vacant bed next to Karianne. Dr. Fagan had told him he did not think it was a good idea to leave his bed so soon. Chris had thanked him for his concern. Gavin thought his partner still looked terrible, but knew there was no way to exclude him. Chris was staring at the sketch that had been derived from the bartender's description. The sketch had had a sobering effect on any thought that the killer would be easy to handle once cornered. Earlier, when Gavin had first seen the drawing, he'd checked his shoulder holster to make sure his gun was with him and loaded. Katz had requested Karianne not be shown the sketch yet, lest the image of the killer's face remain in her mind and interfere with the hypnosis.

Gavin drummed his fingers on the windowsill and looked at his watch. It was one-thirty. Where was Amy? She'd wanted to research the strange word the bartender had heard. How long could that take her? He was getting spoiled by the speed with which she usually found obscure information.

"Okay, Karianne," Katz said in an extremely deep voice. "First I must officially inform you of the obvious. This videotape is now recording our session and will record everything you do or say under hypnosis. Do you understand?"

"Yes."

"And we have your permission to proceed?"

"Yes."

"Excellent. This won't hurt a bit. In fact, you'll find the entire experience very soothing. As for the rest of you, I have a few ground rules. Normally, these types of sessions are private, but under the extreme circumstances, allowances must be made. If you have a question, write it down in ink, not pencil. And write small. I don't want to hear any turning of pages. I will expect complete silence throughout the interview."

Katz placed a musician's metronome on the rolling bedside table, adjusted the tray's height, and positioned it over Karianne's legs so the metronome was directly in front of her. He released it's shiny gold arm, letting it swing freely. The room was silent except for the constant sound of the timer. Tick, tick, tick, tick . . .

Katz sat on a stool by the bed and folded his hands in his lap. "Karianne, I want you to look at the thin, polished arm as it moves back and forth. Take a deep breath and exhale."

Karianne breathed in deeply and blew out as if she were trying to blow up a balloon.

"Good," Katz lied calmly. "Easier with each breath. Listen to the sound of your air. Allow all your troubles and fears to flow away in the currents. Relax. Just keep your eye on the moving arm and listen to the gentle beat it emanates."

Tick, tick, tick, tick . . .

Katz continued to talk calmly to her about her lungs filling up with anxieties and fears and her ability to release them all simply by blowing them into the air. Her facial muscles soon relaxed as she sank into the pillows propping her head.

Though he thought some of the credit could be shared with the drugs she was on, Gavin was impressed. Katz really seemed to know what he was doing. Just ten minutes ago, Karianne had been jittery, her eyes following every movement. Now, with the exception of an occasional blink, she was motionless.

"Now I will ask you a few questions. All of my questions will be simple, and you will be able to answer them easily. All of your answers will be correct and you will not worry about making any mistakes. Do you understand?" Katz said in his low, mellow voice.

Karianne said nothing, staring at the metronome like she was stoned.

"Karianne?"

Nothing.

Great, Gavin thought, reminded of all the times his computer froze or his cell phone lost the signal. Now we have two co-matose witnesses.

"You are hearing my voice and answering in your mind, but you will also answer with your voice. If you understand, say yes."

"Yes," she said after a brief pause, moving only her mouth, the golden metronome reflecting in her blue eyes.

Katz nodded in relief. "What is your name?"

"Karianne."

"And your last name?"

"Stordal."

"Very good. And where were you born?"

"Fagernes, Norway."

"Where do you live now, Karianne?"

"Long Beach."

"You're doing excellently. All your answers are correct and they will always be correct. Now, raise your left arm over your head and do not put it down until I tell you. Your arm is as light as a feather. You will not get tired of holding it up."

Karianne raised her left arm over her head like a child asking to be excused. Gavin frowned, wondering what the purpose of this exercise was. In his peripheral vision he noticed the door open and close. It was Amy. She came quietly in and sat on the unoccupied bed. Katz shot Gavin a look and he motioned for the doctor to refocus on his patient. Amy smiled at Gavin and discretely gave him a thumbs-up. She apparently had information.

Katz studied his subject. Gavin wondered just what it was he was looking for.

"I want you to keep beat with the timer with your right index finger. Every beat represents a moment in time. But time is no longer marching on. It's ticking backward; with each beat time is regressing. You are going with it. Your mind will be alert and you will be able to report what you see. Go back. Back to the last flight you were on."

Karianne remained transfixed on the metronome. Her eyelids began blinking, slowly at first, then faster, until they were fluttering.

Katz nodded silently in approval. "Where are you?"

"In first class," she said, her voice lower and slower than usual, her arm still in the air.

"What are you doing?"

"I'm talking to Norman Sorenson."

"Do you know him?"

"Yes. He's the kicker for the Giants football team. He's cute. I'm thanking him for the football ticket he gave me. I'll see him after the game," she said, smiling. Suddenly her expression changed. "Uh-oh."

"What's wrong?"

"Another bump. A big one. Clear-air turbulence. The seat belt light just went on. The captain announced — Oohhh! That hurt."

"What happened."

"The plane — Oohhh! I wish it would stop. I'm afraid."

Katz frowned. "Are the other flight attendants afraid?"

"No."

"But you're afraid?"

"Yes."

"Have you always been afraid of flying?"

"Not afraid of flying. Afraid of crashing."

"You think the plane will crash?"

"No. Car crash. Like last time."

Katz frowned, but before he could say anything else Gavin motioned him over.

"She had another crash about five years ago in Norway," Gavin whispered in Katz's ear. "It was very similar and we have reason to believe it may have been caused by the same driver, but I didn't know she'd had a rough flight then, too."

Katz nodded, massaging his chin, then returned to the foot of the bed. "Karianne, you've left the plane and now you're in the Seahorse Tavern. Are you there?"

"Yes."

"Is anyone with you?"

"No," she said. "Just me."

"What are you doing?"

Karianne didn't answer. Her hand was still in the air and her eyes were still fluttering, but she remained silent.

"Why don't you answer?" Katz finally asked. "Are you afraid?"

Karianne shook her head.

"Are you doing something wrong?"

A pause, then a nod.

"You're ashamed because you're drinking?"

"Yes."

"How much have you had to drink?"

"Too much. The bartender won't let me have any more. I gave him my football ticket, but he didn't take it."

"Then you left?"

"No. A man told him to give me more."

Gavin reflexively sat up, then looked at Katz, repeatedly pointing his finger toward Karianne as if to say, *That's him!* Katz nodded and motioned for Gavin to settle down. "What did he look like?"

"Big. Strong."

"Were you afraid?"

"No. We drank. I wanted to be with him. Go with him," she said. Suddenly her hand began to lower, then raise again.

Katz frowned. "What's happening?"

"I feel strange."

"Why?"

"I'm leaving, but I'm staying."

Gavin shook his head and waved to Katz. "What's his name?" he mouthed.

Katz nodded and looked back at Karianne. "Did he tell you his name?"

She frowned, then smiled, then frowned again. Her head was rocking slowly, as if her neck was stiff. Then her eyes stopped fluttering and instead blinked slowly. The smile came back. "Of course," she said finally, curiously smug.

Katz looked at Gavin, then back at Kari-anne. "What did he tell you his name was?"

Again she paused with an arrogant smirk. "Who wants to know?"

"I do!" Gavin blurted angrily. Katz immediately drilled him with a hot glare. He could feel warm blood flushing out his neck. Who did she think she was and why was she suddenly asking the questions?

Katz exhaled deeply. "You are feeling very relaxed. You do not need to ask questions. All your answers will be correct. Do you understand?"

"Yes," she said, with a hint of mocking that left Katz frowning.

"What was the name of the big man at the Seahorse Tavern?"

"Krogan," she said matter-of-factly, her voice more in control.

Gavin wrote the name down and saw Amy do the same. Strange name, he thought. Chris whispered something to Amy and she immediately got up with the paper she had just written on and left the room. Chris then brought his right hand to his ear to indicate to Gavin she had gone to give the door guard the name to call in. Amy reappeared through the door. She hopped back on the bed and whispered back to Chris.

"That's all? Just Krogan?" Katz asked.

She laughed. "Krogan is enough."

Katz looked at Gavin and shrugged his shoulders, then looked back at Karianne. "Then what happened?"

She laughed again, loudly. *"Shadahd,"* she said with feeling, as if the word tasted good to her.

"What is *shadahd?"* Katz said.

"Shadahd is *shadahd,"* she said with authority.

Amy's eyes were wide, obviously disturbed by what she was hearing.

"You were involved in an accident, Karianne. Do you remember?"

"Yes."

"Was Krogan driving?"

"Yes."

"Where did he go after the crash?"

"Gone. Later."

"When is later?"

"Shadahd," she said again with obvious satisfaction.

Gavin wrote something quickly and handed Katz a note. The doctor read the note, nodded, then focused his attention back on Karianne.

"Were you ever involved in a crash with Krogan before?" he asked, bracing both hands on the bed.

"Yes," she said.

Katz looked at Gavin and smiled.

"I want you to go back to that first crash with Krogan," Katz said.

"The first crash . . . with Krogan," she repeated slowly.

"Yes," Katz said.

Karianne gave what appeared to be a sigh of satisfaction, stretching her neck back comfortably.

"Are you there?" Katz asked.

"Ken," she said.

"Ken? Who's Ken?" Katz asked.

"Ken. Rishon maaratsah, Krogan."

Katz stood upright. He appeared astonished.

Amy wrote the words down in her book.

Katz seemed like he was going to ask another question, but stopped, apparently thinking better of it. He went over to Gavin and leaned toward his ear. "She answered me in Hebrew. *Ken* means "yes" in Hebrew."

"Hebrew? Are you sure?"

"Absolutely. My parents were very religious. I was taught it as a child and have heard it spoken my whole life. I'm not familiar with the specific dialect she spoke, but it was definitely Hebrew."

"Why is she speaking in Hebrew?"

"I don't know. Maybe she's dreaming."

"In Hebrew?"

Katz shrugged.

Gavin rolled his eyes. "We don't have time for dreams, Doc. Can you get her back on track?"

"I'll try, but it's possible all we're asking is too much for just one interview. The brain, like anything else, needs training in order to perform well. We could push, but if we want accurate data, a little rest between sessions might be necessary."

More sessions? Gavin thought.

Katz paced slightly, lifting an eyebrow in Karianne's direction several times. She still had her hand in the air, presumably indicating she was still under the hypnosis. She wore a curious, almost mischievous, grin.

Katz leaned back over the bed. "Are you still at the first crash?"

"Ken."

"Where did Krogan go?"

"Acharon. *Shadahd.*"

Katz frowned, then looked at Gavin and shrugged again, while Amy took more notes.

Gavin dragged the side of his index finger across his throat. Katz nodded in agreement.

"I want you to come back to this time,

Karianne. Back to the hospital."

The smile that lingered on her face faded and her eyes began to flutter again.

"When I clap my hands three times you will awake rested, unafraid, and able to remember everything you have seen and said. Do you understand?"

"Yes."

Katz clapped three times and Karianne opened her eyes.

"How do you feel?" Katz asked.

"Confused. Like I just had the strangest dream of my life. Only I'm not sure it was a dream," she said.

Katz smiled at her. "You did fine," he said.

"I did fine? I don't feel like I did anything. I felt like a spectator, at least for most of it. I heard you ask questions I didn't know the answers to, and then I heard myself answer them."

"At what point was that?" Katz asked.

"When you asked me the killer's name. I didn't know it, but then I did. It became like a strange dream. I was seeing faces and places I've never seen before," she said, her eyes welling up with tears.

"Now, now. What you experienced was perfectly normal," Katz said, reassuringly. "You simply entered your subconscious.

That's why it seemed dreamlike. In fact, it's quite possible some of what you experienced was a dream state. You were in and out of rapid eye movement."

"But it all seemed so real," she said.

"Well, hopefully some of it was," Chris interjected. "You gave us a name, and that's primarily what we're after."

Katz nodded in agreement. "Yes. But it's possible there is much more than simply a name within our grasp. You revealed a previous encounter with this man and probably know much more about him than you think." He motioned for the envelope on Chris's lap.

"Do you remember now the face of the man you called Krogan?"

"I think so," she said.

Katz pulled the sketch from the envelope and dangled it before her. "Is this him?"

Karianne gasped reflexively. "That's him," she said, shaking her finger at the picture. "That's the man I saw in my dream. I mean my mind. I mean . . . oh, I don't know what I mean."

So much for the suggestion Katz had given her that she wouldn't be troubled, Gavin thought.

"Why did she answer some of the questions in another language?" Amy asked.

Katz smiled knowingly. "The mind is a fascinating thing. She probably entered a semi-dream state and allowed my questions to merge with her knowledge of Hebrew."

"Hebrew? I don't have a knowledge of Hebrew," Karianne said.

Katz frowned. "But you must. Maybe not a direct knowledge, but some connection must exist. Maybe through the airlines or a childhood friend long forgotten."

Karianne shook her head. "None. I speak Norwegian, English, a little German, but definitely not Hebrew."

"How about ancient Hebrew?" Amy said.

"Ancient Hebrew?" Katz said as all heads turned toward Amy.

"Yes. I'm sorry I was late, but today's research took a little digging. As it turns out, *shadahd* is a verb — an extinct form of another ancient word that means . . . ," she held up her notebook, "to ruin, destroy, deal violently with, devastate, despoil, wreck, waste." She put down the notebook and scanned the silent room.

Gavin remembered Karianne grinning eerily after speaking the ancient word. Were she and this Krogan character part of some secret satanist cult that got off on senseless destruction? Was that why she was so conveniently forgetful while conscious, afraid her own life would be in peril if she exposed the members? But why hadn't she recognized the guy when she first saw him at the bar? Was the cult large enough and secret enough that its own members didn't know each other without this ancient password? If so, why had she not recognized the password until she'd had more to drink?

"What do you mean by extinct?" Katz asked. "Most of ancient Hebrew is only a read language, studied by theologians and historians, unused in normal conversation."

Amy nodded. "Let's put it this way. If the word were any older, no record would exist. It was already out of use before Moses, possibly Abraham. According to my research, there are some who believe the roots of Hebrew contain the planet's first language. For all I know, its origin could date back to, I don't know, the Garden of Eden, if there was such a place."

With the exception of Dr. Fagan, who was grinning sarcastically and shaking his head, all expressions were blank. Fagan, who had been so quiet he could have been mistaken for a lamp, uncrossed his legs and leaned forward. "You know, it wasn't bad enough you had to jeopardize the woman's physical recuperation. Now you set her brain on end with crazy conjecture so obviously irrelevant to your case that all it can do is heap fear onto an already steep pile of confusion."

Even knowing Fagan might be correct, Gavin still had to suppress a retort. Obtaining evidence and connecting data was not an exact science; the road to truth was rarely the straight and narrow in the homicide department. Still, Gavin had to admit they were about as far out on a limb as he had ever been. He knew Amy meant well, but did she have to mention the Garden of Eden? She might as well have mentioned Atlantis or Asgard as far as Fagan or Katz were concerned — to those two, any of the above was indicative of a myth.

Amy caught Gavin's attention and motioned she was going to visit her sister. Gavin nodded.

"I can appreciate your concern, Doctor," Katz was saying, "but I believe we are on the brink of something substantial. What we need is another session after Karianne has some rest. I would suggest tomorrow at the latest, if that's all right with you, Karianne."

"The sooner the better, as far as I'm concerned," she said, appearing ready for the session to take place immediately. "How can I rest knowing I'm connected to that . . . beast?" She hitched her chin toward the police sketch of Krogan.

Gavin, too, was anxious to press on. He looked at Katz. The man was deep in thought. The fact the man had shown more than a little surprise several times during the session had Gavin concerned they were stretching past the psychologist's boundaries of experience. He hoped he had the right man for the job.

— 20 —

Gavin called headquarters only to find they had no record anywhere of anyone named Krogan, either as a first name or a last. He decided to check on Amy and Amber. When he walked into the room, Amy was on her knees crying at the side of her sister's bed, her forehead against the mattress as she held her sister's limp hand. She had apparently not heard Gavin enter. He started to leave her to her grief, but hesitated. Watching her made him want to take the sketch he held and blow it to pieces at the shooting range, shot after careful shot. But, no, he needed it — he planned to advertise Krogan's face throughout the metro area like a politician on Election Day. Someone out there had to be able to connect the face with the name. And Gavin knew Gasman would jump at the opportunity to print that name . . . right over the sketch.

"Amber, Amber," Amy was crying over

and over. She looked into her sister's face — peaceful, beautiful, asleep. "You need to wake up. I need you to come back."

Again Gavin thought of leaving. He'd never seen Amy so weak and vulnerable. Maybe she needed him. Maybe she wouldn't want him there. After a moment's struggle, he walked over and gently placed his hand on her shoulder. She startled, but when their eyes met she relaxed and put her hand over his. Gavin couldn't remember the last time someone had been so comforted by his presence. He felt privileged . . . wanted.

"I love her, Gavin. She's part of me."

"I know," he said quietly, softly squeezing her shoulder.

"Have you heard from Reverend Buchanan yet?"

"As a matter of fact, I haven't. I need to check the machine. Either way, I'll call again," he said.

Amy leaned over and kissed her sister on her cheek, then spoke a few words in Japanese to her. After giving Amber a final kiss she stood up and turned to Gavin, her wet, green eyes blazing. "I want Krogan. I want that animal."

"We'll have him soon," he said. "But the line forms behind me."

The receptionist at *The Daily Post* put down the phone and looked up with a smile at Gavin, then at Amy, who was standing next to him. She appeared to be in her early twenties, with short, straight hair that showed her black roots. Her perfume could overpower Lysol.

"Can I help you?" she said, her overly made-up eyes remaining on Amy in an obvious compliment to her looks.

"Mel Gasman, please," Gavin said.

"Mr. Gasman is in an important meeting and won't be available for another half hour. If you like, you can wait over there." She extended her gaze to a black leather couch behind a table of loosely strewn magazines.

Gavin looked at his watch and shook his head. It was already four-thirty. "I think Mr. Gasman would like to know Detective Pierce is here now, but by five I'll be at the *Times* and he'll have lost his exclusive. And I can assure you, he wouldn't be very happy to hear that."

The receptionist paused, then held up a finger. "Let me see how the meeting's going," she said and disappeared through a heavy oak-veneer door that closed with a loud click.

"If I know Gasman, he'll be right out. Let me do the talking. He has a nose like a bloodhound when it comes to a story, and there's a lot here we don't want him to know, at least not yet," Gavin said.

"No sweat," Amy replied. "Like I've told you all along, you won't even know I'm here." Gavin rolled his eyes.

Moments later the door opened again. Gasman looked first to the couch, then quickly to the receptionist counter where Gavin and Amy were still standing.

"Whoa!" he said with a broad smile. "To what do I owe this pleasure?"

"A coin flip," Gavin said. "Best two out of three."

"And who won the first toss?"

"You did."

Gasman laughed nervously. "You're such a kidder. And who is your new partner? Quite an improvement over the old model," he said, surveying Amy.

"None of your business," Gavin replied, then pulled out the sketch. Gasman's gaze locked on the envelope like a dog anticipating a steak. He reached for it, but Gavin pulled it away. "Don't smudge. Only touch the edges."

Gasman nodded eagerly, slowly taking it with a tweezerlike hold on the top edge.

His eyes widened. "Oh . . ."

"I should have figured you'd have strange worship habits," Gavin deadpanned.

Gasman ignored the joke, transfixed on the sketch. "Is this for real?"

"Would I make it up?"

"You couldn't. If I told the art department to draw me the scariest dude they could, it would look like Little Miss Muffet compared to this. This is gold, baby. If this mug goes on the front page we'll sell out."

"Your priorities are so predictable."

"Yeah, well, that's why they pay me the big bucks. Let me make a copy of this and then we'll sit and talk," Gasman said, leading them through the doorway he'd entered by. They followed him down a corridor lined with framed photos of faces and awards, some old, some new. The hallway emptied into a large, florescent-lighted room buzzing with activity. Support columns rose over dozens of cubicle offices. The partitioned walls rose only about waist high, affording a good view, and most of the occupants' necks craned toward Amy as they walked by.

Gasman's office, though nothing to brag about, was a step above the others they had passed. At least he had a door, and his partitioned walls were permanent, with glass on top to help keep the sound down. He pulled a seat away from the wall for Amy and pointed Gavin to its match, then walked around his desk and sat down, quickly locating a yellow pad. He looked at them and smiled.

"Now then. Does it have a name?"

Gavin cleared his throat, looked at Amy, then back to Gasman. "Uh, we have a name we'd like to try."

"Try?" Gasman said, tilting his head slightly.

"We think it might be an alias or nick-name."

"Well, what is it?"

"Krogan."

"Krogan? That's it? No first name?"

"That's it."

"Fantastic. He kind of looks like a Krogan." Gasman eyed the sketch on his desk. "Krogan the Terrible. Krogan the Hun. Hulk Krogan. Man, oh, man. That name, this face . . . Oh, baby! There is a God."

Gavin rolled his eyes. "Earth to Gasman. I'd like you to subtly present the name as a possible alias, not a billboard for a monster movie. If the name is wrong, it might con-fuse someone who really does know whatever his correct name is."

"Sure, sure. No problem. Whatever you say. What makes you think Krogan might be his name?"

"I'd rather not reveal that information at this time," Gavin said.

"Come on, Pierce. You promised me details. Are you gonna give me the story or not?" Gasman whined. "You know me; I'll work with ya. What happened? Did your witness get her memory back? Did she finally confess? Was she calling his name in her sleep? At least tell me what you're afraid of."

"Forget it, Gasman. Take it or leave it."

Gavin spent the next half hour sharing information and updating Gasman on the condition of Chris and Karianne. Gasman continued to beg for more hard details, but Gavin refused. There were simply too many loose ends. And the last thing he wanted was to have to explain to the lieutenant why Karianne Stordal, a Norwegian flight attendant, had been speaking ancient Hebrew, a language she didn't know, while being interviewed under hypnosis.

"I don't want any surprises," Gavin said, echoing the lieutenant's warning as he and Amy left Gasman at his desk staring at the sketch.

"Hey, Pierce, you won't mind if I make copies of this for holiday presents?" His laughter followed them down the hall.

A moment later Gavin and Amy were descending the broad, weathered granite steps of *The Daily Post* building.

"So now what?" Amy asked.

"What do you say we get something to eat and then go boot up your machine and see what we can find on the name Krogan."

"Do you think you can stand my cooking two nights in a row?" Amy asked.

Gavin sunk into overstuffed cushions, sipping green tea at Amy's small Manorhaven home while she busied herself in the kitchen. He had asked if he could help, or at least watch, but was chased out with a wooden spoon. Fine. He would use this time to rest; with the restless sleep he'd been having lately and the pounding of the pavement all day, he wouldn't mind a small nap and the promise of awakening to what looked to be a delicious dinner.

"Hey," Amy called from the kitchen. "While you're doing nothing, why don't you call your answering machine and see if you got a return call from that Reverend Buchanan."

"Funny, I was just thinking of that." With a sigh, he reached for the phone and after a short series of codes and beeps found his machine empty.

"Zippo," he said.

"Well, you still have the paper I gave you with his phone number, don't you?"

Gavin smiled to himself. He liked her feistiness. "I don't need your paper. I remember the number." Surreptitiously he pulled Amy's paper out of his wallet and dialed up Samantha's Farm again.

"Hello?" answered a deep, raspy voice.

"Is . . . is this Samantha's Farm?" Gavin said.

"Yes, sir. How can I help you?"

"Is this Reverend Buchanan?" Gavin said.

There was a pause. "And who might you be?"

"Detective Gavin Pierce. I called you last night but got your machine."

"Ah, yes. I remember. I was wondering what somebody with your area code wanted with us. I don't believe you mentioned you were a detective."

By that, Gavin figured the man had not intended to return the call he'd made last night. "I was hoping I might be able to ask you a few questions."

"About?"

"I'm looking for information on a case."

A moment of silence. "Well, I'm just an old dairy farmer, Detective. I don't know how I could help."

Gavin exhaled. "Well, to get right to the point, I think I'm after the same man that killed your family in Norway five years ago. This guy has the exact —"

"I'm sorry, Detective. I don't know how you found me, but this is not a subject I can talk about, except to tell you I can't help you."

"Sir, whatever your fears are, I can assure you complete protection. Besides, you are one of many whom this man has affected, myself included. He won't even remember you. Five years is a long time."

"Detective, you are correct when you say I am one of many. More correct than you know. But you are very wrong about five years being a long time. Time means nothing to the one you're after . . . I've already said too much. I truly feel for whatever harm you've been caused and I'll keep you in prayer. Again, I'm very sorry. Goodbye."

"Wait! *Please.* There'll be a sketch of a suspect in tomorrow's *Post.* Won't you at least confirm if it's the same man who assailed you?"

"Sorry."

"But why? What harm —"

"I won't recognize the face."

Gavin paused. "How do you know that if you don't look?"

"I know."

"How?"

"Anything I have to tell you would be of no use to you, so please, let me go."

"I don't understand."

"I know. Good-bye, Detective."

"But —"

Click.

"Hello? Hello?" Gavin said through gritted teeth. He hung up, feeling like he now knew less than before he'd called. What had the reverend meant by "More correct than you know"? He knows of others? And what did he mean about time meaning nothing to Krogan? Gavin cursed. He hadn't even been able to ask if the man knew the name Krogan.

Gavin picked up the phone again and hit the redial button. The machine picked up. He disconnected halfway through the little girl's message. He would have thrown the phone if it were his own. He was going to talk again to the Reverend Jesse J. Buchanan. But next time he would not get hung up on.

"Did you reach him?" Amy asked from the kitchen.

"I spoke to him," Gavin said. "But I didn't reach him. Not yet."

— 21 —

Krogan was awakened by the sound of the forklift working at the lumberyard next to his shack of a house. Judging from the angle of the sunlight coming around the yellowed window shades, it was morning. He didn't remember going to sleep. He rarely did. His mouth was terribly dry; his tongue felt swollen and stuck in place.

Before rolling out from under the single thin blanket he paused, checking for any new pains he should be aware of. There were none. In fact, the soreness he'd had for the last couple of days was almost gone. No new aches meant nothing interesting in the newspaper.

He groaned as he sat up on the blood-stained mattress. As thirsty as he was, he didn't want water. Only more liquor would be able to cut through the tacky dryness he felt. He reached for an empty vodka bottle on the floor, the stretch aggravating his bruised ribcage, and held it upside down over his open mouth, hoping for a few stray drops. Nothing. Maybe the refrigerator. He dropped the bottle behind him and heard it roll as he walked stiffly to the kitchen, his bare feet sporadically sticking to months, maybe years, of spilt liquor that added an additional glaze to an already thickly painted pine floor. He glanced lazily at the table as he passed it; a half-full quart of malt beer with a cigarette butt floating in it failed to lure him.

The unleveled refrigerator was old and made a loud hum he no longer heard. He yanked open its door and squinted into the cold shadows. The unlatched interior freezer door above slowly opened by itself as it always did, revealing frozen baitfish, their eyes bulging redly from exploded blood vessels. Below them in the fridge sat a bottle of ketchup without the cap, a few open Chinese take-out containers, a half-eaten apple pie broken from random fingerings, and some Tabasco sauce, also without a cap. Nothing to drink. He cursed and threw the door closed, then turned to the beer on the table. Without pausing, he grabbed its neck and guzzled it down, then spit the butt in the direction of a dented tin garbage can.

He wondered what day it was. Through the window he could see the forklift busy at work. It wasn't Sunday, then. When had he last checked the lobster traps? Ah . . . today's date would be on the newspaper. He opened the front door and stepped onto the small porch. The warm sunlight felt good on his bare mass, but annoyed his unadjusted pupils. With narrowed eyes he searched for the paper and found it laying on the cracked and buckled concrete path that divided the lawn of uncut grass and weeds. With much less difficulty than yesterday, he walked down the porch steps and retrieved the paper. It was bound by a single green rubber band, which he immediately broke off. The paper unfolded in his hands: Friday, August 29.

Krogan turned the paper over and was instantly startled out of his morning daze. The likeness he saw was astonishing for a sketch, so much so that he thought he could have been looking at a photo. He wanted to find a mirror and compare. He was so completely fascinated with the drawing that he didn't at first notice the headline. When he did, he was stunned a second time. Above his face, which took up three quarters of the front page, was his name in giant, bold print: "GHOST

DRIVER OR KROGAN?"

He quickly crushed the paper closed. He felt exposed and reflexively crouched, snapping his gaze back and forth as if he'd been physically spotted. To his right, a couple hundred feet down the street, a large, yellow utility truck was parked. The boom was stretched up over thirty feet to an electric transformer and a man with a yellow hard-hat was in the bucket. To his left, the forklift was still at work behind a tall, rusted chain-link fence. Nobody seemed to have noticed him.

With the paper tightly clenched in his right fist he went back into the house and closed the door. In the bathroom he re-opened the paper and held it up next to the cracked medicine-cabinet mirror. He stared at himself, then at the sketch, then at himself again, and finally decided they hadn't done as good a job as he'd first thought. He laughed and spit at the mirror for being so stupidly concerned. He was the one who was in control, not them. He was the hunter, the trapper, the executioner. And if they caught him — which they would not, could not — he would still be in control.

He left the bathroom and plopped into an old, overstuffed chair with pea-sized burn holes all over the arm rests. Leaning his head back and looking at the cracked plaster ceiling, he tried to remember the past few days. He could imagine someone seeing him good enough to give a description, but how had they gotten his name?

He opened the paper to the story on page three and began to read:

KROGAN?

The Ghost Driver now has a face and possibly even a name. Police have revealed an artist's rendering of the serial killer who uses motor vehicles as his choice of murder weapons and who turns accomplices into victims. Among others, the Ghost Driver was responsible for the recent crash at the Hempstead Harbor Marina that took the lives of Lori Hayslip and Michael Clayborne and left Mr. Clayborne's wife, Amber, in Glen Cove Hospital, where she remains in a coma.

Police have also uncovered a possible alias or nickname for the Ghost Driver: Krogan. Details have not yet been released on how the police obtained this possible alias. Detective Gavin Pierce, who heads up the task force assigned to this case, has detailed only that someone has come forward with the name.

Anyone with information regarding the Ghost Driver should contact either *The Daily Post* or Detective Gavin Pierce at police headquarters in Mineola at 212-555-1455. The killer should be regarded as extremely dangerous.

Krogan threw his head back and laughed loudly. "You don't have a clue, do ya, Cop?" he said. He noted the byline for the story — a Mel Gasman. "And Newsboy called me by name. He wants to be contacted. He thinks being contacted is a *good* thing."

He continued to laugh as he threw the newspaper down on an avalanching pile of old papers at the side of the chair. Heading to the bedroom, he found a wrinkled gray T-shirt and pair of jeans crumpled over a pair of worn work boots at the foot of the bed. The wrinkles in the shirt vanished as he pulled it down over his massive chest and shoulders. He took a moment to stare at himself in an old, cracked mirror leaning against the wall, flexing his muscles hard and long until they started to cramp. The tension and pain felt good as the veins running down the sides of his neck swelled. He looked into his eyes, two silver streaks cutting diagonally across the bridge of his nose like frozen lightning. The eyes of a warrior, he thought. A hunter.

He pulled the boots on over his bare feet and thought again of how the newsboy had called him by name — a name the newsboy was unworthy to speak, much less write publicly for the world to see. He had to be taught a lesson. A lesson the world at large would heed and remember.

He closed his eyes and envisioned himself holding a long pole in the air with the newsboy impaled on it, clearly beaten, clearly punished. He knew the hunt would be pleasurable. He would not simply drive into this one. That was too simple. He would play with this newsboy as a cat plays with its prey. He would enjoy his supremacy — his utter dominance. He didn't know how, but he knew the hunt would be special. And, most important, fun.

He stretched across the bed and reached for the windowshade bottom, then tugged and released. The weak spring gave up when the shade reached the halfway point. Between the shade and dirty windowpane a large spider had spun an impressive web. The spider was busy wrapping up a recent catch. Krogan watched approvingly.

Peering through the clouded glass and the bare branches of a dead tree outside, he could see the electric company bucket truck was still there with its boom stretched out to the pole. He stared at the man and the truck for several minutes and then refocused on the spider, which had clearly conquered the weaker bug. Foolish prey deserve to die; that's what they're there for, Krogan thought. To die. He rolled onto his back and laughed softly before getting up and going to the kitchen. The day would belong to him.

On a cast-iron radiator under the kitchen window he found a Yellow Pages phone book and flicked the pages until he reached the listings for *Aircraft Charter, Rental and Leasing Service.* Sweeping his arm across the table and knocking a few beer cans onto the floor, he pulled the phone to the table's edge and dialed.

"Executive Airways. This is Cheryl. Can I help you?"

"How much advance notice do you need for a flight to Albany in a Learjet?"

"We could have you in the air in an hour, sir."

"Perfect," he said deeply, then looked at the clock. It was nine o'clock. "I'd like to reserve a flight leaving Republic Airport at exactly twelve-thirty."

"And your name, sir?"

"Mel Gasman. I'll call back with my credit card number in about an hour."

"Very good, Mr. Gasman. And thank you for choosing Executive."

With a laugh, Krogan hung up the phone. "Oh, but it is *I* who should be thanking *you*."

He went back into the bedroom and reached under the bed, slowly withdrawing a large black case. Inside the case was his father's ninety-pound-draw hunting bow — a Browning. Mounted in foam rubber on the case's lid were a dozen arrows, three of them already fixed with broadhead hunting tips. He freed one of the arrows and smiled as he saw sunlight reflect off the silvery triple-razor head. He tapped the point with his index finger; a small, round drop of blood appeared.

His breathing quickened with excitement as he pulled his bed out of the way of the window. The old sash weights could be heard as the window opened. The spider dashed away as its web tore in half. The screen was already gashed open with a hole large enough that he didn't have to bother removing it.

Looking out, he cursed. There was a problem. The arc he would need to hit his target was blocked by a dead tree branch. He had to change his vantage point. Quickly snatching his three razor-sharp arrows, he exited through the back door and went left through an overgrown empty lot marked with a No Dumping sign. Judging by the litter, the sign had not been much of a deterrent.

There was no need to hurry; his prey had less of a chance than the spider's bug.

Krogan passed unnoticed behind his target, taking note of a Thermos and clipboard on the seat of the open cab. Perversely, he continued further so his shot would not be too easy — he wanted to make the game interesting. He finally came to an abandoned and stripped car at the curb and set his arrows on its rusted trunk.

He grasped the bow tightly in his powerful left hand. It felt good — even better than it had when he used to target shoot with his father, before he was half the warrior he was now. He picked up an arrow and made sure the three feathers aligned perfectly with the three glistening blades as he had been taught. After a slight adjustment, he placed the arrow on its rest, then drew back on the high-tension string with three fingers of his right hand. His back and shoulder muscles rippled as he dropped to one knee and brought the string to his cheek. He estimated his target at about seventy yards. A long shot, but his bow had enough power to drop a Kodiak bear at that range, if the shot was accurate.

He calmed his breathing as the man working from the bucket fell into his sights. The man appeared to be wrapping up his work. Perfect. If his job was completed they would likely assume he had left to go to his next assignment. Whatever. He exhaled slowly through his mouth, breathed in and held . . . then released, making sure the arrow was safely on its way before moving the bow.

Sssssssssss. The arrow silently whizzed by a couple of inches behind the back of the man's neck and disappeared over distant treetops. Krogan's eyebrows raised; he was surprised he'd missed. He wondered briefly where the errant arrow would land. Hopefully *in* someone, he thought as he nestled out of view.

The man in the bucket had immediately turned around, presumably hearing or feeling the wind as the arrow passed by. He continued to scan the surrounding area for another twenty seconds or so, then went back to putting his tools away.

Krogan's laugh was low and raspy as he set the next arrow. This was fun. The fool didn't have a clue he'd just been granted another minute of life. Back in position, with the bow drawn in full, Krogan adjusted slightly to the left.

Sssssssssppp. Krogan heard the thunk as the arrow found its mark in the man's left shoulder. The man screamed in terror, looking down at the arrow sticking out the front of his light-blue shirt, which was rapidly darkening. He dropped into the bucket, presumably to hide.

"Just when you figure it's a beautiful morning," Krogan laughed as he loaded his last arrow.

With only the man's hand visible on the controls, the boom began to lower. When the bucket touched the truck, the man's anguished face appeared over the top. Krogan drew back again. He knew the man would have to try to get out of the bucket and into the truck. The inexperienced fool was terrified enough to chance that it had all been a terrible mistake. The blood alone would convince him he needed to get to the hospital . . . fast.

As predicted, the man rose, his right hand clutching his shoulder, his fingers split around the protruding arrow. He clumsily tried to lift one of his legs over the rim of the bucket.

Sssssssssppp.

This time the man was knocked to the back of the bucket, the arrow having gone cleanly through the bottom of his neck, held only by the feathers from going completely through. The man then fell forward, back to the bottom of the bucket, where he would surely stay.

The chance his victim was still alive and suffering was exciting to Krogan. He sought to thrill himself further, trying to sense the horror of pain and fear in the man's mind, then remembered what was to come. There was so much to do and he didn't want to be late for his appointment. He hoped the keys were in the ignition of his new vehicle — and that the coffee in the Thermos was still hot.

— 22 —

"Pierce," called a voice, just as Gavin was about to open the hospital entrance door for Amy. They both turned to see Katz walking slowly toward them alongside a short, elderly man with a thick white beard and yarmulke skullcap. The man kept one hand on Katz's left arm. He wore dark sunglasses.

"This is my Uncle Hiram," Katz said with a proud smile.

"Uncle Hiram?" Gavin said.

"Yes. He's spent most of his life studying the ancient Scriptures in their original language. I thought he might be able to help us if Karianne speaks in ancient Hebrew again. As I mentioned yesterday, ancient Hebrew is a read, not spoken, language, but Uncle Hiram reads the Scriptures aloud. Always has. He's used to hearing the language from his own mouth."

Gavin didn't know what to say. He wanted to keep the interrogation as low profile as possible, and Uncle Hiram might be all that was needed to push Fagan over the edge. Gavin didn't exactly cherish a conversation between Fagan and Lieutenant Sandel. On the other hand, the old man might be helpful. Besides, what was he to do — tell Katz to send his uncle back to wherever he'd found him, wasting more precious time and insulting the psychologist he desperately needed? Inwardly, Gavin sighed.

"Hello, sir. I'm Detective Pierce and this is Amy, my assistant," he said extending his hand.

"Oh, thank you, my son," Uncle Hiram said as he took Gavin's hand and held on to it for additional support.

Gavin fell into step with Uncle Hiram and glared at Katz.

"Maybe we should get him a wheel-chair," Amy said.

"That would be excellent," Katz replied.

The old man nodded approvingly.

Maybe we should check him in while we're at it, Gavin refrained from adding.

Tick, tick, tick, tick, tick . . .

Gavin leaned against the window wondering if he too would be hypnotized as he listened to the beat of the metronome and

Katz's mesmerizing voice. He'd had maybe four hours of sleep and was feeling it. He looked at Amy, who sat hunched and bleary-eyed at the foot of the other bed. Last night after dinner she had further impressed Gavin with her computer skills as they collaborated and brainstormed into the wee hours. In all that time she'd failed to retrieve any further useful information. According to Amy's research, Krogan didn't exist.

Chris, who sat next to Amy, appeared in better shape than she, and he was still in a wheelchair. Next to Chris and also in a wheelchair was Uncle Hiram, who for all Gavin knew was asleep behind those dark sunglasses. And watching from the back of the room was Doctor Fagan, who had simply been told Uncle Hiram was an expert linguist.

Karianne's arm was raised, indicating to Katz she was ready. Katz had been right about her being able to slip into her hypnotic state easier the second time. Earlier, Karianne had asked Katz, "What now?" He had explained that the most significant and common thread found in both the conscious world and her hypnotic state was the word *shadahd*. The bartender had heard the killer say it, and though Karianne didn't remember it consciously, she had confirmed her knowledge of it while under. Katz also seemed fascinated by the fact it was an extinct word from very ancient times, something he said his Uncle Hiram confirmed. Gavin worried that Katz's agenda went beyond the case at hand. Regardless, they had all agreed *shadahd* was a logical place to start.

"Karianne," Katz said in his soothingly deep voice, "I want you to go back in time to the Seahorse Tavern. Are you there?"

"Yes," she said slowly in a hushed voice.

"What are you drinking?"

"A Bloody Mary."

"Now you've been there long enough for the big man to come up beside you. Do you see him?"

"Yes," she said.

"He tells you his name is Krogan, correct?"

"Yes."

"He speaks a word to you. *Shadahd.* Do you understand what he means?"

"I . . . I don't understand."

Katz frowned. "Do you tell him you didn't understand?"

"Yes."

"Then what does he tell you?"

"He orders more for us to drink."

"Then does he explain?"

"He doesn't have to. After a few more drinks I know."

"You know what?"

Karianne paused. Her expression seemed to struggle a bit, then stabilize into a grin that made Gavin feel quite uncomfortable. It was the same strange smile from the day before — almost feral. Finally she said, "I knew *everything.*"

Katz looked at Gavin and then back at Karianne. "Why does Krogan say *shadahd?*"

Karianne lifted her chin upward as her expression hardened. "*Shadahd* is a battle cry," she said proudly.

"For what?"

"The war."

"What war?"

"There is only one."

Katz paused at that statement. "When did the war start?"

"Before 'when.'"

Katz frowned again, then straightened up and went to Gavin's ear. "Her answers are incredibly emphatic and real to her even if they seem abstract to us. I'm going to repeat some of yesterday's questions and see if we wind up in the same place. If we do, we'll explore. Maybe we'll find

Krogan between the lines."

Gavin nodded, although he wasn't sure what Katz was talking about and wondered if even Katz knew. He grabbed Katz by the elbow as the psychologist started to turn back. "Just do us a favor: if she starts to speak in ancient Hebrew again, make sure your uncle translates what she says into English, loud enough that we aren't all left sitting here in the dark."

"I'll try," Katz replied.

Katz repositioned Uncle Hiram closer to the bed and found his own spot at the bed's foot. Karianne still had her left arm in the air. Her countenance was proud.

"I want you to go back to when you first met Krogan. Are you there?"

"Ken."

Great, Gavin thought sarcastically. Here we go again with the ancient Hebrew lesson. Now he had to consciously remember *ken* meant "yes."

"Is Krogan with you?"

She nodded with a satisfied smile.

"Where are you?"

"Yecko."

Katz frowned. "Where is Yecko?"

"Maveth nahar al."

Uncle Hiram paused long enough for Gavin to wonder if he even remembered he was supposed to interpret, then said, "I don't understand what she means."

"Don't worry about what she means, Uncle Hiram. Just translate what she says," Katz said kindly.

Uncle Hiram, who had begun nodding while Katz was speaking to him, said, "Death river near."

"What?" Gavin said in a hushed voice.

"In Hebrew the verb comes first, then the subject then the direct object and its modifier, if there is one. If anything, English is backwards," Katz explained. " 'Death river near' would mean 'near river death.' "

"Oh, now I understand perfectly," Gavin said with quiet sarcasm. "Are you sure he's interpreting correctly?"

Uncle Hiram nodded. " 'The river death.' She said she's near the river that dies," he said softly. "Whatever that means."

" 'The river that dies'?" Katz said. "What country or nation are you in?"

"Lo coy. Arabah."

Again the old man took his time. "She said there is no nation, only desert."

At this rate, Gavin wondered if they would be done by midnight.

"You're not in a country, you're in a desert?"

"Ken," she said with a nod.

"Does everyone speak your language?"

She continued to nod affirmatively.

"Why does the river die?"

"Amets. Lo chayah."

All eyes went to Uncle Hiram, whose white eyebrows dipped below his dark glasses rims in wrinkled confusion. "I don't know," he said. "The dialect is broken. It doesn't seem to make any sense, but I think that she's saying, 'Strong. No live.' The river dies because it's too strong to live."

"Too strong to live? How? What's too strong?"

"Melach."

"Salt," Uncle Hiram said.

"Salt? It's too salty?" Katz replied.

"Ken."

Katz's eyes suddenly widened. "Does the river become very big when it dies?"

She nodded.

"Is it also called the Dead Sea or the Salt Sea?"

"Maveth nahar al."

"It is only called the river that dies?"

"Ken."

"Is Yecko also called Jericho?"

"Yecko is Yecko."

Katz's eyes widened as he slowly

nodded. "What is the date?"

"Lo machath."

Uncle Hiram shook his head. "She says there is no date."

Katz looked surprised at the answer and paused, his eyes rapidly looking around the room as if there might be a cue card somewhere to tell him what to ask next.

"Are you aware of what the date is?"

She shook her head slowly.

"Are there other people there?"

"Ken."

"Do they know you?"

She nodded and smiled.

"What do they call you?"

"Ehud."

"You're a man?" Katz said.

"Ken."

"Ehud, I want you to look at your feet. Do you see them?"

"Ken."

"What are you wearing on them?"

"Bilti."

"Nothing," Uncle Hiram said.

Gavin rolled his eyes and dragged his finger across his throat. He had no idea what this was all about, but as far as he was concerned, it wasn't getting him any closer to Krogan, or whatever his name was.

Katz waved Gavin off.

"What are you and Krogan doing?"

"Shathah yayin."

"Drinking. Drinking wine," Uncle Hiram interpreted.

"Have you had much to drink?" Katz asked.

"Lo," she said and laughed coarsely.

Uncle Hiram smiled. "She said no."

"No. Hmm. Okay, four hours have gone by. What are you doing now?"

"Halak."

"She says 'travel,' " Uncle Hiram said.

"You're traveling. Are you on a horse?"

"Lo."

"No," Uncle Hiram said, notably more attentive than before.

"No horse? Does anyone use a horse?"

"Lo."

"You are walking?"

"Ken."

Katz shook his head in apparent disbelief. "Where are you going?"

"Mattah Gaanos."

"She is going to the tribe of Gaanos, whatever that is," Uncle Hiram said.

"Why are you going to the tribe of the Gaanos?"

"Shadahd."

Katz dabbed his sweaty brow with a

handkerchief, then leaned over the bed. "How many times have you met with Krogan since then?"

"Rab."

"Many," Uncle Hiram said.

"Five, ten, a hundred, a thousand?"

"Min."

"More," Uncle Hiram said.

Katz stood upright and blinked. After spending the next few moments staring into space, he took a drink of water from a paper cup, then lifted the index finger of his right hand like a lawyer questioning a witness.

"You're moving forward in time. You are going to the moment of Ehud's death. You will not experience any fear or pain. You will only observe. Are you there?"

She nodded.

"How is Ehud dying?"

"Chanith."

"Spear," Uncle Hiram said.

"Spear?"

"Ken."

"Okay. Move a little further ahead in time. Ehud has been dead for two days. What are you doing?"

"Searching," she said, now speaking in English.

Gavin didn't understand why she was

suddenly speaking in English any more than why she'd understood Katz's English before but only replied in Hebrew. Why didn't she speak English the whole time?

"Why are you searching?"

"I'm uncomfortable. Need rest. Need comfort."

"What are you searching for?"

"A body."

"What kind of body?"

"A comfortable one."

Katz looked at Gavin and shrugged his shoulders, then indicated he would be wrapping it up shortly. Gavin hoped he would. Amy was busy writing in her notebook.

"Did you find a comfortable body?"

"Yes."

"Was it hard to find?"

"No."

"Move forward in time until you come to, uh, nineteen . . . nineteen forty-four."

Karianne's head swayed slowly from side to side, then stopped.

"Are you there?"

Karianne nodded. "Hai."

Katz paused. "Does *Hai* mean 'yes'?"

Karianne nodded again. "Hai."

"Now she's speaking Japanese," Amy blurted out.

Katz nodded and held up his hand toward Amy for silence.

"What is your name?"

"Naoyuki Kamiya."

Gavin signaled for a time-out. Katz tried to wave him off, but Gavin made the sign again and would not back off. Katz sighed. Gavin got up, squeezed the psychologist's elbow, and whispered into his ear. "Kill it now, Katz. Push the pause button or whatever you have to do to shut her off. We have to talk."

"Okay, okay. But remind me to get you some medication."

— 23 —

Krogan listened to the ringing on the other end of the line. From the phone booth at the corner gas station, he had a clear view of the pay phone at the bus stop in front of the *Post* building.

"Good morning. *Daily Post*. This is Angela. How can I help you?"

"Mel Gasman," Krogan said.

"Please hold while I transfer you."

"Mr. Gasman's office," said another female voice.

"Mel Gasman," Krogan said.

"And who should I say is calling?"

"Krogan."

There was silence on the other end. Krogan smiled as he imagined a stunned expression on the face of Gasman's secretary. He didn't hear the line being put on hold. He could still hear background noise. She was probably in eye contact with Gasman, pointing to the receiver and mouthing his name.

"Gasman here. Who is this?"

"Like I told the wench, Newsboy. My name is Krogan and I have information as to my whereabouts," he said, enjoying every second. He didn't usually get the chance to speak to his targets beforehand.

"How do I know this is really you and not a prank caller?"

"Who else would know the informer you won't identify was a blonde babe I picked up in the Seahorse Tavern?"

A pause. "Why are you calling?"

"Not so fast. I don't want to talk on this phone line. I'm shy. Outside your building there's a pay phone at the bus stop. Go there now and wait for my call. If you're not there in one minute, I'm gone," Krogan said, then hung up.

Soon after he was laughing as he watched a short man in brown pants and a white shirt come running from the building to the pay phone. Almost immediately, Krogan dialed it up.

"Hello," Gasman said, breathing heavily.

"Not bad. Forty-five seconds," Krogan said, looking at his new watch, which he'd taken off the left wrist of the dead man in the bucket.

"What's going on?"

"I read your paper today. I don't think you understand where I'm really comin' from. I'd like people to understand me better. I want us to talk. And the picture was lousy. I've got better ones."

"You want to give us a better picture?" Gasman asked incredulously.

"Yeah. Why? You don't want it?"

"No, no! I mean, yeah, of course. It's just unusual that —"

"I'm not usual. Do you want to meet with me or not?"

"Meet with you? In person?"

"Yeah. What'd ya think I meant? On the phone?"

"Well, I —"

"I thought maybe you were someone I could talk to, but if you don't want to . . ."

"No. That's fine. Lots of people talk to me. I am . . . I'm very understanding."

"I thought so. We'll meet at one-thirty, in a public place so you won't need to be concerned about me kidnapping you. I'm really not interested in that sort of thing, but you'll know much better after we . . . meet," Krogan said. He watched his victim-to-be at the pay phone. At that moment he imagined driving the truck full speed, pedal to the floor, right through the bus stop. It would not only take care of

Gasman, but also the people waiting for the bus. But, no, he was enjoying this little game too much and the final result would be far more exciting than a quick fix now.

"Where do I go?" Gasman asked.

"Albany," Krogan said, anticipating his prey's surprise at the location.

"Albany?" Gasman gasped. "You're in Albany?"

"Would I ask you to meet me in Albany if I wasn't there?"

"No, but to meet you by one-thirty I'll —"

"You'll have to take the jet I've reserved for you at Republic Airport."

"How did — ?"

"Shut up and listen. If you don't follow my directions perfectly there's no meeting. Call Executive Airways to confirm your flight and pay them with your credit card. Your flight leaves at exactly twelve-thirty. Come alone. Wear a bright red shirt or jacket so I know who you are from a distance. I'll contact you after you land in Albany if I'm convinced you're alone."

Krogan hung up and watched. Gasman appeared to be speaking. After a moment he too hung up and darted back toward the building, almost knocking over someone waiting for the bus.

Krogan laughed loudly, then started up the bucket truck and headed to Republic Airport for his appointment. He had gotten no more than a few blocks when the dispatch radio came on, apparently looking for the guy in the bucket. "McQuade? Where are you?"

Krogan unclipped the handset on the dashboard, found the side button, and pressed it. "He quit."

There was silence for a moment, then the radio came on again. "Who is this?"

Krogan smiled. "I'm the guy who convinced your boy to quit. And by the way, this truck's a piece of garbage."

"Whoever this is, that truck is private property. Is Jim McQuade there?"

"He's takin' a nap," Krogan yelled, then ripped the radio off the dashboard and threw it out the window, along with the empty Thermos and clipboard. McQuade wouldn't be needing them anymore.

— 24 —

Gavin stood with Katz in the hospital hallway by a window overlooking the parking lot. The nearest ear belonged to the police guard outside Karianne's room, a hundred feet away.

"What's going on, Doc? We're wasting our time. I know you went through the trouble of bringing Uncle Hiram here, but how's this helping us get the killer? All this business about raiding ancient tribes and living who knows where, who knows when, is a fantasy I can't appreciate right now. Can't you jog her memory into today's reality without her slipping into this wild dream she keeps getting stuck in?"

Katz laughed condescendingly. "I have to admit, this is not my specialty, but anyone who studies past lives would trade all they have for an hour with her."

"Past lives, Katz?"

"Exactly!"

"As in reincarnation?"

"Of course."

"Sorry, I don't buy it." Gavin was starting to wish he'd never agreed to this hypnotism stuff. He'd already been iffy about it, but talk of past lives was far beyond anything he was willing to put faith into. He didn't pretend to be a theologian, but he did know enough about God and the Bible to know everyone got one chance at this world and when they left it they were going to one of two places. There were no second chances.

"Well what other explanation could there possibly be?" Katz replied. "Her recollection of ancient history is nothing short of phenomenal. And I have never heard of anyone traveling back even a fraction as far. And she does it with ease. Like it was yesterday. No, like it was today — *now*. To say she has an old soul is the grossest of understatements. Who knows how far back she can remember? And the idea of *two* souls meeting each other in other lifetimes and somehow recognizing each other . . . If I could only hypnotize Krogan to confirm these meetings," he said thoughtfully. Gavin realized he wasn't joking. He was in his own world.

"Have you gone mad? How far back can

you remember? Krogan is a *killer* and he's alive and on the loose, in the here and now. Can you remember what you're supposed to be doing here? What you're paid to be doing here?"

"Pierce!" Katz pleaded. "Just think of what we've stumbled upon. She could unlock mysteries historians and scientists have pondered for centuries. She said she was in Yecko by the river that dies. For the last five thousand years at least, those places have gone by the name of Jericho and the Dead Sea. Jericho is the oldest city on earth and she was there before it was called Jericho — before people rode horses."

"How do you get Jericho out of Yecko?" Gavin said. He didn't want to know any more about this crazy dream, or whatever it was, than he already did, but if he listened he might find something that could bring Katz back to earth.

"Look, Pierce. The letter J doesn't exist in the Hebrew language. Hundreds of years ago Martin Luther translated a ton of biblical information into German for his church and we got that consonant through him. In German a J has a Y sound, so all Ys became Js. By the time it got to us, Yerushalayim had become Jerusalem,

Yeshua became Jesus and Yericho became Jericho. But what was Yericho before that? Yecko?"

Gavin was already sorry he'd asked.

"Good grief! She was part of a tribe of hunters and gatherers speaking an ancient form of Hebrew," Katz cried with raised voice and animated hands. "You could speak Hebrew fluently and barely make out what she was saying. Her dialect could be where the Hebrew language was born. Pre-Tower of Babel. Predeluge, if you can believe it. In fact, she might be able to tell us if the Great Flood was localized or literally covered the entire earth, which is a question that has plagued theologians since the beginning of . . . theology. I'll bring her back to her original lifetime and —"

"Katz," Gavin yelled. "I'm a cop! I've got no time for this reincarnation garbage! And anyway, I simply don't believe in it."

"Oh, so that's it. I should have known. You don't want me to step on your religious beliefs, whatever they are."

"Look, pal, I'm not the one you're supposed to be analyzing. Besides, I might be a little rough around the edges, but I know where to draw the line."

"And I'm a psychologist. Her past affects her present and future. The reasons for her present behavior could be locked up in her past."

"But you're not just talking about her past; you're going after something you're saying she did thousands of years ago."

"Exactly. Don't you find that to be amazing?"

"Too amazing. I just want to know what she did the day before yesterday."

"Can't you understand this could be the find of a lifetime?"

"No, I can't. I can't allow myself to understand that. There's no time to. Not when someone else's lifetime is about to be cut short."

Katz quickly turned and stamped out ten frustrated paces, then stopped and turned again, looking at Gavin with that basset-hound face. He sighed and looked at the ground, silent for a long moment. Then, "You're right, of course," he said solemnly. "It's just that —"

"Look, Doc. Let's go back in there and find our killer. After that, I don't care what you do. Write a book about it. Do some TV and radio. Become famous. Win the freakin' Nobel Peace Prize. But first, let's get this psycho before he creates any more past lives out of present lives — innocent present lives."

Gavin was getting a headache. He was starting to wonder if his psychologist needed a psychologist.

"Gavin. Dr. Katz," called a female voice.

Gavin turned to see Amy in the hall by the bedroom door. She was waving them over. When Gavin got to her she pointed him inside. Karianne was sobbing and Dr. Fagan was trying to console her.

"What is it, my dear?" Katz asked after pushing his way between Gavin and Amy.

"Your suggestion that she would feel rested and unafraid doesn't appear to be holding very well," Fagan snapped sarcastically.

"What's happening to me, Dr. Katz? Why did I see those places? Why do I speak those languages and understand them? What is all this violence and killing? Why was I in a plane aiming for a boat? I wanted to fly into it . . . destroy it."

Gavin looked at Amy, who looked back with wide eyes. Wonderful, he thought. Katz will probably convince Karianne she's a terrorist or a kamikaze pilot.

Katz motioned for Fagan to step aside, then stood over Karianne, holding her hand. "You don't have to be afraid, my dear. Those are memories from another time; they can't hurt you here. They only reveal the past."

"Who's past? Not mine."

"Not your past in this life. Those were other lives — different lives. You are connected now only by your memory of them. But I repeat: they cannot hurt you. They are gone," he said in that mesmerizing kind of way, attempting to pacify her.

Gavin opened his mouth to say that was perhaps Katz's explanation, but not necessarily the correct one. But Karianne was beyond listening.

"No!" she cried, shaking her head back and forth. "I could never have done those things. I don't believe you. This is my life. Those were other lives, not mine."

Katz closed his eyes for a moment, apparently trying to hold on to his own composure. "Karianne, listen to me. We're not going to go there. We're going to stay in your time. If you slip into another time or another place you're not familiar with, we'll stop and come back. It's very important you tell us about the Krogan of *this* time. Is that all right with you?"

Karianne closed her eyes, frowned, and nodded her approval. In spite of himself, Gavin was moved. Up until now he had only thought of her as a means to an end and would just as well have had her locked up for being in the same car as the killer. His heart was changing. She was obviously in extreme emotional pain, yet she was pressing on. She wanted the killer caught. And she seemed willing to go through whatever it took to accomplish that.

Katz put her through a few breathing techniques to help defuse the stress and then proceeded to put her under again. Getting hypnotized was becoming so natural to her that Katz dispensed with the metronome, using a shiny gold pen instead. Other shortcuts were also obvious. The transitional period, where Katz had previously tiptoed into her subconscious with a laundry list of personal questions, was replaced by a few token suggestions. And he no longer asked her to keep her hand raised, apparently confident of her ability to remain hypnotized once under.

"Now I want you to go back just five years, no more, to Karianne Stordal's first accident in Norway," Katz said.

The rapid eye movement began. She squirmed a little and then wrapped her arms around herself as if she were cold.

"Are you there?" Katz asked.

"Yes?"

"Is Krogan with you?"

"Yes, but he's leaving."

"Leaving the car?"

"Yes."

"Is he hurt?"

"Yes. Badly hurt."

"Why is he in Norway?"

"He's found a home there."

Gavin frowned. The guy was from Norway?

"Can you see the other car? The one you hit?"

"Yes."

"Did you just happen to hit this particular car because it was there, or did you have a reason?"

"Krogan wanted."

"Why?"

"Retaliate. Hurt enemy. *Shadahd.*"

"People were killed in that crash. Was that what Krogan wanted?"

"Stop enemy."

"Was the enemy stopped?"

"Yes."

"Hmm. Do you know where Krogan lived in Norway?"

"Never know. Krogan always finds me."

"How? How does he find you?"

"Krogan sees. Krogan wants. Krogan finds."

"When did Krogan come to New York?"

"Sixteen sixty-four."

Katz's eyes widened. He looked at his fingers and counted them one at a time, apparently calculating something. "Wasn't New York called New Amsterdam then?"

"It was New Amsterdam before we got there and took it from them," she laughed.

"We? You were English?"

Gavin could see he was about to lose the psychologist again. He caught Katz's attention with a wave, then sternly shook his head. Katz nodded reluctantly.

"When did Krogan come to New York since the Norway crash?" Katz asked, rephrasing the question.

"I don't know," she said.

Gavin's beeper vibrated in his front pocket. He pulled it out and held it toward the light coming over his shoulder through the window. He didn't recognize the number, but it ended with a 911.

"Do we have a bad connection or is it my pronunciation, Pierce? For the third time: Krogan called me and I'm going to meet him this afternoon," Gasman said from his cell phone in the luxury lounge of Executive Airways. Plush royal-blue carpeting covered every inch of the floor and ran halfway up the sides of the chrome-and-glass reception desk. Through the window that ran the length of the lounge he could see the sleek white jet with a violet tail that would take him to Albany. He had never been on a Learjet before, but he knew under the circumstances his boss would agree to the extra expense. He crushed his cigarette in the fine sand of an ashtray and watched the fuel truck drive away from the plane.

"Where?" Gavin demanded. "Tell me where or I'll lock you up."

Gasman laughed. "For what?"

"For your own protection," Gavin yelled.

"If you don't tell me where the meeting is I swear I'll strangle you."

Gasman checked his fingernails and smiled. "No way, Pierce. As you so often tell me, that's confidential. If he spots anyone he even thinks is a cop, the meeting is off. He might be crazy, but he's not stupid."

"You're stupid. Do I have to remind you who this is you're going to meet? He kills for fun. What's going to keep him from killing you?"

"Don't worry. I've taken measures. Besides, we're meeting in a public place."

"He loves public places. That's his arena. He kills in public all the time. I'm telling you, Gasman. Don't do it."

"Sorry, Pierce. It won't work. Everybody has rules. Cops have rules. Athletes have rules. Reporters have rules. If you want the high ground, you've got to go and take it. The ground doesn't get any higher than this. It's Mount freakin' Everest. It's the biggest story of my life."

"You won't have a life, you idiot. You'll be the story. Why can't you see that?"

"You're just trying to scare me. The truth is you don't trust me. You don't think I can handle it. That's where you're wrong, Pierce."

"Don't be a fool, Gasman. I've already promised you first shot at whatever happens. At least tell me where so I can keep an eye on you."

"Forget it, Pierce. Even if I changed my mind, which I'm not, there's not enough time. The meeting isn't local," he said looking at his watch. "My flight is leaving any minute now."

"*Your flight?* Where are you meeting him? In the airport?" Gavin was frantic now. "Does he know what flight you'll be on?"

"Relax, Detective. We're not talking major airline here. I've got a private charter. And if it'll make you feel any better, I've already asked them about the possibility of a bomb and they said the only one who could have possibly planted any explosives on this baby in the last three days would have to be the pilot himself. And I've seen him. He doesn't look at all like our boy Krogan."

"If it's not a public flight, how would he know what plane to bomb?"

"Because he arranged the charter. He has a lot more at risk here than I do, you know."

"*Krogan arranged it?*" Gavin wanted to go through the phone and wring Gasman's neck.

"Now there you go again, repeating what I say. Look, Pierce, he's just being careful. He wants to know what flight I'm on so he can make sure there are no tricks. He has to make sure I'm alone. He needs to know he can trust me. He *wants* to trust me. If he wants trust, I'll give him trust. If he wants understanding, I'll give him understanding. If he wants to be heard, I'll let him speak."

"He wants your life."

"If he wants my life so badly there're plenty of easier ways he could have taken it. I don't wear a bulletproof vest or drive with three-inch-thick glass. I spoke to him this morning from a pay phone. I was a perfect target. If he wanted me, he could have had me then."

"Maybe that wouldn't have been as much fun for him."

"Maybe you want the first shot at him. Maybe you're jealous," Gasman said.

"Open your eyes, Gasman. This isn't a contest."

"Oh, no? Tell me you don't want Krogan's face in your gun sights. This guy's killed your grandfather and your friend and put your partner in the hospital. Tell me you can't feel his neck in your hands."

Gavin paused. "Look, I admit I want to take this guy off the planet more than anyone could. And if you quote me on that, we're through. But you've got to believe me when I say that has nothing to do with it. I don't know much, but I do know 'understanding' is not high on his list. Destruction is."

"Touching, Pierce, but there's a pretty redhead in a blue suit that wants to escort me to the jet. I'll call you after the meeting. Wish me luck."

"Wait!" Gavin yelled, to no avail.

Gasman put his phone away, picked up his attaché, and followed the woman out of the lounge and onto the macadam where the jet awaited him. He now wished he'd never called Pierce. What had it accomplished except make him feel nervous?

The redhead stopped at the bottom of the airplane steps. "Thank you for choosing Executive," she said with a broad smile. "Rachel, your flight attendant, is on board and Captain Mills and his copilot will be here in a minute."

Gasman smiled nervously and thanked her as he took his first step up. His feet felt as heavy as lead and his knees felt like rubber. Look what he's done to me, he thought. I should never have called him.

He had almost asked the redhead again about a bomb, but knew her answer would be the same. She had used the word "impossible." He repeated the word to himself a few times, then managed the rest of the stairway.

"Good afternoon, Mr. Gasman. My name is Rachel," said a petite blonde, extending her hand. "Is there anything I can get for you? A drink, maybe?"

Before Gasman stepped inside, his gaze quickly darted around the inside of the aircraft's mid-cabin before finally coming to rest on Rachel's cheery face. "Yeah, uh, scotch on the rocks," he said, wondering where he would plant a bomb if he were Krogan. He had never felt claustrophobic before now. But the ceiling was so low he couldn't even stand upright without the top of his curly hair brushing the ceiling. If a bomb did explode, he would stand as much chance as a spider in a gun barrel.

"Johnny Walker Black all right, sir?" Rachel asked.

"Black? Sure. Forget the cubes and make it a double."

"No problem. Coming right up, Mr. Gasman. Find the seat of your choice and make yourself comfortable, sir."

Gasman surveyed the puffy, white-leather seats. Turning toward the cabin, he saw the one he wanted. It was just behind the divider that separated him from the pilot. As he walked toward the seat he nervously twitched a bit lower at each ceiling light. All this luxury and expense and he suddenly decided he would rather be on a 747. Something that had more air in it to breathe.

Before he sat down he peeked into the cabin. The controls looked overwhelmingly complicated and vast. He had never understood how pilots could fiddle with all these dials and lights and still watch where they were going. There was just so much that could go wrong. He peered through the front window. He could see the runway they were going to take off from. To his left was the fuel truck making its way to another plane. He tried to see what the driver looked like, but the angle was wrong. He felt a chill as he imagined the truck colliding with the jet — talk about explosive. He would definitely have to keep watch for that. The rest of the airstrip was clear. To his right, running the length of the airfield's border, was a chain-link fence. It appeared to be at least ten feet high, judging from the yellow utility truck parked on the other side of it.

"Excuse me, sir," said a deep voice from behind.

Gasman turned quickly, startled.

"Sorry, I didn't mean to scare you. I'm Captain Mills and this is my copilot, Bill Nolan," the owner of the voice said, extending his hand. Gavin shook it and then the copilot's hand as well. They both appeared very confident and neither of them looked like Krogan.

"We'll be leaving momentarily. If we could just squeeze by?"

"Oh, sure. I'm sorry," Gasman said.

"Not at all," the captain said as Gasman dropped into his seat.

"Your drink, sir," Rachel said.

"Oh, yes. Thank you," he said, taking the drink from her hand before she could set it down.

"You're quite welcome, sir. If you'd like another, just let me know. I'll be right behind you. And if you would please buckle your seat belt?" she asked sweetly.

Gasman smiled. She sure is pretty, he thought, trying to get his mind off Krogan. He gulped down half of his drink and winced as a shiver went down his spine. As smooth as the twelve-year-old scotch was, the eighty-six-proof alcohol content was hard for his body to ignore. He held the tumbler with both hands to try to keep it from shaking. The tiny ripples on the whiskey's surface were proof he needed more help, so he drained the glass in hope of steadier nerves. He should never have called Pierce.

The engines started smoothly and hummed quietly without any trace of vibration.

"Okay, Mr. Gasman," said Captain Mills over the intercom. "We're about to take off. If you've never had the pleasure, you'll find this little sweetheart is as strong as a lion but as graceful as a swan."

The engines increased slightly in volume and Gasman suddenly realized they were moving. Looking out his circular side window, he could see the fuel truck was occupied elsewhere. He let out a sigh and settled the back of his neck into the soft white leather of the chair's headrest, closing his eyes. What news reporter had ever had an exclusive interview with a criminal as sought after as this one? None. He was on his way to the story of his life. He would be the envy of his profession and overnight would become the most recognized man in his field. Maybe it was the change of thoughts, maybe it was the Johnny Walker, but he was starting to feel better.

The jet made a couple of small turns and then stopped at the beginning of the runway. Gasman listened to the radio chat between the pilot and the tower. As soon as he heard them say all was clear for takeoff the engines began to increase their whine as the pilot powered up. Here we go, he thought.

The jet accelerated forward in steady increase of thrust and speed. It was exhilarating. Gasman leaned toward the window and could see the ground racing by. Forget the 747, this was amazing.

"What is that?" Mills yelled.

What is what? Gasman thought. He leaned forward, trying to see into the cabin, but his seat belt stopped him.

"Tower, tower, emergency. We have a vehicle crossing the runway. Acknowledge," Mills yelled.

Gasman's eyes almost popped out of his head. He unbuckled his belt, grabbed a chrome bar in front of him, and pulled himself up, struggling against the jet's acceleration. He ignored Rachel's plea for him to please sit back down.

"Affirmative, Dan. We see it. Can you throttle down?"

"Negative. Our velocity is too high. What the — It's heading for us. I repeat, the vehicle has turned and is heading at us. I'll have to add thrust and lift her up before we hit it," Mills yelled frantically.

Gasman saw it. The lighting truck from the other side of the fence. Somehow it had gotten past the barrier and was on the runway. His chest suddenly ached in terror. Krogan! "Pull up! Pull up!" he screamed.

"I am. We're going to make it," Mills yelled. "Our engines will probably set that truck on fire, but we'll make it. Sit down!"

Mills's words resonated loudly through Gasman's mind. "We'll make it . . . we'll make it . . . we'll make it," he said, hammering the air with his tightly clenched fist in emphasis. He felt suddenly heavier, like he would in an express elevator beginning its assent. He held the chrome bar tightly and bent his knees under the additional force, realizing he needed to sit back down. The instant he began to turn, however, as the nose of the jet rose, he saw through the speeding truck's windshield a man with blond hair. He hoped Mills was right. He hoped the engines burned the truck to the ground. That it would turn both the truck and Krogan into a smoldering pile of ash. "You stupid fool," he yelled with a laugh of triumph. "Not *this* time."

"Oh, God! The boom is raising, Dan. He's raising the boom," the copilot shouted. "Left! Go left!"

"Not enough altitude," Mills yelled back.

Still, he tried, veering to left what little he could before, in the blink of an eye, the extended bucket passed by the windshield and smashed into the right wing. The force of the impact ripped Gasman's hand from the chrome bar. He bounced off a seat and slammed face first onto the floor. The collision took his breath away and sent a sharp, searing pain into his abdomen. He tried to scream, but couldn't. Everything seemed to be moving slower than it should, as his brain rushed to take in all it could. The round side window displayed alternating flashes of ground and sky; the jet was helplessly spinning through the air and would certainly crash any second. Crash and explode in flames, just like every other jet crash he had ever covered. He was going to die. He came off the floor and in the instant before he heard the brain-deafening crunch from his head hitting the ceiling, he saw Rachel's horrified face. She was still buckled in her seat.

Suddenly, oddly, he no longer felt any pain. He was no longer afraid. In fact, he became more and more detached from the scene until finally he was outside the aircraft, looking in at his own body, strangely twisted and limp, ricocheting about the mid-cabin.

— 26 —

Gavin seethed with anger at his own short-sightedness. Krogan had used the same psychology on Gasman that he himself had used regarding the story exclusive. He'd never even considered the possibility. But whose fault was that? Certainly not Gasman's. Maybe if he had let Katz spend a little more time in Krogan's past he would have picked up more of his tendencies. So what if they were past lives? Who was he to say that sort of thing didn't exist? A good detective looked under every stone. He'd screwed up, and someone had died because of it. Oh, sure, he'd warned Gasman that Krogan would try to kill him. But by then it was too late. He should have known telling Gasman to stay away from a story like the one Krogan offered would be futile — like warning a hungry tiger that the helpless goat tied to the stake might be bait set out by the hunter.

Gavin could still hear himself arguing with Gasman as he walked solemnly about the airfield. Fire engines and ambulances and police cars decorated the acreage with a colorful assortment of flashing lights. Helicopters hovered and camera crews hustled about. Both the FBI and the FAA were already here and it wouldn't be long before they were knocking on his door for whatever information they could scrounge up. He would cooperate, but only because the lieutenant would pull him off the case if he didn't. He would provide them with file data only, though, and nothing more. As far as he was concerned, the FBI would have to wait their turn.

Crime scenes, especially of this magnitude, had a tendency to suck you in and make you oblivious to the world outside. Gavin, though, felt strangely distant. The chaos before him was eerily reminiscent of the hypnotic episodes Karianne had revealed. The thought of Karianne recalling Krogan's past atrocities made him wonder if someone would recall this one someday in the future.

FBI agents were everywhere. They could no longer watch from a distance. As far as they were concerned, Krogan was now a bona fide terrorist. He might not have the organized connections other groups had, but five more lives lost in the destruction of a jet was more than they could pass off to the local police.

The crime scene unit was carefully placing a pair of bolt cutters into a large plastic bag. They'd been found on the ground by the chain-link fence and had been used to cut the fence adequately enough for the truck to break through without the risk of being snagged like a fish in a net. Gavin already knew Krogan's fingerprints would be all over the tool. If anything, Krogan probably wanted the credit for pulling off such a good job — for killing Gasman so utterly and completely . . . and sensationally.

Off in the distance, on the grass by the end of the runway, the fire department was still working on the blazing Learjet. Gavin doubted the bodies would even be recognizable. He'd never really liked Gasman, but that didn't stop him from feeling somewhat responsible for his death. Gavin had played him, preying on his weaknesses. The reporter had wanted nothing more than a good story, and Gavin had taken advantage of that foible; he'd exploited Gasman's tunnel-vision ambition to be famous and it had backfired.

But Gavin had learned one thing new about Krogan from Gasman's death: he was definitely capable of being motivated. This was 100 percent premeditated and as cold as anything Gavin had ever seen. But the thought persisted: if he had been a little more open-minded and less concerned with when and where Katz was bringing Karianne, maybe he could have prevented this.

A hundred feet away stood Krogan's weapon, the Lighting Company bucket truck. Gavin was a little surprised Krogan hadn't driven away with it. Except for the fact the bucket had been torn off the boom, nothing was wrong with it. Another surprise was that there were no beer cans or lobster claws in it. Apparently, Krogan didn't need to be drunk to be deadly. In fact, he was just as efficient a killer, if not more so, without his trademark borrowed party vehicle.

At the marina crash, Gavin had wondered how Krogan could hit the boat so precisely, especially when drunk. To knock a Learjet from the sky with a bucket truck would require ten times the luck . . . or skill. Was there something in this past-life stuff about transferred skill and abilities? After seeing this, how could he not at least consider such craziness? Krogan's timing had been perfect. Near superhuman. He was now at least two for two in highly improbable feats of destruction. Dumb luck? No way. Not this time.

"Hope you haven't eaten yet," one of the forensic techs said as Gavin approached the bucket. Gavin ignored him and continued. He stopped next to a medical examiner who was writing on a pad a few feet from the bucket. The man looked up from his notes and did a slight double take when he saw Gavin.

"Lucky for him he wasn't around for all the excitement. Those arrows killed him hours ago," the man volunteered. "You got a real winner on your hands this time, driving all around Nassau County with a dead man in the bucket. What would he have said if he got pulled over? And then he whacks a Learjet with the guy still in there?" He shook his head in amazement.

Gavin remained silent. He had already instructed the Lighting Company to immediately fax headquarters with a list of the unfortunate employee's assignments along with a probable driving route. If there had been an assignment printout or clipboard in the truck, there wasn't one now. He figured Krogan had tossed it.

That nobody anywhere in the county had reported what was probably a silent murder drastically reduced the possibility of a witness. But, still, the way Krogan left fingerprints around there was no telling what might show up if he could find the spot the truck was stolen from.

He stared at the mangled mess that had been a man. The fact he wasn't shocked or horrified at what he saw bothered him; unlike others around him who were registering their disbelief of the broad-head hunting arrows in the man's shoulder and neck, Gavin wasn't surprised. If Katz was correct, a man with Krogan's vast history would have killed with arrows thousands of times. What would surprise Gavin was if the beast had ever done it without pleasure.

He pulled out his cell phone, called the hospital, and had them page Katz.

"Katz here."

"I want another meeting . . . session . . . whatever you freakin' call it, and I want it tonight."

"The hospital's releasing her as we speak," Katz said. "She's only been here as long as she has to accommodate us."

"Then we'll have it at her place or your place or my place, but we've got to have it."

"I don't know, Pierce. She going to be tired after —"

"Make it happen, Katz. You can hypnotize her and take her anywhere you want to — ten years ago, ten thousand years ago. I don't care anymore, just as long as Krogan's there. I want to know everything about this guy — who he was, who he is, what turns him on, what turns him off, what he likes to do besides killing people . . . everything. I want to eat, drink, and sleep this psychopath until I know what he's thinking, starting tonight. We're out of time. And don't let Karianne out of your sight. The last thing we want is for something to happen to her."

"What if she refuses to do it tonight?"

Gavin looked at the smoldering plane wreck, then at the dead man in the smashed bucket. "Then I'll talk to her. But I don't think that'll be necessary. I think I was wrong about her, Katz. I think she's a good lady who had a bad day. I don't know how any of this past-life connection stuff really works, but I do believe she wants him stopped as much as anyone. If she's his enemy then she's our friend. What's your professional opinion?"

"Uh, ditto."

Gavin managed a fleeting smile.

"Thanks. That was exactly what I needed to hear right now. Oh, by the way. I want some kind of language expert there other than just your Uncle Hiram. I don't want us guessing what she's saying when she starts to speak Greek or Swahili."

"But how am I going to get a language expert on such short notice?"

"You told me this was the find of a lifetime, Katz. I'm sure you can round up someone who wants to be in your book."

Gavin put away his phone. He'd seen enough. He was about to turn and walk away when he noticed something curious about the wrist of the dead man. His left wrist looked the same as Gavin's did when taking a shower . . . when he wasn't wearing his watch. The wrist was tanned except for a watch-sized band. It was possible the guy had lost the thing in the crash, but it was also possible Krogan had stolen it. A souvenir? Or had Krogan needed to know what time it was?

Before he left, Gavin asked someone on the CSU to keep a lookout for the man's watch. Walking briskly back to his car, he was intercepted by a man with a miniature tape recorder.

"Excuse me, sir. Are you Detective Pierce?"

"Yeah," Gavin said without breaking stride.

"I'm Bennett Norel from the *Post*," the man said, holding out a card. Gavin didn't take it, so Norel continued. "Uh, according to the receptionist, Mr. Gasman was heard speaking to someone he called Pierce before he got on the jet."

Gavin stopped and turned to look at the man.

"Look . . . Norel, did you say it was?"

"Yes, sir," the young man said eagerly, his tape recorder at the ready.

"How old are you?"

"Twenty-three."

"You want the big story?"

"Yes, sir."

"Are you willing to do anything for it?"

"Absolutely."

Gavin put his hand over the mike and spoke softly, motioning toward the smoldering remains of the jet. "So was he."

He left the young man staring at the smoking pile of metal. Hopefully Gavin had impregnated him with the kind of wisdom that only hindsight can deliver to the blindly ambitious. The kid reminded Gavin of a young Gasman. If only he could have had such an opportunity to remind Gasman of the dangers of ambition, maybe then he wouldn't have felt so invincible.

Pondering the clarity of hindsight, Gavin picked up his pace. He was anxious to see what Karianne's distant past would reveal, but first he wanted to stop by headquarters to see if the fax from the Lighting Company had come in yet.

— 27 —

Krogan had just wolfed down his third helping of ham and sunny-side-up eggs with home fries, all drenched with Tabasco sauce. The waitress looked at him strangely as she replaced yet another empty plate, this time with a double cheeseburger deluxe and a fresh bottle of hot sauce. Tearing into a nearby plate of hot buttered toast, two at a time, he tapped his empty coffee cup with a dripping fork, then stabbed at the French fries.

"Honey, if you're going for the house record, you've already blown it away. I've never seen anyone drink eight cups of coffee before," the waitress said as she poured.

Krogan said nothing as he poured enough sugar in the coffee to make the waitress frown, then, without stirring the sugar, threw the steaming cupful down like it was a shot of whiskey. The waitress shivered at the sight, then turned to leave. She had only taken two steps before he tapped the coffee cup again.

All the work involved in killing Gasman had given Krogan a ferocious appetite. He didn't even notice, through the diner's window at his right, that the orange glow in the distant sky had finally been extinguished, leaving only wisps of gray smoke. After dressing his burger with the appropriate drowning of ketchup and Tabasco, he took a healthy bite, the hot juices running over the egg yolk on his chin. Two bites later the burger was gone. He was about to tap for more when a throaty motorcycle rolled into a parking space outside the window. The bike was a Harley and it was saddled with some leathered-up guy and his chick.

The guy turned the key to shut off the engine, but hadn't removed it when the bottom of Krogan's boot slammed into his helmet, sending the guy onto the hood of the car in the next space. The guy fell motionless. The girl screamed as Krogan quickly mounted the bike, started the engine, and took off with her still hanging on. Krogan laughed as the girl cursed him and beat on his back as he sped down the road. Finally he leaned back and yelled to her, "Your place or mine?"

— 28 —

By the time Gavin got to Karianne's apartment everyone had already been there for hours.

"Are you okay?" Amy asked, giving him a warm embrace and, after an uncharacteristically shy moment, a quick kiss on the cheek. Gavin hid his surprise, enjoying the moment.

"Fine," he lied. "I had to stop at headquarters and get this fax. It's a list from the Lighting Company of the stops the truck was supposed to make. I need to check these locations ASAP."

"Pierce," Katz called, looking relieved. "We were getting a little worried and wondering if we should start without you. This is Doctor Paul Steinman. He's the language expert you requested. Uncle Hiram had to pass on tonight. Your . . . our pace is a bit too demanding for him."

"Detective Pierce," Steinman said with a

big smile, offering his hand. The man was in his late forties, heavyset with big cheeks and a full reddish-blond beard. His merry, Santa Claus-like face was a contrast to Katz's perpetually sad one.

Gavin nodded and shook the man's outstretched hand, but was in no mood to return the smile. "Where's Karianne?" he asked Amy.

Amy motioned toward the living room through an arched opening a few feet away. Gavin immediately left the foyer to see her. Karianne was laying on a comfortable-looking couch with a southwestern design, her broken leg propped up on a pillow. She smiled briefly, but said nothing.

The living room was not big, but had a very cozy feel to it. Neat but well lived in. To his left the wall was full of photos, most of them of Karianne posing with friends in various outdoor scenes. Mountain backgrounds, beach shots, both snow- and water-skiing. All probably the result of the perks of her job. The other walls were full of small watercolor paintings, wall hangings, and other likely souvenirs. A long table in front of a window behind the couch she was on held a collection of live plants. Everything pointed to a healthy, active life. In other words, there was no obvious evidence of alcoholism or partying. If indeed she hadn't had a drink in five years, she had helped her cause by not even allowing a bottle in the photos or paintings. It was hard for Gavin to easily connect the woman's immediate situation with the one represented in the room.

He knelt down before her on one knee so he would be more or less at eye level. "Thank you," he said as sincerely as he could. "You're quite a trooper. The courage you've shown in allowing us to pursue the killer through you is, at this point, heroic."

She laughed. "Heroic. I'm scared to death. I don't know what I'm doing, how I'm doing it, or what will come next. The only thing I understand is real people in this time are dying. If there's any way I can help, tell me and I'll do it. Everyone else around here is jumping through hoops and giving their 110 percent."

Gavin was comforted by her willingness. It didn't make sense to him that she could have been in the car with Krogan, much less that she had been traveling from one lifetime to another as his sometime sidekick. He wondered if the others that had died as Krogan's passengers were also reincarnated *shadahd* dates. Time-traveling

party souls that had an occasional irresistible impulse to destroy.

Gavin turned to see Amy, Katz, and his
language expert all standing behind him,
waiting to start. The video camera was set
up across the room and an additional tape
recorder, probably Steinman's, was on a
small chair.

Katz brought in another chair and
placed it next to the couch by Karianne's
feet so he could face her straight on.
Steinman took a seat in an overstuffed
beige chair close enough to the recorder
that any of his comments could be easily
picked up by its small internal microphone. Katz also provided Gavin and Amy
with a small dry-erase board on a stand so
they could communicate with him without
speaking.

"Dr. Katz," Karianne said, halting the
psychologist just before he was about to go
to work. "Do you think while you have me
hypnotized you could ask me what I did
with my opening-day football ticket? I
haven't seen it since . . . since that night.
The game is two days away and the ticket
was a gift from one of the players. It's a
great location, too — second tier, right on
the fifty yard line."

Katz smiled. "We'll see what we can do,"

292

he said, then continued.

Karianne slipped into her hypnotic state almost automatically. Gavin wondered if Katz had ever really brought her completely out from the last time.

Steinman was at the edge of his seat. He'd probably never seen anything like this, Gavin thought.

"Now, Karianne, I want you to think about Krogan. Do you see him?"

"Yes."

"I want you to see him smile, see him happy — the happiest you've ever seen him. Are you there?"

Karianne's eyes flickered. Her head moved slowly, as if there was an unseen thickness about her. "Sic. Krogan," she said.

"Krogan is sick?" Katz asked.

"Haud!" she yelled. "Delectatio. Krogan delecto," she continued. Her tone was almost scary. Gavin thought she might be angry she had to repeat herself.

All eyes fell upon Steinman.

Steinman was obviously stunned. "She's speaking Latin! Ancient Latin. *Haud* means 'no.' She said Krogan is not sick but very happy, delighted, enjoying himself."

Katz smiled at everyone, then turned back

to Karianne. "Good! And why is he happy?"

"Congrego."

"Gathering," Steinman said.

"Hmm. Who is gathering together that Krogan is so happy?"

"Refragatio."

"Resistance," Steinman said.

"Revolutionaries?" Katz asked.

"Sic."

"Yes," Steinman said.

"Are you a member of the resistance?"

"Sic."

"Are you happy, too?"

Karianne laughed. "Sic, sic, sic."

"Are there any others from the resistance that are from another time — another life?"

"Sic."

Katz looked around the room. He had the same expression someone would have if they had just found a recipe for a peanut butter and jelly sandwich written in Martian. He was probably imagining his name next to Freud's . . . Da Vinci's. Gavin gave him a warning look, and he turned back to Karianne.

"How many of the resistance do you know from other lives?"

"Plurimus," she said.

"Most or all," Steinman translated.

What she said was startling, even to

Gavin. Amy put her hand on his hand, but continued to look at Karianne.

Katz frowned. "Was that why you gathered? Because you all knew each other in other lives?"

"Haud. Celebritas."

"No. Celebration," Steinman said.

"What are you all celebrating?"

"Neco. Leto ensis . . . nex. *Shadahd*," she said with a snarl.

Steinman frowned, then shook his head slightly before he said, "Put to death. Kill the sword. Violent death. The last word sounds like Hebrew."

"We know what the last word means," Katz said quietly. "Is this an execution?"

"Sic."

"Someone is going to be killed with a sword?"

"Haud. Neco ensis."

"No. Kill the sword," Steinman said.

Katz frowned and tapped his finger on his knee. "You're going to kill a sword?"

"Sic."

"Is the sword a person?"

"Sic."

Katz smiled and nodded at everyone, obviously proud of his perceptiveness. "What country are you in?"

"Y'hudah."

Katz's eyebrows raised and he mouthed Israel to Steinman, who nodded in agreement. "What city are you in?"

"Yerushalayim."

Katz paused. "What are you wearing on your feet?"

"Auarca."

"A leather sandal," Steinman said. "The kind usually worn by a peasant. She's probably visiting from Rome. That would be in keeping with the dialect."

"What is your name?"

"Glaucus Tertius."

"Are you Roman?" Katz asked.

"Sic."

"Who is the emperor?"

"Tiberius."

Steinman leaned so far forward he almost fell out of his seat. Katz ran his fingers through his hair. His hand was shaking as he dragged his fingers across his lips. Gavin didn't know too much about history, but he knew plenty about shock, and Katz was shocked. Which emperor was Tiberius? What was Katz thinking?

Katz cleared his throat. "The one you call 'Sword' . . . is there any other name you call him?"

"Filius."

Steinman exhaled heavily before he

spoke. "The Son."

Now Gavin knew what was freaking Katz out. He didn't need to know much about history to know whom Karianne was talking about. But who was this Glaucus character and who was Krogan that he would gather with a band of people who had been meeting each other through the centuries and were now all in one place, celebrating the execution of the one they all knew as The Sword?

He tapped on the dry-erase board until he got Katz's attention, then wrote *Krogan*. Katz nodded.

"What is Krogan doing?"

"Crapula. Derideo. Accendo."

"She says he's drinking wine, laughing and mocking someone, and trying to get others to do the same," Steinman said.

"Who is he mocking?"

"Deludo deus filius," she yelled, then laughed. "Deludo deus filius," she repeated again and again in an eerie chant as if she too were drunk.

Gavin snapped his fingers several times at Steinman, who was staring straight ahead with his eyes wide open, as though he was afraid to interpret. He looked at Gavin, nodded quickly, and exhaled. "She says he's . . . mocking God's Son."

Amy's hand, already on Gavin's knee, squeezed tightly, intensifying the shiver traveling through his veins.

After a long silence, Katz pulled out a handkerchief and wiped the sweat off his forehead. "What do the people who are not in your resistance call the one who you call The Sword?"

"Haud," she yelled.

"No?" Katz asked, apparently surprised by either her sudden anger or her refusal to answer him.

"Haud," she repeated loudly.

Katz frowned, looked at Gavin, and shrugged his shoulders. "Maybe Karianne can tell us what Glaucus won't," he said in a hushed version of his deep voice. "You are now moving forward through the centuries until you are Karianne again. You will be able to recall all you have seen while being Glaucus Tertius."

Karianne's head began moving slowly from side to side again, like it had before.

"Who are you?" Katz asked.

"Karianne," she said.

"Very good. Now I want you to —"

Suddenly, unexpectedly, Karianne's eyes stopped fluttering and then opened. She looked around the room at each of the faces in it, then screamed and cried convulsively.

— 29 —

"This is a joke, right?" Katz said in disbelief. "You can't be serious, Pierce. She saw Jesus Christ! How many other sons of God were crucified in Jerusalem two thousand years ago?" he said through clenched teeth.

Both he and Gavin quickly looked into the living room to see if their elevating discussion from the foyer had disturbed Karianne. Fortunately, she was still under, with her right hand raised like a flag. "There is nothing bigger than this, Pierce," Katz said in a desperate whisper. "She was actually there. At the crucifixion. Her report is the most . . . most . . ."

"Sorry, Katz," Gavin whispered. "We have to move on."

"Move on? *Move on?* I'm scheduling you for a CAT scan, Pierce. You definitely need your head examined. No one in their right mind would move on from this. For heaven's sake, I'm Jewish and even I want to know more!"

"Katz, we almost lost her. She cried hysterically for more than a half hour and didn't respond to any of those little tricks of the trade you're so hot on. Thank God you finally did get her back under."

"I screwed up. What can I say?" Katz said. "I never expected her to pop out of the trance like that. Very uncharacteristic. She's been the perfect patient up until then. But now I know better," he pleaded. "I won't take anything for granted."

"Neither will I," Gavin shot back. "Whoever or whatever she saw almost drove her out of her mind. If we lose her, we lose our best shot at Krogan. I can't — won't take that chance."

Katz rolled his eyes. "Look, we won't lose her. I promise."

"Sorry."

"But how can you not let me take her back?"

"How can I let you? These questions you're asking her could give her nightmares — could screw her up for the rest of her life!"

"Please! Let me be the psychologist and you the cop. When was the last time you heard someone speaking in premedieval

Latin, asleep or awake?"

"She never actually did say his name. All we got were nicknames."

"Nicknames? Nicknames! 'God's Son'? Render unto me a break, Pierce. When was the last time you heard a nickname like that?"

"The answer is no. You're just gonna have to be patient."

"If you asked every person on this planet whom they would want to meet if they could meet any person from any time, half of them would say Jesus Christ. And you want me to be patient? We could confirm or rewrite the Bible!"

"Leave me out of your professional aspirations, Katz. Leave Karianne out of it. Look, the longer you argue with me about it, the longer it will take us to get Krogan. And the longer that takes, the longer you're going to have to be patient," Gavin said.

"Okay. Okay," Katz said. "If that's what it's going to take, let's get him. He's ruining everything."

Gavin had to laugh to himself as he followed a newly motivated Harold Katz into the living room. The psychologist took his seat facing Karianne with a determined countenance.

"Karianne, I want you to go back to the life of Glaucus Tertius," Katz said, motioning to Gavin, who was already half out of his seat, to relax. "I want you to go back to the next time Glaucus sees Krogan."

Once again, Karianne's head swayed slowly for almost a minute. "No Glaucus," she said. "Glaucus dead," apparently free to answer in the language spoken to her while between bodies.

"How did Glaucus die?"

"Decapitated. Battle ax," she said calmly.

Doesn't she ever die of natural causes, Gavin wondered.

"Hmm. If Glaucus is dead, where are you now?"

Gavin cleared his throat and tapped on the board. When Katz turned, he underlined the same message he had already given: *Krogan.*

Katz mouthed, *"I know."*

"Searching," Karianne said.

"For Krogan?"

"No. Want comfort. Want life. Krogan will come later. Krogan always comes."

"I want you to move forward to the next time Krogan, uh, comes."

After a brief pause, Karianne's eyes sprang open. Gavin reflexively stopped breathing, anticipating that she might freak out again, but she didn't. Her eyes, though opened wide, didn't appear to be moving or focusing on anything in the room. She began laughing. She appeared to be still under, but the laughing didn't put Gavin at ease. It sounded more scornful than cheery.

"Has Krogan come?"

"Sic," she said, still laughing.

Hearing her speak again in Latin, Katz looked at everyone's face and then back to Karianne. "What is your name?"

"Dorjan Maximus," she said proudly.

"What country are you in?"

"Roma."

"And what is Krogan's name in this life?"

"Krogan."

"In every life his name is the same?"

"Sic."

"Does Krogan like his name?"

"Sic. Scribere nomen cutis."

"She says Krogan writes his name on skin."

"On skin? You mean like a tattoo?"

"Sic."

"Are there any other tattoos Krogan likes?"

"Sic. *Shadahd.*"

"*Shadahd*. Hmm . . . Does he do this in every life?"

"Sic."

Katz frowned. "How is that possible? He can't be born with the knowledge of his previous life's name. His parents certainly can't know it. Could he be that in touch with his subconscious in every life? Is that it? Is Krogan somehow psychically linked with others from his past?"

Karianne laughed. "Krogan praevalida . . . firmus. Krogan convinco. Krogan excellens," she said with the swagger of arrogance in her voice.

Steinman looked confused, but relayed what he had heard. "She says Krogan is very powerful, very strong. Krogan overcomes. Krogan is superior."

Gavin wondered if this Dorjan character had misunderstood the question. By the look on Katz's face, he was probably wondering the same thing.

"Krogan maintains his name because he's superior?" Katz repeated.

"Sic."

"His memory is strong — is that what you mean?"

Karianne laughed arrogantly again. "Krogan commorantes praevalens."

"She says Krogan exists very powerfully."

Katz looked around the room. Gavin made note of what she had said and motioned for Katz to move on.

"Who is the emperor?"

"Nero."

"Nero?" Katz blurted. He turned to Gavin. His droopy face looked even more pathetic than usual. Gavin stoically shook his head, then tapped the marker once on the board, where the psychologist's first duty was clearly spelled out. He felt like a stern parent marching his sugar-craving child through a candy store, slapping his hand whenever it came near the object of its temptation. With a sigh, Katz turned back.

"How do you recognize Krogan when he comes? How do you know it's him?"

"Krogan palificare," she laughed.

"Krogan makes himself known," Steinman said.

"How?"

"*Shadahd*," she said proudly.

Katz looked at Gavin as if for an answer, then shrugged. "What is Krogan doing?" he asked.

"Comprehendo discipulus," she said, laughing condescendingly.

"Seizing disciples," Steinman said.

"Christians?" Katz asked.

"Sic."

"Why?"

"Concutio."

"To terrorize," Steinman said.

"Why?"

"Contemptus infirmus, inanis, laudator. Desipio."

"They're useless, weak, contemptible praisers who make asses of themselves."

"What will you do with them?"

Karianne laughed louder. "Cruor. Carnifico. Eviscero. Connubium. Diripio. Deleo," she yelled, her eyes flaming with intensity.

Steinman looked queasy. He paused until Katz finally motioned for him to speak. "She says they will rape and slaughter them. They will behead, mangle, disembowel, and tear them to pieces until they are all gone forever."

Gavin quickly cleared the dry-erase board and wrote, *Don't let Karianne witness this stuff. Find out if Dorjan knows how Krogan dies.*

Katz nodded quickly, as if he had been thinking the same thing.

"Does Dorjan know how Krogan's body dies?"

"Sic," she said delightedly.

"Did you see him die?"

"Sic. *Shadahd*," she proclaimed. "Mons via. Raeda. Abruptus clivas. Petra."

"She keeps speaking in imagery, not complete sentences. I believe she's saying Krogan was on a mountain road in a large horse-drawn wagon full of captives and he drove it off a steep hillside and crashed it into a rock."

"Was that correct, Dorjan?"

"Sic."

"Were you with Krogan?"

"Sic."

"Did you die, too?"

"Sic."

Gavin cleared his throat to catch Katz's attention, then signaled a time-out with his hands and motioned for Katz to follow him into the foyer.

"How's she doing?" Gavin asked.

"She seems to be holding her ground well while in regression. I'll have to be very careful bringing her back to this time, but in the other lives she's remarkably solid."

"How much more can we press her?" Gavin asked, looking at his watch. "It's after ten. We've been at this for more than three hours."

"Actually, we are the ones affected by the time. For all intents and purposes she's asleep. As long as she doesn't pop out like she did before, she'll outlast us."

"Then let's keep going. In each life I want you to key in on what Krogan is doing and how he dies. Find out if he ever gets arrested. And how."

"Are you sure you want to continue? We've already covered a lot of ground tonight. There's always tomorrow."

"Forget tomorrow! The problem isn't if Krogan is going to be stopped. It's when. He's not a pro. He just kills and escapes. He doesn't do much to cover his tracks, and if we wait, sooner or later we'll get him. But in the meantime he'll continue to do just what he's been doing apparently since who knows when. He kills recklessly until he or someone else sends him into the next life. And as far as I'm concerned, his time in this one is way overdue. Now . . . Let's get some coffee and get back to our history lesson."

Suddenly, or so it seemed, morning light invaded the darkness outside the living room windows. Gavin, in disbelief that so much time could have passed, checked his watch. To his surprise, dawn was still keeping its regular schedule. His eyes were burning from lack of rest and his stomach was burning from coffee acid. Katz's speech was slurred and Steinman had to be regularly reminded to translate into English, not German or French or, once, Japanese. Amy, who had been keeping scrupulous notes from the outset, occasionally jerked her head upward after unintentionally slipping into sleep.

Gavin was trying his best to stay objective under the bizarre and sometimes frightening circumstances. Although there was nothing in his training that dealt with past lives and finding clues in historical nightmares, he had been trained to focus and find patterns in the midst of chaos, whether they made sense or not. And there were patterns. They had found that whenever they were together, Krogan was always the leader and Karianne's host, male or female, was always the follower. Krogan, for whatever reason, was always male. Another strange coincidence was that they always seemed to be under the influence; every reunion was one of drunkenness and destruction and almost every life ended in tragedy. They never seemed to live past thirty-five years of age.

Katz sat back in the folding chair and dabbed with his white handkerchief at his puffy, drooping eyes. Gavin didn't know if the tears were from fatigue or sorrow.

Maybe both. "I need a break," Katz said. "If I could just close my eyes for a little while, I'd . . ."

"Get some rest, Doc," Gavin said. "I think we've pushed as far as we can for now. We need to compare notes when we can all think straight."

Gavin also needed a break. The fact all this reincarnation crap was actually becoming plausible to him made him desperate for sleep. A rested mind could function at a level impossible for him now. He had to rest.

Amy stood up and stretched her arms toward the ceiling, then slowly lowered them to her side, moving her head back and forth until a small pop was heard. After a second's hesitation, Gavin walked up behind her, rested his hands on the top of her shoulders, and lightly massaged her neck. She sighed gratefully.

"Would you like me to drive you home so you can sleep for a while or would you rather lay down in Karianne's room? According to Katz she won't need her bed. She's had the equivalent of a full night's sleep by now," Gavin said, hoping she would opt for Karianne's bed. He was too tired to drive and needed only a pillow and a place on the carpet for a couple of hours.

"Neither," Amy said. "I want you to take me for a drive in the country."

Gavin was too tired to repeat himself or be humored. "There's beautiful country just the other side of that door," he said, motioning toward the bedroom.

"Then send me a postcard; I'll go upstate by myself," Amy said, bending over to put her notebook into her handbag.

It took Gavin a second to understand, as if his brain was on some kind of low-battery time delay. "Whoa! Where exactly is it you think you're going?"

"Upstate. The Catskills. I want to talk to the Reverend Jesse J. Buchanan."

"Now?"

"Yes. It's Saturday morning. The perfect time," Amy said, hanging her handbag strap on her shoulder.

"Aren't you too tired?" Katz asked. "The Catskills are a good three hours from here. Can't you simply call him?"

"Hamden is more like four hours and I want to talk to him in person."

Katz shook his head and dismissed her with a wave of his hand. "Then I'll take Karianne's bed."

Gavin watched Katz walk back away and felt the need to control a rising anger. Why did she have to be so pigheaded? "Amy, I want to talk to the Reverend Buchanan, too. But I need to check out the work list from the Lighting Company. We'll both think much better after a little think — I mean sleep. See? I can't even talk straight."

"We'll have plenty of time to sleep when we're dead," Amy quipped.

"The list is just as important as the Reverend Buchanan and has to be done first, while whatever evidence there might be is still fresh."

Amy paused for a long moment. "How long is the list?"

"There are several jobs here but there's an asterisk next to the last stop where work was completed. The truck was stolen somewhere between there and the next job that never got started. The two locations are less than a mile apart."

"You do the list, I'll go upstate."

Gavin sighed and massaged the bridge of his nose.

"What makes this Reverend Buchanan guy so important he can't wait?" Katz said, coming back from the living room. "I don't generally like to butt in, but you do need sleep. A four-hour drive could be dangerous."

"He's a strong lead," Gavin said.

"Strong lead? He was a victim," Katz countered.

"A victim the Norwegian police questioned and released begrudgingly because he admitted to knowing the killer's identity. And Karianne had spoken of him as Krogan's enemy."

"With Krogan's face and name on the front page of the newspaper, don't you think he would call if he had something of value he was willing to share?"

"That's just it. He's not willing," Gavin said.

Amy started walking toward the door. "If you want to get some shut-eye I'll understand."

"You'll understand?" Gavin said.

"Yeah, where your priorities are."

"Oh, and where are they?"

"Eat, sleep, work, eat, sleep, work, eat, sleep, work," she said, motioning with her hand at different imaginary levels in the air with work always getting the lowest level.

Gavin rolled his eyes at her attempt to make him feel guilty, but was too tired to fight her silver tongue. Amy opened the door and without hesitation started to close it behind herself.

"Amy," he called. "Wait."

She stopped, but didn't turn around.

Apparently, the more tired she got the more stubborn she got — just like him.

"We'll do both," he said. "I guess a little change of scenery would do me good and I do want to be there when Buchanan is questioned," he said. "But first the list."

She turned around and faced him. "Do *us* good," she said, the hardness gone from her voice. "I'll make sure you stay awake."

Gavin looked at her — her beautiful eyes now heavy-lidded red slits. He managed a thin smile. "A job you do very well. But who's going to keep *you* awake?"

Gavin dropped Amy off at her house to freshen up then went home to feed a lonely Cedar, shower, and change his clothes. The shower and new clothes felt good, but were no substitute for sleep. By the time he got back to Amy's, she was sitting on the front brick stoop. She slung her handbag over her shoulder and walked toward him. She had traded in her usual play clothes for new jeans, a sage-green V-neck T-shirt, and a blazer that matched her eyes. As she got closer Gavin could also see she was wearing makeup. Gavin wondered if it was possible for her not to look absolutely stunning.

"Excuse me," he said as she got into the

car. "Do I know you?"

"I doubt it," she said with a sly smile and a slanted look.

"I suppose the next thing you'll want is to carry my shield?"

"Some of us don't need a badge to stop traffic," she said smartly.

To that he had no reply.

— 30 —

"Dead end," Gavin said, pointing at the yellow road sign before turning onto the street. He looked at the Lighting Company's work sheet, then up at the street sign, then pulled his car to the side of the road and parked. For the next few moments he and Amy stared in silence at the street before them. With the exception of one dilapidated house at the end of the block, the street was empty of homes. There were no sidewalks, only rubbish-riddled overgrown vacant lots on either side with a few rusted-out, abandoned cars.

"This was where the guy was killed?" Amy finally said.

"This was the last recorded place he worked," Gavin said, getting out of the car.

"What was he doing here?" she said, joining Gavin.

He pointed up to the lone transformer

on a telephone pole. "Working on that gray can."

"Eww," Amy said in a shiver and folded her arms. "This has to be where it happened. No wonder nobody reported it. Who would see anything?"

"You never know," Gavin said, walking toward the pole. "Maybe someone from that lumberyard or that house."

"If anyone even lives there," she said, following slowly.

Gavin stopped and waited for Amy to catch up. Her arms were still folded as if she were cold. "If he was working on the pole when he was shot, the arrow would probably have come from this direction."

"How do you know that?"

"The first arrow was in the right shoulder. Assuming he was facing the pole while working . . ."

"But how do you know what arrow was first?"

"The arrow in the neck killed him. There would be no further need to send another arrow after that."

"Wait a minute. You mean the worker was shot in the bucket and Krogan just left him in there, driving around town?"

"Apparently."

"Could he have still been alive?"

"It's possible."

"Eww." Amy shivered again.

Gavin walked to the abandoned car and looked up at the transformer on the pole. He noticed some fresh scratches in the rust on the trunk and shook his head. "I bet when we get a tech here we find Krogan's prints and traces of the arrows' paint in these scratches."

"Right here," Amy said, pointing.

"Don't touch," Gavin said, pushing her hand away. "He may as well have signed his name while he was at it." He turned around and looked back at the cross street. "He was probably driving by when he saw the truck he wanted right there," he motioned. "Easy pickings. This psychopath has zero conscience."

"Almost like it's all a game," Amy said.

Gavin walked over to the pole and looked at the ground. He'd expected to see blood but realized now it had probably been contained in the bucket. He then scanned the area again in all directions.

"Go wait in the car. I'll be right there."

"Where are you going?"

"Over to that house. Maybe someone over there saw something."

"Do you think somebody actually lives

in that shack? And isn't it too early? It isn't even seven yet."

"It's never too early in this business."

"Well, then, I'm coming with you. This place gives me the creeps. For all we know he might be in one of those cars."

Krogan's eyes opened at the familiar creak of his porch stairs. His newly acquired wristwatch told him it was way too early for friendly visitors. In a moment he was out of bed and peering through his cobwebbed front window. He had to squint; his dilated, bloodshot eyes were not ready for the sunrise. He didn't remember going to bed, but it couldn't have been long ago. His head ached and his parched mouth needed a drink, preferably beer so his thinking would clear. A drink in the morning was the best remedy for a hangover.

His pained eyes widened with surprise. "A ghost," he said to himself as he focused on the two people stepping onto his porch. The man looked familiar, but the woman . . . He didn't need to see her in a bathing suit to recognize she was that same Asian wench that had been on the boat he rammed. Apparently she hadn't been killed. As he wondered why, he suddenly remembered where he had seen the man she was with; he'd seen him get into that van with the cop he'd crashed into. He was probably the detective the newspaper had said to contact. He couldn't remember the name; his mind was still half drunk and asleep.

He watched the intruders a moment longer as they nosed around. "Oh, no. You found me," he mocked in a low, quiet voice that sounded more like a growl. "Found, but not caught." He quietly stole away from the window and reached under his bed for his compound bow.

A moment later he was standing naked at his bedroom doorway, swiftly setting a triple-razor broad-head arrow into the bow. Weapon ready, he stepped to the center of his darkened living room. He was invisible to his visitors, but their bodies were silhouetted against the thin curtain covering the glass window of his door. They were talking to each other, but he couldn't hear what they were saying.

Krogan's attention momentarily detoured to the body of a naked woman on the floor by his kitchen doorway. Then he remembered the Harley in his backyard and how he'd dragged her into the house.

He didn't remember what had happened to her clothes and wondered if she was dead. She looked dead — face down, her arms and legs outstretched and limp.

He returned his focus to the front door. Though groggy, he effortlessly drew back the powerful bow and leveled his sights on the taller shadow's head. His choice of whom to shoot first was easy. The girl would react with fear at seeing an arrow go through the man's head, which would make dealing with her more fun. He could play with her for a while, or have her for breakfast. He was curiously excited, wondering whether she would faint or scream.

The taller shadow reached for the doorbell. Krogan snickered. The doorbell had never worked. Another example of his father starting something and never finishing it. He watched the shadow knock gently on the glass. The wimp. If he was going to call this early he should at least have the courage to knock with authority.

Krogan lowered his sights to the hand. Though his eyes were as blurry as his mind, the hand was a slightly more challenging shot. Besides, only wounding him would set things up for a fun hunt as they tried to hide from him.

The smaller shadow said something and rapped hard on the door, obviously agreeing the detective was a coward. She was determined . . . and probably not the type to faint. The taller shadow pulled her hand away but she quickly snatched it back and said something. She then moved her head about as if trying to peek inside. Feisty, Krogan noted.

"Greetings," he growled, now zeroing the arrow's point on the center of her right palm, flattened on the glass. He was about to release, but paused as a half-sober thought came to mind: maybe he hadn't been found. They didn't have guns drawn and there were no police cars or cops surrounding the house. They must have somehow found out the electric utility truck had been on this street and were probably looking for a witness.

Krogan lowered the bow. As much as he wanted to properly greet his guests, he was now thinking just enough to realize it would cost him. After his fun was over he would no longer be able to return home.

As the shadows finally left the front door he went back to the window to make sure they were leaving the property. For a moment he watched them walk down the block to their car, then he flopped back onto his bed. He could have them later, whenever he wanted. He warmed to that thought as he fell back to sleep.

— 32 —

"Can we go now?" Amy said, standing beside the car as impatient as ever.

Gavin tried to ignore her as he recapped instructions to the uniform cop standing before him, making doubly sure he had conveyed everything and was understood.

"Got it. Don't worry. Go have a good time with your wife before she leaves without you," the cop said, motioning toward the car.

Gavin started to correct him but instead just nodded. He had been mostly appreciative of Amy's help, but he didn't like being rushed away from a probable crime scene. The fact he'd only managed to station a single patrol car at the end of the block to maintain the site until the techs got there was disturbing. He wanted to personally point out his own findings and suggest his own theories, not relay secondhand messages. Experience had shown him more could be learned from the logic produced during random crime-scene chitchat than an entire stack of investigative reports. Amy, though, was driven in another direction. That Reverend Buchanan supposedly knew Krogan was all the logic she needed.

Three hours later, Gavin was driving through the green rolling hills of the Catskills mountain range. The hours of engine hum, wind noise, and flashing road lines had worked as well as any metronome Katz could have produced. Amy was out cold. The lack of conversation, mixed with too much strong coffee, had ignited Gavin's hyper-focused mind. Too many questions with no acceptable answers. Instead of enjoying the fact he was finally getting the chance to drive his little sports car on country roads or that right now he had the soft-top down on a perfect sunny morning with a beautiful woman at his side, he was rehashing last night's session with Karianne. Was any of it real? He felt like he had entered a time machine and taken statements from over two dozen character witnesses from across the ages — witnesses to crimes committed by the same man he was now hunting. Without the videotape, who would ever believe him? He kept rearranging the pieces of Krogan's puzzle — the consistencies and the incongruous. Maybe something would click.

He had never seen Amy so quiet for so long. She'd been sound asleep for almost the entire trip. Earlier, she had opened her eyes only briefly when Gavin pulled the little lever to recline her seat. He glanced at her now as he had done throughout the trip, the one pleasurable divergence he allowed himself. But even that relief was tainted. As she lay there peacefully, the sun warming her golden skin and the wind playing with her hair, Gavin was cruelly reminded of when he'd first seen her twin sister in the hospital.

During the first hour of their trip, when Amy was awake, she'd reread her notes aloud. Noting that Krogan liked to tattoo himself with his name, she'd wondered if he might have had his name put on a vanity license plate. Gavin had told her the department did have some experience in tracing names and a vanity plate check was standard procedure. He then told her he'd already made a note to check the local tattoo parlors, but figured Krogan had probably gotten tattooed abroad, possibly in Norway.

Another pattern Amy had brought up was Krogan's apparent preference for Jewish blood; more than half of Krogan's victims in the interviews, which included the early Christians, were Jewish. Just another tidbit that didn't seem to fit anywhere. And then there was the celebration at Jesus' crucifixion — Krogan's happiest moment, according to Karianne.

Coming over the ridge of the Downsville pass, Gavin could see the small historic town of Hamden in the valley below. Hamden was nestled cozily within pine-clustered mountains and grassy foothills. Running parallel to Route 10, the only main road, was the Delaware River. This far north, the river was barely fifteen feet wide and appeared too shallow for anything larger than an inner tube or kayak.

"Come on, Sleeping Beauty. Time to wake up," Gavin said, patting Amy's left thigh.

Amy stretched her arms upward and smiled. "But I don't want to go to school today." She pulled herself upright by the armrest, with the back of the seat following her. "Wow! We're not in Kansas anymore, are we?" She turned and looked at Gavin for a long moment. "Sorry I fell asleep. How are you doing?"

"Fine," Gavin said.

"Liar."

Upon entering the town, Gavin was halted by a girl wearing a yellow hard hat and waving a bright orange flag. The road ahead was under construction and Gavin had to wait.

"When all of this is over, I'm going to get a job like hers," Amy said.

Gavin suddenly had to shake off a thought that came from nowhere, of Amy directing traffic and then unsuccessfully trying to stop a wild car headed right for her. He shivered as he saw the impact in his mind's eye and then saw Krogan laughing through the car's window.

"What's wrong?" Amy asked, apparently having seen Gavin wince.

"Nothing," he said, not very convincingly.

Amy frowned, but didn't pursue it.

Hamden appeared to be no more than a dozen houses on either side of the road with one store in the middle on the right. The river ran behind the store. A small rectangular sign several yards away read "Hamden, founded 1797." Gavin figured the town had not gone through too many facelifts since. The modern machines tearing up the road appeared out of place next to the old homes surrounding them.

The girl waved them on. A hundred feet further, where the construction actually began, the paved road suddenly became a packed gravel subsurface. Oddly, the gravel gave the old town a more authentic feel.

Gavin pulled over in front of the store and parked. The sign hanging over the old wood porch read "Hamden General Store." A smaller sign in the window revealed it was also the post office. Someone here would know where Samantha's Farm and the Reverend Buchanan were.

They parked and walked up the well worn, creaky steps of the porch. Next to the doorway was a rack of newspapers, none of which were familiar. An overhead bell jingled as they entered the store. The floor was sprinkled with sawdust and in the center of the wide main aisle was a large, black pot-bellied woodstove. Beyond it an elderly woman stood working behind a counter.

"Can I help you?" the old woman asked as Gavin and Amy approached. She was old enough to be Gavin's grandmother, bony and petite, with white hair tied up in a bun. She energetically stocked the shelf behind her as she spoke.

"We're trying to locate Reverend Jesse J.

Buchanan," Gavin said. "We understand he lives here in Hamden at Samantha's Farm."

"*Mr.* Buchanan," the old woman corrected. "You should know he doesn't like to be called Reverend anymore. Are you news people?"

Who is she, his secretary? Gavin thought. He pulled his shield from his pocket and dropped it on the counter. "I'm Detective Pierce. I was hoping Rev— Mr. Buchanan would be able to help us."

The old lady stopped working and looked at Gavin, then his badge, then suspiciously at Amy. "That of course would be up to him. A half mile north, take your first right. The first driveway on the left after you cross the river is Samantha's Dairy Farm. You can't miss it."

— 33 —

"Samantha's Dairy Farm" was hand painted in small lavender letters on the white mailbox. Gavin turned into the driveway and stopped before driving on. A wire fence, probably electrified, bordered the ascending dirt driveway on either side. On the right side of the driveway several brown cows stopped grazing to stare at them.

"Check it out," Amy said, pointing at the cows. "How adorable."

Gavin did a double-take when he saw the cows all had pink bows on their necks. "Can I trust you to not ride any of these?" Gavin said. Amy smiled.

He turned his attention to the house at the top of the driveway — a white two-story with pink shutters and a wraparound porch. Gavin thought it looked like a dollhouse; Amy said it was adorable. To the right of the house was the broad side of a white barn with about two dozen small windows running the length of it, all with pink shutters. Between the windows, large multicolored butterflies had been painted in detail. Several black crows perched along the ridgetop.

"Shouldn't the crows also have pink bows?" Gavin asked.

"Definitely. Look!" Amy said. A large bird circled high over the barn. "That must be an eagle, or a hawk."

Gavin wanted to tell her which it was, but the truth was he didn't know. For some reason he felt embarrassed by that, like he should know such things. The bird circled effortlessly, without even a single flap of its wings to maintain its lofty height, then drifted over their heads. Both Gavin and Amy craned their necks around, following the majestic creature's flight over the valley fields that bordered the river.

The country setting was beautiful and serene, a place Gavin could easily imagine getting used to. But why had Reverend Buchanan come here? Why had he left his congregation in New Jersey? Was it because this was "God's Country"? Was it an escape in the wilderness? Escape from what? Krogan?

Suddenly the great bird stopped drifting across the sky, flapping its wings to hold its position. Then, as if for the thrill of its audience, it tucked its wings and fell headfirst like a meteorite to the earth until the high grass of a nearby field swallowed it up. Gavin and Amy looked at each other with wide eyes then, without a word, unbuckled their seat belts and kneeled on their seats, craning for a better view. The tall golden grass moved lazily in the gentle breeze without evidence anything had happened. Just as Gavin wondered if he had witnessed one of nature's strangest ritualistic suicides, the bird suddenly swept back in the air with a limp animal in its claws.

"Shoot!" Amy said. "How would you like to be that poor little guy? One second you're enjoying a great day in the sunshine, sniffing for roots and seeds, the next second, boom, you're dead . . . in the claws of a giant flying monster."

Gavin said nothing. He could not help but see the bird as Krogan, crashing into Amy's brother-in-law off the fishing pier, leaving his limp, lifeless body half crushed under the car that had pounced on him.

" 'The brave live as long as the coward allows,' " he said.

Amy looked at him quizzically. "You okay?" she asked lightly.

"Yeah." They both turned and slid back

into their seats. "Say good-bye to the muffler," he added as he slowly started what looked to be a bumpy ride up the driveway.

"Not that I'm real up on this, but I've never heard of reverends or ministers or preachers, or whatever you call them, working a dairy farm," Amy said.

"Mr. Buchanan, remember," Gavin warned. "And I get the impression he's no longer a preacher."

"Don't you think we should let him correct us just in case the old lady was wrong?"

"I suppose you're right. Calling someone Reverend isn't exactly an insult," Gavin said.

"Unless he no longer wants to be associated with his old ministry," Amy said after a moment of thought.

"We'll find out soon enough."

"What about you, Gavin. What are your beliefs?"

"Why?" Gavin said.

"Well, if the subject comes up I don't want to be shocked. Partners should know what each other's beliefs are."

Gavin looked at Amy, wondering if she was serious. Her reasoning had merit, but now was not the time to open a possible can of worms. "I'm a Christian. I don't know much about the details, but I know that."

"So you believe in loving God and loving your neighbor?"

"Yeah. And I also believe in my gun inside Krogan's mouth," he said, really not wanting to get into this now.

"Wonderful," she said sarcastically. "Now I feel I really know you."

"Sorry. You get what you see."

"What about reincarnation?"

"What about it?"

"Well, have you seen enough with Karianne to at least believe in that?"

"I've seen enough to know I haven't seen enough."

"Now that's deep."

"What do you believe?" he said defensively.

"I believe there's something going on behind the scenes."

Gavin looked at her again. She was staring at him as if she hadn't appreciated his shortness with her. He knew he should be touched she wanted to know him better. If only he wasn't so tired and wired. He couldn't remember the last time anyone had cared what he believed. "It cuts across my basic beliefs. But to tell you the truth, I'd never really thought much about reincarnation before Katz brought it up."

"And now?"

"Now it's a distraction. Katz can't keep his mind on the case. Look, if you really want to get into this, I promise you my full attention . . . later." She nodded.

Gavin stopped the car in front of a bluestone path that led to the porch entrance. The path was generously bordered by a billowy procession of colorful annuals that extended up to and surrounded the base of the porch. The sweet fragrance brought high praise from the various bees and butterflies that danced about the flower tops. Gavin and Amy walked up the path, he with a newspaper rolled up in his hand. The porch steps were in far better condition than the ones at the store. They felt solid and appeared to have been recently painted, as did the rest of the porch. An assortment of potted plants hung from the roof beam, all of them well kept and flourishing in the southern exposure. The warm, light breeze wandering up the hill would have gone unnoticed if not for several small wind chimes tinkling pleasantly, two of them over a wicker porch swing. Somehow, even the unmistakable scent of cow manure was not offensive.

As he walked to the door, Gavin looked

longingly at the swing with its tufted pastel cushions. The coffee he had been pumping through his veins was losing its battle to keep his eyes open and the cushions looked very comfortable. In fact, the porch floor looked comfortable.

He searched for a doorbell, but couldn't find one. By default, he pinched a polished brass horseshoe doorknocker and gently clacked it three times.

"What have we got here?" Amy said as a snow-white cat brushed up against her leg, purring. "Where's Daddy?" she asked the cat as it prowled affectionately around and between her legs, tail held high.

Gavin tried to peek through a window next to the door, but the white lace curtains made it impossible to see anything. All this dainty femininity. The emphasis in Samantha's Farm was obviously Samantha. Like the old lady had said, you couldn't miss it.

He gave the door three more clacks, then listened hard with his ear close to the door, hoping to hear some movement. Nothing. He backed away from the door with his hands on his hips, turned, and looked out from the porch. The magnetic view and the fact the Reverend was not there was all the excuse he needed to wait in the swing with Amy. But, no. He was certain he would fall asleep and had no wish to awaken to the view of someone's shotgun pointed at his nose.

"Nobody's here," he said, then pointed to the barn. "Maybe there."

The door in the middle of the north side of the barn was wide open. They walked over and stepped inside, looking around. The entrance divided a long center aisle with cows parked in milking stations on either side. Not surprisingly, they also had pink ribbons. "Hello," Gavin called. Turning left, he saw the back of a man at the far end, busy at work.

"Excuse me," Gavin said, walking toward him. The man made no reply. Gavin motioned for Amy to follow him and started down the aisle. The cows were facing away with a single chain to keep them from backing into the aisle. Each chain had a little name plaque dangling from it. Gavin shook his head as he read some of the names. Cutzie . . . Cinnamon . . . Cuddles . . . Fuzzy . . . Sweetie Pie . . . They sounded more like names of little pet rabbits than cows. Just behind each cow's back feet was a gutter drain for their urine and manure to fall into — a scene that hardly went with "Cutzie."

"Hello," Gavin repeated, louder this time. Still the man continued to work under the back of a cow. Gavin and Amy continued until they were but a few feet from him. "Excuse me, sir," Gavin said.

"That's Gregory," said a raspy, deep voice that could have belonged to James Earl Jones after a swig or two of kerosene. "He can't hear you."

Gavin and Amy turned to see a black man of medium build with a little bit of a paunch, bold white hair, and a white mustache. He appeared in his mid-sixties and wore jeans, work boots, and a white T-shirt.

"We're looking for Reverend Buchanan," Gavin said.

"Nobody worth being revered around here. Least of all me." The man held up his hand. "Name's Buck. How can I help you?"

The old lady had been right. But why, Gavin wondered, not buying the humility angle just yet. "I'm Detective Pierce. This is my . . . assistant, Amy Kirsch. We were disconnected on the phone, what was it, two days ago? I don't know anymore what day it is. I'm sorry, but my list of leads is too short to scratch you off."

"You've come a long way, Detective. I'm

sorry if I seemed rude on the phone. I don't like being rude."

Suddenly, there came a noise from behind them. Gregory had apparently been startled by their presence. Buck smiled calmly and quickly spoke to him in sign language. The man signed back and then went back to his work. Gavin was impressed by Buck's choice of a second language.

"Now, Detective," Buck said, returning his attention to them. "Your persistence is admirable and I'm sure it will lead you to the man you seek, but as I tried to tell you over the phone, I cannot help you find him."

"Can you tell us why?" Gavin said, trying to stay calm.

"Well, for one, I don't know where he is," Buck said with a shrug.

"Are you telling us that you do know *who* he is?" Gavin said.

"Detective, I don't mean to confuse you, but you don't know what you're asking me and I can't explain it."

Gavin frowned. "Don't you at least want to know what we know about him?"

The ex-preacher paused, as if the question needed careful consideration. He looked at Gavin and then at Amy and then at Gregory, who was silently tending to his simple tasks. "No," Buck said.

"Buck," Amy said sweetly. "We've traveled far to find you. Won't you please at least hear us out?"

Buck furrowed his bushy white brows and sighed. "You did come a long way. I suppose there's no harm in listening. God knows I've asked the same of a congregation often enough."

Amy winked at Gavin's disbelieving expression. He could have begged and pleaded until the pink-ribboned cows were wearing steak sauce and he wouldn't have been shown anything but the exit. But a few bats of her emerald greens and her foot had slipped right into the front door. Well, he supposed he couldn't fault Buck; he'd been there more than a few times himself.

"Like I started to tell you over the phone," Gavin said. "We believe we are after the same man who killed your family and we don't believe any of it is an accident. We're tracking down leads in connection with the serial killer the media has dubbed the Ghost Driver." He closely watched Buck's expression.

"Forgive me, Detective. I've never heard of the Ghost Driver. The only newspaper I read is a local one that keeps me in touch with some of the needs of the valley. I don't own a TV. I find it distracting. And the only time I turn the radio on is if the Angels are playing the Devil Rays."

Gavin looked at him in confusion.

"I'm sorry. I can't seem to get away from corny pulpit humor," Buck said.

"Oh, yeah. The Angels. I get it," Gavin said. He didn't smile. He wanted to ask Buck if anyone around here watched TV or read the papers. The man did live in the sticks a couple of hundred miles from Long Island, but Gavin still found it hard to believe Buck hadn't heard of Krogan — if not through the media, then at least through local conversation.

"Does the name Karianne Stordal ring a bell?"

Buck's congenial smile evaporated as his eyes froze onto Gavin's.

"Was she in an accident?" he asked with a look of concern, his eyes unblinking.

"Uh, yes," Gavin said, surprised.

"Did she survive?"

"Yes. But what made you think she was in an accident?"

The preacher-turned-farmer had closed his eyes. "Thank you," he said. "Thank you, Lord."

Gavin looked at Amy, who shrugged as they both watched Buck continue to give thanks for the spared life of someone who had been in the assailing car that had killed his family. They waited a long moment until the old man seemed finished.

"Buck?" Amy said softly.

"Passenger-side air bag, I presume?" Buck said, without any explanation of his reflexive prayer response to Karianne's well-being.

"Exactly. But how —"

"I'm sorry, Detective. She was in the car that collided with us in Norway, as I'm sure you know. I just assumed something similar," Buck said, looking in Gregory's direction.

"That's quite an assumption, Buck. I mention her name and you immediately assume she was in a crash? From what we know, the only other crash she's ever been in was with you."

Buck was silent.

"Buck, please tell us what you know," Amy said.

The old man shook his head. "The last time I did that the local media misquoted me, made a mockery of my words, and went behind my back to interview my granddaughter."

Amy looked at Gavin, as if to acknowledge she had missed something in her research. "We're not the media, Buck."

"It doesn't matter. I know nothing that would help you get who you're looking for."

"Why don't you let us be the judge of that?" Gavin said quickly, his natural intensity difficult to mask.

"Did you know Karianne was going to be in another . . . accident, Buck?" Amy said gently.

"I hoped not. I'm glad she owned a car with modern safety devices."

"Who said it was her car?" Gavin said.

"I just assumed."

"I understand," Amy said quickly, before Gavin could say anything. Her look told him to lighten up.

"How bad were the others hurt?" Buck said with concern.

"Who said there were any others?" Gavin said.

"There're always others," Buck said. His eyes briefly lost focus and Gavin was suddenly unsure if this was a conversation Buck was having with him or with himself.

"This Ghost Driver," Buck said. "How long have you been chasing him, Detective?"

"Personally, about a month. Though the calendar seems to be a bit blurry right now."

"And how many other suspicious accidents have there been in that time?" Buck asked, now curious.

"It's starting to get hard to count. Firsthand, I know of four — and one outright murder with an arrow — but I've heard of others," Gavin said, wondering who was questioning whom. "What else do you want to know?"

Buck closed his eyes and shook his head slowly. "Once you start there's no place to stop," he said softly.

On paper, interviews always look so logical, so simple. Painless. See Reverend Buchanan and get information. If he resists, press on until resistance breaks down. Use whatever tool works. Real life wasn't so simple. Buck leaned on a post looking like a man who had just been dropped into a room where every exit read "Do Not Enter."

"Please," Amy said. "We need your help."

"You want me to tell you Norway's problem is now New York's problem?" Buck said.

"If it's true, that's exactly what we want,"

Gavin said. "And anything else you could tell us."

Buck paused for a long moment before answering. "I'm sorry, Detective. I can't do this. The information I have is not information you can use. Believe me when I tell you what I know can only get you hurt."

"Bull!" Gavin snapped. The lack of sleep had worn his patience and tact clean away. The man before him was a witness and he was ready to dig through granite with a toothpick if need be.

"Easy," Amy said.

"Detective, you don't know what you're asking of me. I have to think of my granddaughter first."

"Your granddaughter? What does she have to do with anything?" Gavin asked. "If she's in danger, we can protect her a lot better than you can, hiding up here."

Buck closed his eyes and shook his head. "Not you or your whole department can protect her from him."

"Why?" Gavin demanded. Again, maybe the fatigue was responsible, but he felt tears waiting to spill and knew he was losing it. He wasn't familiar with the interrogation procedures of the Norwegian police department, but he knew for sure that if Krogan had killed a cop's family member, Buck wouldn't have gotten out of there alive without telling what he knew.

"Look Rev— Mr. — Buck. I'm not just some cop investigating a murder. This psycho scum killed my grandfather, my friend, and a reporter that was working with me to hunt him down. He also killed Amy's brother-in-law and put her twin sister in the hospital, where she's been in a coma for the last couple of weeks. And thanks to him, my partner's in the hospital, too. Not to mention the dozens of others that just happened to get in his way in the wrong place at the wrong time. I don't know what you think you can't tell us, but if it can give us even the slightest edge, I want it, and I want it now."

He took a deep, shaky breath and felt Amy's hand slip into his and squeeze.

Buck's poker face seemed to soften as he stared at them. "You won't believe me," he said.

"Try me," Gavin said. "After what I've seen and heard in the last twenty-four hours, I can believe anything."

Buck looked down at the ground and spoke softly. "Don't you think I would tell you if I thought it would do any good?"

Gavin shrugged. "Can it do any harm? He doesn't know we're here. Nobody does.

We left spontaneously after spending all night interrogating Karianne."

Buck quickly looked up. "Did you mention my name to her? Where I was? That I'm still alive?"

Gavin and Amy looked at each other.

"I don't think so," Amy said with a confused frown.

"Are you sure we're talking about the same person, Buck?" Gavin said, wondering how in the world anyone could be afraid of Karianne.

"It's not her I'm concerned with."

Gavin closed his eyes. It was the lack of sleep, he decided. It had to be that. He seemed to be missing something.

"Detective, if I tell you what I know, you will at some point want me to get involved. You'll want me to come with you."

"That's crazy," Gavin said. "All we want from you is facts, not physical help."

"It's not the physical help I mind," Buck said.

"I promise you that you will have nothing to worry about."

"You promise what you can't."

"Hi, Grandpa!" said a cheery voice from behind Buck.

Buck turned and opened his arms. "Hello, Precious," he said lovingly as a young girl skipped energetically to his embrace. The strands of hay weaved into her thick, pony-tailed brown hair, the smudges of dirt on her white T-shirt and cut-off jeans, along with the dried clay on the knees of her skinny legs were all glaring evidence she had just been out in the field somewhere, probably playing with her cows and chickens. This place was an eleven-year-old girl's dream come true. Gavin was suddenly saddened by the thought of shattered dreams and priceless memories whispered into the ears of her oversized pets.

"Samantha, this is Mr. Pierce and . . . Miss Kirsch, is it?"

"Yes," Amy said, giving the little girl a big smile.

"This is my granddaughter, Samantha," Buck continued. "She's the boss here, aren't ya, honey?"

"Yup," she said with pretty, saucer-shaped eyes and a wide grin that showed off perfect white teeth.

Gavin was amazed at how Buck's demeanor changed upon seeing his granddaughter. All the concern that had a moment ago carved his face was now replaced with bright eyes and dimples.

"It sounds like the cows agree," Amy

said, commenting on the stir the little girl produced when the cows heard her young voice.

"Yessirree! What she says, goes," Buck said. "Sammy, why don't you check on Gregory — make sure he's doing a good job. I'm going to show our guests up to the house for a drink of iced tea."

— 34 —

Gavin didn't know he liked the rustic, farm-house look until he sat down in Buck's kitchen. The wide-planked pine floors, the butcher's block counters, the black-iron stove, and the age-darkened hemlock walls brought to mind thoughts of things like fresh apple pie and homemade vanilla ice cream. Not that Gavin had ever had homemade ice cream. He found himself suddenly craving it, wondering what it would taste like. He shook his head. He really needed a nap.

"I'd do anything for her," Buck was saying, placing a large pitcher of iced tea on the kitchen table. The tea was amber in color, with lemons floating in it. "After the crash, I was the only one left to look after her. She liked animals, so we moved to a farm."

"Lots of people like animals, Buck. Why not stay in New Jersey, get a cat?" Gavin said.

Buck gazed into the distorted reflections of the ice-tea pitcher. "To be honest, the crash and all the attention it drew caused me to reevaluate my situation. I . . . we lost so much. I needed to get away for a while. Maybe longer than a while."

"It must have been very hard for you," Amy said warmly.

Buck nodded, then broke his gaze and retrieved three glasses. "I've heard it said death is natural; it's part of life. I tend to think not. God didn't create us to die. He created us to live. Dealing well with death wasn't included in the equipment God originally created us with . . ." He realized he was rambling. "I'm sorry, I guess I could have just said yes. I've a habit of giving long answers to short questions."

"Well, how about a long answer to this?" Gavin unrolled the newspaper with Krogan's name and face on the cover and held it before Buck. "You said you'd never heard of the Ghost Driver. Do you recognize this man?" he asked.

Buck stared for what seemed like a full minute without taking his eyes off the page or saying a word. Then, finally, he looked up and said, "I'm very acquainted with the name, but I've never seen that face before."

Gavin frowned. "Are you sure? Your accident was five years ago and this is only an artist's rendering. You might have to use your imagination a bit."

Buck smiled compassionately. "I am sorry, Detective, but I'm certain I've never seen this face. I may be old, but I have a good memory for names and faces."

Gavin straightened. He snatched the newspaper off the table and dangled it in Buck's face. "This isn't Krogan?" he said, his voice raising.

"Well, no, but —"

"But you're saying Krogan is the correct name?"

"Yes," Buck said. "Krogan *is* the name of the one you're after. I really can't imagine how you found out, but Krogan is the name of the one behind the killings. But you —"

"We've had this face on the front page of a million newspapers. Karianne said she was with Krogan and was extremely confident this was him. And the bartender also described this guy as the one whom she was with," Gavin said, frustrated. "Are you sure this isn't him?"

Buck sat forward. "Miss Stordal told you the name?"

"Yes," Amy said.

"She didn't remember at first, but under hypnosis she clearly indicated the man she was with was Krogan," Gavin pointed out.

"Hypnosis. I see," Buck said, nodding knowingly. "Before I tell you any more, would you two please tell me more of what's been happening with you."

Gavin shrugged. "Of course. To make a long story short —"

"No," Buck interrupted. "I was a preacher. I like the long story."

Gavin took Buck through everything step by step. He spared Buck some of the bloody details because Amy was there; he'd never painted more than a vague picture of her brother-in-law's death and saw no reason to upset her further. Buck listened intently, nodding occasionally as if he already knew what Gavin was going to say. Gavin told him about the lobster-claw roach clips and the unbelievably high alcohol content found in the blood of those who rode with Krogan and how they always turned out to be the vehicle's owner. Through all the talk of destruction, Buck never once so much as raised an eyebrow, not even when he was told of the premeditated attack on the Learjet with the bucket truck. Curiously, he seemed familiar with the ancient word, *shadahd*. Only when he was told of the hypnotic sessions with Katz did his expression change — he was clearly amused by Katz's explanation of reincarnation regarding Karianne's transmillennial encounters with Krogan.

"Thank you, Detective, for divulging what certainly must be some extremely confidential information. I promise to respect your trust," Buck said sincerely. "You've gathered an impressive array of data, but you're still missing the most important ingredient: truth."

"Tell me about it," Gavin said. "Every time I think I'm about to lay hold of the truth, I get ancient history and riddles. Truth is exactly what I'm here for, Buck. Plain, old-fashioned truth."

"You have pieces of truth, Detective. Krogan is not the man's real name."

"Come again?" Gavin said. "We shouldn't be looking for someone named Krogan?"

"Yes and no. Krogan controls the man you have sketched here."

"Controls? I don't understand. Are we dealing with organized crime or some kind of terrorist cell?" Gavin said, suddenly wondering if this old preacher had been involved in espionage. The details of destruction hadn't fazed him. What connections did this old guy have and with whom? That could explain his reasons for not wanting to talk.

"Terrorists? Absolutely," Buck said with a brief laugh. "You're dealing with devils, Detective. Concerned only with their own agenda."

Gavin wasn't sure if he understood what Buck was saying. Krogan was part of another terrorist plot? An operative? Could the FBI have been so wrong? Could he have? With the escalation of all the germ-agents and nuclear threats, who would have thought that an alcohol-crazed killer could actually turn out to be a terrorist?

"So Krogan is in control?" Gavin said.

"Yes, very much so."

"Then who is this?" Amy said, pointing to the newspaper. "If this is not the man who crashed into you, who is he?"

Buck poured the tea. "I don't know. The man who crashed into me is dead," he said sadly.

Buck's answer was as surprising as his concern for Karianne. Gavin looked at Amy and then back at Buck. "We thought Krogan was the one who crashed into you in Norway."

"It was Krogan. I know for sure now. We had eye contact while he was escaping the scene and I had been warned he would re-taliate. I couldn't stop him then and he saw I was dying. If he had known I was going to live he would have finished me off before leaving. Payback for messing with his friends."

Gavin sat back and slowly massaged his eyes. "I don't know. Maybe it's the tea. Maybe one of my coffees was drugged. But I'm having a hard time following this. I thought you said the man who crashed into you was dead. Is Krogan dead or alive?"

"If Krogan is now in control of the man you have sketched here, the man who collided with us in Norway is now dead. Krogan cannot control more than one person at a time."

Gavin nodded, although he had no idea why. He was as confused as ever. Was Buck saying the terrorist chain of command was only connected to one person at a time? "Krogan is not able to control more than one person at a time?"

"No, thank God. Not any more than it can die."

Gavin rolled his eyes. "Krogan can't die?"

"*It?*" Amy said.

"Yes, my dear, *it*. I told you, you're

358

dealing with devils. They're immortal. You can't kill them. They can't die."

There was a long moment of silence.

"Devils as in . . . demons?" Amy said.

"Yes, demons."

"Real demons?" Gavin said incredulously. "The terrorists you're talking about are demons? As in evil spirits, horns, the devil?" He brought his index fingers to his head and mocked a set of horns.

"Gavin," Amy said, pulling down his arms.

"It's all right, my dear," Buck said. "I told you you wouldn't believe me. But you wanted the truth."

Gavin took a moment to let everything sink in. If he hadn't been so tired and far from home he would have simply thanked the preacher and left. But under the bizarre circumstance he had somehow allowed himself to fall into and with the colossal waste of time so completely unredeemable, all he could do was reveal a rare smile while shaking his head. "May I?" he said, reaching for the pitcher of iced tea.

"By all means, help yourself, my son."

"Thank you," Gavin said and filled his glass, then motioned it toward Amy. She nodded and he topped off her glass as well.

"Excellent iced tea, Buck."

"The secret is to not use more than two teabags per gallon and to not squeeze the lemons. Just let them sit and float overnight in the fridge."

"I'll have to remember that," Gavin said, then looked at Amy. If Chris Grella had been sitting in her seat, he would never have let him forget this. But Amy wasn't Chris. She was someone whom Gavin had allowed to enter into an arena she had no experience in. This was not her fault as much as it was his. It was a lesson for both of them and maybe next time she wouldn't be so headstrong.

"Now, Krogan . . ." Amy said, apparently wanting to proceed anyway.

"Yes."

"If he's . . . I mean, if *it's* busy controlling the guy in the sketch . . ."

"Yes."

"Then I suppose there's another demon talking to us through Karianne."

"Exactly."

"Buck, I don't suppose you have anything stronger than tea?" Gavin said, too tired to get mad at Amy for continuing. The smart thing would be to surrender for now and let her finish without interruption, if he could bear it. He would just have to refocus when they got back to the island.

"Wine?"

"I was thinking more like scotch."

"Sorry."

"Does the demon speaking to us through Karianne have a name?" Amy said.

Funny question, Gavin thought. Would Buck's delusion be so complete he could readily provide another demon's name? Or would he have to think about it? Gavin then tried to think of what he would name a demon if he were asked on the spot to produce one. Nothing came to mind.

"Yes, but you must promise me not to speak it in her presence," Buck said.

He's buying time to think, Gavin thought.

"Why?" Amy asked, as if she was actually interested.

"If you speak to a demon without the proper authority they tend to act badly."

Amy nodded. Gavin rolled his eyes.

"You must not take this warning lightly."

"We won't," Amy said reassuringly.

Buck looked at both of them for a long moment. "Sabah. You've been speaking to Sabah. Under hypnosis, Sabah has been talking through Miss Stordal."

Gavin had just lifted his tea to his

mouth, but pulled it back down. "Saahhbaaahhh?" he said, exaggerating Buck's pronunciation. He was sure he could have done better.

"Yes."

"Karianne is really a demon named Sabah?" Gavin said.

"No. Of course not. Haven't you been listening? Karianne is Karianne. Sabah is Sabah. Sabah is no more Karianne than the man on the cover of that newspaper is Krogan."

"Because Krogan's really a demon controlling the man," Amy said.

"That's right."

"Excuse me, but how could you possibly know the name of a demon in Karianne?" Gavin said.

Buck paused thoughtfully before answering. "Detective, have you ever been involved in deliverance?"

"Deliverance?"

"Yes. You might know it better as exorcism, thanks to a particular horror movie in the seventies that sensationalized something that for thousands of years has been treated very seriously by those who know and serve the Lord."

First Katz and his reincarnation, now this, Gavin thought. "I'm listening."

"Three days before the night of the crash in Norway, I was ministering deliverance at what you might call a church meeting, as I often did back then. Many were getting freed from demons of fear, depression, suicide, sarcasm, anger, bitterness, and a host of addictions. It was toward the end of the meeting that a young man pleaded with me to deliver him from a spirit of alcoholism."

"A spirit of alcoholism," Gavin said flatly. He wondered how many patients in psychiatric wards thought they could see and talk to demons. He was also wondering about Amy. Was she just playing psychologist or did she really believe this interview was getting them somewhere?

"That's correct."

"I thought alcoholism was a disease."

"It is a disease, but sometimes it's more."

"Go on, Buck," Amy said.

"I prayed for the young man and commanded the spirit to reveal its name."

"Now why would you do that?" Gavin interrupted.

"One, so I know what I'm dealing with, and two, because demons happen to be very legalistic; not unlike lawyers, they can be very exacting and deceptive. I find that by speaking to them by name, they are easier to deal with."

"If it doesn't want to tell you its name, why doesn't it just not tell you?" Gavin said, thinking this was perhaps even more ridiculous than Katz's explanations.

"Simple, Detective. Because I speak to them in the name of my Lord and they have no choice but to obey, albeit sometimes with quite a bit of kicking and screaming, so to speak. Try to think in terms of what your badge can do for you when it's shown. People obey you because of the authority behind your badge. The name of God carries supreme authority. He is my badge."

"Buck, I'm a Christian. I mean, I'm not beating the church door down every week, but I believe in God. But real demons controlling real lives . . . in this day and age? Come on! This isn't a movie!"

"Jesus spoke about demons all the time, Detective."

"Jesus lived two thousand years ago." Gavin's patience was wearing thin. Amy gave him a warning look.

"Please continue," she said to Buck.

"Well, the demon told me its name was Sabah. The young man had no way of knowing the words that came out of his mouth actually meant 'heavy drinker' in ancient Hebrew."

"You knew that?" Amy asked.

"Yes. I've dealt with Sabah in the past, so I had already done my research. Sabah is also a gabber by nature. A babbling drunk."

Gavin almost laughed. Buck had to be making this up as he went along.

"Sabah pleaded with me to allow it to stay in the young man, but when I insisted it come out, the demon threatened retaliation. Threatened to return with Krogan. Of course, I knew what that meant. I had never met the demon personally, but Krogan's reputation preceded him. I refused to back down."

"Why?" Gavin asked.

"Demons lie a lot and will sometimes say anything to stay in a host they enjoy. I hoped this was another lie. I was wrong."

There was a moment of awkward silence. Gavin hadn't believed a word Buck said, but he could relate to the pain the old man must have gone through.

"You're saying Sabah, the demon in the young man, was cast out and found its way into Karianne before the first crash. And that it's still there," Amy said.

"Yes."

"And this Sabah thing is what we've been following through the annals of time," Gavin said.

"It would seem so, Detective."

"Are the things we're being told by Karianne — I mean Sabah — really true or is it all a lie?" Amy asked.

"Sabah, like most demons, is very crafty, an expert at confusion. It deliberately confuses the truth, conveniently vague and informative at the same time. My friends, you are being played with by a master. In short, Sabah was giving you a guided tour and enjoying every minute of the deception. It will take you anywhere and to any time you want to go, even to before man walked the earth."

"Before?" Amy said.

Buck nodded. "All you would have to do is ask."

"Wonderful," Gavin said. "Amy, you have to promise me Katz never finds out Karianne is capable of going back to the freakin' dinosaurs. We'd lose him for good."

Looking annoyed at his remark, Amy refocused on Buck. "*Shadahd,* Buck. When Gavin mentioned it you gave me the impression you've heard it before."

"Unfortunately, yes. *Shadahd* is not just

an ancient Hebrew word, my dear. *Shadahd* was Krogan's battle cry from the beginning. And don't ask when that was, for it was a time before time as we know it. A time of initial spiritual clashing between darkness and light — or more accurately between reality and unreality."

Gavin decided not to ask him what he meant by reality and unreality.

"What do you mean by reality and unreality," Amy said.

"Simply, God can only abide with perfect truth. When Lucifer, a great angel at the time, wanted to be worshiped like God, he stepped into unreality. God will not have unity with unreality. Lucifer's delusion spread to other angels and a war broke out. Although much ground has been gained and the outcome decided, the war continues. Krogan's total disregard and contempt for God's creation stems from a basic perverted belief that everything should be his, if I may refer to the gender he presently embodies, to enjoy and destroy as he sees fit. Complete unreality."

"But not to Krogan."

"That's right. Krogan sees himself as a god."

"And *shadahd* is a word that means 'to

go out to ruin,' as if to rub in God's face that Krogan has the right to do whatever he wants whenever he pleases."

"Exactly. Frankly, I'm a little surprised you got to meet Sabah through Miss Stordal. When Krogan gets together with his friends, their hosts usually wind up dead."

"Then why do they get back together with him if they know they could die?"

"They live for death, even their own host's." Buck paused and glanced at Gavin. "Detective, you're very quiet."

"Oh, don't mind me. I just have an easier time believing things I can see."

"In my business, Detective, you often have to believe in order to see."

"We're in different businesses," Gavin said.

"You and I are not so different as you might think, Detective. We're both working our way through calamities. We're both experienced in helping others in crisis and we both understand authority. Fortunately, I am not familiar with all you've seen and you should be equally thankful not to have seen what I have."

"I've known a few priests and ministers, but I don't recall any of them speaking the way you do concerning demons."

"I'd be surprised if you had, Detective; there are different types of preachers just like there are different types of other careers. My particular area of expertise is not that prevalent. But like you, I would get the call, show up, and go to work. I was what you might call a hired gun. My job was to corner demons, interrogate them, and escort them out of town, so to speak. When they leave, they remember . . . and never forget. You ever worry about the ones you've put away getting out someday and visiting you, maybe with their friends, Detective?"

Gavin remained silent. He knew cops who had changed their names for just such a reason.

Buck continued. "They don't all retaliate, but some do."

"Krogan?" Amy said.

Buck sighed. "Krogan doesn't wait to retaliate. He strikes first."

"So, for the record, you believe this has nothing to do with past lives or reincarnation," Gavin said.

"Oh, my, no. Not as you understand it. Sabah was just reminiscing about old times. Like most demons, it enjoys masquerading as human thought. Sabah doesn't die and come back to life as someone else. Sabah can't die. It's just homeless until it finds another body to inhabit."

"And when it finds a new home or host it tells them what to do?" Gavin said pointedly.

"It suggests. Sometimes strongly," said Buck sympathetically.

"You speak as though they're victims," Gavin said, the faces of Grampa and Garrity and hospital emergency rooms flashing in his mind.

"Well, they are victims."

"And I suppose you have compassion on the poor host?" Gavin said.

"I try to. Charity comes from knowing the truth."

Gavin's tea glass slammed on the table.

— 35 —

"Time out," Gavin said, making a T with his hands. He'd never been very good at passive observation and this mock interview had gone on way too long. "You know how many guys I've locked up who claim the devil made them do it? I should believe them?"

"Some people, for whatever reason, are influenced more than others. Demons can't make people act, but if someone lays out the welcome mat often enough they can attract company and eventually a kind of partnership can be formed, often without the person knowing it."

"Partnership? Why doesn't God corral these things if they're really there? I mean, didn't God make them in the first place?"

"We're living in a detour in time that is cursed because of misplaced faith. If you have another hour or two we can get into it."

"You must have had a cheery congregation."

"Maybe you find your hypnotist's explanation of reincarnation easier to believe?" Buck said.

"Katz — the psychologist — is convinced. I'm not," Gavin said, wondering what would happen if the lieutenant, not to mention the media, heard about any of this.

"Spirits are often misperceived as a past human life," Buck said. "Does it make sense that Karianne and Krogan and others were meeting each other in life after life after life? That Krogan wanted to keep his name in every life and that his happiest moment was at the crucifixion? And by the way, how did you know he meant Jesus?"

"It was obvious," Amy said.

"Obvious, how? Did she say 'Jesus'?"

"Well, not exactly."

"Not exactly?" Buck said with a smile. "What happened was you asked her who was on the cross and she refused to say his name . . . didn't she?"

"How did you know that?" Amy said, surprised.

"Demons hate to say God's name, unless they're being derogatory. They love to mock and they enjoy it when humans take

God's name in vain. They want us to asso-
ciate the almighty God with the lowly and
common. They find it comforting."

"Comforting?" Amy said, then pulled
her notebook from her purse.

"You mean like, 'God, that's the best
French fry I've ever tasted,' " Gavin said.

Amy wasn't amused. Buck smiled gently.

"I think you know what I'm saying," he
said.

"But that's just normal," Gavin said.
"Everybody does that."

"Exactly, but why?"

"Because, well, because everybody does.
They always have."

"Hmm," Buck said, arching his brow. "I
wonder why that is?"

"Ah, here it is," Amy said, looking at her
notes. "Karianne was asked what she was
searching for after one of her lives had
died. She said she was, 'looking for comfort.' "

"Oh, yes! Like people, demons strive to
be comfortable," Buck said. "Most people
work hard all year long so they can have a
week or two of relaxation. The home is designed for comfort. Some are very particular, some aren't. Some live alone while
others live in a group. Demons are very
much the same. When an evil spirit leaves

a body that has just died, Jesus told us, it goes through formless places searching for somewhere to rest. These spiritually arid periods aren't any more comfortable for them than the Sahara Desert is for you or me. They want comfort. In Sabah's case, comfort meant someone who likes to drink a lot. Like people, demons can be lazy. In Sabah's case, why build a heavy drinker when you can find one?"

"Kind of like house hunting," Amy said. "Everyone has their own personal preference."

"Exactly, and decorate as desired, Miss Kirsch," Buck said. "In the end a demon's favorite home is furnished with weaknesses and perversions that match its own individual tastes. Anger, fear, depression, confusion, violence, power, wealth, fame . . . Our own vanities can make a demon's work very easy. And they don't like it when someone messes up their house. Or worse, evicts them."

"Enough about Sabah," Amy said. "I want to know about Krogan. How do you mess up Krogan's house?"

Buck put his glass down on the table as a solemn look passed over his face like the shadow of a storm cloud. "You don't."

"Explain," Amy said. Surprised at her

level of interest, Gavin looked at her, but remained silent, letting the conversation play out.

"Sabah is content to get high and die, but Krogan thrives on hatred and the ruin of God's creation. Krogan is of a different caliber. Stronger. He isn't content to simply mess with people's emotions and addictions. He wants to make his host a living abomination of hellish destruction. Krogan's hosts aren't tortured as much as they're torturers."

"That's why the host takes on Krogan's name and tattoos it into his flesh," Amy said.

"Tattoos of his name do seem to be a trademark. A possession thing, like the branding of cattle."

"For whom to see?" Amy asked.

"Other demons. Krogan is envied and many will call on him for a . . . 'date.' They've been doing it for thousands of years, maybe longer. They call it *shadahd* to signify what their ultimate intent will be. The demon — Sabah, for example — will plague its host with irresistible, sometimes unexplainable, temptations to drink. When the host has had so much to drink it can no longer mentally resist, the demon takes control. Krogan typically entices the other demon's host to drink until only the demon can function. Krogan says 'Shadahd' as a sort of password. If the host doesn't understand, Krogan gives the host more alcohol. Eventually the password is returned and their fun begins. The next day, if there is one, the host usually remembers nothing, except maybe a bad dream."

"Why Karianne? She seems so different than Krogan. In fact, she's horrified by what Krogan does," Amy said.

"At some point in her life Karianne looked very comfortable to Sabah. The fact she stopped drinking probably upset Sabah, but time was on Sabah's side. To wait five years is nothing to a being that's been around for millennia."

In spite of himself, Gavin was intrigued. "So then why didn't this Sabah just leave and find another alcoholic that's not on the wagon?"

"Sabah cannot leave. When a demon takes up residence, it is there either until the host dies or it is cast out. There is an example in the Bible where Jesus came across a demoniac known as Legion who was a virtual hotel for demons. The demons were petrified when they saw Jesus, but didn't leave . . . because they couldn't.

They begged him to cast them into a herd of pigs. He did, and the demons immediately rushed the pigs into a nearby lake where they drowned, freeing the demons."

"Are there other demons like Krogan?" Amy asked.

"There are many arranged meetings. Dates where the demons pair and gather for *shadahd*. More than you can imagine. But Krogan is one of the worst."

"Can you cast Sabah out of Karianne?" Amy asked.

"Katz wouldn't be very happy about that," Gavin said.

Buck paused. He got out of his seat, walked over to the sink, and leaned on it, staring ahead. Gavin noticed a row of small picture frames, containing photos of what he assumed were loved ones, arranged on the windowsill above the sink. Buck had his own picture graveyard, he thought.

Buck turned and swallowed. "I'm retired. In Norway, I was caught off guard when Sabah retaliated with Krogan — and it meant the lives of my family. I won't endanger the life of my granddaughter by casting out another demon. Sabah alone would not have been a problem, but Krogan is different. Krogan is too strong.

To cast Krogan out one needs special preparation."

"What kind of preparation?" Gavin said, hoping he might finally hear something practical he could use.

"Jesus warned his disciples that sometimes they would face demons of great strength — that they would need to rely on more than their faith. He said they would need to pray and fast. I think Krogan is one of the very demons he was referring to."

Gavin shook his head. "Jesus may have been speaking to his disciples about Krogan?" He couldn't believe this. A large share of a detective's work was spent interviewing people who might somehow know the criminal. Gavin's current list included the likes of Attila the Hun and Richard the Lionheart . . . and now Jesus and the disciples. He wondered if there was something he might have done to his tenth-grade history teacher to deserve all this.

"It's very possible," Buck said. "At the very least he was speaking to them about demons *like* Krogan — demons that require more than simple faith to cast out."

"But how does that help us?" Gavin said, raising his palms to the ceiling in exasperation. "Your story keeps getting crazier and crazier. If Krogan has his pick of the bad guys when he's in the dry land, why doesn't he pick someone with access to nuclear missiles?"

"Krogan doesn't push buttons, he pushes the hosts. The chance of someone in such a position giving his life over to the kind of reckless, irresponsible lifestyle Krogan prefers is unlikely," Buck said. "Krogan enjoys the physical sensation of power and the actual sight of the ruin caused by the host's own hands. He will use a car, boat, or plane as long as the host physically operates it. His carefully picked body must also be able to endure impact and pain. Although if the body dies in the act, so be it."

"I suppose you're going to tell me that the terrorists that flew the commercial jets into the Twin Towers were demonized," Gavin said.

"Would that be so hard to believe?" Amy interjected. Gavin eyed her. Was she actually buying into all this?

"I suppose you're going to tell me Krogan was flying one of those jets?"

"No," Buck replied. "He was probably already in his present host at the time. But whatever demons did orchestrate that event, they were free at that point to search for other hosts. Which, by the way, is why you must be careful not to kill Krogan's host, Detective. If you do, the one you're after will escape your reach and the destruction you are trying so hard to eliminate will continue."

In spite of the fact Gavin categorized Buck's analysis under F for Fairytale, the old man's words hit Gavin like a bucket of ice water. "I have to be careful not to kill the man who killed my grandfather? I *fantasize* about how I'm going to kill him. If you think for one minute I'm gonna give him more than two seconds to comply after 'Freeze or you're dead,' you're crazy."

"Then you'll be setting the real enemy free," Buck shouted, surprising Gavin.

Buck visibly worked to calm himself. "Please understand me: you have to capture him and then keep him from being able to kill himself. Krogan is not one to sit in a prison if he has the choice. If able, he will commit suicide to escape — a common practice for demons who dread the limitations that jail brings. I'm sure you've seen killing rampages that end in suicide. The body dies but the demon simply moves on. The difference with Krogan is the vindictiveness. Krogan will come after you for imprisoning or killing the host."

"Great," Gavin said. "Okay, let's pretend for a minute all this demon stuff is true. How *do* I kill Krogan?"

"You can't. Krogan is immortal."

"Right. Then I would have to capture Krogan alive."

"Yes, but you wouldn't have him for long. At the first opportunity Krogan would overpower his host and convince him to commit suicide."

"You mean I'd have to keep him locked up in solitary in a straitjacket?"

"Something like that. For the rest of his life. And pray the host outlives you."

Gavin stared at him blankly, then at Amy. Her expression matched his. He sighed and stood up. "Well, Buck. I thought when I pulled into your driveway I couldn't feel any more tired or frustrated. I was wrong."

"I'm sorry, Detective. I wish there was more I could do. You do look tired. Maybe you should take a nap before driving back. I'm sure you'd feel better."

Gavin ignored him. "If you think of something, here's my card. If you lose it, I'm in the phone book." He dropped his card on the table and escorted Amy to the door with his hand on the small of her back. She was sweating and Gavin wasn't sure it was from heat or fear.

Outside, Buck followed them to the car. Gavin opened the door, then paused and turned around, meeting the former preacher eye to eye.

"Hired gun, huh?"

Buck said nothing.

"One thing confuses me more than anything else. You're supposed to have this great faith."

"I'm not going after Krogan with you, Detective," Buck said emphatically.

"Krogan retired you?"

Buck looked to the ground. "If I cast it out, it will quickly return to find me. If he finds me he could find my granddaughter."

"Even knowing it will mean others would die?"

"Detective, I got the impression you didn't really believe anything I said."

"But you believe it," Gavin said. "What does that say for your belief in God? Isn't walking away from Krogan the same as walking away from God?"

Buck was silent for a moment, motionless, avoiding eye contact. Then he looked to the horizon. "It isn't fair for you to question. You don't know what Krogan is really capable of."

"Obviously, more than you think God can handle," Gavin said. He got into his car and sped away, leaving Buck in a cloud of dust.

— 36 —

Buck wiped the dust from his eyes as the car left the driveway, the detective's final words still boring a hole into his heart. Was the detective correct? Buck didn't really believe his situation was more than God could handle. Who was Krogan compared to the Almighty God of the universe? But he now wondered if he trusted God's will. Would God handle this situation? Was that what he was asking? He had never allowed himself to think in those terms since the crash. He had always seen Samantha's Farm as a provision for his granddaughter, not an escape from responsibility. After all, was not Samantha his responsibility, too? She was family. He had always taught that family was more important than occupation. But was all that a clever detour he had subconsciously fabricated to keep his eyes off the real question: would God be there for him?

Buck found a large stone a few feet away

and sat on it. He looked out over the picturesque valley, reminiscing. His first experience with deliverance had actually been as a recipient. He had suffered from social insecurities and a severe depression that had started when he was a boy. Finally, when as a young adult his emotions had threatened to overwhelm him for good, a trusted childhood friend convinced him to attend a special church meeting with him. Apparently the guest speaker had some sort of deliverance anointing, his friend had said. Very reluctantly, Buck had agreed to go.

He would never forget that night. He'd found himself in the last row of the old church, frozen to his seat as the minister called on people to come up for prayer. There was simply no way, he'd decided, he was going to stand in front of all those people and be publicly prayed for, with all eyes staring at him. That would be too terrifying. But at the same time, he could not leave. He remembered wondering if what he was seeing was real or just mind-over-matter or power of suggestion? What else could explain some of the behavior he was witnessing? And the control of the exorcist — although no one called him that. He seemed so in command of it all, without all the theatrics Buck would have expected.

After the meeting ended, the church had emptied, except for Buck, his friend, the pastor, and the deliverance guy — Jedidiah Dobbs. It was a name Buck would soon after become closely associated with. Dobbs walked slowly up the center isle toward Buck. He'd been old even then, short and thick and dressed in a gray suit with a pocket watch looped from his vest. As he walked he took off thick, wire-rimmed glasses, cleaned them with a folded white handkerchief, and returned them to a nose that appeared to have been broken more than once.

Dobbs stopped in front of Buck, and with an approving nod his wrinkled face came alive. "It's good you stayed," he said, his voice more hoarse without the microphone.

Buck felt immediately anxious and wanted to run away, but could not. He didn't know why, but his heart was racing. "I almost didn't," he said, wondering why the old man was addressing only him.

"The Lord has a plan for your life, my son. Do you want it?"

That's impossible, Buck said to himself. He says that to everyone.

"In fact, he wants me to tell you he has a

call on your life that would begin tonight. Do you want it?"

Buck was scared speechless. His mind was telling him, "Leave! Now!"

"But first," Dobbs said, "there is something we have to take care of. Or, I should say, get rid of." The old man settled himself down in the pew next to Buck, staring deeply into Buck's eyes. Buck could not look away, no matter how much he wanted to.

"What is your name, you filthy, vile thing?" Dobbs ordered.

Confused and intimidated, Buck felt as though he was looking at the world from somewhere deep behind his eyes — like he was in the backseat of his mind, or at least not the only one driving anymore.

"In the name of Jesus, tell me who you are."

Buck winced, the old man's words stabbing at him — or so it seemed. He was about to tell Dobbs his own name, but when he opened his mouth he said, "Fear."

"Don't get cute with me, lying beast. I want the name the others call you. In the name of our Lord, I command you to tell me now. What is your name?"

Buck felt a sudden constriction around his neck as if he were being strangled. He felt as though something was climbing up his throat and he started to gag. But when he turned his head to vomit, only sound came out. "Dahl," he said, his voice deeper than normal. His friend moved further away, his eyes doubled in size.

"I don't know you, Dahl. But it's time for you to leave," the old man said sternly.

"He is mine," Buck heard himself say.

"He is the Lord's, and in his name I command you to leave. Be gone!"

At that moment the tightening around Buck's neck loosened. He exhaled as muscles all over his body relaxed.

"It's gone," Dobbs said.

"What happened?" Buck said, keenly aware of his surroundings.

"Step one."

"Step one?"

"Yes. The Lord has delivered you from a pest. You've been made clean, and now you need to be made whole. How do you feel, my son?"

Buck thought for a moment. "Lighter," he finally said, with a smile that had been missing from his face for longer than he could remember.

"Good. So, do you want it?"

"What?"

"God's plan for your life, remember?"

With a newfound sense of well-being and confidence, Buck nodded. Dobbs smiled.

The old man spent the next few hours with Buck, praying for the anointing of God's Spirit. In the following days and months, Buck spent much time with his new mentor and was soon ministering deliverance at Jedidiah Dobbs's side. He had continued doing so even after Dobb's death, for many years, until . . . Krogan . . .

"Grandpa!"

Buck's thoughts were suddenly wrenched back to the present. Samantha had been speaking to him. "Hmm?" he said.

"I said I'm going next door to play with Michele and Jackie. Is something wrong with you? I was calling and calling."

"I'm fine sweetheart," Buck said with a forced smile. "You run along and have fun."

Samantha gave Buck a big kiss on the cheek, then ran toward her friends' house. He watched her until she was out of sight, then looked back toward the long road back to Hamden. It was empty.

— 37 —

Gavin was out of view of the farm before he eased up on the gas pedal and turned to Amy. "I figure one of three things is true," he said.

"One, he's crazy," Amy volunteered.

"Yes, but you don't believe that, do you?"

"No."

"I didn't think so. You were so polite and attentive I was wondering if you thought he was your grandfather."

"Nonsense. I'm always polite," Amy said unblinkingly.

"Of course you are, but I still think number one is number one. He sees evil spirits and knows them by name. There are certain institutions where that gift isn't very uncommon, you know."

"Yeah, but he also knew things about Karianne he couldn't have known, lucky or not."

"I'm sure there's an explanation, but for now let's move on to number two."

"Which is?"

"That he's not who he says he is and he knows a lot more than he's telling us and all this demon stuff is either a clever cover-up or just the inevitable perception of a burnt-out preacher. Or maybe he does know Krogan, the man in the sketch, but he's too scared to admit it. I think maybe Katz should hypnotize the Reverend Buck next."

Amy rolled her eyes. "Next."

"What?"

"I said next."

"There is no next."

"You said three."

"Okay. Number three is he's for real."

"And you don't think that's a possibility?"

"No."

"And why not?"

"Why not? Look, Amy, you're great at collecting data, but . . ." Gavin paused cautiously.

"But what?"

" 'When you eat meat you have to throw out the bones.' You can't believe everything you hear."

Amy gave him a look. "Do me a favor: leave the old sayings to me."

"What are we supposed to do, go after Krogan with crosses and silver bullets?"

Amy turned her gaze toward the road before them for a moment, then said, "I wish we could have spent more time with him."

"More? We've wasted enough time already. The eight hours of driving time would have been better spent sleeping."

"I knew I should have come up here alone," Amy said quietly.

Gavin heard her but didn't respond. Her words saddened him and made him wish he'd kept his mouth shut. Without further comment he continued driving for a couple of miles before turning off the main road in search of a private spot by the river where they could take a nap, which was the only advice Buck had given them that made any sense, at least to Gavin. He glanced at Amy several times. She sat slumped in her seat staring into the polished wood grain of the dashboard.

After crossing the river by way of an old wooden bridge, the road turned right, parallel to the flow of water. Soon the road turned from asphalt to gravel to dirt. Gavin pulled the car off to the side of the road under a cluster of pines that bordered a sandy bank. He rolled to a gentle stop, quieting the crunch of pebbles under his tires.

"You okay?" he said, waving his hand by Amy's eyes.

Amy blinked as though Katz had just counted to three and snapped his fingers. "No," she said. "I feel weird."

"Sick?"

"No! Scared. I'm not sick, I'm afraid," Amy snapped. "I'm afraid for my sister, I'm afraid for you, and I'm afraid for me. Why aren't you afraid?"

"Because I don't believe Krogan's an adrenaline-junkie demon."

"Then what's your logical explanation?"

"I don't have one . . . yet. But if I were to believe what Buck says is true, I'd have to change what I do for a living. Trade my gun in for a water pistol full of holy water and squirt it in the face of every psycho that comes down the pike. And believe me, it's a wide road."

"Krogan isn't every psycho," Amy said, shaking her head. "He's different and you know it."

Gavin looked into Amy's molten-emerald eyes and knew there was no point in trying to convince her. How could he? In their short relationship he hadn't once won an argument with her and now was no time to try.

"Hey, I'm too tired to fight," he said softly, covering her hand with his. "Let's see if we can catch a few Z's so we can make it home in one piece. Okay?"

Her gaze fell as she nodded in agreement, giving Gavin a sense of distance between them he hadn't known. She climbed out and walked toward the river, leaving Gavin to scrounge a blanket from the trunk. He caught up with her at a shallow embankment that had probably been carved during the springtime when the water was high, fast, and cold. They slid down to a small sandbar peninsula, Gavin giving Amy a hand although she didn't need the help and didn't appear to want it. He pushed up a small mound of sand in a shady spot to use for a pillow, then flapped out the blanket over it. Without saying a word they both lay down.

The lulling sound of the water, the perfect weather, the little puffy white clouds slowly passing by, and the sweet song of a nearby bird weren't needed. Right now Gavin could just as easily have fallen asleep standing sandwiched on the subway in rush hour.

"You'll feel better when you wake up," he said awkwardly, feeling the need to say something.

"No I won't. I just found out there really is a devil, and if there's a devil, then there's a God."

"So what's wrong with that?" Gavin said, eyes closed, not really wanting an answer right now.

"I don't really know God. I know I'm not on the devil's side, but I don't know if I'm on God's side, either. I feel like I'm in the middle. Is there a middle?"

Why couldn't she have just gone to sleep? At this point anything he said was going to sound abbreviated and uncaring.

"When we wake up we'll call the Reverend Buck. He'll know."

"We'll probably just get the machine," Amy said.

"Then we'll drive back and ask him."

"Yeah, right. After the way we left?"

"Can I have a little more time to think about this?" Gavin said, begging whatever God Amy was referring to, to please let him sleep.

Amy called his name sweetly as her hand warmly caressed his cheek. Again she said his name, her voice so gentle it seemed far away, yet close. He didn't want to open his eyes because he could see her beauty better with them closed. She took his hand in her own, splitting his fingers with her own, pulling him toward her. Everything was so peaceful — so right . . .

"Aghhh!" He yelped as cold water hit his face.

"I said get up."

Gavin opened his eyes to see Amy standing in front of him with two large Styrofoam coffee cups, taken from the trash in his car. Before he could react, the second cup, filled with cool river water, emptied into his face.

"Okay! Okay! Stop! What's going on?" he yelled, hoping she didn't have a third cup ready. His eyelids felt like cement blocks. He desperately wanted to go back to sleep. The Amy in his dreams might even be waiting for him.

"We have to leave now," she said. "My sister woke up and she's freaking out, calling for me."

"How do you know?"

"My beeper woke me up. I knew it was the hospital's number the second I saw it. I had to walk halfway down the road before I could get even a weak signal on my cell phone. They told me she woke up about two hours ago. About the same time we fell asleep."

"Does she know?" Gavin asked.

Amy's instant tears not only answered Gavin's question, but did more to wake him than the water had. He jumped to his feet. In the past week, Amy had not talked much about this moment, but Gavin knew she had been praying for it and dreading it at the same time. With her sister back in the picture, he would lose Amy as a partner; Amber was going to require enormous support. Gavin wondered if that support would get in the way of retrieving information from the only witness he had yet to question: Amber Clayborne herself.

"Your partner, Chris, broke it to her," Amy said between hard sniffs. "I'm sure my parents are there, but it's my name she's calling."

"Then let's not keep her waiting," he said.

Gathering up the blanket, they headed back to the car. A moment later Gavin was downshifting into second as he screeched around the turn, then flooring it over the bridge. He wondered how long the trip would take at a hundred miles an hour. He glanced at his watch. It was just after two-thirty. After being awake for the better part of two days, he'd just had a whopping two hours of sleep.

— 38 —

Amber Clayborne released her mother's hand in order to catch Amy, who had just burst through the door. Amy kissed her on the cheek several times as they both cried. Gavin, who had followed Amy in, was out of breath from the sprint from the front entrance. Across the room he saw Chris sitting in a chair. His partner discretely waved hello with the rise and fall of his right index finger. He was no longer wearing the bandage around his head, but the cast that climbed up his arm and around his left shoulder was still there. His eyes were wet.

"Thank God you're back," Amy cried. "That's all that matters right now."

Amber's loud moans were evidence she did not agree. What was painfully clear was exactly what Gavin had expected: as far as Amber was concerned, her newlywed husband had been brutally murdered just moments ago. The horrible act that had already been realized and digested by everyone else had only now dug its tormenting claws into Amber's soul. Gavin understood the intense need for what was no longer there. He wanted to help, to somehow ease the pain. But what could he say?

Chris slowly got up from his seat with the help of a crutch and made his way toward Gavin, each step clearly difficult. This was the first time Gavin had seen him walk since the accident.

"I'll see you outside," Chris whispered, then continued out the door.

The twins were embracing, with one parent on either side of the bed. Gavin did not feel needed, but their sorrow beckoned him. What could he do? He wanted to join them and tell them everything would be all right. But that would be a lie. Amber's life would never be the same. And to a lesser degree, neither would Amy's. After a few minutes of watching helplessly he slowly backed toward the door, then turned, knowing he'd return as soon as he was done with Chris.

He found Chris on a window seat just down the hallway and sat beside him.

"I'm outta here tomorrow," Chris said.

Gavin was surprised. He wondered if the doctors knew.

"I'm going to see the Giants play the Bears from my own couch. I can't wait."

"It's good to see you out of the wheelchair," Gavin said.

"Yeah, just in time for Amber to wake up. I was hoping it would be your job. It . . . wasn't a pretty scene."

"I owe you one," Gavin said.

"You owe me two. I not only told her about her husband, but I questioned her about the crash."

"You did?"

"It was Dr. Fagan's idea. He thought a strong diversion might help. He was right — for about thirty seconds. It was bad, Gav. As bad as I've ever seen. The nurse had been helping me with my exercise, walking the hall, when she woke up. We were right there," he said, pointing to a spot on the floor by Amber's doorway.

"What did she say?"

"The first thing she said was her husband's name. As soon as I heard 'Mitchell, Mitchell' coming from her room, my heart sank."

"No! I mean, what did she say about the crash?"

"Oh. Not much. The last thing she remembered was the sunset reflecting off the front windshield of the car like it was a mirror. She couldn't see in. The next thing she knew was waking up here."

"Had she ever see Krogan before the crash? He has a habit of going after people that rub him the wrong way. Did you show her the sketch?"

"It never got that far, Gav. Like I said, the distraction idea didn't work very long."

Gavin looked back at Amber's door. He could hear the crying. If she were anyone but Amy's sister, he would give her about an hour and then begin inching his way in.

"Forget it, Gav. Give her at least till tomorrow. She's been through an awful lot and her mind has some clearing out to do. A little time will do wonders."

Gavin sighed. "Yeah, 'Time heals, then it kills,'" he said, then looked at Chris, whose expression begged for an explanation. "One of Amy's Japanese sayings."

"Oh. By the way, Gav. You look like garbage. What did you do, sleep in those clothes?"

Gavin snorted. "I wish. In the last couple of days, sleep has been harder to find than Krogan."

"Speaking of Krogan, where're we at with him?"

Gavin looked at Chris for a long moment without speaking. If his heart hadn't been so wrenched from Amy's anguish, he'd have laughed. His injured partner was probably the only sane person he'd talked to all week. Everyone else, including himself right now, could be ruled "out of their minds." But not Chris. Chris had always been Gavin's voice of reason. The logical one.

"Where are we at? If *we* includes Katz, we're at book signings and talk shows. If *we* includes Reverend Jesse J. Buchanan, we're on a witch hunt."

"Who?"

"Buck is what his friends call him. Amy and I drove up to the Catskills to see him this morning, after staying up all day and night with Karianne. Oh, I almost forgot the breather I got when Krogan took out the Learjet Gasman was on. Who needs a cup of coffee to keep you on your toes with this guy around?"

"I heard," Chris said.

"I told him not to go. I practically spelled out for him he was a dead man if he took the flight. Chris, this guy's bad — real bad — but he's not smart. Why don't we have him yet? There must be something we're not seeing. I know when this is all over I'm going to look back and laugh, or more likely cry, that what we're looking for was right before our eyes."

"Ain't that the way it always works?" Chris said. "It's just that this time you're so personally involved and worn out you can't see straight."

"Thanks," said Gavin sarcastically. "Words of wisdom from the brother I've never had."

"That's right, smart guy. Go home and get some rest. Take tomorrow off, like the rest of the world. Watch the football game and get your mind off the case. Monday we'll both lay everything out on the table and dissect it all with fresh minds."

"This time I'm gonna surprise you. I'm gonna take your advice."

"I'll believe that when I see it."

"No, you'll see it when you believe it," Gavin said, shaking his finger mockingly in the air as he got up.

"What?"

"Nothing."

"Gav."

Gavin turned. "What?"

"Ten bucks says you work tomorrow."

Gavin shook his head. "I can use the ten bucks. You're on."

Back at the room nothing had changed. Amy, who was still sitting on the bed next to her sister, noticed his entrance and immediately waved him over. Amber was sitting up, rocking, with her knees tucked up and her head planted between them, her movement echoing her low moans. Their grief was raw and open.

He didn't even remember telling his legs to move. He just suddenly found himself at their side. He knelt on one knee and took Amber's left hand. He didn't know if she even knew he had it. He felt a hand rest on his shoulder. Amy's mother, he thought, but didn't turn to see. Amy's father sat on the opposite side of the bed, staring tearfully at his ravaged daughter as if he could not find the words to express his anguish. The pain in the room was frighteningly thick.

It was then Gavin knew Amy could no longer be a part of the manhunt. Buck had scared her good and Gavin was almost glad for it now. He would not try to dispel her fears. Krogan would be as vindictive toward her as he had been to anyone who had raised a hand against him. Now at least she was alive and safe from him; Krogan still didn't know she existed. And he wouldn't. She had to be cut off from the case. Amber needed her alive.

The thought of Krogan as the source of

Amber's grief fanned his rage. Effortlessly he envisioned his hand around Krogan's neck, his fist pounding his face. He imagined throwing a handcuffed Krogan at the feet of the Reverend Buck and emptying his gun into the back of his captive's head and shouting into the preacher's face, "Go on. Tell me the cretin's not dead, dead, dead."

Gavin let out a startled yell when Cedar's cold nose found the back of his warm neck. "Snagged me again, didn't you?" he said, rolling over to eye the dog. Cedar just smiled.

Gavin stared at the two digital clocks on his night table until his eyes focused and there was only one of them. Nine a.m. "Geez. I've been asleep for ten hours," he told Cedar.

It was Sunday and he was going to take Chris's advice: a day of rest. He went for the shower, washed, then sat down in the tub, letting the steamy water bounce off his chest and massage his mind. Later, he decided as he soaked, he would leisurely go to the hospital to see Amy and Amber, but not for questioning, unless Amber initiated it.

Gavin had barely finished exhaling a sigh of celebration for his well-needed breather when a crowd of intrusive thoughts raised their ugly heads, vying for position at the door of his mind. Memories emerged of conversations with his grandfather at Coney Island and of working with John Garrity on the Sunbeam Tiger. They were pleasant recollections, but came with a price; attached to them were vicious flashes of their cruel and undeserved deaths. He couldn't see them one way without the other.

He quickly tried to chase them away with more pleasant thoughts. The last thing he needed now was more grief. He tried thinking of Amy, but couldn't do that without thinking of Amber. Relaxing, he decided, wasn't very relaxing. His naturally analytical mind needed to be shut off. What he really needed was a lobotomy.

His thoughts shifted to Reverend Buck. There was no way of proving or disproving anything the man had said. You either had to take what he said in faith or find the more realistic explanation . . .

"Enough," he said aloud. "I get more rest when I'm working." With a sigh he got out of the tub and slipped into a pair of worn jeans, basketball sneakers, and a navy-blue T-shirt. He strapped on an ankle holster and was ready to go when he caught a glimpse of something on his night table that made him pause. He reached for the Polaroid of him and Grampa with the snake on the boardwalk. The smiles on their faces both warmed and saddened him.

Something about the photo bothered him. The snake. He didn't like the way the thing was so at rest on them, as if it owned them. Maybe he was allowing his emotion to read more into the picture than his logic could rightly perceive. Maybe he was simply feeding off the common mythical association that snakes have with evil. Whatever, seeing the reptile spiked a notion he couldn't shake. He might not have any faith in the Reverend Buck, but he could put what he had said to the test.

Gavin saw Katz's car outside Karianne's apartment, so he tried the door before knocking, in case they were in session. They were. He hung back out of sight in the foyer and listened.

"And what is Carry doing now?" Katz said.

"She's taking food out of the picnic basket," Karianne said slowly, the way she spoke when under hypnosis.

"Are you hungry?"

"No. Thirsty."

"What do you want to drink?"

"Whiskey."

"Did Carry bring any whiskey?"

"No. She doesn't like whiskey. Gets her mad. Real mad."

Gavin listened for several more minutes before he stepped into the living room. He hadn't heard a word about Krogan and figured Katz had broken the only rule Gavin had given him: go wherever you want, as long as Krogan's there.

Katz jumped slightly at the sight of Gavin.

Gavin gave him an abbreviated wave with his fingers. Caught you, he thought. He then gave a nod to Steinman, who had been listening because Karianne was speaking in English.

Katz got up and motioned toward the foyer.

"How did it go with Buchanan?" Katz asked in a hushed voice.

"I'm not sure."

"Where's Amy?"

"With her sister. She woke up."

"Thank God."

"Yeah. How's it going here?"

"Phenomenally. I was just speaking to Dr. Charles Gloyd," Katz said, beaming.

"Who?"

"Dr. Charles Gloyd is a Union veteran from Ohio."

"What's a union veteran?" Gavin said, thinking of burly men waving picket signs.

"Union as in Union Army. The Civil War, Pierce. I've already checked with the Kansas State Historical Society to verify what she's been saying. It's all true, and she couldn't have found these facts in an encyclopedia."

"What facts?"

"Have you ever heard of Carry Amelia Moore?"

Gavin thought. "No. Doesn't ring a bell."

"How about Carrie Nation?"

Gavin frowned. "Sounds vaguely familiar, but I don't know. Who is she?"

"At the turn of the century she and her followers were marching through saloons with axes, smashing everything in sight, starting with the bottles. Her zeal was the result of her first husband, who died of alcoholism two years after they were married. He drove her crazy. Dr. Charles Gloyd was that husband," Katz said, beaming.

"A drunk?"

"Yes. Karianne's always a drunk. It's amazing. There's no end to the mysteries she's capable of unlocking. Alcoholism is not only hereditary. Apparently, it can be passed along in the reincarnation process," Katz said enthusiastically.

"Apparently," Gavin said, nonplussed.

"I've traveled five, maybe ten thousand years with her, and in each life, she's a drunk. And so are her friends . . . including Krogan. Do you know she's had at least twenty lives as a pirate, dating back from the first Phoenician pirates, hundreds of years B.C., through the Vikings, and beyond. She even sailed with Anne Bonney, the infamous woman pirate. The only one I'm having a little trouble with is during a time she claims to have been a pirate just after the Vietnam War. The problem isn't verifying that the events happened. The problem is she was already alive as Karianne."

Gavin thought of what Buck had said. "How's our Karianne doing?"

"Great. No more problems. I've installed a shortcut command in her. If I see even the slightest hint of anxiety, I say 'Terminate' and she automatically returns to full consciousness without any memory of whatever unpleasant event she was reliving. And just in case of an emergency, I keep a hypo of tranquilizer at the ready."

411

"You've obviously thought of every-thing," Gavin said sarcastically.

Katz's naturally sad expression became sadder. "What's wrong?"

Gavin paused, looking him in the eye. "I want you to let me speak to her."

"While she's under?" Katz said, taken back.

"Yeah."

"When?"

"Now."

"I don't know. She's not going to recog-nize your voice. It could be disruptive."

"I'll take that chance. Besides, you have your shortcut command."

"I still think —"

"I insist," Gavin said.

"I don't understand, Pierce. What do you want to say to her?"

"One word. That's all. Just one word."

"One word?" Katz found it funny. "Do you think I would spend the time I do, del-icately wooing her mind, suggesting emo-tions and dispelling possible phobias, if I could learn anything by simply walking up and saying one word?"

"Well then you have nothing to worry about, do you?"

Katz shrugged. "Be my guest."

"A simple test to satisfy my curiosity,

Katz. Nothing more."

Katz smiled and graciously gestured toward Karianne. "She's all yours." As Gavin took one step forward Katz held up an index finger and reminded him, "For one word."

Gavin took the seat Katz had been warming since who knows when while Katz sat back in a nearby folding chair. Gavin looked at Katz, who smiled and gestured again toward Karianne.

Karianne looked like she could have been asleep, her eyes closed, hands folded on her abdomen. Gavin had been driven with curiosity all morning, but now, sitting before her, he suddenly felt foolish. He wished he were alone. He could see Katz in his peripheral view, amused, ready to explain to him why some people are cops while others are psychologists. Ah, why not, Gavin thought. It wouldn't be him that was wrong; it would be Reverend Buck. He was simply testing every possibility, as far fetched as it might be, just like a good detective should. And if he was going to do it, he might as well do it right.

"Sabah," Gavin called firmly, as if Sabah was Karianne's real name. Katz looked at him curiously.

Nothing. Good.

Wait . . . Something was happening. Karianne's chin lifted slowly. Her eyelids slitted open, then widened. At first she gazed straight ahead. Then, without moving her head, her eyes shifted and found Gavin.

Gavin was shocked speechless. Of all the times he'd seen her under, he had never seen Karianne open her eyes like this. Her gaze was locked onto his and it scared him. He could not see Katz, but he knew the doctor was no longer smiling.

Karianne pivoted her head until her eyes were centered. "Who called me?" she said evenly, almost authoritatively.

Gavin didn't know what to say. Buck had not said anything about what to do in this situation, only that he shouldn't do what he had just done. Okay, his curiosity was satisfied, but how was he supposed to turn her off? He suddenly wished Buck were here to hide behind.

"In whose name am I called?" she repeated, this time demanding.

A clearly baffled Katz motioned for Gavin to answer her.

Gavin nodded. "Detective Gavin Pierce, Nassau County Police," he said. He could not remember it ever sounding so lame.

She laughed strangely; a scream would

have sounded warmer.

"I don't recognize your authority. How do you know my name?" she said as she dropped her good leg off the side of the couch and sat upright, her injured leg sticking outward in the cast. It was not a position Karianne would naturally situate herself into.

Gavin started to tell her he was a friend of Reverend Buchanan, but hesitated. He didn't know if it would help or hurt. He didn't know anything.

Just then, Katz, who had not been prepped on any of this, came over. He put his hands on Karianne's shoulders, apparently hoping to ease her back down. "I want you to relax yourself and —" he said, just before Karianne threw him to the side as easily as if she was a bull gorilla. Gavin jumped back as he watched Steinman reflexively raise his arms to protect himself from Katz sailing into him. In the next instant they were both sprawled out on the floor.

Gavin instinctively reached for his ankle, pulled out his gun, and leveled it between Karianne's eyes. "Hold it right there," he yelled, feeling ridiculous. There he was, weapon in hand, aimed to kill a twenty-nine-year-old woman who had just gotten out of the hospital with a broken leg.

Karianne looked at the gun and laughed. "Go ahead, Detective Gavin Pierce," she said spreading her arms wide, her eyes unnaturally wide. "Shoot." She rose from the couch like a living scarecrow, effortlessly standing on the broken leg.

Gavin stepped back involuntarily. He immediately remembered Buck warning him not to shoot Krogan. He didn't want to shoot Karianne, but . . .

"Terminate," Katz yelled from the other side of the room.

Nothing.

"Terminate," Katz repeated. "Ter-min-ate."

So much for the shortcut. Karianne was still standing there as if hanging on an imaginary cross, seemingly intent on being shot. Gavin thought of what Buck had said about disenchanted demons wanting to kill their hosts so they could get a new one. If Sabah wasn't doing this to Karianne, then what was? He could not believe what he was thinking, but he also could not believe what he was seeing.

Katz and Steinman came to their feet and hurried toward her. Gavin joined the charge.

Gavin had been on a college wrestling

team, had trained in the martial arts, and had instructed rookies in police defense, but never had he seen quicker reflexes than Karianne's when he, Katz, and Steinman closed in. A simple but blindingly fast backhand lifted the two-hundred-plus-pound Steinman into the air and dropped him unconscious to the floor more than fifteen feet away. Gavin himself was certain he had her by the right arm when suddenly the arm he thought he had, had him. She gave him a snapping jab under his left eye and then with astonishing speed grabbed his shirt with the same hand, lifted him up by the chest, and threw him down at her feet. The strength in that one arm was hydraulic. His gun jarred from his hand, flying into the chair's cushion.

As Gavin took in his bearings from his new floor-level position, he saw the drug-filled hypo nearby. Karianne was turning toward Katz, who let out a loud groan and then crumpled. As fast as he could, Gavin grabbed the hypo and stabbed it into soft vascular flesh behind Karianne's knee joint, burying the plunger into the hypo's barrel in the same motion. He only hoped whatever was in the syringe was fast acting.

Karianne reacted instantly, and with a flick of her leg, Gavin was thrown against the wall, collapsing the plaster between the studs. He fell back to the floor. As she came toward him he dove for the over-stuffed chair . . . and his gun. If he didn't shoot her now, she would kill them all. He found the gun quickly and spun to fire, but when he turned, she had already stopped. She blinked once . . . twice . . . then fell to the floor in a heap.

— 40 —

"One word, you said. 'I just want to say one word.' What was that word?" Katz yelled, shifting a bag of frozen peas from his swollen left eye to the back of his head. Gavin ignored the question as he placed a package of frozen blueberries on the back of Steinman's neck. He didn't want a psychological explanation to what had just happened; he wanted to talk to Buck. He reached for his cell phone before he remembered he had left it charging at home. He quickly looked around the room.

"Where's the phone in this place?" he said. The bruised and confused psychologist pointed to the kitchen.

With the receiver of the wall phone pinched between his cheek and shoulder Gavin searched his pockets and then his wallet for Buck's phone number, to no avail. "Great, Pierce," he said sarcastically. "No cell phone, no number. Can you at least remember the freaking city and state?"

The information operator gave him the number for Samantha's Dairy Farm. He dialed. One ring . . . two rings . . . the answering machine. He cursed. "Buck! Buck, are you there," he yelled into the receiver, hoping the preacher would pick up.

After a moment of silence the machine beeped and disconnected. Gavin redialed, going through the machine process again.

"Just like you to know while you're enjoying your country retirement, all hell's breaking loose down here — literally. Why did you even mention not saying 'Sabah'? You knew I would!"

He slammed the receiver again. Even if he had reached Buck there probably wasn't anything the ex-preacher could do over the phone except remind Gavin he had told him not to call Sabah by name in the first place. Now what was he going to have to do? Have Katz keep Karianne unconscious until he could drive all the way to the Catskills, kidnap Buck, and drive back? He'd probably strangle Buck first. But what other preacher would know what Buck knew? Maybe they all did. Maybe none did. How could he find out — look up *Demonology* in the Yellow Pages? He went back to the living room.

"You okay?" he said to Steinman, who was sitting on one of the dining room chairs, his elbows on his knees and his face in his hands.

"A little dizzy, but I'll be all right," he said.

Gavin looked at Karianne, who was now back on the couch as if nothing had ever happened. He was a little concerned about the broken leg she had been standing on, but much more nervous about who or what would wake up when the drug wore off. And what could Buck do even if he *was* here — cast the demon out of her so it could find another host and come back to get them? Wonderful, he thought. Now *he* was calling it a demon.

Gavin needed time to gather his thoughts. There had to be a logical explanation. Maybe Karianne had some kind of mutant, metaphysical, psychosomatic thing going on and maybe Katz could eventually figure it out. Yeah, right. And maybe he had not really woken up this morning and this was all a nightmare. The thought actually made him wonder.

"How long can you keep her out?" he asked Katz as he uprighted a lamp table. The lamp was broken in half, but Gavin put it on the table anyway.

"Why do you want me to keep her under?" Katz said. "Are you afraid she'll still —"

"How do I know what she'll do? The only thing I know is she didn't pay much attention to your shortcut."

"What does it mean?"

"What?"

"The word you said to her, Pierce. What do you think I'm talking about?" Katz replied in exasperation.

Gavin was wondering what to tell him when his beeper went off. He recognized the number at police headquarters. On a Sunday? He went back to the kitchen for the phone, hoping he hadn't broken it.

"Homicide. Sergeant Maloney," said a voice through the receiver.

"Sarge, Gavin Pierce," he said, then winced as he touched his left cheekbone. "You page me?"

"Yeah. Sorry to disturb your Sunday, but the lieutenant thought you might want to know there's been another crash and it looks like your boy. He fits all the physical descriptions, a dead ringer for the sketch, drunk as a skunk, and was driving the passenger's car. The only difference is he didn't get away. Fingerprints and hair samples are still pending, of course. Again, I know it's Sunday, but the lieutenant figured you might want to identify him."

Gavin was stunned speechless. He knew, of course, the possibility had always existed that Krogan would be caught this way, but somehow he'd thought . . .

"Hello? Pierce. Are you there?"

"Yeah, yeah. Listen, it's extremely important he be put on a suicide watch."

"That won't be necessary."

"What do you mean?"

"He's dead. Killed in the crash."

"He's dead?" Gavin squeezed the phone so hard he heard the plastic creaking. "What kind of crash was he in?"

"He drove into the broadside of a bus with a big pickup — hard. Sent it into a deli. Fortunately there were only two passengers and the deli was closed. He put the bus driver and the two passengers in the hospital, but nothing serious."

Nothing serious? "Are you sure it's him?"

"Well, we couldn't find any ID, so we won't know for certain until the prints come in."

"No ID? Does he have a tattoo?"

"Hmm. Don't know that."

"Can you ask someone?"

"Hold on."

Gavin held for what seemed like an eternity. Another pickup truck, he thought. Hitting the side of the bus also reminded him of Garrity's crash.

Maloney finally returned. "Nobody remembers seeing anything, but they weren't looking."

Gavin cursed. "Where is he?"

"The morgue."

"Okay, call the F.M.I. and get him to tell whoever's down there I'm coming in for an ID."

"Now?"

"I'm on my way," Gavin said and hung up.

Back in the living room, Katz had found the overstuffed chair.

"What's going on, Pierce? And don't tell me you don't know," he said.

"Later, Katz. That was headquarters. They've got Krogan."

"Seriously?" Katz said.

"He's dead."

Katz paused. "Well, what else is new? He's been doing that for over five thousand years."

"You have no idea, Katz. I'll be back as soon as I can. In the meantime, keep her out."

— 41 —

Foregoing the formalities of the front entrance, Gavin hurried down the vehicle ramp to the lower level of the Nassau County Medical Examiners building. As expected, the large steel door was open, a parked ambulance van in its bay.

"Can I help you, sir?" asked an attendant who intercepted Gavin as he rounded the van. The lanky man wore green sanitaries and had his reddish-brown hair tied back in a ponytail.

Gavin showed his shield. "Detective Pierce. I'm here about the vehicular homicide that arrived this morning. A big guy?"

The attendant nodded. "That was fast. I just got the call you were coming. He's still on the gurney. Follow me."

Gavin followed the young man into the building. He had seen about every violent act and consequence there was to see on the street and had no problem digesting his food after a particularly gruesome day. But the clinical atmosphere of this place and the people who worked here was something he had never gotten used to. The attendants did nothing to help that perception, even purposely enhanced it with what Gavin perceived as an exaggerated nonchalance whenever visitors like himself toured.

The attendant pushed open a glass door marked "Autopsy." Once inside, Gavin's eyes were immediately drawn to a white sheet covering a large mass that was still on the ambulance gurney, just as the attendant had said.

"Any tattoos?" Gavin asked, as the attendant circled to the other side of the dead body.

"As a matter of fact, yes. I remember seeing something on one of his shoulders."

Gavin's heart raced as the attendant peeled the sheet completely off. The forehead had a deep, open gash that ran diagonally from left eyeball to blond hairline. The face looked similar enough to the sketch to work, and his size fit the testimony of the bartender from the Seahorse Tavern.

"The tattoo?" Gavin asked.

"Right here," the attendant said.

Gavin hurried around the table. Ever since he had heard Krogan's name he had wanted to see it attached to a dead man. Now, after the impossible reaction Karianne had had to the name Sabah, he didn't know what he wanted.

"I've seen better," the attendant said as they stared at a snarling tiger head with blood on its teeth. Compared to the tattoo Gavin had expected to see, this one looked like a harmless kitten with milk on its whiskers. He wasn't sure of much these days, but he was sure of one thing: this wasn't Krogan.

Gavin was only two miles from Karianne's when his beeper sounded again. Of all days to have forgotten his cell phone. He thought of waiting to use the phone back at Karianne's — until he saw the number. He recognized it as the hospital's, although he didn't know the extension after the number. Maybe Amy needed him. He needed a phone and he needed it now.

At the next intersection he saw a pay phone at the corner gas station. He drove in and jumped out of the car, ramming a quarter into the machine and dialing.

"Community Hospital."

"Extension two-five-seven."

"Thank you."

"Hello?" said a voice Gavin recognized.

"Chris?"

"Gav! You owe me ten bucks. I called your house and no answer. I knew you couldn't do it."

Gavin sighed in relief to hear Chris's voice. "I'll give you twenty. I thought you were going home to watch the game."

"Ah, they said I need a couple more days. At least I get to see the game here. It's a great game, too. It's halftime and the Bears are up ten to three. Boy, I'd give anything to be there right now."

"You sound like Karianne," Gavin said, more relaxed. "She had a ticket and lost it in the crash somehow. I think it was right on the fifty, too."

Chris laughed. "Yeah, Krogan probably stole it. He's probably enjoying himself at the game right now. The camera will catch him and the creep will wave to us on TV."

Gavin didn't laugh. He mind was turning over a sudden, horrible thought: Krogan would look at football as a human demolition derby. Karianne had not been able to find her ticket. She thought she might have lost it at the Seahorse, and the bartender had said she offered it to him, but he never took it. She would have been too drunk to realize or remember if Krogan took it.

A moment later Gavin was screeching out of the gas station, the phone receiver left dangling from the cord, Chris still talking.

— 42 —

Gavin had the gas pedal crushed and a small red flasher blazing on his dashboard. Top speed in the Tiger was around 140, but the stock brakes were undersized and would fail at that speed, so he tried to keep it under 120.

Everything he had picked up over the last couple of days with Katz and Buck told him Krogan was at the game. He had to get there before the game ended. Chris said it was halftime. Giants Stadium was an hour away in New Jersey. The game would be over in about an hour and a half. He wanted to call for backup, but he couldn't chance Krogan being shot. He wasn't sure how he would handle him, either, but he would cross that bridge when he came to it.

He turned the radio on to the game, noting in frustration that the Bears had scored another touchdown. Unlike Chris, he didn't care which team won the game; he just didn't want the game to be a blowout. If Krogan got bored with a lop-sided rout, he might leave — or try to create a little excitement on his own.

As Gavin approached the parking area to Giants Stadium, he pulled the plug on the flasher, fearful the Goodyear blimp would spot him and televise his approach. The thought was highly unlikely, but he didn't care. He had never been to the stadium before and was not about to get sloppy now if he could help it.

He was surprised at the number of people still in the parking lot. The game was inside, yet the parking lot was full of tailgate parties with televisions and radios tuned in to the game.

He was about to turn the flasher back on when he considered that might draw the crowd rather than disperse it. Instead, he shifted into reverse so hard the gears ground, then floored the gas. The Tiger raced backward with a high-pitched whine. He spun the steering wheel and bumped onto a sidewalk, then screeched to a stop.

In an instant, he was dashing across the spacious parking lot, threading through tailgate parties and impromptu touch-football games. And barbecue smoke; there seemed to be enough rising into the air to whet the appetites of the blimp crew. Open coolers filled with ice and beer became hurdles for him as he searched for the straightest line to the entrance.

At the entrance gate he waved his shield to the confused but obliging faces of the stadium staff. Taking the steps two and three at a time, he headed for the second level by the fifty yard line where Karianne had said her seat was. As he ran through the concession corridor he saw the passageways to seating were listed by sections, not yard lines. Which one should he take? He ran through one of them.

All at once he was one of eighty thousand people. The game was in progress and he was even with the twenty. He approximated the distance to the fifty, then disappeared back into the corridor, his navy blue T-shirt soaked with sweat.

The next time he emerged into the sunlight, he was at the fifty. Gasping for air, he leaned over with his hands on his thighs and allowed himself a moment to catch his breath. When he straightened up he saw nothing but the back of heads. He hoped Krogan's big, blond hairdo would stand out among the crowd.

He made several sweeping scans before looking at the scoreboard to see how much time was left. The fourth quarter had just started. The Bears were still two touchdowns ahead, but the Giants had the ball. From the sound of the crowd, they weren't having much success moving it.

Where was he? Someone Krogan's size shouldn't be too hard to find, even in a crowd like this. Gavin started slowly down the center aisle, looking more carefully at each row. How could he not be here? He felt like arresting everyone for *not* being Krogan.

He walked down a little farther, then turned his back to the game. Maybe he would see the face in the sketch — the face he imagined even in his sleep, often riddled with bullet holes.

"Excuse me," said a husky voice from behind.

Gavin spun quickly.

"Easy," said a heavy, balding man with a black beard.

Gavin sighed and stepped aside. He walked the rest of the way down to the balcony railing, turning to pan slowly across the heads below him in the first tier, although he knew that wasn't where Kari-anne's seat was. An out-of-bounds tackle at the fifty caught his attention. An official threw a flag and several cameramen were helped off the ground. A penalty was announced for unnecessary roughness and another official marched off the damage against the Giants. The football players scrambled back into their respective huddles near midfield. On the other side of the field, the Bears' coaches were applauding the call.

The other side . . . Gavin suddenly flushed hotly with adrenaline. He was an idiot. His eyes immediately scanned the second level, but it was too far away. He was turning to run up the aisle when he noticed a nearby woman with stadium binoculars.

"Miss," he yelled as he pulled his shield from his back pocket and held it out. "I need those binoculars. Seriously! It's urgent."

At first she looked at him like he had to be kidding, but apparently thought better of it and passed them over. Without a thank you, he grabbed the glasses up and shot his gaze back to the other side, traveling quickly from one face to another. Right to left, bottom to top, one row, then another, then another.

He got to the top of the section, moved

to the other side of the center aisle, and started again at the bottom. No . . . no . . . no . . . no . . . Wait! Go back! He froze in place, unable to blink, as blood rushed into his face. It was him. *It was him!* The object of his rage was sitting stoically in sharp contrast to the smaller, more animated, fans surrounding him — the sketch come to life. He looked as big as anyone on the field.

"Here," Gavin said, handing off the binoculars, then sprinted up the steep center aisle and into the curved corridor. He had him. He definitely had him.

"Hey, there's no running in here," a security cop yelled as Gavin flew by. "I said stop!"

Gavin couldn't have slowed even if he wanted to. The adrenaline flowing through his veins was more than he had ever experienced. He expected the guard, who was still yelling, would radio his troops and try to intercept him. Good. The more help the better. Besides, Gavin didn't have any handcuffs with him, and they probably did.

He was amazed at Krogan's gall. To steal Karianne's ticket and then show up in her seat. He must have thought she'd died in the crash. Or was it possible he just didn't care? Whatever, Gavin would show him just how big a mistake he had made.

Ahead, two security guards stepped into the corridor. Calling his name to warn them, Gavin reached into his back pocket and pulled out his shield. Seeing it, they made no move to resist him.

"Come on," he yelled, waving them to follow. He called over his shoulder for one of them to radio the police and tell them the Ghost Driver was at Giants Stadium. One guard dropped back. Gavin suddenly wanted all the help he could get. And in a place like this, he wasn't afraid of armed help. He figured the chances of a fellow cop actually firing a shot off in Giants Stadium with seventy or eighty thousand people around was slim. He would finally have Krogan, and he would have him alive.

By the time he got to the other side of the fifty yard line six more guards had joined him. He was breathing so hard he could speak to them only between gasps.

"The Ghost Driver," he said, trying to catch his breath. "You know who I'm talking about?"

They all affirmed with nods.

"He's down in the first row." Gavin reached down to his ankle holster and pulled out his gun, then stuffed it into the front of his jeans and let his T-shirt fall over it. "I'm going down to introduce myself. I want half of you to go down the next aisle so he can't run. The other half of you can follow me. Wait until I'm halfway there."

Gavin was glad they all agreed because he was going with or without them. He hurried halfway down, then slowed himself. The killer was easy to see as long as the fans around him stayed in their seats. He stepped into the second row and politely excused his way through, hoping nobody would complain and draw attention to his location.

Krogan was so close he could practically smell him. The big man wore an olive-drab tank top, and Gavin's racing heart picked up when he saw the lettering tattooed across the back of the man's shoulders. The shirt covered half the height of the lettering, but there was no mistaking the word it spelled: Krogan.

Moving slowly up behind him, Gavin touched the gun barrel to the back of Krogan's head, to the sudden consternation of those around him, and spoke the words he'd longed to say: "The game's over, Krogan, or whatever your real name is. You're under arrest."

Fans quickly exited from the first three

rows and the guards rushed to fill the vacuum, surrounding Gavin and Krogan but allowing Gavin to make all the moves.

Surprisingly calm, Krogan looked over his shoulder. Gavin stared in the deep, freaky, empty gaze. Was he even human? Gavin didn't care. Whoever or whatever he had, he had him.

"Turn your ugly face back around and stay where you are or I'll take your head off," Gavin said, then motioned with his left hand to one of the guards for his handcuffs. His need was quickly satisfied as cold steel slapped into his palm.

"Hit him!" Krogan yelled toward the field. "Take him down."

Gavin couldn't believe it. Krogan was being arrested for multiple murders and he was more concerned with the Giants' inability to cope with the Bears' running game.

"Okay, Krogan. Real slow, put your left hand behind your head," Gavin said, pressing the gun harder against his neck.

"Here," Krogan said, raising his right hand. "I'd rather wear them on this hand. The nice watch that electric man gave me is on my left."

Gavin remembered the tanned outline he had seen on the dead utility man's wrist. Krogan's arrogance was astounding.

"You unbelievable scum," Gavin said, snapping a cuff on his right hand.

"Now I'll miss the end of the game," Krogan growled.

"Shut up and put your other hand behind your head or you'll miss the rest of your life!"

Krogan suddenly stood up and turned around. Gavin followed him up with the gun, for the first time looking his foe full in the face. Krogan's defiant smile was eerily reminiscent of Karianne's smile before she collapsed. The similarity was chilling.

"I'll tell you when to get up. Turn back around and put your hands behind your back."

"You're the detective that newsboy said to get in touch with, aren't you?" Krogan said, his smile widening. He snatched the handcuff away from Gavin's hand and closed it on his own right wrist, next to the other circlet. "I always wanted a bracelet like this," he said in mock admiration.

Gavin wished he had real cops with him. He couldn't expect these stadium employees to do anything more than look threatening. And Krogan was acting anything but threatened.

"You shouldn't have done that," he said,

not really knowing what else to say.

"You mean now I'm in more trouble?" Krogan laughed. "What are you going to do, shoot me?" He laughed louder. "Go ahead — shoot."

Gavin felt helpless. He finally had Krogan trapped, but he could do little more. He wanted to shoot him, at least in the leg to force cooperation, but to discharge a firearm in a stadium full of people was something he would save for a last resort. Besides, he couldn't get out of his mind what Buck had told him. After what had happened earlier with Karianne, he was now confused. Could it be possible the one he was after was really inside this giant? Was that why Krogan was so at ease with a gun staring him in the face? Gavin had never seen anything like it.

Just then, the radio on a security guard's belt came on, announcing the police had arrived at the gate. Thank God, Gavin thought. "Looks like I won't have to shoot you after all."

"Your friends have come to play?" Krogan mocked. "Good."

"You won't be wearing that smirk for long. Today's payday, Krogan. And you've run up quite a tab," Gavin said. Spontaneously, he added, "And we've got just the cell for you. One you'll be in for the rest of your life. And I'll make sure it's a long, safe, lonely life. Compliments of Sabah."

The smile that so confidently decorated Krogan's face vanished. He obviously recognized the name. In fact, Gavin actually thought he caught a tinge of concern in the killer's expression. He stared straight into Gavin's eyes. Gavin stared back, but didn't feel as confident as he would have liked. He blamed Buck — it was the preacher's fault he was now thinking he might be facing a demon, not a man. "A demon other demons envy for his power," Buck had said. It made Gavin edgy when he most needed to be in control.

"They're here," said one of the security guards.

Now it was Gavin's turn to smile, as he heard the sound of feet hastening toward him and knew Krogan saw his end approaching.

It was in the split second Gavin glanced in the direction of his rescuers that Krogan made his move. Before Gavin could respond, Krogan spun around, hurdled the railing, and was gone. Gavin sprang to the barrier. The drop was over twenty feet to the field-level seating. To his surprise, Krogan wasn't sprawled out on the ground. He had pulled himself up to his feet and taken off down the aisle toward the field. Below, where he had landed, a small crowd was circling around the two people who had apparently broken his fall.

Gavin heard the men behind him radioing what had happened and the perpetrator's new position. Radioing to whom? Stadium guards? The real police, who had responded to the call, were all up here with him.

"Agghhh," Gavin screamed. He grabbed hold of the rail, his knuckles turning white. His only real chance of getting Krogan now was to jump after him. Desperate, he blew out three times in rapid succession, closed his eyes, and threw himself over the metal bar. Just as his hands released, he felt arms grabbing and pulling him back.

"Are all you Nassau County guys crazy or just you?" said one of the New Jersey police. "You trying to kill yourself or just whoever you land on?"

Gavin didn't answer. He watched Krogan, who was knocking over cameramen on his way to the sideline. The psycho was headed for the field and anyone who got in his way was instantly smashed to the ground. So enraged that he felt beyond sanity, Gavin did the unthinkable — the unfathomable — for such a place as Giants Stadium. He pointed his gun at Krogan. If Krogan went out onto the field, maybe Gavin could get off a clean shot. Hopefully the bullet would not kill him. He sighted on his target . . .

A hand came from Gavin's side and seized his arm, pushing his gun into the air. "Snap out of it, man. You're going to get someone killed and start a panic. He can't get outta here without running into us. We'll get him," a New Jersey cop said.

Almost in a daze, Gavin looked at the cop in disbelief, then back at Krogan.

Krogan had broken out onto the field while a play was already in progress. The Bears had the ball and one of their running backs had broken into the secondary and was headed for the end zone with nobody left to stop him. Krogan, whom everyone had expected to try to escape, was now trying to tackle that running back.

Watching the scene, Gavin was reminded of the graphic scenes Karianne had spoken of — tales of the Roman coliseums and the delight Krogan had exhibited as he publicly murdered helpless Christians, running them down with a chariot. Was Krogan now taking a time-out from his escape to relive an old thrill, or was this part of the escape?

Down on the field, the football player had seen Krogan coming and now held out his arm to stop him. Krogan hit him so hard the entire stadium recoiled on impact. Krogan then scooped up the fumbled ball, leaving the Bears' number thirty-one motionless, face down in the turf. As he ran through the end zone, two security guards leaped before him. Krogan rifled the football into one face, then lowered his shoulder and rammed the other. Then he disappeared into the service tunnel.

A moment later Gavin found himself running through curved corridors and down stairways until he was in the service tunnel. There, security guards were tending to the broken bodies of the ones who were supposed to have stopped Krogan.

The killer was gone.

— 43 —

Amy came back into Amber's room with a glass of orange juice. Amber was sitting up in bed; no one else was there. Earlier, Dr. Fagan had given Amber a clean bill of health but told her she was going to have to remain in the hospital for at least the rest of the week for precautionary observations.

"Thanks, sis," Amber said as she took the juice. She sipped, then set it on the table next to three open tissue boxes. On the floor next to the table was a trash-can half full of used tissues. Scattered around it were others that had missed the basket.

Amy snuggled up next to Amber and put her arm around her. Amber melted into her loving sister's embrace and Amy squeezed her hard enough to assure her sister she still wanted to be there, even after spending all last night in that same position. As far as Amy was concerned, she was going to remain there until her sister was released.

As exhausted as Amy had been, her night's sleep had been interrupted constantly, haunted by her sister's grieving moans as she relived memories of happier times. At each gut-cramping groan, Amy's mind was tortured afresh with her own memories of her brother-in-law.

Grief was not the only thing to blame for Amy's lack of sleep. There was also fear — a living, growing, nagging fear brought on by Buck's explanation of who or what Krogan was. Amy could not comprehend why Gavin wouldn't at least consider Buck's story a possibility. She had determined, though, that his opinion was not going to blind her. As far as she was concerned, Katz was probably wrong and Buck was probably right. She wished it were the other way around, but she was not going to hide from what she believed to be the truth just because she preferred the convenience of reincarnation over demonic possession. Truth was truth and she was not going to believe that grass was violet just because violet was a prettier color than green. Grass was green and Krogan was a demon.

Thinking of Gavin made Amy want to

tell Amber about him — how close she felt to him and how she wanted to get to know him more. But she didn't dare — not with her twin hurting so. Hopefully someday soon.

"When they let you out of here, you'll move in with me for a while," she said to Amber.

"Amy, I can't. I need to —"

"You need to do nothing. And I need to know you're all right. You'll move in with me where I can keep my eyes on you and that's final. I need that."

Amber's swollen red eyes filled with fresh tears as she held Amy tightly. Amy closed her eyes and rested her head against the propped up pillow. Her hand found Amber's black hair and stroked it gently while her mind drifted again to Gavin. She wondered where he was. She appreciated his respect and patience in not interviewing Amber, but she found she missed him. She glanced over at the phone, wanting to hear his voice. But, no, this was Amber's time. Everything and everyone else would have to wait, including Gavin. And Krogan.

Amy's parents quietly entered the room, apparently wondering if the girls were asleep. Amy saw them, but didn't say anything. Even simple hellos seemed somehow inappropriate now. Both parents silently kissed their children, then took seats without a word. There was nothing that could be said and no questions that couldn't be answered with one look at Amber in a near fetal position, holding Amy near.

The food cart appeared in front of a young woman in a red-and-white-striped uniform. She smiled silently and placed Amber's covered dinner on the mobile bed tray. "I'll just leave it here," she whispered, apparently thinking better of disturbing anyone.

"Come on, Amber," Amy said, pulling the tray over the bed. "Whether you want to or not, you have to eat."

"I don't think I can," Amber said. She unwrapped herself from her sister and sat up.

"Well, we're going to try," Amy said, pulling the cover off the plate to reveal steamed chicken, carrots, mashed potatoes, and apple juice, with one cube of jiggling red gelatin for dessert. The meal did nothing to stir Amy's appetite, and she was sure Amber was likewise unenthused.

"Okay!" Amy said, stabbing a small carrot and bringing it to her sister's mouth.

Amber obliged, chewed, then curled her lip slightly. "Tastes like nothing," she said.

"That's okay. You have to get your body used to food again. Next week at this time we'll be eating a lobster dinner together."

"Lobster?" Amber said, wrinkling her nose. "I don't think so."

"Why? You've always loved lobster."

Amber shook her head slowly. "Not anymore. I saw this crazy guy tear a live lobster in half and eat it right in front of me. It was the grossest thing I've ever seen. I can't even think of a lobster without seeing his face."

Amy smiled to hear her sister talking about something other than her husband's death. "And when was this?" she said, trying to stimulate the conversation further.

"It was the morning before the crash. Some lobster fisherman. We got too close to the back of his boat while he was pulling up traps. He was furious, although we hadn't done any harm. Mitchell just wasn't used to handling such a large boat. Mitchell . . . Oh, Amy. I want Mitchell back," she cried.

Amy cradled her sister's tear-swollen face on her shoulder, thinking about what Amber had just said. She frowned. "You came too close to the back of a boat?"

"Uh-huh."

"Did you see a name on the boat?" Amy asked as calmly as she could manage, although she suddenly felt like shouting.

"Oh, what was it? I was staring right at it for what seemed like an eternity, and now I —"

"Try Amber," Amy said sharply, drawing frowns from her parents.

"Shanghai . . . Shangri-La . . . Shha—"

"Shadahd?" Amy finally said, much louder than she'd meant to.

"Yeah! That was it. *Shadahd.*"

Amy had to leave. She didn't quite know yet what she was going to do, but she knew she had to move. She was shaking.

"What's wrong?" Amber said as Amy slid off the bed.

"I . . . I need to —" She was about to say "make a call" but realized she didn't want Amber to overhear the conversation. What would happen to Amber if she suddenly realized her grossed-out lobster fisherman was the man who'd killed her husband, simply for sailing too close to his boat? "— talk to Gavin's partner, Chris Grella," she said to three frowning faces. "I'll be right back."

— 44 —

Amy forced herself to walk calmly until she was out the door. Then she ran to Chris's room, almost sliding by his doorway as she tried to stop on the freshly waxed floor. Inside, she found Chris watching football. She started to tell him about the lobster boat, then realized she could not. What if Chris called the police and they found and killed Krogan before Gavin could insist they capture him? If there really was a demon, it would be freed.

"Age and treachery always win over youth and zeal," she said to herself, quoting another of her sayings. Not this time. Krogan had had a millennia's worth of age and treachery. And she still had the element of surprise.

"Hello, earth to Amy," Chris was saying as he waved his hand. He turned back to the TV set.

Amy blinked. "How are you, Chris?" she

said, wishing she had simply used the cell phone in her handbag back in Amber's room.

"I'd be a lot better if Gavin would return my page," he said. "I've beeped him three times."

"Why don't you call his cell phone? Maybe he's left his beeper at home."

"Actually, he left his cell phone home. That's the problem. The last time I spoke to him was almost two hours ago. I think he went to Giants Stadium to find Krogan. And from what I just saw on TV, I think he found him."

"*What?*"

"When he called me before, I joked that Karianne couldn't find her ticket because Krogan probably stole it. The next thing I knew, Gavin was gone. It wasn't until I hung up that I realized how much sense it made. Then," Chris said, pointing to the TV, "halfway through the fourth quarter this big, blond maniac stops the game by running onto the field and tackling the Bears' running back. What a hit he laid on the guy! The game stopped for almost fifteen minutes while they got the guy back on his feet and sorted out all the confusion."

"Did they catch him?"

"That's what I've been trying to find out. I called headquarters, but they don't know anything. I called the stadium, but they're not talking. And I can't get Gavin to call me back. My money says Gavin flushed him out onto the field somehow."

"So maybe they've got him."

"I don't know. The blimp showed a lot of activity outside the stadium and the announcers were all asking the same thing, which makes me doubt they did. I wish I could get out of here."

"You stay where you are," Amy commanded. "If Gavin calls you, tell him to call me on my cell phone." She turned to leave.

"Where are you going?" Chris asked.

"Fishing."

— 45 —

Amy parked her father's car at the Hempstead Harbor Marina under the only shade tree she could find and exhaled nervously. She didn't know if the butterflies in her stomach were more from excitement or terror. Her father hadn't been happy about giving her the keys without her telling him where she was going, but he finally did at her promise it was urgent and that she would bring it back before visiting hours were over. She had stopped at her house in order to confirm the *Shadahd*'s registration. She had also tapped into the county's system to see where the boat was docked. She found a commercial boat named *Shadahd* was owned by a Karl Dengler and was docked at the Hempstead Harbor Marina. She changed into cut-off shorts and transferred what she wanted from her handbag to a fanny pack, trying to look like she belonged by the boats.

Before getting out of the car, she paged Gavin with her cell phone number. She knew Chris had tried unsuccessfully to get him, but maybe he'd been busy and figured he could call Chris later. Maybe if he saw her number he would respond faster. She liked to think so.

She took another deep breath, exhaled, and got out of the car. Act natural. Casual. Relax. She had taken no more than a few steps when a mussel smashed onto the blacktop before her. She gasped, jumping back, then relaxed as a seagull swooped down and snagged the now cracked open morsel of tasty food and flew off. She frowned, angry at her jitters. What was there to be afraid of anyway? The sun was shining, people were fishing on the pier, the beach was lined with sunbathers, and a not-so-small crowd was watching a man attach the wings on some kind of strange-looking seaplane. She wondered if he was the same guy Gavin had told her about.

Enough of this nonsense. Back to the original plan. Relax. Just another day. Walk down to the boat slips like an owner or at least a friend of an owner.

Before taking the ramp to the slips a good eight feet below, she surveyed the boats. She was no expert, but the three large, commercial-looking gray crafts at the end of the dock did not blend in very well with the spit-and-polish pleasure fleet that occupied the rest of the marina. She exhaled once again and walked on.

The bottom of the ramp was on wheels in order to adjust with the tides; judging from where the wheels were now, it was high tide. She wasn't sure what type of hours fishermen kept, but it was after five on a Sunday. She passed a couple of young men hosing off fishing rods. They paused to smile at her. She returned their smile and, seeing a large cooler full of iced-up fish, gave them a thumbs-up. See? She belonged there. Fish were cool.

"Want one? We've got plenty," said one of them.

"Yeah," said the other, the water from the hose he was holding now going into their boat.

"Uh, no thanks," she said as she continued, feeling a little more like she was in her environment.

So far so good. As she neared the fishing boats she could see piles of lobster traps on the dock next to them. She also could now see they weren't actually in slips, but tied to the dock's side. She walked by the first one and looked at the name on the stern.

"*Bass Ackwards*," she said to herself. Cute. About sixty feet later she came to the stern of the second boat. "*Osprey*," she read.

The last boat was the largest by about 50 percent. She paused at the bow and touched the cold, gray hull. She wondered if there was anything evil and unseen guarding it for Krogan. Maybe Krogan was getting a vision of her right now. She knew so little about what Buck had told them that she now found herself stirring up fears from old ghost and horror stories. Keep moving.

A little further down the bow, she came to a small porthole. She glanced over her shoulder to see if there was anyone watching. Nobody, not even the two young fishermen. Carefully she cupped the light away from her eyes and peeked in through the dirty glass. The interior was spacious enough, but half full of junk haphazardly strewn about. Frayed netting, broken pieces of algae-soiled Styrofoam buoys, various sizes of rusted chain, a gross-looking mattress propped up on bent lobster traps . . . and a shotgun next to the mattress.

Amy left the porthole and casually walked past the stern to the end of the dock, paused, and walked back. There was something about seeing the ancient word spelled out in bold black letters that sent a shiver through her body. *Shadahd.* She wondered if the man, Karl Dengler, even knew what the word meant. On second thought, he probably did. Maybe more than she. Maybe even more than Buck.

She continued back toward the pleasure boats. Mission accomplished. Now she could tell Gavin and the police could lay a trap for the killer. She didn't know what, but Gavin would figure something out. She was sure they could easily wait until he was on the boat, then bust out of the woodwork and surround him. Eventually he would have to come out. If they got impatient they could use some tear gas or something. There would be so many police here they could even pick up the boat and carry it to jail, she joked to herself, feeling better.

But what if Gavin didn't care about taking him alive? He hadn't believed a word of what Buck said. He had told Buck he would give Krogan two seconds to give up and then shoot.

The shotgun. She stopped as the thought hit her. If Krogan had a shotgun, someone was going to get shot.

Not *someone*. Gavin was going to get shot.

Without thinking, she turned and ran back. Going into the boat was insane, but so was leaving the weapon for a monster who couldn't care less about killing. She made up her mind. Taking one quick look around, she hopped over the side of the boat, crouching, crawling, moving quickly like a crab to the cabin door. There was a padlock, but it wasn't latched, apparently used only to keep the door closed. She reached up and slipped the lock out of the loop, then placed it on the floor. A moment later, she was inside, sliding the door closed behind her.

Inside she gasped and covered her mouth and nose with her hand. It didn't help. The place was hot enough to bake bread and smelled like dead fish. To her right was the steering wheel and controls. Straight ahead was a small stairway that led down into the bow, where the gun was. With no time to waste, she scurried down the stairs, almost slipping on empty liquor bottles. There was a garbage can, but it was full to spilling over. What a pig, she thought. How did he ever get a boat like this in the first place?

The shotgun was leaning on the stained

mattress. Amy's arms were beaded with sweat and her shirt was starting to stick. She didn't want to touch anything, for fear of contracting some lethal disease from whatever toxic and viral strains were mutating in the filth around her. The first thing she was going to do after tossing the gun into the water was go home, throw her clothes in the garbage can, and take a long, hot shower. On second thought, she would go for a swim before even getting back into the car.

She took a step and, balancing on one leg, reached over to retrieve the gun without touching anything else. As she touched the barrel, her cell phone rang. She gasped, the noise startling her back onto two legs. She quickly unzipped her fanny pack as it rang again, the noise alarmingly loud.

"Hello?" she said breathlessly, trying to look through the slimy porthole to see if anyone was coming.

"Hi! Are you alright?"

"Gavin!" She was relieved to hear his voice.

"I got your page, but I didn't have my phone. I just stopped home on my way to Karianne's. You're not going to believe what's been happening."

"Neither are you," she said.

"Yeah, well top this: I said the word 'Sabah' to Karianne when she was under hypnosis —"

"Buck told us not to do that."

"Uh, well, anyway, she nearly killed Steinman, Katz, and me with her bare hands. Fortunately we were able to tranquilize her. Then —"

"You found Krogan at Giants Stadium?"

"How did you know?"

"Chris saw it on TV, with the rest of the world."

"Chris . . . I have to call him."

"Now my turn," Amy said, anxious to hear his surprised reaction. "I'm inside a lobster boat named, get this, *Shadahd.*"

"What?"

"Krogan is really Karl Dengler and he's a lobster fisherman. An endless supply of lobster claws."

"Amy! Get out of there! Now!"

She held the phone away from her ear. "Believe me, that is exactly what I'm going to do as soon as I get this shotgun and —"

"Where are you?" Gavin screamed.

"Hempstead Harbor Marina. Gavin, he was right here under our noses all the time and we di—"

The phone was grabbed from her hand a

split second before she crashed headlong into a tangled pile of netting, then rolled onto a rusted chain and barnacle-encrusted anchor.

"Hello, pretty girl."

— 46 —

Krogan stood there, seemingly in thought. His mass shrunk the room. His rippled arms were cut and scraped and his tank top was torn and soiled. Amy's heart hammered. Apparently he had heard enough of the conversation to surmise his situation. The longer he stood there the angrier he appeared. Finally he let out a primeval scream and kicked the garbage can, sending bottles and broken glass everywhere. He then brought the cell phone to his mouth.

"Gavin, huh? I didn't expect to be speaking to you again so soon."

"Krogan?" came Gavin's voice through the receiver, barely loud enough for Amy to hear.

"Very good. That's why you're a detective. You're good at figuring things out. I'm a detective, too. You know what I just figured out? I figure this nosey wench just put me out of the lobster business. She'll die for that. But not before I have some fun with her. If you want my boat so bad, you'll have to pry it out of another. I never was a big fan of freedom or New York. You think you're so smart, figure that one out, Detective."

Krogan smashed the phone against the wall and turned to Amy with a smile. "Well, pretty girl. Anyone who looks for me as hard as you deserves my best. Just whisper in my ear if I'm moving too fast."

Amy was scared less by his ominous presence than by what she knew about him. She didn't know if Karl Dengler knew anything about Krogan's past, but she knew the demon in him found his comfort in terror and destruction and she wasn't going to worry anymore about killing him. So what if he disappeared and popped up in someone else? At least it would be someplace else, and right now that seemed like a good thing.

She glanced at the shotgun and knew by the way he followed her eyes that the weapon was loaded.

Krogan took a step in her direction and she dove for the shotgun. The instant she grabbed the stock, he grabbed the barrel, snatching it away from her with a laugh.

"All right," he said. "This is my lucky

day." His hungry, wild eyes were a vacuum of darkness, feeding like a shark off her terror.

She leaned back hard into the netting as he approached until all she could see was his enormous bulk.

— 47 —

For one horrified instant Gavin stared at his phone. Then he was bolting for the door. Cedar saw him coming and scrambled to get out of the way, his paws slipping on the oak floor. The aluminum storm door slammed against the handrail as Gavin landed on the walkway, then cleared the chain-link fence . . . and stopped. There was a white pickup truck in his driveway and someone was getting out.

Five minutes ago there was no one in the world Gavin would rather have seen than the man who emerged from the truck. But right now all he wanted was to get to the marina as fast as possible.

"Detective Pierce!"

"Buck, I don't know what you're doing here but you've got to let me out of the driveway — now."

"I came as soon as I got your message. I told you not to —"

"*Get out of the driveway!* Krogan's got Amy in a fishing boat. I've got to stop him before he gets out of the harbor."

Buck's expression stiffened. "I have to come with you. We'll take my truck. You drive." He threw Gavin the keys, which Gavin immediately threw back.

"You can come if you like, but we'll take my car," he yelled as he hopped into his Sunbeam Tiger and started the engine with a throaty roar.

Buck quickly backed his pickup out of the driveway to the opposite curb. He hurried to Gavin, carrying an old wooden chest the size of a milk crate.

"What's that?" Gavin said.

"A tool of the trade."

"Come on. Put it in the back and get in already," Gavin said, folding up the seat for him. He watched impatiently as Buck stored the chest.

Before Buck had the door closed Gavin hit the gas, whiplashing Buck and leaving a cloud of exhaust behind them. Keeping the pedal to the floor, Gavin threw the four-speed into second and then third, chirping the tires each time. He then put the flashing red light on the dashboard before shifting into fourth.

"I think I can understand why we took

your car," Buck said loudly enough to be heard over the engine and wind.

Gavin handed Buck the cell phone and told him to dial 911.

"That would be a huge mistake, Detective," Buck said.

"A mistake I should have made this afternoon. Now dial," Gavin commanded. "We're going to need all the help we can get as soon as we can get it."

"They're going to kill him and Krogan will be free. You have to believe me when I tell you your fight is not only against flesh and blood."

"Tell me about it," Gavin acknowledged.

"You mean Sabah?"

"You got it."

"I told you not to."

"That's why I did it. I had to know."

"What actually happened?"

"Later. Call 911. We'll surround him and he'll have to give up."

"Please, Detective. You've faced him. You've followed him through five thousand years. Stop listening to your police training and tell me: is Krogan going to give up? Is he going to let anyone take him alive?"

"Then we'll kill the monster. We'll catch him the next time, or we'll kill him again and catch him the time after that. At least

Amy will have a chance."

"Krogan knows you'll do this. He's counting on it. You can't match his craftiness with your logic and emotion. Your men will swarm him from every direction and he'll kill Amy so they'll have no choice but to kill him. When he found out his host's fun-filled life was going to change he had to have been very angry. The faster he can find a new host the better for him."

"But if we don't catch him, he'll kamikaze some party boat and kill himself and Amy and half the people on board. I can't let that happen," Gavin said, downshifting to second for a hard turn, then slamming it into third.

"Then we have to catch him. It's our only chance of keeping everyone alive," Buck pleaded.

Gavin growled in frustration. "Then dial this number," he said, handing him his beeper.

Buck dialed the number and handed the phone over to Gavin.

"Hello?"

"Chris!"

"Gav! Where are you? I've been paging —"

"I can't talk about it now. There's something you've got to do for us."

"Shoot."

"Two boats: *Freedom* and *New York*. Find out what they are and where they are, then call me on my cell phone. They could be anything from an old tall ship to a navy vessel to a party boat to a tour boat. Fast, Chris."

"You got it, pal."

Gavin hung up and concentrated on driving. A few minutes later he was fishtailing into the marina parking lot, alternately downshifting and speeding up as he wove through the cars. He soon found himself racing down the same fishing pier Krogan had when he'd crashed through the fencing and into the sailboat. By the time he skidded to a stop at the temporary barricade that had replaced the broken railing, Buck's hands were splayed against the dashboard and a couple of fishermen were clinging to the pier's outer rails.

Gavin was out the door in a flash and up onto the barricade, his hand blocking the sun from his eyes as he searched the harbor's mouth for the lobster boat. Nothing.

"Did either of you see a lobster boat leave the marina?" he yelled to the shaken fishermen.

They both nodded, one of them pointing out of the harbor.

"And I'll bet it was going a lot faster

than the five-mile-per-hour speed limit," Gavin said.

The fishermen nodded, then looked at each other oddly, as if they thought he was going to give a lobster fisherman a ticket for speeding in the harbor.

Gavin ignored them. Down to his left were the boat slips. Several boats were slowly maneuvering in and out, but they were mostly sailboats and cabin cruisers and would have little chance of catching up to the lobster boat. To his right was the boat ramp, with boats going in and out of the water. Maybe he could use one of the ones already in. He scanned the half dozen or so waiting their turn, but saw only little ski boats and runabouts. Why was it that every other time he had come down to the marina, he had been wowed by at least one or two ocean racers, yet now, when he needed one, there were none?

Frustrated, Gavin hopped back in the car and slammed it into reverse. Next to him Buck sat with eyes closed.

— 48 —

Amy lay face down on the rotten, liquor-bathed mattress. Before Krogan showed up, she had tried her best not to touch it lest some horrid disease invade the pores of her skin. Now she was trussed up on it like an animal awaiting slaughter. Her hands were tied so tightly to her ankles she could barely feel her fingers anymore. Another droplet of blood crawled from the cut over her left ear along her bruised, sweaty cheek to her lips.

Fortunately, thanks to her phone call to Gavin, Krogan had been in a hurry and hadn't taken the time for any indulgences. Of course, nothing would have been easier than for him to kill her outright, but he seemed willing to keep her alive, at least for the moment. If there was anything to be learned from the sessions with Karianne — or rather Sabah — killing was to be savored. Looked forward to, like dessert after a fine meal. Krogan had pretty much told her so, beating her only to the point that she would allow him to tie her up. He wanted her fully alert and horrified at whatever he had coming.

He had taken the shotgun with him. Through the open doorway she could see him from the waist down. He was at the steering wheel and she hoped he would stay there. In one hand he had a fifth of clear liquor. Whatever it was, he was downing it fast. She wondered how long she had before the inevitable crash. Knowing the Krogan that Sabah had revealed, she knew his target would be large, yet sinkable. Something the size of a yacht, she thought. A ferry maybe. What kind of boat would be in the water, full of people on a Sunday evening before sunset? Whatever and wherever it was, she wasn't about to just lay there and let it happen.

She rolled to her side and tried to lower her tied wrists under her buttocks. She could not. She rolled back to her abdomen and struggled to raise her rump, dragging her chin on the mattress until she was up on her knees. Next to her was another dirty porthole, opposite the one she had originally looked through. She wished she had never peeked in; after all her good intentions, Krogan still had the shotgun.

Peering out the window, she saw they were about a thousand feet off a shoreline she did not recognize. The very fact the shoreline was off the left side meant they were traveling west, toward Manhattan. She was surprised at the speed they were traveling at — for such a large boat *Shadahd* could move.

"I'm sorry. You wanted a view?"

Amy turned her head as far as she could without falling to see Krogan crouched down, staring at her through the shallow doorway. The engines suddenly slowed to an idle; the excess momentum made Amy fall forward onto her face. Terror snapped at her mind like an uncoiling viper and she fought to control a scream. What perverse ideas were marching him toward her . . . alone in the water . . . tied up and at his mercy?

Her eyes widened as Krogan slowly knelt down beside her. He looked her up and down, examining her like an unwrapped gift. Then he closed his eyes and whispered close to her ear, "Listen . . . can you hear it?"

Amy couldn't answer. She sensed whatever she said might snap him into a violent rage. But then, so could her silence.

"Your heart. I can hear your heart. It's

beating for me. Boom, boom, boom, boom, boom," he said, slowly at first, then faster and faster until Amy could swear he actually was in rhythm with her racing pulse.

"*Boom!*" he yelled, his eyes popping open, his face inches from hers.

Amy startled. She jerked again as he touched her leg.

"Very smooth," he said, then brought his nose to the back of her thigh and licked her. "Mmm . . . Did you shave just for me?"

Amy began to tremble uncontrollably. She had been determined not to cry, but her shivers turned to whimpers. Krogan began to laugh, and she felt his hot breath against her. She struggled violently to gain control of herself and to get his slithering, slimy tongue off her.

"You coward," she screamed.

Krogan laughed loudly. "Brave girl. We'll see how tough you are."

— 49 —

The moment Gavin pulled into the boat-ramp parking lot, he saw the boat he wanted. Sitting on a huge trailer hooked onto a Range Rover was almost thirty feet of streamlined ocean racer, its bow taking up at least three quarters of the boat. Perfect. The boat should be able to catch Krogan fairly rapidly — if, that is, they chose the correct direction once out of the harbor.

Both Buck and Gavin got out of the car, but Gavin motioned Buck to remain there. He didn't want this scene to be any more confusing to the boat owner than it had to be. The man in the Range Rover frowned as Gavin ran toward him, his shield out and in clear view.

"Sir. I'm Detective Pierce of the Nassau County Police Department and this is a police emergency. I need the use of a boat and driver to apprehend an escaped felon."

"Yeah, right," the man said incredulously. He looked at his buddy in the seat next to him and laughed.

"I'm serious."

"And you want to use me and my boat?"

"It's a matter of life and death," Gavin said.

"Don't the police have any more boats or helicopters?" the man said as he laughed again.

Gavin was too desperate to feel like a fool, but he didn't have an answer that would make any sense. He couldn't very well tell the guy he was afraid of involving other policemen, and he didn't have time to explain why.

"If you're worried about your boat, I'll take personal responsibility for it. We'll go right now to the front of the line. You'll be a hero tomorrow whether we catch him or not." Gavin was lying; for doing what he was doing, he'd probably be fired by this time tomorrow.

"Personally responsible? Do you have any idea what you're talking about? Do you know what this boat cost? And what are we going to do, get shot at? Sorry, pal, I gave at the office. Besides, nobody's going anywhere until the wild-man with the flying machine gets his crazy contraption off the ramp . . . again. Now there's someone you should arrest."

Gavin didn't even remember running toward the ultralight, but suddenly he was there.

"Hey, uh, Bill, right?" he said, grabbing the man by the arm as he was climbing into the pilot's seat of his experimental seaplane.

"Huh? Oh, hi, Detective. Look, I'm really sorry for the holdup. I didn't open my gas valve all the way and it conked out right here. But as you can see, the engine's back on and purrin' like a kitten. I'll be outta here before you can tell me to, uh, get outta here."

"Forget that," Gavin said, shaking his head. "The last time I saw you, you said you would take me for a ride sometime."

"Yeah, sure. But didn't you say you were afraid of heights?"

"This is an emergency. Did you happen to see a lobster boat leaving a short while ago?"

"You mean *Shadahd*? You bet I did. I've always got an eye peeled for that guy when I'm around here. He hates me — always gives me the finger for no reason. For the life of me, I don't know what I ever did to him. I think he's dangerous."

"More than you know. He's the Ghost Driver."

"No way! Him?"

"That's right. And right now he's on the run with a hostage on board."

"Seriously?"

"Dead serious. Will you help me catch him?"

"Me?" Bill said, his voice rising. "Now? In this?"

"Yes, yes, and yes. Please, we have to do this fast."

"But —"

"I can't tell you anything else. This is all extremely confidential. I'm desperate. Please!" Gavin tried very hard not to think about the fact he was asking to go into the air in a glorified kite with a motor. All he could focus on was Amy.

Bill took a brief pause to frown suspiciously. "Why would this be confidential?"

"That's also confidential."

Bill rolled his eyes. "Okay, whatever. You don't have to explain yourself. A ride is a ride. Get in!"

"One more thing," Gavin said, seeing Buck approach with his wooden chest. "There's two of us."

Bill turned to see Buck. "Him?"

"Me," Buck chimed in.

"What's with the chest?" Bill asked.

"It's . . . confidential," Gavin said with a shrug. "I don't even know."

"Weird," Bill said, nodding. "But three is illegal."

"I'm a cop."

"I don't have any extra helmets."

"Then don't crash," Gavin said, ready to explode with anxiety.

"The extra weight will make takeoff a little harder and our airspeed a bit slower, but we have the power."

"Then let's go, already," Buck said.

"Okay, you get in the seat," Bill said to Buck. "And you sit in front of his seat, Detective. Hold on tight to the back of my seat and keep your feet on the mono-float."

In a few moments all three were snuggly in place. Gavin sat in front of Buck's feet on a six-inch pipe, the main body of the plane to which everything appeared to be either bolted or strapped. His fingers dug reflexively into the back of Bill's seat as the pilot throttled up. As the ultralight rolled down the rest of the boat ramp, Gavin looked to his left, then wished he hadn't. Everyone around was staring at the spectacle. Their expressions mirrored the thought Gavin was desperately denying:

they were doomed. He closed his eyes and prayed. He begged for God's immediate attention. After all, wasn't he chasing one of God's mistakes? He held his eyelids tightly shut as the roar of the engine behind him grew louder and louder until the engine was screaming like a dozen lawnmowers and the waves blurred by, slapping with increasing frequency against the frame in a drumroll of noise. "Please remember Buck is with us on this thing," Gavin verbally added to his prayer. "He's on your side."

Just then, the barrage of watery noise stopped. Gavin's eyelids remained stoically shut. He felt like he was in a confused elevator — weightless, then rising against gravity, then weightless again. The engine itself continued its steady roar. That was a good sign, he hoped. He cracked open his eyes, although he refused to look downward, focusing instead on the back of Bill's white helmet and noting the microphone arm that jutted from the side.

"How are you doing?" Buck yelled, tapping Gavin on the shoulder.

Gavin released the grip of his right hand just long enough to make an OK sign, then quickly regrabbed.

"We should be able to see them soon, no matter what direction they went," Bill yelled over his right shoulder, inches from Gavin's face.

"Aren't you ever afraid of this thing crashing?" Gavin yelled back.

"Nah. It's a lot stronger than it looks. Besides, if there's a problem, there's always the ballistic chute," he said, tapping a white canister the size of a two-quart soda bottle mounted over his head on the front of the wing. "It fully deploys in a second and a half with a pull of the lever under my seat. And if that fails, I have a smaller version attached to my vest. I like to know I can abandon ship if I need to."

Gavin suddenly wanted his own personal ballistic parachute.

— 50 —

Amy's terror-filled eyes widened as Krogan drained the last of his bottle and dropped it on the floor with the others. She turned her head away, then squealed in pain as he grabbed her hair. She was tense with fear and anger. If he were going to rape her he would have to tear her pants off because she was going to fight as hard as she could.

Krogan laughed casually and pushed her face into the mattress until she couldn't breathe. She fought desperately to lift her head or turn it to the side, but he was too strong. Her concern about composure vanished as she screamed hopelessly, her muffled panic swallowed in cotton. Something cold, hard, and abrasive dragged against her calf and then ankle. Suddenly her legs were free. A rusty knife was now on the side of her neck. She felt faint and didn't know if it was from lack of oxygen or raw fear.

Krogan grabbed a fistful of hair, yanked up her head, and slid the knife to the front of her throat. The serrated blade was corroded but painfully sharp as she gulped for precious air. The cabin was stiflingly hot and sweat saturated her clothes, but there was a chill in his grasp that nothing could warm. He pulled back on her head and met her eye to eye. The foreign calmness of his handsome smile was more frightening than if he'd had the head of a jack-o'-lantern. Deep in his eyes she could see a different life, more animal than human. She suddenly believed Buck's claim to be able to see beyond the man-host. In that instant she knew Karl Dengler was not the one whom she was looking at. She was facing the immortal, Krogan. She didn't know how she knew, but she knew. The many faces he had worn through the centuries could not hide who he was in Karianne's vivid descriptions, nor could the human face of Karl Dengler. She looked away.

"Do you know what a figurehead is?" Krogan whispered, his breath reeking of cheap tequila.

Her breathing came fast and shallow and she feared she would hyperventilate and faint into the knife.

"During what you would call ancient times, figureheads were carvings of idols and deities mounted on the bow, supposedly to scare away evil. The fools. They were invitations. Of course, eventually the carvings were mostly of women. I think this boat deserves a figurehead for its final voyage. Now, we can go up there the easy way or the hard way. Personally, I prefer the hard way."

He took the cold, rusty knife, which had probably been used to cut bait, from her throat and stabbed it into a crusty Styrofoam buoy. He yanked her off the mattress and steered her with his hand, holding her hair in a vise grip. Her legs felt strangely weak and shaky. She tripped over the bottles, but did not fall; his strength held her upright. As much as she wanted to kick him, preferably in the groin, she knew that was exactly what he wanted. Not that he needed an excuse to beat her. She didn't know what hideous plan he had for her, but at least she was out of that hellish cabin and into fresh air.

She breathed in deeply as he maneuvered her onto the bow and considered jumping into the water if given the chance. With her hands tied behind her back, she would probably drown. If she managed to somehow stay afloat, he would surely run her down. It all sounded worth it just to be free of his cold, slimy hands.

"Kneel," Krogan commanded, forcing her to her knees. Her left ankle was quickly tied to the boat, then her right. He then tied one end of another rope around her abdomen and fed the other end through a cleat at the tip of the bow.

Her heart banged against her ribs. What was he doing?

He drew the line, pulling her forward on her knees. A few feet from the tip of the bow, the ropes tied to her ankles caught. Krogan yanked, slamming her down until her face hit the deck just before the front cleat. He fed some slack into the ankle ropes, then pulled again from the front, dragging her forward until her head was completely beyond the bow and out over the water. He then tightened all the ropes, stretching her out until she was nearly raised off the deck.

She grunted as he kneed her back. The wind was forced from her and the cleat on the deck dug into the center of her chest. Krogan's sodden breath fanned her ear.

"Now, isn't that better? You have a view, like I promised, and can catch a tan at the same time. Did anyone ever tell you you'd make a perfect figurehead?"

The fact she was being spoken to by a demon conjured up fears Amy had never known existed. Looking back to one side and then the other, she could see she was hopelessly tied to cleats on either side of the boat. The friction from the rope was already burning her back.

Whatever Gavin was doing, she only hoped he would hurry. She didn't care if he brought the entire police department and killed Krogan right off. She abhorred the thought of Krogan returning in someone else, but if they didn't kill him, he was going to enjoy killing her and, from what she could glean from his plans, himself, too.

— 51 —

"That looks like them over there," Bill shouted over his left shoulder.

Gavin forced open his eyes and in doing so almost fainted. Buck grabbed him by the shoulders, steadying him.

"Right there," Bill yelled, pointing. "At ten o'clock. They're stopped."

"Are you sure it's them?" Gavin yelled. He saw the boat, which looked like a toy from this height, about two thousand feet up and a mile away.

Bill bent over and pulled a pair of binoculars from a small metal box near his feet. When he leaned forward, so did the joystick he was holding with his right hand. Consequently, the plane dipped, enough so that Gavin tightened his already finger-cramping grip on the seat. When Bill sat back up, the plane straightened out again. Gavin wondered if Bill was aware or simply did not care.

Bill brought the binoculars to his eyes and kept them there as he spoke. "That's them all right. I can just about make out the name. Someone's on the bow . . . Wait! They're moving. And someone's still on the bow. Take a look," Bill yelled, handing the binoculars over his shoulder.

Gavin froze at the sight of the binoculars. He would have to let go with one hand. Bill motioned again for Gavin to take them. Gavin released the grip of his left hand, then slowly, very slowly, extended his hand toward Bill's, half focused on the seat he would grab if he had to.

"I've got you, Detective," Buck said, lightly touching Gavin's shoulders to reassure him of his presence.

Gavin took the field glasses and brought them straight to his eyes. The illusion of everything becoming larger and closer was somewhat settling, but the movement of the ultralight made focusing on any one thing difficult and the tighter he held on to the tubular frame the more the flight affected his vision. He exhaled and slowly eased his death-grip on the frame. His more flexible position helped him to stabilize the binoculars. He tried not to think what a sudden gust of wind would do.

After a moment he found the boat and

focused in on it. He grimaced at the sight of the body sprawled out on the front of the bow and his own fear of heights suddenly dwindled like tissue in flame. Amy's head appeared to be beyond the bow. He could not see the ropes, but he knew she had to be tied there. What was Krogan going to do — use her as a battering ram?

"Hang on," Bill yelled as he veered left over the peninsula of Sands Point, straightening his angle to twelve o'clock.

"Ahhh . . ." Gavin stiffened at the sudden change in direction and almost lost the binoculars. "How long till we catch them?" he yelled.

"I don't know. We've picked up a head wind since we turned west. Our airspeed is about sixty, but with the wind in our face, we're only doing maybe forty to fifty ground speed. That's only about five or ten more than him."

Gavin didn't have to ask the obvious. He knew they would never catch them in time. All they would do is get close enough to clearly witness the unthinkable. "Oh, God," he said quietly. He didn't have much faith, but he was in desperate need of help. He thought of Amy's fear and pain and he begged. "Please, God, please, God, please," was all he could say as the lobster boat gathered speed. If God really could read his thoughts, there was nothing else that needed to be said.

"Are there any speed boats in sight?" Buck yelled.

Anything was better than watching Amy get further and further away. Gavin would not be denied as he had been at the boat ramp. If a speed boat was already in the water, he would take it — like a pirate if he had to — and deal with the consequences later, including the fact he had never driven a powerboat before.

"If you want an ocean racer, I might be able to get you one," Bill yelled back.

"Now?"

"Maybe."

"How?"

"A good friend of mine is selling one. I was supposed to meet him for dinner at City Island."

"Where's City Island?"

"Right there," Bill said, pointing to a small island at two o'clock, not far from the Throgs Neck Bridge.

"Are you kidding me?"

"The boat's a twelve-year-old, twenty-six-foot Welcraft, and he only wants fifteen thousand for it. It's in perfect shape and the two engines can push over eight hundred horsepower. The thing's a rocket. I could try to radio him. He might still be on his way to the island."

"Get him!" Gavin yelled. "I don't care what it costs."

The aluminum tube Gavin was sitting on had become unbearable. He tried shifting himself while Bill spoke on the radio. He could not hear the conversation over the noise of the wind and the engine, but he could see Bill's mouth moving. As he waited, he spared a moment to wonder about the incredible coincidence of getting this boat. It seemed almost too farfetched to be possible — that Bill had dinner plans with the owner . . . on the island they were currently flying past. Had God heard his prayers? At this point he was willing to believe anything.

"My friend wants to know if you need for him to drive," Bill yelled over his shoulder. "But I'll warn you: he's a little crazy."

"Yes! Just do it!"

Bill talked a moment more, then signed off.

"That's all he had to hear. We'll be seeing him any minute. To save time, I'll fly directly over him. When I get close enough, you two can jump into his boat."

"Your friend isn't the only one who's crazy," Gavin yelled.

Holding firmly to the back of the seat, Gavin bravely raised himself until he could see over Bill's left shoulder, hoping they were a little closer to Amy. They were not. The lobster boat was now passing under the Throgs Neck suspension bridge that connected Long Island with the Bronx. On the other side of the bridge sat a Merchant Marine ship that was permanently docked and used as a school. Gavin hoped it was not named *Freedom* or *New York*. He wondered what was taking Chris so long in coming up with a boat to match the names, then realized Chris might have been calling or paging him without him being able to hear over all the noise.

Suddenly the angle of the plane shifted downward.

"I see my friend's boat leaving City Island," Bill yelled. "We can gain some ground on them on the way down. Increasing the angle of attack increases our airspeed. Our extra weight will speed us up on the way down, too."

He suited actions to words. The increase in speed made the craft vibrate. Gavin looked doubtfully at the colorful translucent fabric wings held in place by a few tubular struts and thin cables and waited for everything to suddenly fold in half.

"*Shadahd*'s changing course," Bill yelled. "She's headed straight for a fishing party boat."

Gavin looked over Bill's shoulder again. The path made by *Shadahd*'s wake had veered right. Dead ahead lay a party boat, just as Bill had said.

"No!" Gavin screamed. He turned his head away, unable to watch. Then, unable to stand it, he looked back, unable to *not* watch.

— 52 —

Before Krogan turned *Shadahd* toward the *Flounder Filet II* party boat, Amy had been having a difficult time holding her unsupported head up, her muscles cramping as she tried to arch her neck and back. Now, however, she was unconcerned with spasms. Her head was raised toward the broadside of the charter boat before her, which quickly filled her vision until she became too horrified to keep her eyes open. The top of her scalp tingled wildly as she waited for the impact.

"You might feel a little pinch," mocked Krogan with a deep, boisterous laugh.

Amy peered over her right shoulder to see he had opened his windshield. She could not remember if she'd ever seen anyone look like they were having more fun. He was sucking in life through her fear while crowing over her undignified, helpless position.

Unable to keep from glancing ahead

again, in the hope the fishing boat could stage an unlikely emergency maneuver, she saw the fishermen were no longer interested in their rods and reels. Their boat was twice, maybe three times the size of Krogan's, but would that be enough to save them? At this speed *Shadahd* would certainly plow a sizable hole into their hull. Steel against steel. What could they do to prevent it? Who could save them on such short notice? If she could see them, then so could Krogan, probably taking in each individual expression as it evolved from casual interest to disbelief to helpless terror.

Suddenly the fishermen's gaping faces shifted to her right as the lobster boat veered left. She too looked and saw why. Several rows of large, rolling waves, probably from a tug or barge or distant tanker, were making their way through the otherwise moderate waters. Krogan had turned directly into them. Their audience on the *Flounder Filet* was still frozen in place. Hopefully one of them would have enough sense to call the police. But what if someone did? A police boat would only be another fun target for Krogan, another hard surface for her skull to crush against. Where was Gavin?

The first wave sent the bow frighteningly high. She had always enjoyed roller coasters — the slow, suspenseful climb to the crest followed by the scream-sucking free fall and hairpin thrust . . . all while locked into a seat designed for maximum safety. Before getting into that seat, you witnessed all the passengers before you that had survived and even returned to do it again. But no one was in line for this ride and there were no previous survivors. As the bow fell, mercilessly pulling her down with it, she could hear Krogan screaming in mock panic. "Oh, no! Oh, no!"

Amy inhaled, stiffened, and closed her eyes. The dark, cold salt water gushed upward from the V-hull like a geyser before the solid body of the wave met her face with an impact that felt like hitting a wall.

Flounder Filet had apparently been crossed off the menu of horrors. Why? Did Krogan want to attract attention or did he not care? Was he simply trying to scare her or was it more than that? Was he showing off? Showing her off? Was she some kind of trophy? Suddenly Amy felt as though she'd been hung out for display like a head on a wall — like a dead tiger under the heel of a hunter posing for a trophy photo with a pipe in his mouth. A visual proclamation to worlds both seen and unseen that Krogan was in control. Krogan was his own god.

— 53 —

"He turned away," Bill yelled.

Gavin's immediate relief was tempered by the distance they had to cover to catch the boat. Amy was still hostage in this horrific cat-and-mouse game.

Instead of traveling directly toward each other, Bill and his friend were aiming for a common intersection, angling toward the fleeing lobster boat. The racer slowed to the speed of the ultralight as Bill aligned with it, about fifty feet above. Gavin eyed the boat, which was long and narrow, like a bullet. *Sudden Pleasure* was marked on the yellow ocean racer in bold orange letters with black shadows.

Bill lowered the ultralight until the inflated monofloat pontoon was but a few feet from the racer's windshield.

"You first, Detective. Move slow and steady. You've got to hang from the pontoon mount and drop. Easy as pie," Bill yelled.

Gavin could not have been happier to get off the flying machine and into a boat. He quickly and confidently shimmied down and hung from the pontoon. He had no fears at this height. The worst that could happen would be that he missed the boat and got wet. He let go and fell softly to a crouch on the engine cover. He looked back up and saw Bill motioning for Buck to follow.

"No!" Between the noise of the ultralight and the boat Gavin couldn't hear Buck's cry, but could read his lips clearly. The preacher, who had shown no fear while flying through the air at two thousand feet in little more than a motorized kite, had drawn the line. Gavin, not wanting to lose a second of precious time, motioned angrily for Buck to try. Obviously knowing his limitations, Buck refused.

Gavin considered going on without him. But what if things turned out like that ordeal with Sabah? How much worse would Krogan be? Frustrated, he hopped into the plush, vinyl cockpit alongside Bill's friend, who appeared to be in his early forties. The man turned to Gavin, offering his hand. His wide, friendly grin made Gavin feel like he already knew him.

"Hi! I'm Vinny."

"Gavin. I'll buy the boat and give you whatever you want for driving," Gavin said.

"Forget the driving fee," Vinny said with a dismissive wave of his hand. "It comes with the boat. But you could put me down for one of those PBA badges."

"Done. Did Bill tell you who we're after?"

"Yeah. That's another reason the ride's free. I've been docking at the Hempstead Harbor Marina for years. I didn't know the guy who got killed, but the owner of the sailboat that idiot wrecked is a good friend of mine. No one has any idea how many long hours he put into that boat, trying to make a business of chartering it," Vinny said, shaking his head. "But why Bill and me? Where's the police?"

"I am the police and there's no time for backup. But Bill's going to have to land that thing to get my friend off," Gavin said, pointing over his shoulder with his thumb to the bobbing aircraft.

Vinny nodded, glancing up at Bill and pointing out ahead of the boat. Bill visually acknowledged with a thumbs-up, then veered away like a huge, rainbow-colored prehistoric bird. Vinny pulled back on two chrome levers, throttling down the powerful engines to a low, bubbling rumble. For the first time since takeoff, Gavin could hear, though a buzzing sound in his ears remained.

Unlike the takeoff, the area needed for landing was short. Once the pontoon touched the water, the aircraft slowed to a stop quickly. Bill shut the engine off as Vinny pulled up next to him under the wing. Buck wasted no time in unbuckling his seat belt and stepping onto the pontoon. But when he tried to hand off the mysterious wooden chest to Gavin, a wind gust hit the wing and separated the two crafts, leaving Buck with a decision to make: either drop the chest and grab onto the ultralight's rising struts, or fall into the water with the chest. He dropped it.

"Get it," he pleaded urgently to Gavin. "Don't let it open."

"We don't have time for this," Gavin screamed as he took his cell phone from his pocket, tossed it to Vinny, and jumped into the water. The chest was beginning to sink, but Gavin reached it before it vanished with its unknown cargo. He swam to the rear of the boat and handed the chest up to Vinny, then climbed up the ladder Vinny had unfolded for him.

Buck had already scrambled onto the

boat and Vinny was powering up again when Gavin's phone rang. Gavin grabbed it.

"About time," he said into the receiver as the racer shot forward, leaving Bill and his plane to take off again behind them.

"About time? This is the third time I've called. What's going on, Gav?" Chris said.

"Can't talk about it now. What have ya got for me?"

"A Coast Guard boat called the *USS New York*. An eighty-foot sailboat called *Freedom*."

"Where's it kept?"

"Montauk Point."

"No. Next." As he spoke, his eyes scanned the area ahead of them, searching for Krogan and Amy. He hoped the delay wouldn't prove deadly.

"*Miss New York* and *Miss Freedom* are two of the three ferries that leave Battery Park for the Statue of Liberty and Ellis Island every half hour. The third one is *Miss Ellis Island*."

"Anything else?"

"Yeah, about fifty variations on the theme, but then we're talkin' dinghies, rowboats, skiffs, and small ski boats."

"Then I guess that's it."

"What's it? What are you talking about?"

"Gotta go," Gavin said and hung up. Buck was examining his precious chest.

"What's in that thing?" Vinny said over the noise of the engine.

"A one-room apartment," Buck said, opening the chest and peeking inside.

"You okay?" Gavin said.

Buck nodded. "Just fine. Did your partner find any boats with the right name?"

"Too many, but there's a *Miss Freedom* and a *Miss New York* that ferry tourists to the Statue of Liberty. That's the direction Krogan's heading. But why go all that way when he could have done the same damage to that party boat?"

"To be honest, I don't know. Like people, demons have varying personalities. They all stand before a watchful arena of spirits, both light and dark. They're all proud and like showing off to one another. Demons also spend a lot of time trying to own what doesn't belong to them. Krogan's host is a fisherman and there are fish markets in the waters near the Statue of Liberty. It's not inconceivable that one of the ferries happened to get in his way at one time or another. Vengance is a big part of why Krogan does what he does."

Gavin inwardly shook his head. If Buck

had tried to tell him this spiritual stuff even this morning, before Sabah, he would simply have laughed and rejected it. Now he wasn't about to argue with him about anything.

"In other words, Krogan might have a score to settle with one of the ferries and might have a better opportunity with this host than his next," he said, amazed to find spiritual logic coming from his own mouth.

Buck looked impressed. "Very possible."

"Can we get to the Statue of Liberty before the lobster boat?" Gavin asked Vinny.

"I don't know." He radioed to Bill, and a minute later the ultralight was flying a straight path toward the Statue of Liberty and *Sudden Pleasure* was roaring under the Throgs Neck and then the Whitestone Bridges with little more than the propellers touching the water, Manhattan's jagged skyline straight ahead. The racer's chrome throttle levers were all full ahead and Vinny's face was set like stone against the seventy-mile-an-hour wind. His focus at this speed was intense.

Gavin's eyes widened as a large tugboat crossed ahead of them. Vinny adjusted their path to avoid it but the tug's steep, rolling wake was coming up fast. "Hold the bar," was all Vinny said. He gave a light-ning-quick nod toward a chrome bar on the padded dashboard before him. A second later they hit the wake and were airborne. After a long moment the racer landed with a thump and aggressively settled back into its rhythmic gallop. The Rikers Island Prison passed by quickly on their left.

Gavin suddenly glanced at his watch and cursed. *Katz.* He'd forgotten about Katz. Crawling into the long, dark cabin, where the noise was slightly diminished, he dialed Karianne's apartment, hoping Sabah's voice would not be the one to answer.

The phone rang twice and Karianne's machine picked up. This was not an unexpected option. Throughout all the hypnotic sessions her machine had intercepted all incoming calls. After listening to a breezy, pre-accident message, Gavin yelled for Katz. If everything was all right Katz would hear him and pick up.

No answer.

After a long, confused moment Gavin hung up and called again, hoping Katz had been in the bathroom.

Again, no answer.

There were a dozen reasons why Katz wouldn't have answered, but at the moment Gavin could think of only one.

With a sigh, he climbed out of the cabin, bracing himself with every step. Buck sat on the thickly padded bench seat in front of the engine cover, holding on to the chrome bar with his left hand while his right cradled the chest. His eyes were closed. Probably praying, Gavin thought.

He glanced at Vinny, whose eyes were wild and unblinking. There was certainly enough for Buck to be praying about.

54

Amy tried to lift her tired head to let the wind rid her face of her hair, soaked with the polluted waters of the East River. The tide was at its highest and the murky water foamed on either side of the boat's hull. The East River was fabled for its mob executions, Amy remembered. She imagined an underwater city of people with concrete around their ankles. Soon she would join them.

Amy's hatred of Krogan was growing disproportionately to her fear of the monster that steered the boat into every large wake he could find, howling raucously each time the wave smacked her stinging face. What had she done to deserve this? What had her sister, Amber, done? Even as she asked herself these questions she remembered another Japanese saying: "Self-pity is always the beginning of the end."

She now hoped the police would not come. She thought about it as the pain in her chest grew with each bounce on the bow cleat. Her anger had finally tipped the scale. She would rather die than have Krogan go free.

Krogan laughed heartily as another wave sprayed the front of the boat. Amy closed her eyes and prayed for Gavin to find her.

Suddenly she heard a thumping sound swelling above her. She opened her eyes to see a blue-and-white helicopter drop into the clearing beyond the bridge they were going under. Her heart sank as she read the abbreviation on its side: NYPD.

The police.

One of the hundreds of people who had seen her had actually decided to call the police. The cops would be quick to confirm this was not your ordinary Sunday joyride. There was no way she could disguise the fact she was in mortal trouble. Tied up and positioned the way she was, a human figurehead, what else could they believe?

"Police! Stop your vessel. Now!" came an amplified voice from the helicopter.

"Oh, no! What am I going to do now?" Krogan mocked, his words slurred. He must have found another bottle.

The helicopter maneuvered to the front of the boat, facing head on and flying backward, its downdraft flattening small waves and spraying Amy's face. Squinting, Amy could see the pilot and co-pilot. She shook her head desperately, pleading for them to go away. Krogan's speed remained steady and the helicopter lowered to a few feet off the water, apparently hoping to intimidate. The pilot obviously had no idea who he was dealing with. He repeated his command.

Krogan answered.

The first blast from the shotgun sprayed the windshield, cracking it but not penetrating. Amy winced, knowing the buckshot had to have been traveling mere inches over her head. The second shot followed immediately, and the helicopter instantly jerked upward, the pilot obviously surprised by the gunfire exploding onto the windshield in front of his face. Amy watched in horror as the front of the helicopter rose and the tail and rudder prop dipped, hitting the water. The aircraft immediately flipped over. With a whine of propellers the craft crashed upside down into the swirling, inky currents.

"*Shadahd!*" Krogan roared, making no effort to steer away from the mess before him. Amy screamed as the helicopter came quickly upon them, the landing gear sticking upright from the water like metal skis set to shear her head off. The skids were only inches from her paralyzed eyes when they were sucked downward by the current. The lobster boat cut the police helicopter in half as easily as if it were a cheap toy.

Amy was surprised to be alive. Still breathing, albeit in quick, shallow gasps. Apparently, Krogan's plans for her death were flexible. He simply did whatever he wanted and whatever happened, happened. She wanted to let her head fall limply, but the steel cleat tenderizing her sternum now shot pain through her chest like a branding iron, the slightest touch forcing her to arch her back, further cramping already knotted back muscles. Even the minor back support found by pulling with her fingers at the frayed cloth of her cut-off shorts came at the expense of Krogan's lewd, verbal observations.

She again looked out before her as they neared what could only be the Brooklyn Bridge. In the lower right-hand corner was posted a bold white sign that read "Pier 17 South Street Seaport." She exhaled loudly as she thought of the possible targets Krogan could find there. The children's center, the *Titanic* memorial, the ocean library . . . Would she have to endure any more heart-pounding near misses? Perhaps one of the several historic tall ships docked nearby would meet Krogan's fancy. Or the Fulton Fish Market; surely, as a lobsterman, he'd had to deal with many people there — people who might have angered him enough to want to retaliate in some vicious manner.

Amy suddenly noted movement out past the seaport and the fish market. About a quarter mile away two helicopters took off from the Port Authority Heliport. The downed chopper had apparently grabbed their attention. Flying straight toward Amy and Krogan, the sky's crimson glow reflecting off their windshields, they looked like angry wasps whose nest had been disturbed.

Krogan's throttle remained wide open. Was his gun still loaded? He had fired two shots, hadn't he? If the gun had been fully loaded, he would have three or four shots left, Amy figured. As if they had come to the same conclusion, the two choppers simultaneously increased their altitude. Amy followed them over her shoulder as they banked and took up positions behind them at a safe distance, one at ten o'clock, the other at two.

Krogan appeared typically unfazed, draining the last of another bottle and tossing it into the river. Such detachment seemed impossible. The muffled sounds of sirens drew Amy's attention to the right, where flashing lights kept pace along South Street, paralleling the river's edge. She looked forward again and saw two, no, three large white boats, each with a thick diagonal red stripe. She assumed they were Coast Guard. They motored into the mouth of the river like ducks in a row. Another large boat with bold lettering came from the Brooklyn side — Police Patrol. Centered maybe a mile beyond the challenging armada was the Statue of Liberty, three hundred and fifty feet tall. The statue appeared to be looking right at Amy.

Yet another police boat entered the picture. None of them advanced, probably waiting for the lobster boat to leave the highly populated, busy confines of the East River. They wanted Krogan in the open waters. And after what had happened to the first helicopter, Amy was reasonably confident there would be no more warnings. They would want him to pay dearly for that.

Krogan's speed quickly closed the gap between the boats. Uniformed men armed with black rifles lined the boat sides. This had to be what Krogan was waiting for. They would try to cage him in and he would drill them in the side head first — her head. They would never expect that. They might open fire, hoping to kill him, then get out of the way of the unmanned boat. Then they would have to somehow chase the boat down and get on board before it crashed into something else.

From nowhere, two F-16 fighter jets roared by and circled around. Amy assumed they came from one of the patrols that had manned the New York airspace ever since the attack on the Twin Towers. They were obviously focusing on Krogan as a terrorist.

"I give up! I give up! There's too many of them. I'm frightened!" Krogan cried out in mock fear. "Oh, no! Oh, no! I can't slow down. What do I do? What do I do?"

"Uhhh!" Amy gasped as something struck her back — hard. Whatever it was made a clanking noise as it fell to the deck at her side. She turned to look. The throttle lever — Krogan had broken it off with the boat at full speed. So much for the hope of a safe rescue.

"Oh, no! Oh, no!" he continued, then laughed ferociously. "What do you like better, police boats or Coast Guard boats?" he yelled to Amy, then laughed again.

Amy was no longer physically able to brace herself for impact. She could not even muster the strength to see the faces of the riflemen on the boats they were seconds from hitting. If they were smart they would dive off now and save themselves.

With *Shadahd* showing no sign of slowing down, the wall of boats scrambled to separate, apparently realizing the bluff they were trying to call was no bluff. Krogan shot through the middle of their small fleet with mocking laughter, leaving them to maneuver and race to catch up. Other smaller and faster police boats had just arrived, running in the same direction just ahead of Krogan; from the choppers it would almost look as though he were chasing them. Amy saw hope in this strategy. If they could sandwich the lobster boat as it caught up to them, then they could conceivably control and subdue it.

The police boat at the far left slowed until it ran even with them, then carefully closed in. The far right police boat did the same. At this rate they would be on him just before he crashed into Liberty Island.

"Oh, no! The whole world is closing in

on me," Krogan yelled. "I'm so scared. Go away! Go away!" Just then, he cranked the steering hard to the right, heading straight for the nearby police boat. The boat tried to respond by turning with him, but didn't react fast enough. Amy screamed as the starboard bow of the lobster boat slammed into the port bow of the police craft, missing her by inches. The sound of the collision was loud, leaving her badly shaken and in tears. If Krogan was trying to scare her to death, he had nearly succeeded.

The police boat fell back, having been rocked badly from the unequal angle of attack favoring Krogan, then struggled to catch up. Turning to her left, Amy could see the rest of the armada also in chase. She looked upward at the Statue of Liberty. How ironic to be so helplessly enslaved before such a symbol of freedom . . . and the audience now gathered on the island's granite shoreline. Amy couldn't bear to look at them. She looked forward — and froze.

"*Miss Freedom.*" She silently mouthed the words on the upper hull of the 135-foot tourist ferry. There was an audience there, too, but Amy no longer felt embarrassed. If Krogan had been thinking of a sensational crash to end it all, this was it — a statement only his demon onlookers would understand and applaud.

Unable to control herself, she fought frantically against the tight cords tying her wrists, rubbing and jerking her hands back and forth, moving them no more than a fraction of an inch each time as the rope wore into her flesh. The steel hull she would be crushed into drew closer by the second. The more she struggled, the louder Krogan laughed.

Before them, the ferry had picked up speed in a hopeless attempt to escape. All the increased velocity would accomplish would be to relocate the point of impact from center to rear. Regardless, the lobster boat would plow into the tourist-laden vessel like a guided missile, the end of another small chapter of Krogan's ongoing existence of terror and the end of Amy's entire life. Krogan would die with her.

Die . . . With her?

She was going into an unknown dimension, but he was going into a world as familiar to him as the world he was leaving. More familiar. He probably had friends there. He definitely had friends there. Would she be at his mercy there as well? Their mercy? Engines roared, sirens wailed, helicopters clattered, ships' horns blared, and water gushed, pounding against her face, yet she could not blot out Krogan's raucous laughter. In fact, his laughter became all she could hear. Moments before certain death, he was downright excited. Confidently excited. About what? Death? Why? What was next? What did he know that she didn't? Everything! The possibility of her life extending into another world, another dimension, with Krogan there to greet her, was horrifying.

With eyes tightly shut, Amy stiffened like a wooden beam, every muscle in her body braced. She could no longer struggle; her fate was as inevitable as if she were falling from the sky without a parachute. She could not keep her brain from counting down the seconds to impact. A strange weakness came over her as sound and motion slowed.

"God!" she cried out.

She was silenced by the explosive impact.

55

"Yes!" Gavin shouted to Amy, who had turned to see him shaking his fist triumphantly in the air. She was still alive and he was bent on keeping her that way.

The impact of the ocean racer into the side of *Shadahd*'s bow had thrown Krogan from the steering wheel to the floor, allowing the powerful engines to drive the lobster boat off course, barely missing the rear of the ferry. The top left bow of the racer was badly damaged from the angular slam; loose and shattered pieces of fiberglass flapped in the high wind. Gavin was wet with water — and sweat from seeing Amy nearly crushed before his eyes. Buck was on the floor. Gavin was unsure if he had been knocked there from the impact or if he was praying again. Perhaps both.

Vinny, now a certified mental patient in Gavin's mind, had assured Gavin they would make it with inches to spare — as if an inch could actually be determined while flying along at seventy miles an hour. He'd been right, though, give or take an inch. His only concern had been whether or not Gavin would still buy the boat if it were damaged. When Gavin assured him he would buy it even if it were completely destroyed, a small, frightening grin had appeared on Vinny's otherwise intense expression and never left.

Vinny continued to keep pressure on the lobster boat's bow, pushing it left toward the rear of Liberty Island. Krogan reappeared by the steering wheel, a lone trickle of blood tracing the border of his right eye socket. He no longer wore the smirk he'd had at Giants Stadium — the smirk he'd had only seconds before. Gavin considered that a small victory. He managed a brief smile as they made eye contact, fluttering his fingers in a mocking salute intended to irritate Krogan. He thought Krogan might be more likely to slip up if he was mad.

With a roar, Krogan yanked the wheel to the right, his huge arm muscles rippling. Vinny also turned to maintain his angular advantage. Even though the ocean racer had the speed to catch the lobster boat and the quickness to outmaneuver it, Krogan had the leverage of sheer weight and power on his side.

Gavin looked past Krogan toward Liberty Island. The granite bulkhead surrounding the island did not continue all the way around to the west shore. In one section a cobblestone shoreline had been installed, sloping from the high tide mark to a chain-link fence. On the other side of the fence was lawn, a few trees, and several weather-beaten brick homes, presumably where the park staff lived.

"Run him aground there!" Gavin shouted to Vinny, pointing past Krogan.

"I'm trying! I can't!" Vinny yelled back, shaking his head, fighting desperately to maintain his position. Suddenly his eyes widened and he spun the steering wheel to the right, banking hard and away from *Shadahd*. Before Gavin could ask why, there came a deafening blast and the windshield by his head exploded. He winced, the left side of his face stinging from tiny glass projectiles. Vinny dropped to the floor, keeping one hand on the wheel, wanting to put distance between them and the shotgun.

Gavin was emotionally torn. He'd already done the unthinkable in having Vinny chase down Krogan, but how could he ask him to continue after being shot at? The man wasn't a cop and didn't even know the truth of what he was up against. Gavin made his decision.

"Stop the boat, Vinny," Gavin yelled. "Ellis Island is an easy swim from here. You'll be safe there. I've got to go back." Gavin pulled his gun from his ankle holster and slipped it into his pant waistline for easier access.

With a nod Vinny pulled back on the throttle and made a tight U-turn. Krogan, who had been heading away since the gunshot, was now making a wide turn. Oddly, he was still traveling at full speed. Vinny looked glumly at the nearby south shore of Ellis Island, obviously not wild about Gavin's proposal.

Ellis Island had dramatically changed since the 1800s and early 1900s, when it had been the country's only immigration bottleneck and later a jail for alien enemies. For the past half a century it has been little more than a deteriorating monument. From the south shore all that could be seen of the once busy facility was a dilapidated three-story building that reminded Gavin of his Long Island elementary school, with its once spectacular, steeply gabled Spanish-tile roof. Now, abandoned for decades, doors hung off hinges and an overgrowth of strangling vines crept up walls and into broken windows. Its greatest value was to the pigeons that lined its ridge and swooped through gaping holes in the roof. It was a home for the homeless, inhabited by ghosts, compliments of the unswimmable currents of the merging Hudson and East Rivers. Only its grand history, holding the promise of future restoration, kept the bulldozers away.

Gavin could not waste time with Vinny's indecision. Some of the Coast Guard and police boats were closing in again. They had apparently divided around Liberty Island to block off any escape to the south. What they didn't know was that Krogan had no intention of escaping. He wasn't trying to live. He was trying to die while causing as much damage as possible. Gavin wished this could have remained between Krogan and himself.

The demon was angrier than Gavin had ever heard mention of in any of Katz's sessions with Sabah. If Gavin had learned anything about Krogan, it was that he was compelled to attack whatever he was angry at. And Gavin had just made him mad as hell, literally. In one day he and Amy had combined to wreck the football game, destroy the lobster business, and thwart Krogan's dream of crashing into *Miss Freedom*. Gavin didn't have to be psychic to know what Krogan wanted — needed — to do before dying. Could he work that predictability to his advantage?

Just then a shadow moved across the boat. Gavin looked up, expecting to see a chopper filled with Emergency Service Unit troops. He knew they would be on the scene. ESU troops trained for situations like this and taking out Krogan would be easy for them. Their motto was, "When people need help they call the police. When the police need help they call the Emergency Service Unit." But it wasn't the ESU that flew overhead. With all that had been happening, Gavin had forgotten about Bill in the ultralight.

"Oh, no," Vinny said, watching the ultralight fly toward Krogan. He grabbed the radio handset off the dashboard. "Bill! Come in, Bill."

"Let's get 'im, Vin."

"Bill! He's got a shotgun."

"I know. I've been watching. But he can't hit what he can't see. Over and out."

"What did he mean by that?" Gavin asked.

"I don't know, but I'm not going to sit

here and watch Bill get blown out of the sky like that helicopter we passed," Vinny said, pushing the throttle.

Relieved that Vinny had made a decision, Gavin grabbed the chrome bar as the boat lunged forward. "You okay, Buck?" he yelled to the preacher, still on the floor. Buck motioned with his right hand that Gavin needn't worry; with his left hand he held tightly to his precious chest. The man was as mysterious as they came.

Krogan had completed his circle and was coming directly at them, as expected. The sun was in his eyes. Gavin hoped that wasn't what Bill had meant about not seeing. If so, the ultralight would be downed like a lone mallard flying over a duck blind.

Racing toward Krogan, Gavin saw the shotgun leveled at them out *Shadahd*'s front window. "Keep your head down," he yelled. He glanced back to make sure Buck was still on the floor. "Pray for bad aim, Buck."

Vinny pressed a black spring-loaded switch that read "Trim." The bow began to rise and a rooster tail of jetting water appeared off the stern. The angular degree-change slowed the racer, but created a shield Krogan immediately tested. A basketball-sized chunk of the high-gloss yellow bow edge exploded, leaving ravaged strands of fiberglass blowing furiously about. The hit was followed immediately by the sound of the gunshot, the slower speed of sound playing catch-up with the deadly lead buckshot. Gavin and Vinny ducked as most of the debris careened off Vinny's windshield.

The ultralight, a robotic bird of prey, swooped toward the charging lobster boat. With Krogan's shotgun pointed out the window and the gap between them narrowing fast, they looked like two jousting knights.

Another hole blasted into the bow. Gavin cursed, knowing the shotgun was firing just behind Amy, barely missing her head each time. If she survived this she would be shell shocked. And what was Bill doing? Gavin half expected the Statue of Liberty to glance over her shoulder and ask the same question. Krogan was apparently curious enough to allow the ultralight closer. Then again, Bill had mentioned a tense relationship between them. Maybe Krogan was waiting for a point-blank shot.

Gavin could see Bill holding something in his hand. His vest? He was going to throw his vest at Krogan? Gavin was about to question Vinny when, like magic, a huge white sheet appeared below the ultralight, directly in front of the lobster boat. Bill's emergency ballistic chute!

The ultralight banked away as the lobster boat rode full speed into the fully deployed parachute. The canopy covered the entire front of the boat, including Amy and, most important, Krogan's windshield.

"Hold on," Vinny yelled, then hung a sharp U-turn. A moment later the lobster boat was once again a few yards off the port side of the racer, both boats pointed at the shallow bulkhead of Ellis Island. Krogan's arm appeared out the draped window, reaching, pulling, struggling with the chute. The violent yanking and wrenching of the giant white blindfold pulled harshly against Amy's head; the contours of her face were defined like a pale mannequin in the tight fabric.

"He's gonna break her neck," Gavin yelled.

Vinny turned hard left, slamming *Shadahd* just below Krogan's arm, which disappeared behind the blowing cloth.

"If we get much closer I won't be able to turn away," Vinny yelled, looking dead ahead at the ghostly shoreline, desperate for immediate instruction.

What was crucial was that the lobster boat be held on course until its grounding was inevitable, while leaving enough time for the quicker, more maneuverable, racer to throttle down and turn away. Though the granite bulkhead ended only about a foot above the water, at almost seventy miles per hour their survival, should they hit it, was anything but certain. The lobster boat, made of steel and twice the size of the racer, would most likely survive intact, skidding to a halt somewhere on the uncut lawn. There, Gavin needed to apprehend Krogan before the approaching armed forces turned him into used ammo storage.

"Pull away," Gavin was yelling to Vinny when he was struck in the left shoulder by something blunt and hard as a cement block that sent him crashing into Vinny's dashboard. Without a second to lose, Vinny pulled all the way back on the throttle levers and cranked the steering wheel to the right. The racer broke off from the lobster boat, but for only a few yards. Then it slammed back into *Shadahd*.

"He's got us!" Vinny screamed.

Still stunned from the hit, Gavin turned to see Krogan at the side of his boat, gloating with smug triumph. A large, rusted anchor held the side of the racer like a grappling iron, its heavy, corroded chain wrapped around *Shadahd*'s trap pulley. Gavin immediately grabbed the anchor, but the tension between the boats was way too strong. Krogan laughed tauntingly at the useless attempt.

With no time to jump from the boat without hitting granite shore instead of water, Gavin and Vinny dove for the floor next to Buck. The carpeted deck offered nothing to grab hold of. Gavin clenched his teeth and futilely tried to relax. He was about as flexible as glass when the two boats hit the solid rock. At the point of impact, his face dug into the hard floor. A moment later, he was weightless, flying feet first toward the bow along with everything else not tied down, including Buck and Vinny.

There was instant silence. In the sudden rush of quiet, Gavin found himself in the racer's dark, shallow cabin, fists still clenched. As the buzzing in his ears cleared he heard the approaching Coast Guard and police boats cutting through waves, their motors at full tilt. Also drawing near was the *whump-whump-whump* of helicopter blades and distant horns and sirens.

Amy!

Cat quick, he sprang forward, then just as quickly fell to his knees, grabbing for his side with a wincing cry. Struggling to pull himself from the darkness of the long cabin, he found a jagged piece of wooden decking, ugly enough to slay a vampire, had speared him low in the right side. Frantic to get to Amy, he took a deep breath and ripped it out with a scream. Blood blossomed on his shirt and jeans.

Vinny lay next to him, moaning and moving slowly. To his right, Buck lay motionless, bright blood puddled at his nose. Gavin touched Buck's neck, searching for a pulse. He was alive.

"Don't move," Gavin said to Vinny, who had shakily struggled to his hands and knees.

Amy.

Gavin climbed to his feet, all his weight shifted to his left side. The chute still covered the front of the lobster boat and he could see the shape of Amy's body still there. There was no movement or sound.

Was Krogan still in the boat or was he already on the run? Gavin craned his neck, hoping to see him. It was possible Krogan was dead, or at least injured or trapped by the crash. Gavin touched his left rear pocket and felt the hard, curved steel of handcuffs taken from the stadium security. The sooner Krogan was wearing them, the better. Every second of unshackled freedom could mean a second more of recovered strength, a category Krogan needed no handicap in.

Amy.

Gavin hurdled the side, landing on his left leg, then both hands. Groaning, he scrambled like a wounded spider to the front of the lobster boat. The bow angling upward; Amy was out of his reach, but the canopy wasn't. He jumped up, pushing from both legs, punctured muscles and flesh sending shock waves of searing pain as a handful of silky cloth filled his hands. He fell backward, disrobing *Shadahd* and covering himself. The cloth was too strong to tear, but he fought the feather-light material, folding, compressing, and finally tossing it aside. He looked up again.

Amy's long black hair hung straight and heavy across her face, her head hanging in limp surrender. She wasn't moving.

"Amy?" he said hoarsely.

She remained still — dead still.

"Amy!" He grimaced as he struggled to his feet.

Ever so slowly, Amy's head turned and her hair fell away from her face. With a groan she opened her eyes and focused at him. "Gavin," she said weakly as water dripped down her face to hang from her cracked lower lip. "Untie me."

Ignoring the pain, he jumped, grabbed a cleat, and pulled himself up until his face was next to hers. "Are you all right?"

"I will be, now," she said with a sigh.

Something heavy hit the ground on the other side of the lobster boat. Their eyes widened.

"It's him," Amy said. "He's getting away again. Hurry, untie me."

"No," Gavin said, dropping to the ground. "You'll be safer here."

— 56 —

Gavin focused grimly on his opponent. Krogan, shotgun in hand, was limping toward the ghostly ruins of what used to be the detention complex of Ellis Island. His gait strengthened with each step.

There was only one thing in the world that could keep Gavin from immediately untying Amy's tortured wrists and ankles: the chance to finally get his hands on Krogan. He would shoot Krogan in the leg — both legs. Two shots in each leg and then the remaining five in the arm holding the shotgun. The thought of shooting the monster energized him as he imagined the bullets zipping through the air, each in honor of a fallen friend. Grampa . . . Mitchell Clayborne . . . John Garrity . . . Mel Gasman and the flight crew . . . all the other unnamed innocents . . .

In anticipation Gavin reached for his gun. Nothing.

He reflexively checked his ankle holster. Nothing.

Frantically, he looked back toward the racer and then back to Krogan. There was no time to look for it. Krogan was getting away . . . again. He was on an island surrounded by Coast Guard and police, and he was going to get away. Gavin knew it. A wild seething rage filled him. The only scrap of human reasoning that remained told him death to the creature equaled its freedom and capture meant its death. It was an unacceptable paradox.

Gavin picked up a baseball-sized rock that had been unearthed by the plowing steel hull of the lobster boat and then another. His mind on fire, he bolted after the object of his madness, ignoring the crippling pain in his side.

"Gavin! No!" Amy cried, desperately craning her neck to watch.

When Krogan spun around, Gavin was already halfway to him. He leveled the shotgun and appeared ready to fire. Gavin screamed into the face of the barrel, unwilling — unable — to stop himself. To dive out of the way or serpentine his straight line of attack was suddenly unacceptable.

Krogan laughed loudly, his eye fixed behind the gun sights.

Less than thirty feet away, Gavin's blind rage saw something that horrified him more than the thought of his own head being blown apart — something so unexpected and devastating he could only dive to his left with a choking cry, hoping the shot would find him . . . and not Amy. He didn't understand why, but Krogan had shifted his sights to Amy, which made as much sense as a hunter shooting at a caged animal when a deadly tiger was about to leap at him. But Krogan was not a hunter. He was a monster. He was a demon beyond understanding.

Horizontal in midair, Gavin heard the firing pin strike . . . but no resounding blast followed. Krogan pumped, aimed again.

Click.

Gavin was galvanized. As he hit the ground in front of Krogan, he threw one of his rocks at Krogan's head. Krogan quickly deflected it with the shotgun, like a pro ballplayer bunting a wild fastball. He laughed.

"You can do better than that," he sneered, then set himself in a mock batting stance and deflected the other rock.

Undeterred, Gavin dove at full speed for

Krogan's midsection.

"Please don't hurt me," Krogan said in a mock little-girl voice, then laughed as he fell backward.

Without the slightest hesitation Gavin sprang to his hands and knees, ramming his right knee into Krogan's groin and smashing a hard, straight-armed fist into Krogan's Adam's apple. There wasn't a man on earth that could remain conscious after such a combination; most would die outright. Not Krogan.

In a deeper and raspier than usual voice, he said, "Should I pass out now so you can cuff me? I don't want to spoil your fun."

Astonished and enraged and sitting on Krogan's abdomen, Gavin hit the monster's jaw with the hardest left cross he could manage, then a right, and a left, and right and left, his splitting knuckles smearing blood on Krogan's face. "I'll . . . wipe . . . that . . . smirk . . . off . . . your . . . face," he said, hitting Krogan again and again with each clearly enunciated word.

"Not likely," Krogan said, then grabbed Gavin by his right arm, his giant hand closing around Gavin's entire bicep, and threw him off him as easily as he would a kitten. He stood, leaving the empty shotgun on the ground.

Enraged, Gavin rolled to his feet and charged, refusing to yield, the adrenaline pumping through his veins.

"Enough," Krogan bellowed, swatting Gavin off his feet with the back of his left hand. The move instantly reminded Gavin of Sabah.

Before Gavin could rise again, Krogan was on him, his knee on Gavin's chest and one of Gavin's baseball-sized rocks in his hand.

"I'll see you in hell," Krogan thundered, his crazed gaze boring a hole through Gavin's head. He drew back his arm, giving Gavin a moment to focus on the rock about to crack his skull.

Gavin spit at Krogan's cold, volcanic eyes. "Do it!"

Krogan didn't even blink as the saliva hit his face. "Very nice. For that, I just want you to know I'm not going to leave the rock in your head. I'm going to take it out and leave it in your girlfriend's head," he said matter-of-factly, motioning with his eyes in Amy's direction.

There was movement behind Gavin. Krogan's eyes shifted. His expression suddenly changed; the smirk engraved on his high cheekbones vanished as his jaw dropped. Gavin looked over his shoulder to see what had hijacked Krogan's attention.

The Reverend Buck.

— 57 —

Buck dropped to his knees fifty feet away, the wooden chest cradled in his arms. Blood dripped from his nose to soak the antique wood. His cheekbone was swollen, throbbing; the ground moved and slid under his feet. Nauseated, sweat and saliva dripping from his chin, he fought for consciousness. The chest fell from his embrace, hitting the ground with a thud. He fell onto it, gagging. He knew if he passed out, he would never again open his eyes. Krogan would make sure of that.

"You!" Krogan said, unable to hide his shock. "You were dead. I killed you in Norway." Below him, Gavin lay still, watching the exchange.

"There is one who lives in me who will deal with you today, evil one." Even to his own ears, Buck's voice sounded weak.

Krogan laughed. "Look at you. You are nothing."

Krogan's voice was fading in Buck's ears, his words swirling with the darkness that threatened to swallow him. He fought for consciousness.

"Where have you been, Preacher? Hiding from me? Afraid?" Krogan mocked loudly.

"I am here," Buck said, shaking.

"You are not strong enough for me, old man. You're a fool to come here, but I'm glad you did. Killing you will make this a most excellent day."

Buck slumped, his forehead hitting the top of the wooden chest. Darkness.

Krogan turned back to Gavin and drew back his arm again, the jagged rock staring Gavin in the face. "Is that your secret weapon? An old man?" he scoffed. "Men like him have tried before, Cop. They always fail in the end. Always."

Gavin winced as Krogan's arm began its downward swing. His only regret was Amy. He heard her scream his name.

"Cease! Be still!"

Gavin waited for the stone's impact. When it didn't come, he forced his eyes to open. Krogan was straining to drive the rock into Gavin's face but nothing was happening. Gavin quickly jerked his head away as Krogan dropped the stone, apparently unable to hold it any longer. He looked toward Buck. He could not believe what he saw. Lying on the ground next to the chest, Buck was pointing at Krogan. What Gavin could not do with his fists, Buck was doing with his finger. Or so it seemed.

Krogan's face flushed redly, swollen neck veins rippling as he strained against an invisible weight. His wild eyes, transfixed on Gavin, moved slowly in Buck's direction.

Gavin did not know what would happen next, but he didn't want to be under Krogan when it did. With Krogan unable to move anything but his eyes, Gavin clawed at the surrounding weeds and grass until he was out from under the hulking statue of a man. He thought better of his first instinct to go toward Buck; if there was some kind of invisible force traveling between them, Gavin didn't want to cross it. He tried to run, but the insanity that had blocked the pain in his side was gone. He fell to his hands, then crawled like a wounded animal until he was about twenty-five feet away.

Amy was still tied up, obviously in pain, but watching the scene unfold. Gavin wanted her untied and with him, but worried that her own hatred toward Krogan would cause her to try to help Buck. That was the last thing he wanted to see. Regretfully, he left her where she was.

There were no earthly explanations for what was happening between Buck and Krogan. Power of suggestion or hypnosis could not begin to explain what he had witnessed today — what he was witnessing now. The gray area between belief and unbelief was gone. There was nothing more to read between the lines. Nothing left for interpretation . . . or even imagination. This was what it really was: a battle in the universe's oldest war — the war from which all other wars were made. Or, as Sabah had stated, "The only war." Two beings from opposite worlds engaged in a contest not commonly seen or understood by human eyes. Light against darkness. Good against evil. God against . . .

Suddenly Buck and his finger collapsed to the dirt. Just as suddenly Krogan's fist pile drove the ground where Gavin's face had been. Krogan quickly looked at Buck's motionless body. He shot Gavin a drilling glare, but said nothing. He was not laughing anymore. He took off toward Buck.

Whatever this gift was that Buck had, it

did not seem to have much effect on Krogan now. Without Buck, Gavin figured he stood zero chance against Krogan if they tangled again, which was sure to happen once Buck was dead. Gavin bolted toward Buck, stifling a scream as white-hot pain shot through his side.

Gavin saw motion enter his peripheral vision to the left, but couldn't turn to see what it was. He pumped his legs hard, watching as Krogan reached Buck and grabbed at the old man's short-cropped silver hair. Just as Krogan lifted Buck's head out of the dirt with his left arm and drew back his massive right fist, Gavin hit Krogan in the side at full speed, tackling him away from Buck and to the ground. Krogan rolled to his feet like a panther and faster than Gavin could react he found himself on his knees with Krogan's right hand around his neck. How had he moved that quickly? The demon stood upright, dragging Gavin up with him like a weightless rag doll.

"Hold it right there, big guy. You twitch and you're dead," yelled a voice Gavin didn't recognize.

Gavin was held so tightly around the neck he could barely breathe and could only look out the corner of his eyes to see two ESU officers outfitted in bullet-proof Kevlar helmets and shields with assault rifles at their shoulders. More officers were pouring in from every direction. Some were headed toward the lobster boat to attend to Amy.

Krogan smiled and opened his arms wide, now holding Gavin out at arm's length on his tiptoes. "Go on. Shoot me. Shoot me or I'll kill him."

"Don't shoot!" Gavin gargled, holding his right hand out while his left pried at Krogan's fingers. "Don't shoot him!"

As other officers circled, Krogan's grip tightened around Gavin's neck. Gavin pried at Krogan's hand as his air supply was cut off.

"Come on. What are you afraid of? You said you would shoot. *Shoot me!*" Krogan demanded. "Shoot or I'll rip his head off."

"Release him now or I *will* shoot," the ESU officer ordered.

Krogan laughed.

The officer fired. Krogan remained standing, blood dripping from the arm that was holding Gavin. The officer fired again into the same arm. Nothing.

"You missed," Krogan taunted. "In the face. Don't you want to shoot my face?"

"Let go of him, Krogan," Buck said

weakly, conscious again. "In the name of him who conquers all, I command you to release him."

Slowly, Krogan's grip weakened. Gavin inhaled, coughed, and finally fell to his knees as Krogan released him.

"Be still," Buck commanded as Krogan took a step in Buck's direction. Again, Krogan found himself straining fiercely to move, blood dripping down his arm and off his fingertips.

"Get down on your face! Now, mister," the ESU officer ordered, his and several other rifles aimed to kill.

"Stay out of this," Buck said to them without taking his eyes off Krogan for even a second. He drew himself to his knees and opened the wooden chest. The confused ESU troops looked like they would like to contest Buck's authority, but something in his manner stopped them. Instead they stood uncertainly at the ready.

Buck reached into the wooden chest and lifted out what looked like a large, brownish turtle with a domelike shell — an old, dirty army helmet with bumpy, stubby legs and head. He placed it on the ground before him where Krogan could clearly see it. It momentarily tucked into its shell, but then a curious head poked slowly out, followed by its legs, although it did not move from its place.

A turtle? A freaking turtle? Gavin thought. This was Buck's secret weapon? Not a big, jewel-laden gold cross or an artifact from a holy crusade? Not ancient shackles that had once held an apostle or saint? Not even balloons filled with holy water? Gavin didn't know what he had expected, but . . . a turtle? Gavin spared a glance at the ESU officers; he could only imagine what they must be thinking.

Apparently, though, Krogan saw something in the turtle that Gavin did not, because shock rushed into the demon's face. Buck closed his eyes for a long moment, then fixed his gaze upon the man before him.

"Krogan," he spoke firmly. "In the authority of the Lord of lords and King of kings, whom I serve, I loose you from the man, Karl Dengler and bind you into this tortoise . . . *now.*"

Krogan roared. His face, his whole body, appeared pained. He took one step toward Buck, his leg straining as if deeply rooted into the earth. "Who are you to command me?" he hissed.

Most of the ESU officers took a step back.

"I am nobody, Krogan. But in the name of him whom I serve, come out. *Now*."

Krogan buckled sharply as if punched in the abdomen, then fell to one knee. Sweat dripping off his face, he struggled to get back to his feet, grunting and groaning loudly as if lifting a great weight. Gavin could have imagined reading about something like this in some isolated, remote part of the world, but seeing it played out before him in real life right here in New York made him wonder if he was dreaming. He saw Buck, Krogan, and the tortoise. They were right there. Amy was watching them, too, as were a dozen or more of the ESU, albeit in disbelief. They could not all be having the same dream. This was really happening.

"Now!" Buck repeated.

Krogan's gaze snapped skyward and his mouth dropped open in sudden silence. He did not even appear to be breathing. Gavin reflexively followed his line of sight, but saw nothing. Just then, Krogan collapsed.

As soon as Krogan's — or actually, Karl Dengler's — face hit the dirt the tortoise was on the move . . . away from Buck. No longer paying any attention to the man with his face in the dirt, Buck went for the tortoise and carefully picked it up from behind. Its previously sleepy head was now animated, snapping vainly for Buck's hands. Without a word Buck put the animal into the chest and shut the lid.

The ESU converged toward Dengler, who was struggling to get back to his feet, but Gavin held up his hand, badge in palm, asking for them to wait. He limped toward the man whom he now felt confident was just a man. He grabbed a handful of shirt and stood the man up. "*Shadahd* this," he growled and roundhoused his right fist as hard as he could into Dengler's jaw, sending him back to earth.

"Next time, ask your tenant for a reference," Gavin said. He massaged his right hand for a moment, then pulled out his handcuffs, slowly crouching down so he could shackle the man's hands while the ESU crew waited. With Krogan's consciousness supposedly gone, he wondered if Karl even understood what was happening.

"In case you feel like you just got here, pal, and you're wondering what all the fuss is about, you killed my grandfather," Gavin said, then motioned to the ESU to take their man. They swarmed around Gavin and helped him off Dengler, pinning down the fallen man's head, cuffing his ankles, and yelling out his rights. Outside the circle of men, Buck was still on his knees and had latched the chest with the tortoise inside. A couple of officers helped him to his feet and tried to hold the chest for him, but Buck insisted on holding it himself.

Gavin turned to look for Amy, who had finally been untied and helped off the lobster boat. Several policemen were gathered around her, apparently advising her to be still until medical help arrived, but breaking free and ignoring their calls, she hobbled toward Gavin and Buck, collapsed into Gavin's arms, and wept. "I thought I would never see you again," she said.

"It's over," Gavin said, as the police passed by with a heavily manacled Karl Dengler, his feet plowing the dirt as they pulled him by the armpits. He appeared drunk — very drunk and beaten. Strangely, Gavin no longer hated the man with the same intensity as he had. The reality had finally registered: the enemy was not the man being dragged away. For the first time Gavin saw him as nothing more than a host, albeit a now used and empty host. This new logic demanded that his hatred and anger be refocused onto the being in the tortoise. This was what Buck had spoken of. No wonder the preacher had always been able to stay so emotionally detached from the people the demons were using. The people were pawns — pawns who had allowed themselves to be used, but pawns nonetheless.

"Not over yet," Buck said, stepping up to them with an officer at his side and the chest in his arms.

"Huh?" Gavin said.

"We'll take him from here," Amy said to the officer, who nodded and left them.

"Sabah," Buck said.

"Katz!" Gavin said. Borrowing a phone from a nearby officer, he tried calling Karianne's number. The phone rang four times before the answering machine picked up. Gavin yelled for Katz to pick up, but there was no response. He called again and then once more before slapping the lid shut on the cell phone.

"Something's wrong. Something's definitely wrong."

— 58 —

The NYPD wanted to know everything Gavin could tell them, but considering everyone's condition and Gavin's request for an immediate ride home, they had thanked the weary group for their heroics and smuggled them away, hidden from the media. Gavin, Amy, and Buck were chauffeured by an Officer Andrew Syrotick back to Long Island. During the ride Gavin tried once again to get through to Katz, but again reached the machine with no response.

"Why don't we get away for a while?" Amy said to Gavin as she snuggled under his arm in the backseat of the unmarked car.

"Sounds good to me," Gavin said. "I've got some time coming to me. Did you have any place in mind?"

"Actually, yes. How about —"

"Wait!" Gavin interrupted. "Maybe this isn't the place to be discussing future plans and destinations." He motioned to the front seat, where Buck was sitting with the wooden chest at his side. Gavin had no idea of Krogan's capabilities, if any, within his tortoise jail cell and was not sure if even Buck knew, but why take the chance?

Gavin settled Amy more comfortably at his side, and she closed her eyes and dozed while he spoke to Buck in the front seat. Gavin had wanted her to go to the hospital for treatment for the rope cuts on her ankles and wrists and the deep bruise on her chest, but even the mention of being separated from him and Buck appeared to terrify her.

"Why a turtle, Buck? Why not a snail or a slug or even a crocodile — something a little more fitting of the slime's personality?" he asked.

"It's not a turtle. It's a young tortoise."

"Turtle, tortoise . . . either way it seems pretty ridiculous."

Buck rearranged himself in his seat so he could look back at Gavin. "Tortoises live to a very old age, much older than either you or I will — more than a hundred and fifty years under the right conditions. And I plan on making sure he gets the right conditions. When Jesus cast the demons into a herd of swine, they immediately ran into the sea and drowned themselves to escape. I wanted an animal that couldn't commit suicide very easily. A tortoise. They are designed completely for defense. They can't hurt and they can't easily be hurt."

"So you feel good about this? As a prison, I mean."

Buck paused thoughtfully. "With the power of prayer, Krogan will be like a lion in a den of Daniels."

Gavin made a mental note to refresh himself on the story of Daniel in the lions' den. "And without prayer?"

"We die."

Officer Syrotick, who had been pleasantly quiet for most of the ride, glanced curiously at Buck and then back at the road.

"Where did you get the tortoise?" Gavin asked.

Buck paused, looked at the officer, then said, "The little fella's on loan."

"On loan? From where?"

"I have a good friend at the Bronx Zoo."

Officer Syrotick had another glance at Buck and then at the wooden chest next to him.

"Does he know his tortoise is going to have . . ." Gavin glanced at Officer

Syrotick. ". . . uh, some company with it when he gets it back?"

"Of course."

Gavin was surprised. "And he was okay with that?"

"He's a friend and a brother in the faith. We share the same priorities, same enemies. He'll keep a watchful eye on Jeremy."

"Jeremy?"

"The tortoise's name is Jeremy," Buck said. "Most of the animals at the zoo have names, especially the endangered ones."

"Endangered? Ha! If they only knew," Gavin said.

"Have you ever done this before?" asked Amy, who had been following the conversation with her eyes closed.

"No," Buck said. "Honestly, I was not even sure it could be done."

"Then you came with a weapon without knowing if it had any ammo?"

"My faith grew after seeing the initial look on Krogan's face when he saw the tortoise. I knew we had a fighting chance."

"His face didn't look too good when he first saw you, either," Gavin said.

"That's why I stayed on the boat's floor. If he'd seen me he would have immediately made us his primary target or killed himself with the shotgun."

In the rearview mirror, Gavin could see Officer Syrotick frowning.

"Will Sabah recognize you, too?" Gavin asked, hoping the demon was at least still in the apartment.

"Somehow, they all recognize me. When I first started casting out demons many years ago, the recognition helped build my faith. But I guess I was recognized one too many times, and my family . . ."

Gavin put his hand on Buck's shoulder. "Without you, Buck, Amy and I would be dead now."

— 59 —

By the way Officer Syrotick said good-bye, Gavin knew he thought they were all crazy. The policeman wasted no time in leaving once they had gotten out of the car. Before today Gavin would have done the same. Ask no questions and get no answers you really don't want to hear. Syrotick's story of their ride would no doubt make good coffee conversation back at the station.

At the door of Karianne's apartment, Gavin told Amy to wait in the hallway with the wooden chest. Even though Krogan was supposedly in the tortoise, Gavin still did not like the idea of leaving Amy alone, but better with a caged animal than a free one. Buck was to keep back also, but at the ready.

Gavin quietly opened the door and cautiously stepped inside. He didn't have his gun, which was probably still in the boat somewhere. He felt naked without it. Not that it would do him any good with Sabah. Before taking another step he needed to recognize Karianne and Sabah as being one and the same. He did not want to hurt the woman and he did not want the demon to deceive him into letting down his guard.

The foyer was dim, the only light being a yellow glow creeping around the corner from the living room. The quiet was disturbing. He imagined Katz and Steinman dead on the floor with Sabah waiting to pounce on him, or worse, Sabah gone.

Footsteps.

Gavin wasn't sure what to expect, and looked to the door to make sure Buck was still close by.

"Aghhh!" Katz, who had just rounded the corner, jumped back, startled.

"Katz!" Gavin was startled as well. "You're all right."

"Pierce! Are you trying to give me a heart attack?" Katz said. The swollen left eye Karianne — or rather Sabah — had given him earlier had gotten worse. It was now black and had spread over the bridge of his nose, making him look sadder than ever. "Pierce, you look terrible."

"Why didn't you pick up the phone? I called a dozen times."

"Sorry. I turned the ringer off and turned down the volume on the machine. I didn't want to take the chance of any noise disturbing and waking her. I don't know what her tolerances are to the anesthetics she's on, so I dosed her a little on the light side."

"Then she's where we left her?"

Katz waved in her direction. "She's still out cold. Right after I spoke to you I went back to my office, raided my medicine cabinet, and set her up on intravenous. Steinman wasn't so happy about baby-sitting her, but I told him I'd be back as fast as I could. Which, by the way, is what you told me." Katz held his wristwatch up. "It's almost ten o'clock. You've been gone for, what, twelve hours?"

"Where's Steinman now?"

"He went home with a splitting headache. A concussion will do that. I just hope he'll come back. Thanks to you and your little —"

"We got him, Katz. We got Krogan."

Katz paused. "Dead?"

"No, the guy in the morgue wasn't him. It's a long story. But we got him and he's alive," Gavin said, tempted to tell Katz they had brought Krogan with them.

Katz nodded. "Excellent." Gavin wasn't sure if Katz was glad the killer had been caught or glad he could finally get on with his research unshackled by Gavin's authority.

Katz's gaze went past Gavin to Buck and Amy, who were peering around the doorjamb.

"I wasn't sure how safe it was," Gavin explained to Katz. "I don't believe you know Mr. Buchanan."

Katz shook Buck's hand as they all walked into the living room, then turned to Amy, who was carrying the chest.

"Let me take that from you," Katz said. "You look . . . tired."

Tortured was more like it. Amy's eyelids were puffy and red, her T-shirt ripped and dirty, and her wrists and ankles wrapped in gauze and adhesive tape.

"I'll take that," Gavin said, intercepting the chest before Katz could get to it.

"What's this, Pierce?" Katz said, frowning suspiciously.

"You'll see," Gavin said, then walked over to Karianne. With the exception of the intravenous tube taped to her arm, she appeared just as she had when he'd left her this morning, but the picture of tranquility before him did not deceive him. Not anymore.

Amy plopped into the overstuffed chair and drew her knees up to her chest. Gavin wished he could take her home with him and deal with everything else in the morning — preferably late morning. But this couldn't wait.

"She'll need to be woken up," Buck said, pointing to Karianne. He took a seat on a chair with the wooden chest at his feet.

"Stop the flow, Katz; it's time to bring her around," Gavin said.

"To do what?" Katz demanded.

"You may need to hypnotize her again. She needs to be in the state she was in before she was drugged," Buck said.

"I thought the idea was to keep her out of that state," Katz said.

"Don't worry, Katz. Buck's here," Gavin said with a rare smile.

Katz glanced at Buck — at his white hair and tired, rumpled appearance — and looked back at Gavin as though he were crazy. "Don't worry? That's what you said this morning. One word, you said. You just wanted to say one word."

"It wasn't a word, Katz. It was a name."

"Whose name?"

"If I told you, you wouldn't believe me."

"I don't believe you anyway. And what's in that chest?"

"Fine, Katz. Disconnect her and I'll tell you everything."

"And if I don't?"

"Then I will."

"Then I won't hypnotize her," Katz said, folding his arms defiantly.

"Doctor Katz," Buck said. "What needs to be done can be done whether she is conscious or not, but it would be better for her and easier on us if we only had to deal with her subconscious."

Katz took a long moment. He looked at Buck, then at Amy, who were both staring back at him. "Okay. But before she comes to, tell me what this is all about."

"Well, I know this is going to ruin your plans of making Karianne a poster girl for reincarnation, but she hasn't been reliving her past lives for us."

"She hasn't?" Katz deadpanned. "I suppose you're going to tell me she knew how to speak all those languages and made up those stories from what she learned of ancient civilizations in school."

"No. The fact is she hasn't said anything to us. We've been speaking to another."

"Someone else has been speaking through her?"

"Some-*thing* else," Buck said.

Katz turned to Buck. He looked at the chest by his feet, then at Amy, then turned back to Gavin, his blank expression giving way to a smirk. "You? Detective Gavin Pierce? You've got to be kidding me! You, of all people! What now — an exorcism?"

Gavin said nothing. He knew there wasn't much Katz could say. The psychologist couldn't very well protest what they planned — not with all the liberties he himself had taken with Karianne.

Katz noted the stoic faces of the others, then shrugged and chuckled lightly as he shook his head. He clamped the tube and removed the needle from Karianne's arm, then stepped back with a mocking bow.

"Now, if you can wake her up we'll —" Gavin started.

"I kept her dosage fairly light, but she's still going to need a little time before —"

"She's going to need less time than you think, Doctor," Buck said.

Katz smirked. "You certainly are sure of yourself, aren't you?"

Buck didn't respond, but Gavin was confident in the old man. "Just start doing your thing, Katz. It's been a long day."

Katz requested silence, set his metronome on the lamp table behind Karianne's head, and turned it on. He reached for a chair, then turned back to Karianne — and jumped.

Her eyes were wide open.

"Karianne!" Katz said, surprise obvious in his voice.

She said nothing in return. Her eyes fixed on his for a moment, then rolled left toward Gavin.

"Hi," Gavin said with a wave. If he were communicating with the real Karianne, she would take his gesture as friendly, but if he were speaking to Sabah . . .

"You mock?" she said.

Katz backed hurriedly away, right over the chair, apparently recognizing the familiar, arrogant tone and not wanting another beating.

"I'm not here to mock, Sabah," Gavin said, addressing the demon within Karianne. "I'm here to say good-bye. You're leaving."

"I'll kill you for speaking to me by name," she snarled, rising from the couch.

"I don't think so. I've brought a friend whom you might know. He's not the vengeful type, but I think in your case he'll make an exception. At least I hope so."

Before Gavin could finish, Karianne had snapped her gaze left and found Buck. Like Krogan, Karianne's eyes filled with shock. Buck's gaze remained unflinching, hard and cold as black ice. The preacher was old, but his mind was sharp and within him resided a recognized power that struck terror into his ancient foe. Unlike Krogan, Sabah seemed to know from the outset there was no contest.

"It's over, Sabah," Buck said, tapping on the lid of the chest between his feet.

Karianne looked at the chest. "Have you forgotten what happened last time you interfered, Preacher? Have you forgotten Krogan?"

Buck opened the chest and carefully took out the tortoise. Its legs clawed at the air as it tried in vain to snap at Buck's hand. "No, Sabah, I haven't forgotten anything . . . especially Krogan."

Checkmate, Gavin thought as he saw reality wash across Karianne's stunned face. She stared, shaking her head in disbelief. "Hiola kielyatie, Krogan."

The tortoise stopped snapping and looked straight at Karianne. Gavin had no idea what she had just said and judging by the frowns around the room, he doubted anyone else knew, either. But unless he had lost his mind — which at this point he considered a definite possibility — the tortoise understood.

Karianne quickly looked around the room, desperate for an escape. She turned toward Katz, who immediately stepped backward. Her chin hitched toward Gavin. He knew an animal was most dangerous when cornered, but he steeled his nerves and kept his feet in place.

"You're history," he said boldly. "I imagine it's gonna be a little cramped in there with the both of you."

Karianne's eyes appeared ready to burst into flames, but the second she started in Gavin's direction he heard Buck speak the simple command that had overcome Krogan: "Cease."

Karianne's body froze in midstride. To Gavin's relief, she did not demonstrate anything near the level of resistance Krogan had.

"In the name of him who will judge you in the end, I loose you from this woman and bind you into this tortoise."

Gavin rushed to catch Karianne as she fell limply. There was something that had sounded ridiculous in the way Buck said, "into this tortoise," but, holding Karianne, Gavin could hardly poke fun at the results. Buck's power — and power was exactly what it was — was no joke.

In an absurdly anticlimactic gesture, Buck calmly put the tortoise back into the chest and shut the lid as if it were a paddy-wagon door. "Lay her down," he instructed

Gavin. "She'll need to sleep off the rest of that drug you had her on." He looked at Katz, who appeared to be in shock.

"I think you'll find the history lesson is over the next time you hypnotize her," Gavin said as he laid Karianne's head down on the soft pillow on the couch. He reached past her head and shut off the metronome, then turned to the rest of the group.

"And now, if you all don't mind, I'm going to go home and sleep for about a week." He looked at Amy. "You coming?"

Amy nodded and came to his side. He took her hand. "Buck, I'll catch up with you later, okay?"

"Don't worry. I'll take care of our two friends." Buck patted the chest. "My friend at the zoo is waiting to hear from me."

Gavin nodded. Then, without another word, he led Amy out. His last view was of Katz, standing speechless in the middle of the living room, staring at the silent metronome.

— Epilogue —

Exactly four weeks had passed since Krogan and Sabah had been imprisoned. With the cooler weather, sugar maple leaves and kids' cheeks were beginning to blush. Gavin and Amy were walking the winding pathways of the Bronx Zoo. The last time Gavin had been here was with his grampa. Such fond memories now came with a price: the more cherished the moment, the deeper the pain . . .

Amy squeezed his hand, mercifully bringing him back to the present — back to their Sunday walk, back to excited children pointing at the lazy lions and asking for giant New York pretzels. Somehow she had known he needed to be comforted. It was a sensitivity she was allowing to grow as their time together increased.

Gavin returned the hand squeeze, trying not to dwell on the past, seeking rather to refocus on the present and future. That was becoming easier to do with Amy around.

"Excuse me," Amy said to three teenage boys passing by.

The three stopped, gawking at the beautiful woman before them. From the looks on their faces, they would do whatever she wanted.

"Could you take a picture or two of us?" she said sweetly, pulling a strapped camera from Gavin's neck.

"Sure, yeah, yeah," came a chorus of agreements.

Amy handed the camera to one of them and after a brief instruction pulled Gavin in front of a nearby statue of a rhino.

"We shouldn't get too far away from them, Amy. That camera isn't cheap."

"Then we'll run them down and arrest them."

"*You'll* run them down."

"Shut up and kiss me," Amy said, then pulled his face to hers and gave him a kiss he was sure would melt the film. The kids catcalled and guffawed as they took the picture and returned the camera. One of them gave Gavin a big thumbs-up. Amy laughed at Gavin's expression.

"At least we've given them something to talk about," she said as the boys walked on, giggling and pushing at each other.

"Dream about, is more like it," Gavin replied as he opened and studied the zoo map that had been handed to them at the entrance gate. They had just passed the sea lion pool and the big cat cages were now to their right. Lions and tigers and leopards and panthers usually impressed Gavin. Not today. Yes, they were beautiful animals. Yes, it was Sunday — his and Amy's day off. Yes, the weather was perfect and just ahead to the left, the zoo was showing off their prize possession: a zoo-bred baby elephant and its mother. But, no, he wasn't interested. Today was business.

"Oh, Gavin, the children's zoo is still open. Next week it'll be closed until April," Amy said cheerfully, tugging on his arm.

"First, the reptile house," he said. "Business before pleasure."

Amy pouted. "But the baby goats."

"Amy —"

"Pleeeeease?"

"I suppose, seeing it's on the way," he said. Amy was the one doing the asking and he was the one giving the permission, but there was no mystery as to who was in charge here. In spite of himself Gavin smiled. He'd been doing a lot more of that lately. In the last few weeks he had seen Amy every day and he was planning on continuing to do so. He didn't want to think about a future without her.

The children's zoo was self-contained within the main zoo, surrounded on all sides by a tall, wooden fence decorated with plywood cutouts of foxes, iguanas, raccoons, and other cute animals, each one a different color. Out in front sat a small cedar shack with a metal corrugated roof and a bunny-shaped sign that read "Photos." As Gavin and Amy rounded the shack, a couple of service trucks came into view. Several men were working on an open section of the tall fence. A park attendant met them as they walked up.

"Sorry folks, this exhibit is closed today."

"Closed? Why?" Amy said, disappointed.

"Some small repairs. It'll be open again tomorrow."

"Tomorrow? Tomorrow's Monday. We work tomorrow."

"And he's working today," Gavin said. With an apologetic look at the attendant, he put his arm around Amy's shoulder and steered her back to the path, stopping at an intersection a few feet away to read a sign post with arrows pointing in every direction.

"Wild Area . . . North America . . . Africa . . . World of Darkness . . . Snow Leopards . . . Ah, reptiles. That-a-way." He pointed left.

"Little do they know the Reptile House is the *real* World of Darkness," Amy said.

Gavin found no humor in what she'd said. He'd had the exact same thought just before Amy said it.

"Look, a live rhino," Amy said, tugging Gavin toward a nearby pen.

"On the way back, Amy. First things first."

"Oh, wait! I have to have a pretzel." She again detoured Gavin, dragging him to the edge of the path, where a green-and-white concession stand on wheels was parked.

"A pretzel? They're the size of a pizza. We just ate breakfast an hour ago."

"But we didn't stay for dessert."

"With breakfast?"

"It's my day off. If I want dessert with my —"

"Okay, okay! Have two."

No sooner had Amy taken possession of her monster pretzel than she pointed to yet another exhibit.

"Look! The Mouse House."

"Later."

She sighed and continued on with Gavin. According to the map the Reptile House was in the middle of the zoo, just around the next turn in the path. As they rounded the gradual curve, the side of the building emerged through the heavy brush and trees.

"There it is," Amy said.

"Yeah, right where the map said it would be. How 'bout that?"

"Looks creepy," Amy said.

It did look a little creepy, with ivy growing all over the old brick walls. Gavin didn't know the history of the zoo or what buildings had been around the longest, but he guessed this was by far the oldest. "Reptiles" was carved into a stone beam held up by two columns over a very dark entrance. There was no light visible beyond the doors and the building would have looked closed except for the occasional traffic in and out.

"Gavin, the gorillas and apes — over there," Amy said, pointing and pulling with baffling enthusiasm. Against his will Gavin took three steps toward the ape building on the other side of the path before stopping.

"What's going on, Amy?"

Amy's magnetic green eyes lost some of

their shine as she looked over Gavin's shoulder toward the Reptile House, then back to Gavin. "I . . . I don't want to go in there," she whispered, then drew closer and leaned her forehead against his chest. "I don't want it to see me. I want it to forget me."

Gavin sighed as he embraced her, slowly massaging her back. He warmly slid his hands up to her shoulders and held her at arm's length.

She looked down. "I'm sorry."

He took her hand and led her to a long green bench just outside the Reptile House entrance. As they sat down, a half dozen pigeons waddled indignantly away. Amy still hadn't taken a bite from her pretzel; the pigeons would be the likely beneficiaries if they were patient.

"Wait here," he said. "I have to see it. I have to know it's there — know it's . . . secure." And, he added to himself, he wanted the demon to remember him.

Amy nodded and gave a weak but reassuring smile.

Gavin exhaled and got up. He walked up to the entrance, paused and exhaled again, then pushed on the dark glass door. Sensing someone behind him, he held the door.

"Thank you," Amy said.

"What are you —"

"Suppose you didn't come back out?"

Gavin shook his head. "I think, after all this, seeing the tortoise is going to be a bit anticlimactic."

"Let's hope so," she said, taking his hand. Gavin noticed she no longer had the pretzel. The pigeons had probably already teamed up to pull it into the bushes.

He led the way through an old, painted turnstile into a dark and gloomy corridor. The little light available spilled in through a large viewing window to their right. The deep jungle habitat on the other side of the glass wouldn't be for the tortoise. Curled up on a limb under leafy foliage was a huge snake. According to the sign on the window it was a twenty-four-foot python. Gavin was glad it was on the other side of the thick glass. He wasn't fond of snakes and thought this one looked like it would have made an appropriately scary home for Krogan — better than a boring tortoise, at least.

"Gavin!" Amy said, pointing to an area where the hall widened to a dim, but better lit, room thanks to a large greenhouse extension. On the floor before the greenhouse, in the midst of wandering tourists, were two giant bronzed tortoises. With Gavin in tow, she stepped around an elderly man in a zoo attendant's uniform and peered into the beachlike setting within the greenhouse, hoping the statues were advertisements for the real thing.

No. Even before they got to the safety rail they could see the crocodiles, their massive bodies submerged in a clear, simulated pond with only the top half of their prehistoric heads afloat. Looking at them, Gavin wondered how Krogan would have liked spending a lifetime in one of them. Probably too much, he decided, noting the massive teeth lining the crocodiles' mouths. He looked back at the bronze statutes behind them and shook his head. He was just going to have to trust Buck on the tortoise thing.

Following the flow of traffic, they entered into a second hallway as dimly lighted as the first. Dozens of smaller windows revealed what the planet had to offer in the way of lizards, frogs, and finally turtles. A large window just ahead held the attention of several spectators. Gavin paused. Amy held his left arm in a vise grip with both her hands, also looking at the large window.

Several viewers moved away. The empty

space created a vacuum that drew Gavin and Amy in.

"Huh?" Amy said.

A small sign on the window noted that the exhibit held an Alligator Snapping Turtle. In another fake pond swam a turtle the size of a guitar case with a spiked shell and parrotlike beak that could chomp off a man's leg.

"So where are the freaking tortoises?" Gavin whispered angrily. Uncertain of where to go, he remembered the attendant. "Come on," he said, pulling Amy toward the old man.

"Excuse me."

The attendant's eyebrows raised above the rim of his bifocal glasses. "Yes?"

"I thought the tortoises would be in with the reptiles, but I don't see them here. Where are they kept?"

"Half of the year they are in here, but in warmer weather they're kept at the children's zoo. The kids love them and the sun and fresh air is good for the tortoises."

"But the children's zoo is closed."

"Well, yes, that's true," the man replied. "We had a little accident last night," he said in a hushed voice.

"Accident?" Gavin said, a knot tightening in his gut.

"The man told us they were just doing a little repair work," said Amy.

"Well," the man whispered, scratching an ear with his index finger. "One of the maintenance crew guys accidentally drove through the fence with a dump truck after hours."

"Was he drunk?" Gavin blurted.

The attendant's surprise, followed by a nervous scratch of the neck, gave Gavin his answer.

"Was anyone hurt?" Amy asked.

"No, nobody was hurt. Well, I shouldn't say nobody. Around here, animals are people, too. One of our young tortoises was killed in the crash. Little guy was in the wrong place at the wrong time."

Gavin could feel Amy's fingernails digging into his arm.

"Jeremy?" he asked.

The attendant looked over his bifocals. "You know Jeremy?"

Gavin couldn't speak or even nod. His knees were suddenly weak. Amy leaned against him for support.

The attendant shook his head somberly. "It's somethin', how that tortoise went bad."

"Bad?" Amy said.

"Oh, yeah! One day just like any other

tortoise. The next, mean, aggressive . . . That's why they had to separate him from the others."

"And that's why he got killed?" Gavin asked.

"No, that's why he lived."

"He's alive?" Gavin and Amy blurted out in unison.

"Yeah, Franklin's the tortoise that died. Jeremy had been removed to the adjoining pen just a few hours before the accident. He was biting the others, you see. Funny, though . . . If the accident'd happened a few hours before or later, Jeremy probably would've been killed, too. He was digging his way back in."

Gavin looked at Amy, who looked back at him in horror.

"Can we see him?" Gavin said.

"Oh, I'm afraid that's impossible until the children's zoo reopens. He's confined indoors until then."

"Isn't there a safer place for him? Maybe you people could —"

"I wouldn't worry, sir. There's never been an incident like this before and, believe me, it won't happen again."

"Right," Gavin said. "Look, my, uh, girlfriend here is the worrying type," he said motioning toward Amy, whose eyes had widened at the introduction. "And I wouldn't mind getting involved in the cost of a safer pen with, maybe, concrete walls and a deep foundation."

The attendant frowned in confusion. "Sir, I can assure you that —"

"Who would we talk to about this?"

The man looked at him suspiciously, then shrugged. "Zoo management."

"And where would we find them?" Gavin said.

On their way to the administration building, Gavin flipped open his phone and dialed.

"Samantha's Farm."

"Buck? Gavin. We've got a problem," he said, then explained what had happened. "I think you're going to have to come up with a Plan B."

"This *is* Plan B," Buck said.

"Then what's Plan A?"

"What it's always been: prayer. I suppose you think it's just a coincidence Jeremy is still alive?"

Gavin took the phone away from his ear and frowned at it as if it embodied the voice it was delivering.

Amy tugged on Gavin's left arm. "What did he say?"

Gavin held up a finger, then returned the phone to his mouth. "Are you trying to tell me that you've been praying for the turt— tortoise's safety, and that's why it survived?"

"Yes, Detective. The prayer of faith is our greatest weapon. We need to fight spirits with spirits."

"Spirits with spirits? Can't we just find a safer home for it? Get the zoo to put it behind reinforced concrete and bars . . . like Dengler?"

"Precautions can sometimes be beneficial, but true wisdom will lead a man to prayer."

Gavin paused. "But what if something were to happen to you? Are there others praying with you?"

"Detective, who would have more reason to pray for the tortoise than you and Amy?"

"Us? Are you kidding?"

"What is he saying?" Amy said, tugging again.

Gavin looked in the direction of the administration building. "Here," he said, handing Amy the phone. "He wants to talk to you. I'll be right back." Amy took the phone and held it to her ear with both hands.

"Buck?" Gavin heard her say as she followed behind him. Then silence as she listened. "Yes . . . Uh-huh. I will . . . Yes, of course. Don't worry, we'll be there . . . Thanks, I'll tell him. 'Bye!" She handed the phone back to Gavin.

Gavin took it, staring at her. "We'll be where?" he said suspiciously.

"Buck wants to see us."

"When?"

"As soon as we're done here. He said he would have a cold glass of your favorite iced tea waiting."

"Amy, he wants us to be like him."

"What do you think — that God won't listen to us?"

Gavin thought about that.

"Everyone's at the top of God's list, Gavin. We need to start taking our own stand — get with the program."

"Did Buck just tell you that?"

"Yes. He said we needed to get filled with truth."

"Truth. Do we know for sure it's the truth?"

"Gavin, an empty bag will fall."

"What?"

"You know — a bag with something in it is heavier and can stand firm. An empty bag will just blow away or fall. I don't want us to be empty bags," Amy explained.

Gavin smiled thinly. "Buck's beginning to sound like your Japanese grandmother."

Amy took his arm and leaned into him as they walked. "That *was* from my grandmother. And she can't wait to meet you."

Gavin rolled his eyes. He had no idea what he was getting himself into by dating Amy. She was definitely a handful. Strangely, though, he was not at all worried.

They were going to be just fine.